FORENOTE

The takeoff point for *The Lucifer Comet* is the planet Erth, which some readers will have encountered in others of my stories. Erth is not Earth; but it is so much like Earth that every reader can easily settle in here, despite occasional differences from Earth.

As they pursue the story, some readers will be increasingly reminded of a famous Earth-mythos. As always, however, the Erth version is rather different.

I think it appropriate to quote a generalization by Peter S. Prescott who, in *Newsweek* of November 20, 1978, was reviewing a novel unrelated to this one: *"The business of a novelist is to create a world that is true only to whatever purpose he intended."*

—IAN WALLACE

Novels by Ian Wallace (with dates of eras)

Adventures of Minds-in-Bodies:

EVERY CRAZY WIND (1948)
* THE WORLD ASUNDER (1952 and other eras)
* THE LUCIFER COMET (2464 and a prior era)
PAN SAGITTARIUS (2509 and prior eras)

The Croyd Spacetime Maneuvers:

* Z-STING (2475)
CROYD (2496)
DR. ORPHEUS (2502)
* A VOYAGE TO DARI (2506)

The St. Cyr Interplanetary Detective Mysteries:

THE PURLOINED PRINCE (2470)
DEATHSTAR VOYAGE (2475)
THE SIGN OF THE MUTE MEDUSA (2480)
* HELLER'S LEAP (with Croyd, 2495 and 2494)

* Available in DAW editions.

THE LUCIFER COMET

Ian Wallace

DAW BOOKS, INC.

DONALD A. WOLLHEIM, PUBLISHER

1633 Broadway, New York, N.Y. 10019

FIRST PRINTING, DECEMBER 1980

1 2 3 4 5 6 7 8 9

DAW TRADEMARK REGISTERED
U.S. PAT. OFF. MARCA
REGISTRADA. HECHO EN U.S.A.

PRINTED IN U.S.A.

DIVISIONS OF THE STORY

Conjointly, to
ALAN
who long ago gave me part of the idea
and to
LISA
for reasons best known to Alan

Prevoyance One

Methuen, with absolute circumstantial clarity, in 2464 previewed the first 2465 attack upon Erth. Without warning, and without any evident reason or cause or means, the Saturn-satellite Nereid ceased to exist; and with it evaporated Erth-world Headquarters, which was located on Nereid.

The instantaneous evaporative destruction occurred at 0600 hours on 10 January 2465, (Interplanetary Time Convention) and was observed on Manhattan monitors at 1059 the same day. A frantic call for confirmation was immediately dispatched to Nereid, while backup monitors on Erth and in space churned Nereid-vicinity with scanners; but no reply to the query, even if Nereid still existed, could be anticipated before 2058 hours. However, between Nereid and Manhattan there was hourly normal traffic, and no communiqués had been received by 1259. It was, to understate, ominous.

Acting in terms of acute danger, the Chairman of Erth-world Council called an emergency visiradio meeting of the Council and of the presidents of all Erthworld constellations at 1445 hours. Intensive brainstorming elicited no notion of an attack source; but all were convinced that no agency on Erth or in the Sol System could or would have brought this off unless it were some high-placed suicidal paranoiac on Nereid itself. The conference turned then to the question, what should be done on Erth if the destruction of Nereid should be confirmed? The unanimous decision among the world leaders was to keep the business under wraps for at least a week until the secondary echelons on Erth could achieve some sort of provisional governmental stability. Should the newskenners get wind of the disaster, the Council Chairman was authorized to admit it and apprise the newskenners of measures that were being taken. Meanwhile, all military and civilian intelligence services would be pressed into top-priority, top-secret service in an attempt to determine the source and reason for the attack; and all military branches would be placed on red alert.

The Council adjourned until 2200 hours the same evening.

At 2200, the Chairman gravely informed the Council that no message had been received from Nereid, and that no spaceship had been able to locate Nereid. . . .

Methuen awoke from this dire prevoyance with the number *546* reverberating in his mind. At that time, in early summer 2464, Methuen was an Astrofleet commander.

Part One

MULTI-MILLENNIUM SPREAD

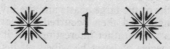 **1**

Narfar was heavy with doom-feeling. Over distance had come into him a telepathic warning that his brother Quarfar was orbitally present, cruising Narfar's planet Dora, spying on Dora quite uninvited; had touched down repeatedly during a full year. Quarfar had come here following the same celestial trail that Narfar had blazed. It had to mean that Narfar's wise brother would take over again, undoing everything that Narfar had tried to do. And Narfar, having learned much from his brother on that other planet, thought that here he had been doing *so* well.

Now Narfar huddled on the glacier, cloaking himself with his great wings, helpless before the impending doom of himself and all that he had accomplished. Should he fly out to meet Quarfar and settle it in space? He was not ready to decide that.

(On faraway Erth, at this time, the year was something like 48000 BC.)

On that earlier world, too, Narfar had thought for a long time that he was doing well. He had found that world swarming with all kinds of beasts, among them a relatively hairless two-legged creature—much like himself, only skin-colored beige, and without wings. This fairly hairless creature had interested Narfar not at all; he was far more engrossed in the beasts, protozoa and insects and fish and mammals alike, whose attributes were so precisely tailored to their several life-styles, whereas those of the two-legged creatures were so useless. Finding himself lord of that world, Narfar had encouraged the beasts, including some so small that almost hairless men could not see them. To Narfar's delight, these beasts preyed on each other and on man, while man sometimes fought them off with primitive weapons (rocks, clubs) and sometimes huddled in fear around chance lightning-spawned fires as Narfar was now huddling on his ice. He fostered the beasts, he cultivated their excellences; with the result that man was on the verge of extinction, dying in tribal hordes by combined assaults of the large beasts and the invisible beasts.

An afterthought had then occurred to Narfar. Man was just another beast, but rather interesting, and it was not desirable that any species of beast be wiped off his world. On an impulse, he had called to Quarfar for help.

And Quarfar had stepped in, on that other planet. Oh, *how* he had stepped in!

Almost before Narfar knew it was happening, Quarfar had adopted man as his own. The first stunning surprise for Narfar came when Quarfar took to lumping the females in with the males and calling both *humans* instead of merely *man*. The next shock came when Quarfar began to teach this little group and that little group of surviving humans how to *use* the fire which came to them by chance, even how to *make* it. Women began to *cook* meat for the men—how revolting! no longer *raw* meat?—while the men, under Quarfarian tutelage, created and mastered all kinds of skills which eventually began to even up the score with large beasts that Narfar found more attractive, although Quarfar neglected to help humans against the invisible beasts.

The ultimate brother-shock came when Narfar began giving special favoritism to the occasionally emerging *funny children*. And Narfar realized hideous climax when the funny children grew up to be a new and formidable species of human which inexorably crowded Narfar's people into despairing extinction!

Narfar now understood that his brother Quarfar, who was wingless and much less handsome than Narfar, had to be put away. But Narfar unaided could not do it. He formed a wicked plan, and he prided himself on this plan because it was rather farsighted for him. Noticing that humans put something they called a *soul* into everything, and that they propitiated these souls (beast-souls for self-protection, weapon-souls for hunting mastery, and so on), Narfar began to cultivate in selected humans the idea that these souls were in fact collective souls, that the collective souls were superhumans called gods and goddesses who dwelt in high places, and that the greatest of these soul-gods was the god of lightning and thunder. Bye and bye the humans began to worship their new gods, particularly the highest god. Whereupon Quarfar, seeing that he was no longer needed, retired himself to a high place and brooded there with mental vultures preying upon his mental liver.

But eventually, with Quarfar safely gone, Narfar discovered an unhappy consequence of his own innovation. The humans were thinking and saying: If the good gods and goddesses could get about the sky unaided by wings, what sort of being was this winged Narfar who whispered to them while they were asleep? Eventually Narfar was declared to be The Enemy of Humans, continually at war with the sky-gods. And again, Narfar was reduced to impotency—this time, by ritual human rejection.

In this dire impasse, it occurred to Narfar that his wise brother Quarfar might help him with wisdom, if only Quarfar could be propitiated. Accordingly, one evening, Narfar flew to the high place of Quarfar's agony; and Narfar demanded of his brother: "How can I regain my mastery of this world?"

Snarled Quarfar, understandably infuriated: "Your mastery was already done before mine was done, and you are a menace to this world. I am going to put you out of it. If you have any particular distant world in mind, I will fling you there; if you refuse my offer, I will kill you. Choose now, brother!"

It was Hobson's choice ages before Hobson. Mortally afraid of his brother, Narfar chose. He scanned the night sky; and to Quarfar he denoted the constellation which was his favorite because he fancied it looked like himself, and the particular star which seemed to be the head of the creature depicted by that constellation. Studying the star, clairvoyantly Quarfar sensed that it owned an inhabited planet; and to that planet Quarfar hurled Narfar.

Arriving on that planet in a burning instant—on *this* planet, *Dora*—Narfar found the world inhabited by beasts such as he loved, plus a handful of groveling humans. And here he began a creation of his own, fancying that he may have learned a thing or two from his brother Quarfar without in any way knuckling down to Quarfar's weirdest ideas.

(In the simultaneity of faraway Erth, Narfar's arrival on Dora occurred somewhen in the fifty-seventh millennium BC.

What Narfar did on this new planet, which he christened Dora, meaning Nubile Nymph, was (he considered) a mas-

13

terful compounding of his own interests with what he thought he had learned from his brother.

First, he gathered all the shivering humans together, informed them that he was a god and their king, and promised to lead them out of darkness into respectful dominance over the beasts, including the sicknesses. And thus he abandoned, with regret but of necessity, his old primary love of lower beasts; and he consecrated himself to the good of humans, without in any way threatening bestial welfare.

He taught humans as *goods* all the qualities which Quarfar had banished as *evils*: superstition, ritual, status-pride, security-worship, and unquestioning obedience to an acknowledged master. And rather than allow them to domesticate and use fire, he taught them that on Dora it was sensible to dwell, not near the northern and southern regions which were perpetually capped with glacial ice, requiring much energy expenditure just to exist, but in the central belt, which was always jungle-warm; so the northern and southern regions became tabu, and it was the equatorial regions of Dora which spawned the pre-civilization of Narfar.

There Narfar taught the preservation of order and the bridling of creativity. He had diagnosed as the primary cause of Quarfarian disorder, not creativity alone nor progress alone, but the twinning of these themes and their association with the infuriating nonsense idea of *endless*. He praised creativity in the arts and crafts, but only for its own sake and without reference to social progress. And since he had intuited that *endless* was a meaningless word, *progress* was understood to mean advancement toward some definite Narfarian end; and once that end would be attained, the idea of future progress beyond that end would be ridiculous.

All these modes of living could be preserved by Narfar's commanding presence, without special methods. He found in this world, however, two perpetually self-reproducing evils which were physically alive, one being human and the other subhuman bestial. He could have annihilated both evils; but to Narfar, any human or animal killing (except for purposes of food or clothing, or in one-to-one combat) was repellent. After generations of study, Narfar partially found and partially created an inescapable *box;* and into this box he conveyed every specimen of these two evils which he found. Mysteriously they kept reappearing; inexorably he kept boxing them, right up to the moment when he sat hunkered on ice worrying about Quarfar.

In the beginning, Narfar reigned over merely a thousand people, most of whom were children, all of whom were nature-reduced to abject savagery, which territorial squabbles often changed to angry savagery.

This condition was only the takeoff phase of the god's grand plan. Dwelling always among his people as a man, universally recognized as Supreme Ruler because of his power and his wisdom and his wings and his skin color and his flaming hair, Narfar proceeded with patience to educate his world. Using first a small core of pupils who in turn became teachers and teachers of teachers, he led them to comprehend his system of defined ends, and to work toward its total perfection. Minor but persistent human foibles were redirected in simple ways, which proved effective given the persistent god-stimulus. Skills (including athletic skills) were substituted for territories, so that contention for excellence replaced territorial combat. Ambition, distorted into a craze under Quarfar on that former world as a by-product of Quarfar's "endless progress" concept, became friendly rivalry for the favorable attention of one's chief or father figure who locally represented the god, culminating at the highest levels in friendly bidding for the favor of the god himself.

The god through his representatives controlled all of Dora including all beings thereon; but what might lie beneath the surface of Dora was tabu. All fire was tabu; so that when a fire started spontaneously by lightning or other agency, the only permissible concern with such a fire was to put it out as an evil.

The first god-defined imperative was: To learn how to survive and help each other and the god, using only animals and vegetables and water and such minerals as might be found on the surface without digging; and these only within the limits defined by the god (for this planet must not be wasted as that earlier planet was sure to be wasted). People quickly found that they could subsist, without cooking, on meat and on the beaten-out pulps of certain vegetables; later, fermented ensilage became a delicacy. They became able to build shelters (against rain and predatory animals and direct sun, cold being absent) from materials within the defined limits.

When creative people began ornamenting shelters, Narfar knew that his ends had been finally attained. His pleasure from now onward would be to preserve it all in unchanging vigor.

15

But now, at the apex of his achievement, Narfar had learned by long-distance telepathy that Quarfar was reconnoitering Dora, obviously with the purpose of destroying the serene pre-civilization of Narfar and substituting Quarfar's own sort of mess!

Fear-filled by this intimation (for the powers of Quarfar were dreadful), Narfar entrusted his government temporarily to his deputies and fled to the far north, to squat miserable upon a glacier and decide what he must do about the threat—whether to go out and attack Quarfar in space or to wait here defensively and meet the enemy as he might come.

And Narfar was no coward. Driving himself into counteraggressive action, he lifted off the glacier to meet the enemy aggressively. . . .

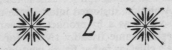

Early in the summer of 2464 AD, the spacedragger *Ventura* was out after ice-comets. And since these had been declared an endangered species in the solar system, naturally the *Ventura* was not infesting the comet-concentration in the neighborhood of Neptune, but was cruising instead in a different star area entirely. She was lazily circumnavigating Bellatrix, a high-hot blue-white helium star in the constellation Orion, right ascension 0524 hours, declination 6°19′, magnitude about 1.7, distance from Earth about 470 light years; Bellatrix had a comet-concentration with no inhabited planet to proscribe comet-collection. The ship's cruising speed was a sleepy 1000 C at a radius of six parsecs off Bellatrix, completing each circuit in twenty-one days.

The *Ventura* was a tight little ship, a hybrid of a destroyer for speedy maneuverability and of a tugboat for tow-power. Her class had been originally designed to clear the interstellar shipping lanes of space junk like asteroids. Lately a number of these craft had been diverted for the ice-comet industry. As polar glaciers on Earth continued to recede, there were fewer and fewer icebergs for oceanic barge-draggers to ensnare and tow equatorward for water supply to the peoples of the expanding deserts. It had long been known that comets in general tended to have varying concentrations of water ice, or of methane ice which could be oxydized to form water with a carbon spin-off, compacted into the space debris which composed them. Once it had been determined (a) that there was a species of comet which contained more ice than rock, and (b) that star systems other than Sol's had concentrations of such comets, spacedraggers had been drawn into the problem, and gradually comets were replacing icebergs.

On the *Ventura*'s tight little bridge, Lieutenant Saul Zorbin (exec, co-pilot, and astrogator), who was tight on his instruments, raised his normally low voice a little as he announced an ice-comet about twenty-two parsecs off. (The *Ventura* deployed a twenty-five-parsec detection field within which information arrrived almost instantaneously.) The reason for Zorbin's arousal was that this comet was moving at unheard-of comet-velocity: more than three percent of light-velocity, about 9800 kilometers per second.

Skipper B. J. Methuen jerked his head around toward Zorbin as the exec dropped his voice to read off trajectory specifications. Methuen, in rank a commander, at thirty-eight still young enough to be thrilled by the challenges of his missions, ordered pursuit and shipcast the alert: "Now hear this. This is the skipper. All stations comet-ready. For now, that is all."

Then Methuen bent to his controls, training his ship on a screen-pip which denoted comet position, jerking the ship into high acceleration from which he and his crew were largely protected by the *Ventura*'s inertial screen. Zorbin was giving him readings of the comet's ice and mineral composition, its mean diameter (just over two kilometers), its mean specific density (about 0.67 grams), its overall gravitational mass (about twenty trillion kilograms or twenty billion tons), its relative inertial mass or momentum (an enormous kilogram number, gravitational mass raised to the eleventh power, because of its ghostly velocity). Methuen whistled low: a direct snatch of this hurtling monster would have about as much chance as a harpooning of a twenty-five-meter whale from a one-man kayak using a tarpon line. Nevertheless it would be necessary somehow to pull the monster out of its inertial orbit into a direct tug-line toward Earth. It would have to be

17

done in tactical stages, each one so chancy that it might prove ship-lethal.

There was also a question of strategic judgment: even outside the Sol System, would it be scientifically ethical to ensnare for destruction a comet so unique? Methuen had to make his own judgment: in these years before nearly instantaneous iradio communication, he was more isolated from home base than a seventeenth-century sea captain in the farthest quarters of a remote ocean—a radio message, limited to light-velocity, would take 470 years to reach Earth and another 470 to return. Methuen could of course dispatch a robot carrier, which would reach Earth and bring back a reply in a mere three weeks, and meanwhile he could be tailing the comet; but that would lose him three weeks of fishing time and could bring a reprimand.

Dark, lean middle-tall B. J. Methuen was an uneasy perfectionist whose inter-conflicting ideation in the planning stage did not stop him from reaching reasonably quick decisions and staying with them during action—uneasy all the way as perfection eluded him, and not at all happy if he attained only ninety-eight percent of perfection. It was the turbulent planning-balancing process that was inwardly agitating sober-faced Methuen while the *Ventura* closed distance between herself and her prey.

Presently Methuen queried: "Zorbin, do you know what I've been thinking about?" His quiet middle-baritone falsely expressed whole serenity.

Zorbin replied promptly: "First, ethics. Second, tactics—but you really haven't reached tactics yet."

"Right. Pray zero-in on ethics. What might be all the consequences of catching and bringing home this extra-large extra-fast comet?"

"Call her Gladys. She'll be your seventh."

"All right, Comet Gladys. Consequences?"

"The Sahara Desert will receive a water bonanza. And the entire astronomical world will be mad as hell because they weren't given a chance to study Gladys alive."

"Which of the two will mean more to Astrofleet?"

"The Sahara, probably. Besides, science will have our report together with detailed behavioral data."

"Is there any chance that Gladys might reach the Solar System if left alone?"

"Most unlikely. A comet orbit rarely exceeds a few light years, a parsec at most. Anyhow, if she did reach Sol, it

18

wouldn't happen at her present velocity for another fifteen millennia. But to be sure about the orbit, I'll need more tracking figures."

"Thank you, Mr. Zorbin. Now: consequences if we bypass her and report when we reach home that she was too interesting to stop?"

"Maybe not too bad, if we come home with another ice-comet. But science will still be mad as hell, because we didn't bring Gladys in for study."

"Science gets mad either way?"

"With science, you can't win."

"If we bypass Gladys, how do you calculate our chances of coming home with twenty billion tons of other ice?"

"We aren't likely to find another comet this big, Skipper. With great luck, we might snare two or three totaling that mass, but it's unlikely, and you know how tough it is to bring in two or three altogether. Gladys is a *big* bastard."

"Thank you again. Any recommendations?"

"None, Skipper, none at all. I've told you all I know."

"Then we'll continue pursuit, and decide what to do when we catch her." And Methuen went into tactical discussion with his exec, meanwhile increasing acceleration until they settled into sprint-pursuit speed of forty thousand times the velocity of light.

In sixteen hours, Gladys was overtaken.

As they came in on Gladys, they were braking under heavy *g*-force. They veered into her wake, and they kept on braking until they were down to Gladys-velocity.

Methuen queried: "Mr. Zorbin, do you have enough tracking figures to plot her orbit?"

Zorbin threw him a peculiar look. "If my figures are right, it's a hell of a funny orbit. I really ought to have another twenty-four hours."

"You have them, sir. Meanwhile we are locked on behind her at her own velocity, which makes the comet and the ship together a relatively stationary unit. Why don't you bring in your relief? And then, let's you and I go out and inspect our catch."

Gladys was a real beaut. They circled her in the tender. She was dark on space-side, of course; but on Bellatrix-side she ice-gleamed like a miniature moon disc. They took particular notice that the comet surface was deeply and complexly

19

crevassed like a glacier surface, which meant that Gladys had never passed through a planetary atmosphere which would have melted surface ice with friction heat and produced a vitreous exterior.

The two officers, alone in the tender, were doing more than eyeball-gazing. Methuen manned a battery of instruments which measured parameters like stratification (layerings of comet-magma, comparable to tree rings in three dimensions) and comparative densities cubic meter by cubic meter all the way in to the core. Zorbin watched other instruments having equal penetration but measuring other parameters, particularly chemical analysis by cubic meters; he was also localizing significant foreign inclusions which had been picked up in the comet's travels, such as siderites.

They were making their second circuit of darkside, on a new angle of declination, when Zorbin said, very low: "There is something peculiar almost all the way in, deep at center; I had a hint of it on brightside, but I get it more sharply here without light interference."

"Oh?"

"Wait till I get the coordinates right. Latitude 49°2′, longitude 82° even" (by convention they had laid off coordinates using the comet's leading direction as polar north), "depth 0.92 kilometers—that's about 0.09 this side of gravity-center. It's funny—"

"What's funny?"

"Relatively tiny inclusions composed almost entirely of organics."

"Got any shapes yet?"

"Wait till we've made about two more passes at twenty-degree declinations."

On the next pass, Zorbin said, "I have to tell you now that the distribution of organics is roughly what you'd expect to find in mammalian bodies."

"Way down in there?"

"Way down in there."

"How about shapes?"

"Not talking yet, Skipper. One more pass."

And during that fourth pass, Methuen was informed dead-voice by Zorbin: "There are two organic bodies, both about Erth-human size. One of them looks like a plain ordinary human—like you or me, or perhaps it is a female. The other looks like a human, too—only, a human with large wings."

Methuen meditated; Zorbin studied. Methuen said, "Chemical analysis in agreement?"

"Affirmative."

"Nothing else? We aren't kidding ourselves?"

"It's hard to imagine what else those inclusions could be."

"Mr. Zorbin, it's just as hard to imagine what you say they *are*. Apart from your wings—how in hell would they have gotten themselves caught in twenty billion tons of high-speed comet?"

"Skipper, do you expect me to tell you?"

"They aren't smashed?"

"Not smashed, as far as instruments can tell me. Well: mammoths have been found in glaciers—"

"That's different."

"Yes."

"My own studies are about through for now, Mr. Zorbin. Want another pass for confirmation of yours?"

"That I'd appreciate. Pray change the declination by forty degrees this time."

When the final darkside pass was more than half done, Zorbin said crisply, "No change."

"Wings and all?"

"Affirmative."

"Those wings—could they be accidentally associated inclusions?"

"I have a holograph built up during five passes at varying declinations totaling a hundred twenty degrees of arc. The wings are wings, and they are connected to one of the guys. And the guys are frozen face-to-face down there, for love or for war."

Steady pursuit continued, while Zorbin or his assistant plotted tracking figures.

Over lunch next day, Methuen used a lull in small talk to inquire casually: "Saul, do you think you can plot an orbit now?"

Zorbin frowned. "I can, B.J., and it will amaze you."

"Want to tell me now?"

"Absolutely straight linear orbit. No curvature at all."

"No question?"

"No question. If Gladys should veer from the straight line, something new would be pushing or pulling her—and at her velocity, that would have to be quite a something."

Methuen meditated. He had planned a complex and dan-

21

gerous procedure for pulling this monster out of some orbit to which she was tenaciously glued with a momentum of 6.168×10^{24} kilograms. For practical purposes, that was her rushing weight. Get ahead of the comet, turn, match speeds with her, snare her with transponder beams going past, slow her a little, release her; repeat the maneuver, repeat, repeat; and if they didn't either sprain all their transponder guns or get pulled into Gladys by her gravity and space-wind, they'd have her tamed whereafter they could simply tug her at gradually increasing velocity in the direction they would choose, which would be toward Erth. But if the orbit was linear, this procedure might be somewhat simplified. . . .

"What," he queried, "is the direction of this linear orbit?"

Zorbin swallowed another mouthful of rehydrated eggs, then told his plate: "Directly toward Erth. No change of orbit required."

After thought, Methuen said carefully, "Apart from understanding that this reduces our tactics to utter simplicity—do you comprehend how unlikely this is?"

"Except," said Zorbin, "for something I noticed yesterday. Remember toward the end of the chase we crossed the comet's orbit?"

"Right."

"Just as we crossed it, the instruments showed a slight Erthward slew. Our position at that instant was, right ascension 0546, declination minus nine degrees forty-one minutes."

"Well?"

"Well, B.J.?"

Having thought, Methuen murmured, "I'll be damned!"

"You're thinking what I'm thinking?"

"The five-forty-six gradient."

"That's what I'm thinking."

"Way out here, Saul?" In his fearsome prevoyant dream, that number 546. . . .

"Way out here. Spotted eleven prior times by various ships, but never farther out than eighty-nine parsecs from Erth."

"Saul, my thoughts are multiple and confused, but three thoughts are standing out."

"May I guess, B.J.?"

"Pray do."

"One: that Comet Gladys may be riding the gradient, which would account for her horrible speed."

"Two?"

"That now we won't have to pull her out of orbit; we can

22

simply get ahead of her, latch onto her with transponders, and ease her up to the kind of velocity we will need in order to reach Erth as soon as you deem desirable."

"Not necessarily the order of my thought, Saul, but you do have two of them. What's the third?"

"That we should follow the comet's example and stay on the gradient in order to maintain the same Erthward speed with reduced thrust and less engine wear."

"Saul, somehow what remains of lunch has lost attraction for me. How about you?"

"I'm with you, B.J. Let's hit the bridge."

They bypassed Gladys, got in front of her, hooked her, and began the patient procedure of pulling her faster and faster. Methuen hit the PA: "Now hear this, this is the skipper. Well done all hands; very nice. Gladys is under control and we are making for Erth. Move into towing routine. That is all."

He snapped off the PA and said low, "Mr. Zorbin, please bring her gradually to nine thousand C, and hold that velocity until we are one astronomical unit off Pluto-orbit."

"Will do, sir."

"What do you think, Mr. Zorbin? Does the gradient extend indefinitely out into space? Does it hold that line of 0546 by minus 0941 indefinitely, or does it eventually begin to show curvature? And since comets normally have closed eliptical orbits, what has Gladys been doing before we found her? Did she in some curved orbit intersect the gradient and straighten out and speed up? Or has she been traveling the gradient since origin?"

"Plenty to talk about, Skipper, during our two weeks going home. I'll add a couple of wonderings. How did two humanoids get themselves caught in the center of a comet without being smashed? And did you ever before hear of a humanoid with wings?"

"There are angels, perhaps, Mr. Zorbin."

"There are also perhaps devils, Commander Methuen."

The remark convoluted the Methuen stomach: devil in the comet, dream of a next-year Erth-attack from space, 546. . . . Resolutely he reminded himself that he did not believe in prevoyance; but from that moment onward, he had a developing thing about Comet Gladys.

23

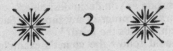

3

Soon after Dorita Lanceo reached the age of fifteen (in a year which her planet Erth counted as 2462 AD), her school achievement began to decline—not nearly to the point of failure, but to a level so far below her usual stellar performance that faculty began to wonder. Dorita was a petite long-haired blonde, round-faced, blue-eyed, kiss-lipped, shaped like a poet's divine dream, and popular with faculty because of the childish gaiety that pervaded her mental brilliance. Eventually her counselor questioned her about her sagging scholarship; Dorita passed it off by making a little face and confessing that these days she was thinking about boys a lot. She wasn't. She had already weighed boys (that is, two boys and one faculty man from another school during the past two years) and had found them wanting, not as thrill devices, but as matters of sustaining interest for herself specifically.

What undermined her scholarship was her calculated decision to shift some of her left-brain-lobe attention away from school work and into the wonderfully powerful and nearly occult searchings that her right lobe was bringing off.

Dorita's prime mover, formulated at the age of nine, was a fixed belief that anything forbidden without convincing reasons required testing, and that she was the one to do this testing. Of course, you couldn't always determine what was forbidden; you had to come face-to-face with the forbidding; or else you had to infer that something was forbidden, simply by noticing that it wasn't being done.

As for the convincing reasons which might justify a forbidding, they were extremely hard to learn without committing a violation and experiencing the consequences. From first-remembered childhood, Dorita had been violating this and that, including (at seven) her mother's locked diary. She had learned how to open it with a bobby pin and had been caught in the midst of engrossment. Frequent incidents had drawn punishment, some of it corporal; but early on, she had decided that intentional punishment was merely part of the forbidding attitude and did not in itself constitute a convincing reason for desisting.

Traumatically, her mother died when Dorita was entering puberty, leaving her father to guide her through and beyond it. Her father was a good beloved buddy; he often took her on vacations and roughed it with her in the mountains; but he wouldn't touch the area of sex education. This hit Dorita as being so senseless that it must be an irrational tabu; and that was why she entered into her first seduction when she was thirteen and reinforced her findings twice when she was fourteen. The series had satisfied her tabu-blasting compulsion in *that* direction, and she dropped it to move into more interesting areas.

She never made any attempt upon her father, not even when alone with him in a night camp. Long ago she had comprehended the dangers of interpersonal stickiness, which was why she had eschewed her male classmates. She and her father were great buddies, and she wanted it to stay like that. Dorita was ruthless only when she was homing on a defined target.

Her decision at fifteen to shift her major attention from scholarship to more arcane concerns resulted from a dismaying discovery. She had run out of locked doors to open; and therefore she put her right lobe to full-time and her left to part-time work in a survey of the potential field.

Dorita had the misfortune to come into her world a bit late: her society had already largely cleared the old tabu-tangle. (This would have been accomplished a lot earlier had some prior society, say the 20th century West, been blessed by the existence of Dorita.) All but a few minority religions (and these did not interest Dorita) smiled benignly at almost every sort of blasphemy and vice, regarding these as wild oats which needed to be sown before the young sinner could be religiously domesticated. There remained in her world no minority prejudices of any consequence, and every imaginable vocational field was wide open for qualified women. In terms of Dorita's assumptions, all of which were zeroed-in on the concept of unprecedented door openings, there existed practically no locked door worth breaking through—except, perhaps, some interesting aspects of the laws.

Her inventory of promising illegalities narrowed to a mere

tetrad of possibles: vice (not as a victim or tool but as an entrepreneur), murder, rape, fraud or stealing. But she detested both murder and rape: both victimized, and both were confessions of one or another kind of inadequacy. The purveying of vice at first seemed more appealing, if one could avoid victimizing nice guys and gals, if one could concentrate on rich and irresponsible customers; but when you analyzed that to the wall, you found that you had to victimize nice guys and gals in order to please wealthy debauchery; Dorita hated hurting good-hearted people, so that was out.

The only tabu left for consideration was fraud or stealing.

At first glance, either fraud or stealing would directly or indirectly victimize nice guys and gals. But Dorita quickly saw that the world was full of fat cats who had got that way by one or another sort of victimization, if only by exploiting workers or by paying no interest on checking accounts. Therefore, with her left lobe critically prompting her wide-ranging right lobe (while her left lobe casually collected B's and C's in her school work), Dorita began to lay plans for becoming the most untouchable and large-scale-successful defrauder and burglar since Robin Hood, with all of Robin's penchant for sharing the wealth with the needy.

When she first began to practice her new craft on schoolmates, Dorita discovered that she had two unfair advantages. Great!

Advantage One: Studying a female classmate who was standing and haltingly reciting in answer to a teacher-question, Dorita found that somehow she was anticipating every word that her classmate was saying. Trying this on others, she discovered that she could read what was forming just below the surfaces of their conscious minds. Trying it eventually on teachers, having a strong feeling that she could read their evaluations, which were developing as recitations proceeded, Dorita tested by getting into teachers' classbooks at times when she sensed that the teachers were distant, and in every case she found that the anticipated evaluation had been marked down. Right-lobe achievement, brought under left-lobe control!

Advantage Two: Pussy-cat-sitting on her bed in her room, meditating, idly eyeing a half-finished glass of ginger ale on the table beside the chair she had just departed, Dorita whimsically reflected how nice it would be if the ginger ale would just come to her; and then, remembering that telekinetic ability was not infrequently linked with telepathy, which she had, she seriously *willed* that the ginger ale come. It came, all over her, without the glass. Laughing while she cleaned herself and theorized, she guessed that you had to have a full mental definition of what was to come, before you tried moving it— and also a restrictive definition, so that the table would not come along with the glass of liquid. This ability, too, she honed. Same lobal interplay.

Soon classmates were beginning to miss things out of their lockers—and to discover them back there within hours—although the lockers were palmprint-locked. Dorita had not bothered to fake palmprints, which she thought maybe she could have done. But she understood now that she must for certain know what she wanted out of the closed place before she tampered; a couple of times she had merely asked for the locker contents, not knowing what those contents might be, and nothing had come.

Before long, teachers began to miss class record books which had been in locked drawers, and to find them in there later. It became more subtle: a teacher, examining her classbook, would find a certain student marked A for yesterday, although she could swear that she had entered a C or D; but the A was in the teacher's own hand, with no evidence of erasure. The student beneficiary was never Dorita; nor was it, except by accident, ever a favorite classmate, just somebody who needed help.

The best-heeled student in school missed a hundred-note from his billfold. That one never came back to him; but five indigent students discovered unexpected twenties in their billfolds or purses.

Dorita now went a step further. Finding an excuse to interview the principal, she detected in his mind an intent to put a fire-insurance policy in the school safe that night. Next day, the policy was gone from the safe, but it turned up in the safe again the following morning. Dorita had successfully put together mind-monitoring and body-snatching.

After high-school graduation at sixteen, she refused college, explaining to her irritated but not altogether mystified father that she had to get a job and find herself. (Her most recent test scores had been so high that a dozen top colleges would have bid competitively for her, despite her shaky scholarship; even the educational achievement measures were high: both her lobes had been involuntarily soaking up stuff.)

She went to the Big Apple in mid-2463 with a small grub-stake from her father, found an apartment with a roommate (female), and located work as a waitress in a fast-food operation. Her roommate was rather attractive, which reminded Dorita that she hadn't yet broken the homosexual semi-no-no; but with a roomie you avoid such things, they breed only living trouble. There were plenty of attractive young men around, too; but Dorita, having already scored in that game, had little time for them.

What she did have time for was banks, on mornings soon after they opened and before her day's work began at eleven, and also on bank-open Monday evenings between eight and nine. She sampled five banks, all main offices, before opening her first account on her first payday.

Her procedure was the same in all five banks. She would enter, look ingenuous, saunter around sizing up the physical and mental terrain. When she sensed that a guard or a customer consultant had eyes on her, she would let her head drift around until she spied that person, and to him (or her) she would mouth from across the room: "Can you help me?" Their sense always was that this wide-eyed round-mouthed blonde kid of perhaps fourteen (as remarked, her age was sixteen) was looking for her father or mother. When the employee would beckon to her, she would approach and plead: "Sir" (or "Madam," the approach worked on either ·sex), "I have a little money that I'd like to invest, can you help me?" And after several minutes of earnest conversation, preferably with an assistant manager, she would produce five credits. The employee would smile tolerantly and aver that there was little he could recommend other than an ordinary savings account. She would inquire intently about such matters as withdrawal privileges and interest; then, all indecisive, she would stand and say, "Thank you so much, but I really will have to think about it—"

She would depart with a good deal of mind-tapped information about that bank's operations, but without opening an account because accounts in more than one prey-bank could lead to trouble. Probably some of the assistant managers from diversified banks would tell each other, at exchange or drinking clubs, the story of the wide-eyed blonde kid with five bucks to invest; if two of them had seen her and compared notes, they would probably chuckle and wonder how many banks she would visit before investing—"Some

28

little comparative shopper!"—and let it go at that; no harm done.

By the time she opened her first checking account with a hundred-credit deposit, which was most of her first two weeks' pay, she knew the generalities of what she needed to know in order to bring off a telekinetic heist. Refinements were needed; amd she had figured excuses to go up the management pyramid in order to get them telepathically. But telepathy alone was not enough: she had to reason out what questions to get answered. And before moving to get any money, she wanted to know the hazards involved in getting rid of it.

Meanwhile it became evident that she needed more capital than she could earn in fast food. Without too much difficulty, she found a job as a waitress in a fairly decent night-spot restaurant on Fifty-Second Street; the restaurant had a lot of business-dinner trade, so she went for the five-to-one shift and got it. The salary was half again her fast-food pay, and her tips doubled the salary. Two weeks later, she had what she needed for operations.

Having set aside ninety-five credits in small bills, she visited a branch manager in a sixth bank. Producing the money, she told the official that a man on the street had given it to her in exchange for her wristwatch, and she had got to thinking that it might be bad money or even hot money; could he help her, please? The official scrutinized every bill (some new, most worn); he got out a book of teletyped serial numbers, sampled the bills, and checked the sample against the book; then, smiling, he returned the bills and assured her that to the best of his knowledge and belief they were neither counterfeit nor hot; but he warned this little girl against taking money from strangers. Dorita departed with all the information that had been going through the man's mind about identifying hot bills and laundering money.

She checked and filled out the information as follows. Compiling a list of five small private detective agencies listed in small type in the yellow pages, she visited each of these dicks, showed him the money, and gave him the story about the wristwatch. After seeing all five and paying their advisory fees, her cash had dwindled to forty-five credits: she had paid fifty credits for a gold mine. True, she was now superficially known to six banks and five private eyes—but to what end?

29

Approach to final operation:

Dorita telekinetically forged a line-out and correction in her checking account passbook; the correction reduced a ninety-credit deposit to eighty credits. Patiently then she stood in line at the window of the same teller; and when her turn came, she showed him the correction, told him she hadn't noticed it until just now, assured him that the original ninety-credit entry had been the correct amount. He studied the entry, shook his head, muttered that he just never did that sort of thing; but he had to admit that the correction was in his handwriting. He couldn't out-check it, his vouchers were long since filed; she'd have to see an assistant manager—and, since she was such a piteous pretty little girl, he left his window, conducted her to the official, repeated the story, and left her there. The assistant manager said kindly that the vouchers weren't available to him, Dorita would have to see the cashier.

The matronly cashier was hostile at first, but Dorita's abashed girlhood brought her around. "Let me show you what the problem is," the cashier said; and she conducted Dorita into the open bank vault. "Have you ever been in one of these vaults?" Wide-eyed, Dorita negated. The cashier pointed in turn to three rooms, each barred by a locked grill. "In *there* are private deposit boxes rented by our customers—*you* can rent one, Miss Lanceo, whenever you choose, if you have valuable papers or wish to keep ready cash there. In *there* we keep deposited cash until it is collected for storage in a Brinks warehouse." Dorita caught it that this happened every Thursday. "Now, in this third room, we store what is related to your problem. Here we file all our vouchers on individual transactions for a period of seven years, and then the vouchers are destroyed. You see, even a microflake wouldn't show the type of error that you are reporting; we have to keep the originals. Now, my dear, just look through those bars at those stacks and stacks of vouchers. It would take one of our busy people at least an hour of lost work to probe into those stacks and produce the voucher that would settle your question about a mere ten credits. Really, if you don't mind, I'd rather give you the ten credits out of pocket." Dorita caught it that she meant, out of contingency cash.

"You're just awfully nice," murmured intimidated Dorita, "and I can see how my problem seems awful little in comparison with all the money in that other room. Your teller was probably right, anyway. I'd rather just drop the matter."

The cashier hugged her arm. "No, I insist, my dear. You just come back to my office, and I'll give you a nice ten-credit bill."

Dorita brought off a blush. "Well, if you insist. But I'd rather you'd make it five credits, that way neither of us would be out more than five."

The cashier gave her an impulsive hug. "Honey, come over to this gate where all the money is. How much cash do you guess is in there? If you come within a million credits of the right figure, I'll give you ten; if you miss, we'll make it five."

Dorita read the figure in the cashier's mind; deliberately, she guessed too low by millions.

And now Dorita had all she needed.

When the Brinks people arrived on Thursday morning, they were greeted by an abashed bank staff. All the money from the past week was gone.

The afternoon papers headlined: FIVE MILLION CR BANK HEIST!

Dorita serenely continued to work in her restaurant. The telekinetically stolen money was stashed in a locus easily available to her alone. Nobody else could possibly find it.

That right brain lobe of Dorita's was incredible! First it had provided her with sure intuitions, then with telepathic readings, then with *projective* telepathy (she could compel a person by telepathic suggestion), then with telekinesis—and, surely the final revelation, with *tempo*kinesis.

Her left lobe kept trying to rationalize her right lobe's developing powers. In the end, her left lobe had to content itself with guiding and controlling those powers.

The concept of reading or partially controlling another person's mind was deceptively easy for her left lobe to accept and even to rationalize. Even the concept of mentally compelling an object to move instantaneously from one space-locus to another was semi-rationalizable, though the question *how* it might be done put the left lobe into a symbolic blur. But movement in *time*. . . .

Can't happen! insisted Left. *No possible conceptualization!*

To hell with your conceptualization, Right retorted. *Excuse me, not to hell with it—just use it to find a way for us to try movement in time!*

31

It had to be a checkable thing, and simple at first. Her initial thought was to send something into the future by a few minutes: she could check its vanishing and reappearance by her cutichron. Right objected: *Not future! something wrong with that. Try past.* Left didn't have the theory of uncrescesced probabilities, which was what was wrong with futuring; but Dorita did accept that the test must be a transition into the past. And that sort of transition would be infinitely tougher to test. Besides, neither Right nor Left had the faintest idea how to gauge whether a thing would go into the past, once sent, by one day or by twenty or what.

Encouraged by her teleportations, Dorita devised a combinaison. On 20 August 2463, she wrote a note to a friend, predating it to 10 August, asking her friend to phone her on 21 August for a special reason. She mailed the note, *willing* as it dropped into the box that it be delivered on 11 August. On 21 August, her friend phoned: "Dorita, I have your note—what's up?" Dorita queried: "When did you receive it?" "That's a funny thing," the friend said; "it came two weeks ago, but it was dated 10 August, only ten days ago. Dorita, are you slipping?"

It did not occur to Dorita that she had created a tiny time-paradox (which anyhow could have no effect on the world's growth). Dorita only exulted in the sure knowledge that she had brought off a backtime passage with merely a forty percent time-error on her first try. During several ensuing months, she worked on the new art, refining it progressively.

Thus, when she stole the bank money early in 2464, Dorita was able to hide it unfindably: in her own apartment—two days in the past.

She laundered the stolen money, developing a simple generalization: every letter in all the serial numbers would be changed to the next one in the alphabet, and each number would become the prior number. And then she simply willed it to happen, and it happened. To crack that would take a cryptographer looking for a change-code, an utterly improbable police hypothesis. She had worked around letters W through Z, knowing from her mind-taps that they had not yet been used in the official serialization.

The next problem was the one that plagues authors: distribution. She set aside twenty percent for herself: a million made a very nice grubstake As beneficiaries of the remaining four million, she built a list of twenty charities; but the difficulty was, how to deposit an average of Cr 200,000 into the treasury of each charity without unbalancing books or otherwise raising eyebrows. Much of her time during the next few weeks was methodically devoted to visiting each charity in the guise of a cub reporter for one or another newskenner, asking to see the books, and locating the cash depository; in this operation, her projective hypnosis worked well; her treatment included a stipulation that they would notice no change in their cash balances, and indeed that they would permanently forget her visits. Wasn't it Jesus who had exhorted, "Give in secret?" Once all that was accomplished, it was easy (relaxed in her apartment) to change all their books and send money to all their safes. Presumably, deserving people would benefit, although you never knew about a charity.

As for her own million, it would have been nice to invest it at interest; but any large investment by previously impecunious Miss Lanceo would be sure to arouse curiosity; and since all investments were centrally registered in Erthworld Union Headquarters, any combination of small investments even under pseudonyms would eventually be brought together by somebody. So she played it safe, economically devouring her own capital, drawing it up from the past of her apartment and spending it as needed, while continuing at the restaurant as a waitress for self-screening and for laughs.

Eventually she dared a dangerously desperate thing. Instead of merely calling up money, she *moved herself* into the past to fetch it—having not a clue in the world as to whether she could ever find her way back to the present with or without the money.

After a number of erroneous backtime drolleries comparable to repeatedly missing your ways in the mirror-maze of a funny-house, quite by accident she found herself again in the present with a fistful of notes.

For quite awhile afterward, the intricacies of learning how to timedive (right lobe somehow initiating, left lobe trying to control) totally engrossed her off-duty interest. But shortly after she had seduced Marc Antony away from Cleopatra, the fascination of time-diving palled.

And it left her facing a life-problem.

Having eliminated all career-objectives other than stealing or fraud, she had brought off one high-level stealing with an associated number of ancillary frauds. And along the way, she had mastered telepathy receptive and projective, some degree of clairvoyance, telekinesis, *tempo*kinesis (a bastard word), and even *self*-tempokinesis. All that was left for her was to go onward and upward in the same lines. And since now she knew from experience that she *could*, with systematic preparation, bring off anything along these lines that she might want, all the way up to removing the gold from Fort Knox or bamboozling the SEC, it seemed really silly to make the effort.

So there was nothing. All the future. Nothing.

Unless she could think of something absolutely *cosmic*. . . .

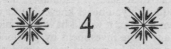

Narsua flittered the forest floor, seeking prey, seeking also not to become prey. Narsua's movements were less than systematic: she would pause, peer and smell around, feel temporarily safe, contort herself to nibble clean the hair on some of her legs, leap erect, peer, smell, contort again to do other legs, leap erect, peer, smell, work her way onward.

Instinct-fear made her jump two yards sideways: the webshot meant to ensnare her missed narrowly, entangled a fallen tree branch, then elastically sproinged around the branch as its shooter bit it loose from herself. Narsua did a dart-spin poised stiff-legged ready with her abdomen swung beneath her legs so that her tailgun was aimed for action: before she had consciously located the adversary, already her tail had shot, and the foe was entangled. For this one more time, experienced Narsua was predator, not prey.

Having cut her web, she straightened out her body and moved with leisure toward the entangled one: an almost identical eight-legged replica of herself. Eight eyes glowered into eight eyes.

Narsua mindspoke ritual: *As with thee, some day with me*

also. Meanwhile, I eat thy knowledge. May all our eggs be blessed.

Responded her prey, reluctant but compelled: *As with me, some day with thee also. Meanwhile, eat my knowledge. May all our eggs be blessed.*

Narsua fanged. Then Narsua activated her eight mouth parts.

Sated, Narsua lumbered out of the forest, around-and-back-alert for possible attackers, but herself no longer on the prowl. Being sated, she had time for the occasional pleasure of indulging in the only wonder that she knew.

This wonder was *not* the sky of her world. That sky was a featureless gray by day, except for clouds which periodically would grow and blacken and bring flooding rain; no sun, only perpetual unvarying diffuse luminosity which faded at night until darkness in her world became total without moon or stars. Even the concept of sky had not occurred to her.

The *wall* was her wonder.

The wall towered indefinitely above her: sheer, smooth-polished bare rock rising a hundred meters (although Narsua could not measure) concavely like the inside of a bowl; above that, jagged rock, practically vertical for most of its height until it lost itself in sky; arising so suddenly out of ground that Narsua had been able to mount the base curvature only a little way before she had been hopelessly balked by impossible steep slipperyness.

The wall went on and on, as far as she could see in either direction. A long time ago, Narsua had set forth on a journey along the base of this wall, pausing each hunger-time only long enough to dart into the forest after viciously backfighting food, pausing at nightfall to sleep serenely (because nobody was hungry then). At the end of many eights of hungers, the wall had only brought her back to her starting point, and she had found no outward passage anywhere.

Did it wall her in from something, or wall her out of something? It was not a question too complex for Narsua, who had been caught within things and who had eaten the knowledge of many sisters who had been caught within things. She thought it must wall her *in*: for she had ranged her forest exhaustively, and wherever she might come out from among trees, she would always see the wall.

She snapped alert: during a few moments, wonder had overwhelmed her, monopolizing her consciousness, and that

35

was dangerous. But there were no attackers in sight, naturally: most of her kind held to the forest.

Wonder gave way to fear. The wall was a solid tabu, dangerous even to look upon. Yet wonder crept back into her: what *beyond?*

Disaster struck! Crumpling, terrorized Narsua wrapped protective legs about her abdomen and rolled helpless with shock upon shock.

Half a thousand kilometers from Narsua's world, a pocket of gas which had been accumulating pressure for centuries reached a level of intensity which the thin planetary crust above it could no longer withstand. Gas blasted the rock, driving into sky dust and pebbles and boulders of ice. Precisely at the center of eruptive force, a billion-ton iceberg was catapulted into sky at a beginning velocity of twelve kilometers per second.

The year of Earth-simultaneity with events on Narsua's planet was something like 48,000 BC.

Narsua's world convulsed and shook, slamming Narsua against a tree at forest edge. She clung, shriveled, to the tree, playing dead, while the world-trembling dislodged great boulders from the wall's height and rolled them down upon her in avalanche. Behind and beyond the rock-rolling noise there was a deep rumble-thundering which continued for time-immeasurable and gradually diminished into silence.

After a prudent while, Narsua allowed herself to appear alive again, although the ground continued to quiver. It had been many eights of eatings since she had experienced that sort of chaos, and this episode had been the most violent. Perhaps it was her punishment for questioningly prowling the wall.

Soul-shriveled, she scuttled back into the forest. Perhaps tomorrow she would ask gods about it. She might even ask God. But God and the other gods probably could tell her no more about the cataclysm than they could tell her about whatever lay beyond the wall.

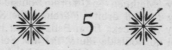

5

The news of Ice-Comet Gladys reached Erth long before the *Ventura* did. Methuen, soon after pulling away from Bellatrix in the wake of his quarry, had fired a report to Astrofleet HQ via a robot carrier which, having no living cargo and therefore needing only a small inertial shield to protect its engine, was able to reach Erth in a week which was half *Ventura*'s time. And once he had reached the periphery of the Sol System off Pluto-orbit, Methuen could open radio communication requiring (at that time in that year) no more than six hours each way; and this time shortened with each planetary orbit overpassed inbound. (He could have talked with the Erthworld capital on Nereid in one hour each way from Pluto, but he hesitated to go so high.)

Capture of a comet was fairly routine. Gladys was very large but not quite the largest ever. The report of the weird organic inclusions was another matter entirely, especially when it was coupled with the comet's uniquely high velocity. Astrofleet was inclined to keep the business under wraps pending extensive scientific consultation; but there is always one crewperson who doesn't get the message, and this time it was an assistant PR spokesman who learned the news just before a newskenner conference and blurted it out there. Questions were fired, the PR man backed and filled, and newsmedia blared MONSTERS COMING IN ICE-COMET! The public fuss wasn't much, in these advanced days of an interstellar Sol/Centauri League, and the newskenner interest waned.

But Dorita Lanceo, on the prowl for a purpose, had caught the first stories and went into furtive investigative action.

An unencumbered starship coming in on the Sol System at nine thousand times the speed of light could simply rotate presenting her stern repulsors to Erth and brake down to a glide-in. It wasn't that simple when you had twenty billion tons of comet in tow at about thirty thousand times a comet's normal velocity. Methuen and Zorbin, outside Pluto, went into a decaying freefall orbit all around the Sol System. It had been nearly two weeks from Bellatrix, at high speed, to an astronomical unit outside Pluto; the first Sol System orbit of 3.7×10^{10} kilometers, which would take light nearly thirty-five hours to course, took the *Ventura*-plus-Gladys thirteen seconds.

With succeeding orbits, the effect of the circular vectors without compensating acceleration was to slow Gladys until she began to pull back on *Ventura;* and when after a number of orbits their velocity had declined to a hundred C, Gladys was tame enough so that Methuen could do increasingly tighter orbits inside the Sol System. Inwards of Jupiter, but outside the asteroid belt, he chanced another 180° turn, so that Gladys was dragging *him;* his ship resisted, and they ended by moving into Erth orbit in freefall just outside the band of communications satellites.

All this orbiting had required five tense days. Both Methuen and Zorbin were thoroughly pooped because of numerous complications such as avoiding planets and large asteroids and space-ships en route.

Advice was streaming in to Methuen from very high levels; it appeared that even Erthworld Chairman Marta Evans was interested. It was unsteadying, but Methuen drove down the temptation to be heady about it and went to work mentally sorting the diversified advice.

Vertura and Gladys remained in Erth orbit for the best part of two weeks. The first visitors from Erth were, of course, Astrofleet officers and assorted scientists; the latter, apart from questioning Methuen and Zorbin in far-and-deep-ranging detail, besides scrutinizing all their instrumental data and their qualitative notes, circumcruised Gladys over and over again, using instrumentation far more sophisticated than the *Ventura's*. At the end of a week, after endless argument around tables in Erthworld Headquarters in Manhattan, with Methuen present at most conferences for expert advice (while Zorbin remained in deputy command aboard the *Ventura*), diplomats and scientists and Astrofleet had arrived at decisions for carving up the comet and disposing of the pieces.

The cutters arrived in *Ventura's* orbit. Gladys was laser-cut (and she submitted without a quiver) into fifty-million-kilo ice chunks—four hundred thousand pieces, all dirty amalgams of ice and rock. Each chunk was coated with a thin silicon derivative for insulation against reentry heat; and then each chunk was pulled out of orbit by a cutter and first tugged and then launched in a precalculated trajectory into one of several hundred-square-kilometer processing basins in the Red Sea.

One fifty-million-kilo ice-chunk was otherwise handled. This was the precious core of the comet—a core of relatively pure ice—containing the two humanoid inclusions.

Entrapment of two apparently unmutilated humanoids in the ice of a comet was in itself unique; and wonder piled upon wonder. On none of the three planets in the interstellar Sol/Centauri League (Sol's Erth, and Alpha Centauri's Vash and Rab), nor on any of the other two dozen planets in various star systems with which Sol/Centauri maintained trade relationships, did anybody know of a humanoid having any kind of wings.

Consequently, some investigating scientists had spent much time questioning the *Ventura* officers and poring over their instrumental flakes in an effort to ascertain or at least surmise the total orbit of Gladys, and in particular, the planet of her origin (assuming that, like numerous other comets, she had originated in an explosion on a planet), but the trajectory of Gladys as plotted by Zorbin was so clearly linear that a closed elliptical course could not be established, and there was even speculation that her total course might have been hyperbolic. These uncertainties led to the wildest speculation as to her possible origin, some surmises making her extra-galactic; but excluded as origin-points were all the stars in and related to the Sol/Centauri League, since beings unknown in the League had been trapped near comet-center and therefore at or near comet-origin.

The central chunk underwent five days of intensive instrumental study at the Erthworld Interdisciplinary Science Center in Manhattan, where the ice-block was stored in a deep-freeze laboratory. Thereafter the institute chief, lean fiftyish Dr. Xavier Almagor, reported as follows directly to the Cabinet Secretary for the Department of Education, Science, and Culture: that the two humanoids were indeed humanoids, that they were frozen into a central comet-

39

stratum which was apparently between 48,000 and 53,000 years old (adjudged by radioactive study of associated mineral inclusions)—and, most arrestingly, that the humanoids were indeed undamaged, were quite possibly not dead but in a state of cryogenic suspended animation. Almagor added that by a careful process of unfreezing the chunk in several successive strata, combined with slow radioheating techniques common in modern cryogenic unfreezings, it might be possible to restore the specimens to full life in a witnessable length of time.

The Secretary immediately reported these findings to Erthworld Chairman Marta Evans. The result, a week later, was a hell of a good show: a cosmic unfreezing before a select group of notables in the five-hundred-seat theater of the Scientific Center. The unfreezing was attended by carefully culled statesmen, diplomats, scientists and newskenner people from Norwestia (the host constellation in which Manhattan was located), Centralia and Cathay (the other two most powerful constellations) and the other eight constellations composing Erthworld Union.

Commander B. J. Methuen, who by this time was restive under a great deal of favorable notoriety, was awarded two seats in a good location. He brought along Lieutenant Saul Zorbin. Hints had been dropped to Methuen from high Astrofleet staffers that he was now in the slot for special promotion; that part of it pleased him, but he did not at all like some signs that the promotion might subtract him from line duty and put him into public relations. He was so preoccupied with strategies and tactics to sidetrack so disgusting a development, without besmirching his escutcheon by declining promotion, that in the theater it required great effort for him to concentrate on the important business at hand.

Also present, on a newskenner pass which she had obtained by a modification of the methods used with the bank, was Dorita Lanceo.

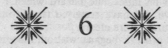

6

Under complex lighting on the big stage squatted the enormous core-cube of relatively clean ice: forty million kilograms of it, sixty-four cubic meters, more than four meters along every edge, beginning to surface-melt sluggishly on the refrigerated stage, whose temperature lighted was ten degrees Celsius.

The lighting changed: the markers hitting the front face of the cube were statted down to ten percent, the floods at the sides and above to fifty percent, while the floods behind stayed full. The cube went translucent, revealing largely in silhouette but dimly in fullness the semi-shadow shapes of the frozen humanoid and the batwinged monster at cube-heart. The spectators were rigid; Dorita heard some gasps, one of them her own.

From among the five doctors who flanked the cube gravely contemplating its contents, their chief Dr. Almagor stepped forward; there was no lectern, the stage had concealed voice-pickups everywhere. In a professionally conversational voice he told them:

"Gentlepeople, all of you have received advance copies of the comet story outlining the unsolved questions about its origin and trajectory and noting also the difficulty of how these two creatures could become entrapped in the comet, without personal damage, perhaps fifty millennia ago. Be reminded that civilization on Erth is only seven or eight millennia old. I will assume that you have read this material, and I will move right on to explain our planned procedure today. There will be a decision for you to make on the spot.

"We will melt their present ice environment by an adaptation of radiant heating. The ice will be melted in successive layers. As we approach the terminal melting, enough of the heat will have penetrated these bodies to thaw them.

"Now, we have every reason to believe that these creatures are still alive, in suspended animation. When they are entirely

41

free of ice, I expect that they will be alive and awake. This fact will present an immediate hazard which I will defer explaining until we will have removed two layers so that you can see the creatures more clearly."

The melting process began, with the doctor laconically describing it. Each melt-layer had been pre-indexed; and as the sludge-milky water ran down into drains, it was being collected below in labeled containers for study. Thus science would learn more about the comet cores, and perhaps more about the humanoid inclusions.

When the second layer had been removed, the creatures were so near the surface that everyone could see both of them rather clearly.

The unwinged man was a naked demigod, apparently brown, and he still-brandished a long spear at the monster—which was a hairy-naked gnarled male, apparently green confused with red, whose big front teeth protruded in an angry grin and whose batwings were spread for fight or for flight.

The theater was pervaded by comet-chill.

Said Almagor: "Now we must call upon you people to decide an issue. It depends on the fact that these specimens must have been somehow deep-frozen instantly while in a combat situation. When the last pieces of ice fall away from them, they will be entirely alive, with no clear memory of anything having happened to them, with no immediate sense of disorientation. Undoubtedly they will go into combat-action.

"Should the humanoid kill the monster, the sequel would perhaps be controllable. But should the monster kill the humanoid or flee on his wings, obviously there would be a peril. The monster must not be let loose upon the world, and consequently we have sealed all openings in this theater; but by the same token, all of you would be confined in a place of great hazard, and there might be injuries or even deaths before we could bring the monster under control.

"On the other hand, we could use a different technique which would leave both of them in suspended animation. But this would rule out the scientifically interesting spectacle of their reactions face-to-face. And we do have methods of bringing one or both of them under control, although we cannot guarantee immediate success.

"Gentlepeople, I think you understand the problem. We

42

will be ruled by you. Please caucus among yourselves for just a few minutes, and then someone may arise and offer a solution for *viva voce* decision."

After silence, a mutterbuzz. Nobody consulted Dorita; she stayed silent, gazing at the icebound combat-tableau. And there were diversified stirrings within her.

The chief representative of Centralia arose, and the mutterbuzz died. "Dr. Almagor, as my party perceives it, we are select people here, we know how to deal with risk—and we are even dispensable." Nervous chuckles, very short. Centralia proceeded: "Our curiosity dictates that you unfreeze them alive and free. But we will listen to a different opinion." He sat.

The silence was total. Dorita found herself agreeing vigorously. Methuen, despite his eagerness to see the combat spectacle, was having another sort of thought.

Said Almagor: "Hearing no further suggestion, I will call for the ayes and nays. And I fear I must request that the newskenner people remain silent; once the vote is in, if any newskenner person or anyone else wishes to depart ahead of the action, please come forward and I will let you out by a backstage exit before the final unfreezing. I now call for the ayes—"

Coming clear on his thought, Methuen stood and barked: "Doctor, I have an alternate suggestion."

All turned to him. Almagor remarked: "This is Commander Methuen who brought in the comet. Yes, Commander?"

Said Methuen, quietly, clearly: "I would like to see the combat, and I can take a risk. However, one or both of the specimens may die, and that is a high price to pay for instant curiosity. Can you keep them in suspended animation, for a subsequent awakening separately and in confinement?" When he sat, there was a small scattering of applause.

Responded Almagor: "I had hoped for that sort of suggestion. The following can be done. I can prolong the suspense of their animation, de-ice them, move them somewhat farther apart, confine them separately in transparent capsules so they can see each other, and then awaken them—right here, all in a matter of minutes."

The Secretary for Education, Science and Culture arose annoyed: "Pray do that, Doctor—and I don't know why you didn't offer this alternative in the first place."

Almagor gently chided: "It had to come from you people,

Madam. And now I will call for the ayes and nays on Commander Methuen's suggestion as amended by me; if the ayes have it, this will be done; if not, we will consider the recommendation from Centralia—"

The ayes were unanimous. Dorita was disappointed, but she saw the sense of it. Nobody ever learned whether any of the newskenner people or anyone else would have arisen to depart if the vote had gone another way.

A capsule-floor of nine square meters was placed immediately behind each creature, and a chair was centered on each floor. Assistants who stood behind each creature, outside the diminished ice cube, caught the specimens as they fell backward when the last ice dropped away, dragged them to the chairs, got them balanced sitting erect with drooping heads, got out of the way. Over each creature was then lowered a bottomless transparent box constituting walls and ceiling for each capsule; in each, one wall was high-doored for magnetically controlled ingress or egress; there was a small door opening off an inside shelf in each capsule, obviously for introduction of food and water; and along the back wall of each capsule was a washing-and-stooling unit. An air-tube led from each ceiling. Almagor had been entirely ready for this decision, obviously he had hoped for it; but Zorbin reflected that Almagor hadn't managed his crowd very well in order to get it. Technicians adhesive-sealed walls to floors. The two capsules now stood five meters apart; they were slide-pushed toward each other a meter along the stage floor until they were no more than a meter apart, with the inert specimens facing each other.

The specimens were awakened.

Integrating swiftly, they came out of their chairs; the bat-creature slammed himself against the capsule-glassoid while the humanoid shattered his spear against the glassoid of *his* prison. The calmly intent humanoid was much taller than Almagor, slender, beardless despite millennia in space, fair of hair and brown of skin, with a penile semi-erection in combat. The monster had the head and crouch of a Neanderthal; he was yellowish green, wings and all, and coarse orange-red-haired all over except as to the naked-skin wings; the forehead was back-sloped, the post-orbital ridges prominent, the chin shallow-receding although the jaws were heavy; he had long tip-yellow fangs, his fingernails and toenails were

44

dirty-sharp-long, his combat-erectus was total; his batwing-spread was three evil meters.

Both of them seemed instantly to comprehend that they were somehow thwarted; the humanoid sank infuriated into his chair, roaring nonsense in basso profundo, while the winged brute laid big flat hands against his glassoid and falsetto-gibbered defiance. Some zany in the audience began to applaud, and a few suggestibles joined in: it was almost as good as a real fight; Dorita stared around, Methuen glared around—*these* were *VIPs?*

The creatures, evidently hearing the applause, became aware of the spectators. The humanoid came erect, and both creatures swiveled to study the theater; seeing this, Almagor signed to somebody backstage who raised the theater lighting. The specimens looked at each other; they looked at the spectators. The humanoid said something to the batwing, who spread wide arms in a universal gesture of puzzlement; both continued staring at spectators. There was no need for Almagor to comment (and he did not) that evidently each had reoriented himself and realized that something astounding had happened to him.

Dorita had an idea and could not resist calling out from her seat: "Doctor, I have a suggestion!"

Almagor and many spectators looked for the source of the voice. The doctor requested: "Madam, will you please arise and identify yourself?"

"Identification not necessary," seated Dorita purred; "my suggestion will stand on its own feet. It is clear that both creatures are speaking intelligently, using language, and they understand each other; but the humanoid sounds like a recording played much too slow, and the monster sounds like one played too fast. Tell me, are the sounds of these creatures being flaked?"

"Of course, and I think I anticipate your excellent suggestion. You want me to play back the sounds of the humanoid faster and those of the monster slower."

"Right, sir."

But before this could be done, the humanoid went into astonishing action. With dignity he began to harangue the audience, in basso profundo largo, standing erect without concern for his nakedness and slowly turning to address all quarters of the theater. And all the time the humanoid was doing this, the bat-creature crouched, obviously gibing, chittering squeaky counterpoint to the rumble-roar of the orator.

Now the humanoid paused, stared, spread arms and hands in broad exasperation, dropped them in defeat, sat, stared helpless at his enemy—who squatted silent-glowering. Both were now entirely detumescent.

Said Almagor: "I will play it all back in modified tempos as the lady has suggested."

He replayed everything. The humanoid's voice came through with speed-up as rich low baritone, speaking what was clearly language, excited at first as it imprecated the foe, calm and measured as it addressed the audience. The slowed voice of the bat-creature was jerky guttural tenor, equally language, first angry-aroused, then possibly jeering—some of the listeners sensed untranslatable profanity. Both creatures were startled by the replays, then most attentive, perhaps recognizing their own voices, perhaps not. . . .

Zorbin, a Tellenic Sinite, whispered to his chief: "Believe it or not, in their talking I get a faint sense of bad Tellene." Methuen stared at the humanoid: his features might be Tellenic, and then again they might not; as for the bat-creature, he was Neanderthal—or he was Satan.

Feeling personally involved, Methuen stood. "Doctor Almagor, it must be evident to all present that these are intelligent creatures from a remote planet or perhaps from two planets. In view of our ignorance about the comet's trajectory, it is even possible that one or both of them lived on Erth in the era which we call paleolithic. It should also be clear that the humanoid despite his nakedness may well represent a civilization or pre-civilization; and that the other despite his monstrous appearance at least represents a culture.

"I propose that they be confined separately in comfortable circumstances for medical study and for questioning by selected people in several disciplines. I would hope to be one of those selected; and my aide here, Lieutenant Zorbin, who has a sense for language among his many excellent qualities, ought also to be selected if I am selected." He sat.

ESC Secretary Farragut asserted from her seat: "Good idea; I endorse it. My department will be able to provide any sort of expert required."

Interjected the legate of Centralia: "We can provide an expert in linguistics; this will be fundamental."

Others wished to speak, but Almagor interrupted. "Mr. Secretary, we are in Norwestia and I do sense political implications. I leave the decisions to you."

46

By discussion's end, a rather cumbersome task force had been designated: Commander Methuen (embarrassingly as chairman), Lieutenant Zorbin (as staff consultant), and ten expert scientists to be named within the week by the ten Erthworld constellations other than Norwestia (which Methuen would be representing). It could prove an ill-assorted task force with some useful disciplines overlooked and others duplicated; but this was a speedy method of reaching action-agreement, and the task force could be refined with more experience. The Secretary expressed hope that Dr. Almagor's people would meanwhile be proceeding with all related scientific studies; Almagor gave assurance that this was already in progress and would continue, and he added that close rapport between himself and Chairman Methuen would advance the work of both.

Methuen stood again; he felt hideously under-ranked for chairing so potent a task force, but he was resolute to do the job. "Excuse me, Mr. Secretary, but I should like permission to conduct beginning interviews with the specimens as early as tomorrow, and the other task-force members may come in as they may arrive." This was granted; it was a chairman's prerogative. The General Commander of Astrofleet, who was present, made a mental note to promote Methuen tomorrow; Methuen was evidently ready, and it would strengthen his hand as task-force chairman.

Dorita, of course, had no part in the arrangement. But the business had inflamed her curiosity and her ambition to action-pique, and she was determined to be in somehow. And Dorita thought she knew how.

 7

It was no trouble at all for Dorita to locate Methuen, knowing his name, rank, and service. It was promising to learn that he lived in a bachelor apartment building. Since he was new-back from space, he probably. . . . On the other hand, he had looked and sounded like an officer who was ambitious, clever, self-contained, and project-oriented; perhaps tonight he had brushed the woman question aside in order to meditate the extra-planetary-creature question. She was perfectly capable of getting in to the alien creatures at night alone; but it would be helpful if she could do it in company with the commander. It looked like a job for shrewd sex; she hadn't practiced that much, just a little bit to hone a useful skill; but perhaps a new-unspaced Methuen might overlook gaucheries.

She chanced phoning him at 1930 hours. He was in, wearing (as the visiscreen showed) fleet dress pants and an open-collar white shirt which he probably hadn't changed since this afternoon, although presumably he had gone out to eat. Methuen was immmediately interested in the image of his caller: Dorita had fixed herself up, not much but enough.

She told him, pouring on girl-coo: "Sir, my name is Miss Dorita Lanceo, I am a teaching fellow at Smith College. I was present at the creature-unfreezing today; I am the one who suggested the tempo-changes in the audio." The part about Smith College was crap, but he'd probably accept it for now.

He was courteously cautious. "What can I do for you, Miss Lanceo?"

She stayed business-cool, but three buttons of her own shirt were open. "My field is extraplanetary psycho-anthropology, so naturally I have a professional interest in these creatures. Perhaps I could be of some help to you. Could I meet with you this evening, to discuss possible futurities?" For now, she omitted throwing him an affirmative suggestion, wanting to see how it might go without that.

She could see him examining frankly her face and more furtively the top of her shirt. He said presently, "Could you be here in an hour?"

"Perfect."

"You know my address, since you know my telephone number?"

"Right. Is that all for now?"

"I look forward to meeting you, although I can't promise anything. Out for now."

En route in a robocab, she decided that Methuen would be interesting, no ordeal at all.

Still dressed the same, he welcomed her and seated her in a compact and rather straight chair, although there were easy

48

chairs and a sofa. He offered a drink; she specified bourbon and water, half and half; he nodded; when he returned with two drinks, it was evident that he had Scotch and water—she knew the color difference. She had a long cigarette in her fingers; he lit it for her, but apparently he carried a lighter only for courtesy. He relaxed in an easy chair, sipping, watching her. She sat prim with her knees together, but she still wore her partly open shirt.

Each waited for the other to begin. The drinks were half consumed and her cigarette was done and stubbed out while they watched each other.

Methuen was finding her enormously desirable, and this made him enormously wary. Once, when he had been a young ensign getting ready for a clandestine date with an older single, an experienced and cynical barracks-mate had told him: "Watch out, B.J., because you aren't the kind of guy who ought to play around, you will feel unnecessary guilt and make some bad mistakes." Methuen had tossed this off; he had gone ahead and seduced the woman (without much trouble, later he had realized), and thereafter had gone into constrictions of ambivalent guilt, conscience-certain that he should offer to marry her, ambition-sure that he wanted to stay unencumbered. It had turned out to be a silly conflict because the woman was a free soul. On the other hand, the next time a similar thing had happened and he had played it cynical-free, the girl had come up as an innocent thing who got pregnant and *did* want him to marry her; and the two-way laceration incident to his tortuous operation of cutting himself loose was an experience which still haunted him. Since that time, Methuen had played it with great care, practicing for the most part a priestly continence. Once, on a far planet, he had experienced high romance; even this had ended in frustration, because the woman had ultimately tossed him over in favor of her husband.

Despite his mercilessly self-appraising introspection, Methuen could not measure the degree to which these woman-experiences had influenced his meticulous caution in the planning stages before committing himself to action. Perhaps it was merely that he was a consequence-projecting kind of joe; and whenever he had rashly abandoned consequence-projection with women, disaster or at least guilt had resulted—which confirmed, for him, the rightness of being meticulous in *all* things, *for him*. He held no brief against those who could succeed intuitively-impetuously; *he* could not do so, that was all. Besides, conscience he did have, and his conscience was an astutely rigorous master, and he wanted it so. Impetuous winners broke lives; he thought it unright to do this when it could be avoided. Whenever he balanced consequences, these were primarily consequences for Erthworld and for Astrofleet, secondarily for individuals affected, tertiarily for Methuen; but he had to remember that if his way was good, he must preserve himself in order to preserve his way.

He was not at all self-righteous. Rather, more than the average man, he was aware of his weaknesses, and he wanted to surmount them if he could.

As now he looked upon child-seductive Dorita, who obviously was ready to use her sexuality in order to obtain something from him, he was balancing the consequences of this indulgence, first for Erthworld and Astrofleet, secondarily for this Dorita who could be hurt, tertiarily for himself. Before he could decide and act, he needed to know more.

Dorita, who had been reading all this thought-web (admirable in him but time-wasteful for her), leaned toward him, allowing her young breasts to blossom beneath her shirt, and told him softly: "Sir, let me begin by saying candidly that I am not associated with Smith or any other college; that was a number to get through your door. I do feel that I have qualifications to help you with these extraplanetary creatures. I will do anything, anything at all, to help you."

It might not hurt to test her, the response might establish a thing or two. He leaned toward her: "The situation here is a bit stiff, Miss Lanceo. Could we perhaps talk better in bed?"

Finding this a splendid idea, Dorita nevertheless played it cute. She caused her face and what showed of her bosom to flush, her eyes widened, her mouth went round, and she answered quite evenly: "I am complimented, but perhaps you do not understand that I came here tonight entirely on business."

He pressed it, not sure what he would do if she should yield. "My dear Miss Lanceo, you are not being realistic at all. You are a beautiful young thing of—what? sixteen?"

"Eighteen," she lied by one year; it might give him more confidence, he was not the sort who would pruriently want to play around with adolescent girls.

"Eighteen, then; but sixteen is how you look, and that happens to be a woman-age peculiarly seductive to a sex-hungry

50

spacer. You come at night to my apartment, offering no genuine credentials, saying you want to help me but not explaining how, insisting that to help me you will do anything at all. Either you are sexually aroused by my notoriety, or you have some ulterior motive. Either way, I suggest that bed is the best place to discuss it." And as she raised a hand and opened her mouth, he amended: "Or, if bed is too messy, you may prefer to hit the carpet. You'll notice that it is new shag." Sipping, he watched her.

Making her flush very deep, Dorita stood, pouted angrily down upon him, opened two more shirt-buttons, and told him coolly: "You take it from here. I won't be fighting."

Feeling his own arousal, Methuen rode herd on it: he could be getting Erthworld and Astrofleet and her and himself into deep trouble. He drained his drink and told her calmly: "Maybe later, Miss Lanceo, but we need to talk here first. Pray button-up and sit down while I make myself another drink. May I sweeten yours?" He arose with his glass and went for hers.

Her complexion went from crimson to pale. Taut, she said: "Commander, I'm sorry, I misjudged you, my approach was wrong. In all honesty you do excite me and I would enjoy doing this for you, but I know that you are testing me and this isn't the way I should be tested. I do want very much to help you with the comet-creatures; and the main way I can help you is, that I am a telepath. So I know everything that you've been thinking. And I really am only seventeen, but believe me, I'm plenty precocious. But we shouldn't make love first, because a man like you will then feel obligated to me, and you shouldn't. So let's talk business first, and you make your decision about me one way or another—me helping you with the creatures, I mean. And after that, either way your decision goes about my help, we can still hit the shag if you want to—or not if you don't."

Astonished, he gazed at her. Slowly she rebuttoned the two buttons, leaving the top three open, keeping her eyes on his eyes. He said at length, gruff: "Sit down, I'll be back." And he went to replenish drinks.

They were on his sofa now, discreetly separate, talking earnestly, sipping slowly. He had begun the talking on his return:

"You say you're a telepath, Miss Lanceo."

"Right. I guess you get my point. The comet-creatures

51

don't talk Anglian or, probably, any live terrestrial language. But with my telepathy, I can be a two-way translator."

"Miss Lanceo, we expect a linguistic expert from Centralia any day now."

"As soon as tomorrow?"

"Well, probably not—"

"But you want to start interviews with the creatures tomorrow. At least for tomorrow, you'll need me."

"You said you'd read all my thoughts tonight. Tell me what they were."

She told him, in near-total detail, to the extent that long before the end of her recital he was persimmon-grinning into his drink. Laying a gentle hand on his shoulder, she appealed: "Don't feel offended, these thoughts demonstrate that you are really a very kind man. Believe me, a telepath knows a lot of other kinds, and so does any woman."

He looked at her: "Can you cut it off?"

"Sure I can. I did *not* read anything since you returned from the kitchen."

"How do I know that?"

"You have to take my word."

"I ought to test your telepathic ability more objectively. Miss Lanceo, can you condition your reading so that you read only what I want you to read and nothing else?"

"Absolutely I can do that. I'd prefer that."

"What am I thinking now?"

"You are thinking, *Next year in Jerusalem,* and you are thinking it in Sinitic. But I don't think you are a Sinite."

"I learned the phrase from my executive officer. Very good, Miss Lanceo. But of course, I'll have to get government clearance—"

"You have to delay for *that?*"

"No delay. Come over here." Arising and taking her hand, he led her to his recorder-communicator. "Just flake-in your full name, birth date, birthplace, parentage, and ID number; and then I'll have to take a retinal photo."

All this was done, with one small delay: "My ID number? Oh, dear, I *never* can remember *that.* Let me go to my purse—"

Presently he transmitted. "We should have a reply in a few minutes," he told her. "The computer is open all night. I do have to say, though, that it may not be possible to get you appointed as a paid staff member."

"I am volunteering," she assured him. "I don't need pay."

"Shall we have another drink while waiting?"

"Do you have some cream sherry?"

"Of course. Will Harvey's do?"

"Exquisite! On the rocks, please. But first I have to make a pit stop."

When she returned, he met her with two glasses of Harvey's on the rocks. She read his thought, *On the rocks yet!* Grinning, she accepted one and sipped. Saying, "Enjoy and excuse me," he set down his glass and hit the corridor. She was pleased with his thought about the rocks: with Harvey's it was blasphemy, and she agreed, but the rocks had sounded nicely naïve. She was sacrificing for a role, he for courtesy.

When he returned, she was standing beside the recorder-communicator, staring at the print-out which it was emitting like an impudent white tongue. She had removed her sandals; she was barefoot on the shag. He ripped out the communication and read it aloud: repeat of the data she had fed in; then: "Father, executive Nellbrook Enterprises, Chicago; mother, homemaker, deceased 2459; no adverse record father or mother. Subject graduated High School No. 5, Chicago, 2463; no known further education. Employed waitress Zingfood Restaurant No. 21 Manhattan 2 July 63 to 7 Sept 63, waitress Shoshone Steakhouse Manhattan 8 Sept 63 to present. Finances: checking and savings accounts main office Hazlitt National Bank Manhattan; av bal checking Cr 97, savings Cr 481; end financial information. No adverse record subject. Cleared for constellational work with access to matter classified CLASSIFIED but no higher pending further information."

He looked down at her face. "If you're an employed waitress, how can you work with me tomorrow?"

"I just quit. I'll tell them tomorrow."

"But you said you don't need a salary. With shoestring finances like that, how can you quit your job?"

Fast lie: "Daddy does fine; he'll grubstake me. But that limitation, matter no higher than CLASSIFIED?—is that bad, Commander?'"

"The comet-creatures are classified CLASSIFIED, no higher, pending further information. You're in for now."

She took the print-out from his hands, read it rapidly, dropped it on the floor. She turned up a tremulous face, saying, "My bare feet like your shag."

Somewhen in the delicious course of that night, Methuen

fell in love with Dorita. He didn't tell her so, because he wanted to think about the question calmly, away from her.

She knew it anyway, and idly she wondered whether she had reciprocal feelings; but acute erotic pleasure tended to glare-out that sort of deeper soul-sensitivity.

Prevoyance Two

Just before he awakened, Methuen sweated through a preview of a second 2465 attack. In his dream, he was an Astrofleet captain attempting to depart Erth aboard his space frigate; the ship proved absolutely lifeless, no system responded at all, 546. After an hour of intensive diagnosis, he had to decide that his ship was inexplicably dead; he could not even send a radio call to headquarters, 546. Quitting the ship, he found a base telephone and put in a priority call—and he learned that no ship anywhere around could be activated, 546. He was ordered to attend a Fleet Admiral's Call in one hour. (The date was 15 January 2465.)

At the conference, the admirals and captains of Norwestia Astrofleet were informed by the Fleet Admiral that, so far as could now be determined, every grounded ship in every Erth-world constellation was out of commission. No cause had been assigned, 546. . . .

It was meaningless dreaming, of course, he adjudged on reawakening to the realities of 2464; and the dream-recurrence of the number *546* could be related to the recent comet-prominence of the gradient. On the other hand, *546* had occurred in his *first* dream, *before* the comet.

Part Two

THE QUARFAR-NARFAR
QUANDARY

8

Methuen and Zorbin and Dorita met in the front lobby of the Science Center. Any trepidation that Methuen had felt about her working attitude was dissipated when she greeted him with impersonal cordiality and a cool handshake. On this morning after, Methuen was no longer sure that he was in love. He liked Dorita very much, and her savoir faire at this morning's meeting added to that. Perhaps he should pursue last night's relationship; perhaps not. He back-burnered the question.

He presented her to Zorbin as "Miss Lanceo who has some interesting qualifications as a telepath."

Zorbin shook hands cordially, remarking: "I understand how your talents may prove helpful, but it will be difficult."

They were admitted by a pre-advised attendant into a small darkened room. "That wall," said the attendant, "is a one-way screen; we thought you might wish to observe unseen. When you are ready to enter the other room where the specimen is capsuled, use this door. If you want me, just call; I will hear you." He departed.

Through the one-way screen, peering into a lighted chamber, they watched the humanoid, who still was naked. Within his tiny capsule, interestingly, he was jogging in place, disregarding the resultant floppery of his respectable genitals. The two men and the women gazed in something like awe: this humanoid was human, his brown body was athlete-perfect, his blond semi-long hair had just a touch of natural wave, his gray eyes were clear, his expression was serene.

"That," Zorbin growled, "is an inhumane way to confine him."

"Agreed," said Methuen, "but maybe we can get that corrected. Are both of you ready to go in to him?"

Passing through a door, they stood before the encapsulated humanoid, who paused in his jogging and turned to regard them with interest.

The attendant had provided three chairs outside the capsule; Methuen took the central one, he was in command, the lady must follow; Dorita sat at his left, Zorbin at his right. Dorita saw the subtle point of the Methuen seat-maneuver, and it worked: inside the capsule, the humanoid also seated himself, and the whole affair took on the tone of a meeting rather than a confrontation. It interested Dorita that the humanoid was unembarrassed about his nakedness in the presence of a strange woman who was clothed. She wondered whether they should undress—and then she grasped that the humanoid was also undisturbed by their clothing.

Methuen began to talk soothingly; the words did not matter in the absence of common language, they would anyhow sound to the slow-basso man-creature like bat-twittering. The interviewee got the idea; and when Methuen fell silent, instantly the humanoid responded with his reverberating roar, not taking too long over his response, merely indicating that he was willing to talk if a way could be found.

Part of the way could be mechanical: Methuen carried a pocket recorder, and he played back his own voice in slowed tempo while the creature listened attentively but with a look of confusion, then the creature's roar in speeded tempo while the creature showed new interest and several times nodded eagerly. Still there was no real communication; but Zorbin muttered, "I keep having that sense of distorted Tellenic, and I swear I heard the Tellene word for *man*."

The Astrofleet officers were thinking; Dorita was ready to act, but she waited. At length Methuen turned her loose: "See what you can do."

Standing, Dorita advanced to the capsule wall; the captive stood also, he was more than two meters tall. Dorita pointed, first to her mouth, then to her ear, then to her forehead; the prisoner nodded. Repeatedly Dorita tapped her forehead, then pointed high to the creature's forehead; he went into thought, then his eyebrows rose and he nodded rapidly.

"Record all this," she ordered Methuen. Then she spoke aloud for the flake, while mind-projecting the statement to the creature: "I am a woman," she said, and with both hands she indicated her breasts. Instantly he replied, *I am a man;* and he pointed to his phallus. She told Methuen's recorder: "He said, 'I am a man.' " Indeed, Zorbin noted, a word somewhat like *anthros* had been pronounced.

So was laid a foundation for language-cracking.

In his ad hoc assignment as Chairman of the Interconstellational Task-Force on Ice-Comet Aliens, Methuen had been detached from Astrofleet and attached to an assistant secretary of Education, Science, and Culture. Shortly after noon that day, Methuen phoned his new chief with a report that preliminary communication with the humanoid alien had been established, that this alien was intelligent and cooperative, and that for him, some degree of freedom under supervision would be far more productive than continued capsule-confinement. Responded the assistant secretary, "I leave the arrangements to your discretion, Captain—including the matter of clothing."

It was Methuen's first intimation that in fact he had been promoted.

So the problem of alien humanoid disposition was Methuen's, and he hadn't the least practical idea how to discharge it. Zorbin suggested his own apartment, he had a spare bedroom; but Methuen felt that the chairman should personally assume responsibility.

Unexpectedly Dorita suggested: "You three men could move in with me."

Demanded Zorbin: "You have three extra bedrooms?"

"No, wait, I mean this. There's an apartment in my building with three bedrooms, I can get it. This creature can have one bedroom, you two men the others, I'll bunk on the sofa, I get along fine with sofas. That way I'll be round-the-clock available for translations."

Methuen had his emotional reservations, but Zorbin's presence would help calm things. It was agreed, and Methuen dispatched her to make the arrangements while he and Zorbin would take a preliminary look at Batwing.

Dorita went home. Visiting the landlady, she proposed a swap of apartments between herself and the family who occupied the three-bedroom suite, accompanying the suggestion with an implanted mental imperative. Necessarily agreeing, the landlady phoned the family and asked for the move before day's end. The shocked wife-mother demanded to know why. Dorita got on the phone and pleaded an urgent need, meanwhile directing a sympathy-imperative along the phone's carrying beam. The woman instantly saw the point (didn't she?) but raised a question as to how she would convince her husband and three chidren to move immediately into a one-bedroom apartment. Dorita assured her, "Believe me, you'll have no problem at all," meanwhile implanting in the woman a radiant imperative which would guarantee consent by the others. By 1800 hours, it was done; moving was a minimum difficulty because both apartments were furnished. If there was injustice and even hardship for that family, Dorita was untroubled: it wasn't her usual style, but the need was absolute, and she planned to route their way a few thousands out of her squirreled bank loot.

Having dispatched her mission, she phoned the Science Center. After a five-minute wait, Methuen's face appeared on visiscreen. Dorita said cheerily, "It's fixed, Commander. If you have a pencil, I'll give you the adress and apartment number—"

He interrupted: "Dorita, first let me tell you about Batwing."

"I'm listening—"

"He's gone."

"Pardon?"

"Vanished. Lock, stock, and wings, Neanderthal forehead and all. Zorbin is here trying to convince the attendant that it's really true."

"But *how?*"

"Nobody can begin to explain it. The attendant let us into a viewing room just as before, and there Batwing was, in his capsule, sort of abject and wing-droopy. After we'd studied his apathy for a few minutes, we went on into the room where his capsule was. Well, he wasn't in the capsule anymore. And the capsule was firmly locked; the shocked attendant saw to that himself."

"Are you telling me that it happened before your very eyes?"

"As near as possible, yes. We had our eyes off of him during the few seconds it took us to pass through the door."

After brief meditation, Dorita said, "I think we need some answers from Quarfar."

"From whom?"

"Quarfar. Didn't I tell you? That's the humanoid alien's name."

"For that, Dorita, we need *you.*"

"Later, but not much later. You and Zorbin arrange for the transfer of Quarfar and get him here about 2000 hours; we can dial dinner here. Go ahead and get on with it, Commander." Disconnect.

Methuen, beginning to wonder who was in charge here, turned to Zorbin and relayed the command.

Command?

One 546 dream was bad enough; the reinforcing second dream was dismaying, and it was Dorita who had been in bed with him when he dreamed it; now the 546 comet-Satan had gone on the loose in Dorita's presence, and Dorita was beginning to control Methuen. Well, Methuen could reassume control over Dorita, but not over his possibly prevoyant dreamings. Quarfar would have to undergo a lot of questioning.

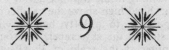

9

Methuen had, of course, immediately reported the escape to his new chief. "Not your fault, Captain," pronounced the assistant secretary, "and we'll put that in the record; but a lot of public hazard could result, and I'll see to that." The assistant secretary alerted the Manhattan police, the Constellational Bureau of Investigation and Interpol: fiend on the loose; then he sat back, grim, to await developments.

This time Methuen was unstartled by being called Captain; he'd received official verbal notice. He told Zorbin—who would tell Dorita, for whatever that might be worth. But he did not yet change his rank insignia pending an official printout; he considered it bad luck to jump guns.

Zorbin had gone shopping in a tall store for creature-clothing, having a good eyeball-idea of the Quarfarian dimensions. He returned to the Science Center with sport shirt, undershorts, Bermuda shorts, elastic socks, adjustable sandals (luckily it was summer, the tricky shoe-size problem could be bypassed). Quarfar, released from his capsule, accepted the proffered clothing and donned it; he seemed to comprehend the use of each garment after brief inspection, but it took him several minutes to master touch-zippers. The sandals were tight, but he managed. Then Methuen said to Zorbin, "Let's not hold him, but be ready to grab him if we must."

Zorbin queried: "What about guiding him?"

"Right," Methuen acknowledged. "I'll do it with an inoffensive arm-touch or two."

Quarfar brought his spear with him; they had seen him shatter it, but now somehow it was whole; it would never leave him, even in bed.

They steered Quarfar into a skimmercab, told the cab where to go and settled back studying the mighty humanoid while he peered about at the remarkable sights of Manhattan. Almost no communication was attempted; even a stab at it would require the clumsy flake-playback procedure for voice-frequency correction. Zorbin made one attempt with a monosyllable: pointing to the top of Quarfar's head, he said, "Tall"; raising his hand high above the cab-floor, he repeated, "Tall"; then, pointing to a lofty building, he reiterated, "Tall." Having studied the skyscraper, Quarfar turned back to Zorbin. Pointing at the scalp of the lieutenant, whose height was below average at 170 centimeters, he profundoed "Meeko." (That would be the approximate phonetic of what they heard.) Holding his hand close to cab-floor, "Meeko"; pointing to a two-story building, "Meeko."

Semi-dazed, Zorbin turned to Methuen—who repressed a smile as he commented, "You know, I think *meeko* means *short*."

"In fact," Zorbin uttered, "ancient Tellene for small was *mikros*."

At dinner in the fifth-story three-bedroom apartment, the two officers ate silently, feeling excluded, watching Dorita and Quarfar engaging each other in animated mind-chitchat. The nose of Methuen, in particular, was disjointed; his intimacy with Dorita had been associated with her entrée to this alien who now monopolized her, although Methuen was chairman of the alien's committee. Methuen knew now that for sure he was in love, but accurately he felt used.

After a quarter-hour of it, the new captain found an official excuse to intervene. "Dorita, how about flaking translations of some of this? We're making no progress with this language." She relayed the request to Quarfar; looking surprised, the alien mind-responded. Dorita explained to Methuen, "He says that would only slow his own progress with *us*. Cheer up, Captain, I'll give you a full report later. I have perfect telepathic memory." And again Dorita and the alien were off.

Giving up for now, the officers watched. And they noticed that as Quarfar grew more and more animated, Dorita grew more and more disconcerted. Presently the alien leaped erect,

pulled Dorita out of her chair, and drew her into the kitchenette, where he pointed at one gadget after another; and there
was conversation over each gadget, disturbed on the part of
Dorita, exuberant on the part of Quarfar. At length she
brought him back to the table, and things calmed for a bit.

Over wine, though, Quarfar went into a brood, during
which Dorita and Methuen and Zorbin mutely consulted each
other. At length Methuen said, "See if you can get him to
bed, Dorita, and then let's talk out here."

She consulted the alien; he nodded absently. She refilled
the alien's wineglass and, carrying it, conducted him to his
bedroom. Inside, Quarfar examined the bed, sat on it and
bounced to test the springiness, shed all his clothing and
reached for the wine. She surrendered it and waited, wondering what this demigod would do. Quarfar drained the glass,
leaped raw into bed, drew up the sheet, turned on his side
away from Dorita, embraced his spear, went to sleep.

Batwing Narfar cruised the new exciting city by night.
Presently he sensed a lone lorn female readiness. Following
the mindscent downward on a long gradient, he paused where
the scent was highest: at a seventh-story window in an apartment house. He window-peered; it was a bedroom, and a
woman tossed in the bed, and the woman was no longer
young but her need was definitive. Unfortunately, she was
one of the funny people; on the other hand, Narfar had seen
only funny people on this planet, and ultimately a hungry
woman was a hungry woman.

He proceeded according to instinctual techniques, project-
ing through the glassoid window a sexual summons blended
with a suggestion that the woman was asleep and dreaming.
She somnambulated out of bed, came to the window, saw the
grinning Neanderthal face and the batwings, murmured, "O
my god," opened the window. He snatched her to him and
flew aloft with her. Once with him nearly did her in; and
when he redeposited her in the bed, she smiled contentedly
with closed eyes and went into real sleep.

Self-satisfied but not yet sated, Narfar lazily cruised on,
looking for another mindscent: this city was challenging. The
next two scents, however, he had to pass up after examining
the situations: one was a young girl yearning for a first lover;
another was the wife of a traveling salesman, a wife yearning
specifically for her husband. These were tabu areas for Narfar; and even though it was he who had established the tabus,

they governed him nevertheless—or, perhaps, all the more. And there must surely be further tabu-free clients. . . .

Sure enough, before the night was out, he had found and satisfied five more true frustrates, always under the guise of a dreaming. Dawn approached; Narfar found a lofty shelter, hung himself upside-down by his knees and fell asleep invisible.

Six had been consoled supernally, and guiltlessly, because for them it had been only a marvelous and uncontrollable dreaming. None had been hurt, their species being reproductively nonviable with Narfar. Nothing would be reported. Narfar was almost content here.

"What I'm going to report," began Dorita, curling her legs on the sofa, "you aren't going to believe. Lieutenant Zorbin, I need a drink, a long one; the makings are in the kitchenette; Scotch and water, half and half." Methuen requested the same, and Zorbin departed for bartending.

Methuen complained, "But Dorita, we haven't advanced a single step toward language interpretation—"

"Be calm," she counseled. "I'll put in several hours on interpretative flakes tomorrow morning. I can talk with Quarfar now, in a limited way, but the mindstuff still is easier."

"All right. Tell me what I won't believe."

"The batwing Neanderthal is named Narfar. He is Quarfar's brother. And Narfar is king of a planet."

"No!" Might it be the 546 planet? Was Nafar indeed winged Lucifer?

Zorbin said, returning with drinks, "You mean, Narfar *was* king of a planet. About five hundred centuries ago. I doubt that he's king any longer."

"Touché, Lieutenant!"

"Please call me Saul," Zorbin urged.

"And lay off that Captain stuff off duty," Methuen added. "Here in our apartment, I'm just B.J., remember?"

Dorita shot: "Stands for what?"

Glancing at Zorbin who would know he was lying, Methuen answered blandly: "My parents christened me B.J. to let me match my own names to the initials. I never bothered. Let's get to business. Apparently Quarfar was also on that planet, since they got caught by the comet together. How about that?"

She frowned. "Quarfar was vague about that; I don't think

he's ready to answer the question. But he was there, all right, and he wants to go back."

"What planet? What star?"

"I asked him about that, but I don't know how we can identify either. He tried to give me a few guidelines—want to get into that now?"

"Absolutely!" Methuen affirmed. Zorbin nodded.

"Well, here, I don't know much about astronomy, but he tried to specify some stars in the planet's neighborhood; and I'll just have to tell you what he told me, if it makes any sense to you. The planet is called Dora, and it is the third planet out from its sun—"

Zorbin inserted: "How many planets altogether?"

"Well, I'm afraid we didn't get into other planets. Anyhow, the sun is a blue-white star. Quarfar mentioned some dominant element in it; his word meant nothing, but I got a mental sense of an atom having two electrons. I was lousy at chemistry—"

"Helium!" Zorbin snapped. "Blue-white, okay; you're sure of this color-meaning?"

"I sensed visually the color he had in mind. It was our blue-white."

"How large a star? Did he say?"

"He said it was bigger than most stars, but not the biggest he knew. He thought it might be a lot bigger and hotter than our sun, but he couldn't tell for sure, because he didn't know how far out we were from ours."

The officers exchanged long looks. Methuen commented: "Type B[0], helium dominant, pretty damn big, pretty damn hot. How many are there like it, Saul?"

"About eleventy-seven million. But it's a start. Go on, Dorita."

"Well, I got thinking about our constellations, and I asked him about Dora's constellations. He said that in Dora folklore, the most important one looked like a giant mizdorf—that's the word I got, mizdorf—flung headlong out of the sky by a demon and falling upon their planet while the demon watched on high. I know that sounds pretty weird, but that's what he—"

Methuen prodded: "What's a mizdorf?"

"That's like the other creature in the comet."

"Like that batwing Neanderthal? Like—Narfar?"

"That was Quarfar's picture."

67

"Did you ask Quarfar what he thought might have happened to Narfar—here on Erth, I mean?"

Dorita was chagrined. "Sorry about that, boss."

Zorbin urged, "Let's stay with the constellation. Dorita, is there any chance that you could draw it for us?"

While she meditated, Zorbin went to the desk and found paper and stylus which he handed to her with a book-backing. Hesitantly she drew a picture; labels were added later as she discussed it.

The men mused over it. Zorbin muttered, "Yes, I can see how it does resemble a down-plunging mizdorf with a bright demon overhead. B.J., do *you* know any space-place where some constellation looks like that?"

Methuen shook his head in slow negation, remarking, "However, Saul, remember that the identification of constellations is a traditional thing in any culture on any planet. If you and I could shake off our own traditional identifications, it's possible that we might be able to make up this sort of diagram out of stars in our own Erth-sky."

"Question of gestalt?"

"Exactly. Dorita, did Quarfar give you any details about the stars in this mizdorf constellation?"

She closed eyes, concentrating. Eyes open, she began to lecture, diagram-pointing. "He said that the brightest one as seen from Dora was right *there*, it is the demon who flung down the mizdorf; it's another blue-white star even bigger and hotter than the Dora-sun. The next-brightest is right *there*, in the right wing of the mizdorf when you look at him from the back, another blue-white but not nearly as big or as hot as the Dora-sun—"

"Great," Zorbin growled. "So far, three B-type stars, counting their sun. Unique identification."

"Wait," Methuen urged. "Dorita, concentrate—what was the *next*-brightest—did you get that far with it?"

She nodded. "Forgetting the Dora-sun, the third-brightest is right *there*, the left knee of the mizdorf, another blue-white about as hot as their sun. The fourth is right *there*, just below the knee of the same leg, blue-white again, about like their sun. The fifth is another one like their sun, *there*, the left foot. How am I doing?"

"Fine, I guess," grated Zorbin.

"Stay at it," urged Methuen, proud of her; you could not call this a hot trail because of the plethora of B-type stars, but my god, this girl was marvelous. . . .

Dorita thrust ahead, lost in her detail memory. "The sixth-brightest from Dora is *there*, the head of the mizdorf. That one is different, its color is orange-red—hey, so was Narfar's hair! That's the coolest of all the stars in the mizdorf, if you can call a star cool; its major chemical component has twenty-two electrons—"

Zorbin barked: "Type M! Titanium! Finally, a different kind of star!"

Methuen murmured, "Like Betelgeuse—"

"And," amended Zorbin, "like at least eleventy-seven other named stars ranging from Antares to Yed Prior. Dorita, do you remember any others?"

"Quarfar mentioned three more. The seventh-brightest star is another blue-white, again like their sun, here in the right wing. The eighth is the hottest blue-white of all, here in the *left* wing. The ninth again is different, yellow-white, hotter than the orange-red head but cooler than all the others: this one, the right knee. In Quarfar's mind I saw other stars in the pattern, and I put some of them in this drawing; but the nine I named are the brightest as seen from Dora."

The officers looked at each other—this kept happening. Methuen remarked: "Legs, wings, but no arms."

Zorbin shoook his head, commenting, "Probably no problem, folklore does have a way of simplifying star patterns. Incidentally, Quarfar's grasp of science must be fairly sophisticated if he was able to identify dominant elements in the star-spectra."

Dorita added, "He also mentioned three nebulae."

"Nebulae?" Zorbin shot. "In that constellation? He knew they were nebulae?"

"Nebulae is my word; he called them star-like clouds which were not stars. Two here in the right wing between the second and seventh brightest stars, and a third here in the left wing beyond the eighth-brightest star."

"How do the nebulae rank with the stars in magnitude as seen from Dora?"

"He said one of the pair in the right wing was bright and beautiful."

Methuen arose to refresh his drink, not thinking about his companions. When he returned, he met Zorbin going in for a refresher; Dorita sat nursing her drink and some thought. Methuen gazed upon her: she was a tiny, appealing, petulant Dresden doll. Abruptly he comprehended that his love for her

69

was an urge for fatherly possession sharpened by a sexual memory. This he would have to sort out. . . .

He sat, forcing his mind back to the problem of the comet's origin. "Dorita—did Quarfar give you any indication what quarter of the Dora-sky the constellation occupies?"

She frowned prettily, staring past him. "Yes, but this is hard for me to translate. He told me that the best place and time to see the mizdorf constellation is in the heart of the jungle at midnight when the orange-red head of the mizdorf is right at the top of the sky where the sun is at noon. Does that help you any?"

Zorbin mused, "That would have to be the date when Dora is precisely between its sun and the mizdorf. It just might mean that their celestial equator passes through the orange-red star."

"What's a celestial equator?"

"I can only tell you how we establish ours, here on Erth. We take the plane of Erth's equator and imaginatively expand it into infinity, and we call that the celestial equator. We use that as a basis for plotting star coordinates."

"Want to give me a for-instance?"

"I'll give you a for-general. Across the equator plane from Erth we extend an imaginary line in the direction of an arbitrary point in the constellation Pisces, and we call that line *east*, and from it we go around the equatorial circle to plot the directions of stars—"

"Permanent directions?"

"Permanent within limits."

"The world turns, the sky does not?"

"The sky does turn, but not fast enough for us to notice during centuries; and the stars within a couple of thousand light-years from Erth hardly change their relative positions during many thousands of years. Now: from Pisces or east, we mark off that celestial equator into three hundred sixty degrees like any circle; but for convenience, we designate each segment of fifteen degrees as one hour on a twenty-four-hour clock, with east being zero hours. This clock-hour measurement around the equator is called the Right Ascension of a star. Thus one o'clock Right Ascension is fifteen degrees clockwise from east, two o'clock is thirty degrees, and so on."

"So twelve o'clock Right Ascension is celestial west?"

"You can say that, but forget about north and south: they're up and down, it would only mix you up."

Dorita nodded. "Then I understand Quarfar's mind-picture, partly. He didn't use clock-hours, but I get it that you might say, the head is at zero o'clock relative to Dora, and the body along with the overhead demon spreads maybe to 0300. But that only handles the horizontal spread; how about the up-and-down stuff?"

"Glad you noticed that, Dorita. Well, for up and down, we take another celestial circle at right angles to the equator, and we mark it off in degrees, and we don't use hours. That's called Declination. So if you know the Right Ascension in hours and the Declination in degrees, you can plot any star on a map."

"Just like Erth geography? Right Ascension is longitude, Declination is latitude?"

"You're a quick read!"

"Well," she sighed, "I can't help you with the declinations. Have I helped you at all?"

"Not much," Methuen ruminated, "if you mean that these data might help us find Dora. You see, Dorita, Quarfar's conventions may be entirely different; he may not use Dora's planetary equator as a celestial equator, although his remark about jungle-heart suggests that; and the axis of Dora may not even be tipped the same way as Erth's. Did he say anything about their seasons?"

"He said the concept of *season* does not apply to Dora. There it is always warm in the central latitudes and cold at the poles and moderate in between. No changes."

"He did use the idea of *poles*?"

"Yes, I'm pretty sure."

Zorbin interjected, "Then evidently Dora's axis isn't tipped like ours, it is tangent to their sun-surface; their sunrays always come in directly at the equator and become more oblique northward and southward until the angles near the poles are most acute. So no seasons."

"On the other hand," Methuen pointed out, "Quarfar does have the concept of *season*, since he denied it for Dora. Which may mean that he came to Dora from some other planet which *does* have seasons. Well, Dorita, you've been most helpful, but we're keeping you out of your sofa-bed."

He rather sweated the response, but she said with a girl-smile: "No problem for me, you guys can retire when ready. And I won't be bothering either of you."

Repressing his meld of disappointment and relief, Methuen returned, "Then we'd better all sack-out, tomorrow is a big day, the first two members of my task force are scheduled to check in. Oh, that reminds me. They won't want to see Quarfar right away, they have to be briefed first, and we'll want to go over the medical findings. So Quarfar may as well stay here with you, Dorita."

"Sure!"

Methuen wet his lips. "I don't think you should be alone here with him, however, so I'm detailing Saul to stay here with you."

Zorbin's eyebrows went up, Dorita's down. She demanded, "You don't trust me alone with Quarfar?"

It made Methuen grin. "Dorita, I don't trust you as far as I can throw you, but that isn't the point. We just don't know enough about Quarfar. He is the one I consider the more unreliable."

"I can take care of myself—"

He drew on his patience. "Yes, Dorita. It isn't rape that worries me, and I don't read Quarfar as the murdering type. It's—just an uneasy feeling about Quarfar. Put it this way: rather than have even Saul guard him alone, I'd want you to be here too."

She, mollified: "What are we supposed to watch for?"

"I don't know. But watch."

She nodded slowly, seeing it. Then she arose, went to Methuen, kissed his forehead, went to Zorbin, kissed *his* forehead, and struck a stance, pointing toward the men's bedrooms.

✳ 10 ✳

After a few hours of sleep (all he ever needed), the mizdorf called Narfar awakened hungry at sunrise and went cruising to find his first food in fifty thousand years. He wasn't unusually hungry, although he hadn't eaten during two days awake. And in contrast to his sensual delights of last night, he found little to tempt his belly this morning: it was a city of skyscrapers and hard pavements, nothing at all like voluptuously sylvan Dora. A few people were about, but he wasn't a people-eater. He cruised. . . .

Finally, Central Park offered promise. There were just a few people, mostly asleep; and there were trees in spate. He had forgotten about oaks and acorns, but the fruit looked interesting, and presently he spied a squirrel eating. Consciously following ancient ritual, he first gathered all the acorns off the tree and buried them in various places, eating one to propitiate the tree, although it wasn't acorns that he was after. Burrowing underground then, he moled around the succulent tree roots in a double circle, chitter-singing praises to the tree spirit, imploring forgiveness for what he was about to do, assuring the spirit that her substance would be many times reproduced and meanwhile would be constructively expended in his own spirit.

He then ate all the tree's root-hairs—easily twenty kilograms of the precious tree parts that suck in water and nutrients from the soil. He knew that the tree would not fall immediately; she might survive by regenerating root-hairs; or else she would die standing, gradually returning her substance to the soil via the mediation of insect larvae; and all her acorns would make a large chunk of new forest.

Having drowsed beneath the oak roots for an hour or so, Narfar the mizdorf came fully awake, sated but no longer lethargic and therefore in the best possible shape for reflection. He had a good brain, and the forebrain was well developed

73

despite the sloping shallow forehead. However, his reflecting was limited by the fixation of his habits; or perhaps to some extent they were instincts, but one of his instincts was to learn habits, and so the distinction is difficult for us to arrive at; luckily it had never occurred to him to introspect the question. Just now, he was concerned to get himself oriented; and the more he labored at this, the more perplexing it became.

Eventually, in this pleasant burrow redolent of soil-dank, he thought of recapitulating his recent memories. Well, there was the just-past root-nibbling, and before that he had hung himself to sleep, and before that a joyous orgy by night in this new city, and before that. . . . Eh. . . .

Clearly he remembered the chill in his heart and in his butt when—day before yesterday?—he had hunkered on a northern glacier seeking a decision as to what to do about the brother-enemy who from that earlier planet had come all the way to Dora and now clearly wished to slay his brother and take things over. Well, Narfar had decided to attack; and he had wing-risen high into the sky above the pole; but Narfar was the last of the mizdorfs, and they were able to stay vital without light or heat or air just as long as their spirits were high. Curious that Quarfar had been called his brother; for Quarfar had been a funny child, different from any mizdorf and far brighter and more daring; and yet they did seem to have owned the same parents, both long dead, both mizdorfs. . . .

Distantly now he had sensed Quarfar on the prowl for him. Narfar had hurled a challenge across supra-Dorian space: *Quarfar, go away, you evil!* Quarfar had responded: *Narfar, both of us are good in different ways, but you are no good to run a planet for people. When I sent you here, I warned you to do it my way, but you did not do so. You must go away and leave Dora to me; otherwise, now finally I will simply have to kill you.* Narfar had mind-howled: *I not go away. Instead I kill you!*

Now, in the weird, hard undiffuse light of the Dora-sun in outer space, they could distantly see each other as half-creatures, one half light and the other half nothing. Narfar could not see the right hand of Quarfar which was unlighted, but he surmised that the hand carried a stone-beaked spear; as for Narfar, he relied on his wings and fangs and talons, on his angry heart and brute strength. . . .

Only, something happened. What it was, Narfar did not

now remember; he only recalled being trapped and losing heart, awakening to find himself confronting spear-armed Quarfar, but both he and Quarfar were confined within invisible walls which neither could see, and many funny people who looked vaguely like Quarfar were watching them out of shadow.

At that instant, Narfar now bitterly reflected, he had the power to pass through the invisible walls and come to grips with Quarfar. But no matter how much power you may have, it is useless unless you think to use it. And Narfar had not thought of this; instead, again he had lost heart, and only yesterday had he remembered his power and escaped, Quarfar no longer being findable.

Well, so now mysteriously he was in this place. It could not possibly be his planet Dora. Had he perhaps been returned to that earlier planet where he and Quarfar had first sought compromises between enmity and grudging mutual help? This unreal city of high buildings, all made of something that gleamed and that you could see through, was nothing at all like that earlier planet or Dora either; yet something about the taste of the tree's root-hairs, something about the wild creatures who played beneath and in the tree, nostalgically reminded Narfar of that earlier planet. Perhaps he and Quarfar had cooperated and contended in some other part of this same planet. Perhaps what Narfar needed to do was to rove this planet, seeking the land from which Quarfar had dispatched him to Dora.

But even if Narfar could find his original takeoff place, how could he get back to Dora without the help of Quarfar?

Well did Narfar remember that night, uncountable human lifetimes before the two had met in conflict above Dora. Narfar had eye-fixed a constellation of stars which was his favorite because it looked like a mizdorf; and surrendering to the stern demand of Quarfar that he go to some other planet, he had picked the star which seemed to be the head of the mizdorf. Quarfar, pointing his stone-beaked spear, had shot a mind-trail through space to Dora, which just then had been on the hither side of the star. Narfar had embarked on the trail, smelling it richly; the smell was alive in him now. Instantly Narfar had found himself on Dora.

Of all the smells in the multi-smell memory of Narfar, none was so peculiar, none so surely recognizable, as the smell of that space-trail.

He had no notion whether the trail still began in the same place where Quarfar had projected it and Narfar had consummated it. The best of all possible ways to start seemed (although he didn't clearly formulate it) to explore this planet and find that original starting point, to learn whether the trail was still there.

Because, of course, there was no hope of getting the Quarfar-like funny humans of this planet to help him get back to Dora. Just no hope at all.

 11

At the Science Center, Methuen confronted the first two members of his task force. The three had been inter-presented by Dr. Almagor; the Centralian, Dr. Olga Alexandrovna, was a stolid blonde Moskovite linguist in her forties; the black-haired Cathayan, Dr. Chu Huang, a small yellow-brown anthropologist in his thirties.

In a small conference room, they sat at table, giving primary attention to the medical and astronomical data which Almagor had handed them. Almagor had excused himself and departed; it was just these three. Alexandrovna and Chu silently studied the data, occasionally darting appraising glances at their chairman; the Centralian glances were hostile, the Cathayan glances noncommittal. In between inter-glancing, somehow they all absorbed the data.

Methuen, having brought under his control the medical data, most of which he had seen yesterday, sat back and watched the other two while they worked back and forth between medical and astrophysical information. The new members, comprehending that their stranger-chairman was ready for discussion before they were, felt a certain whelming; they crowded this down, concentrating on the data, each privately resolved to show up the chairman before long.

Methuen waited, knowing that he would be tested. But so would they.

After much time, Aléxandrovna the Centralian linguist

raised her head. "Mr. Chairman, I think I am ready. I don't know about my colleague from Cathay."

Chu acknowledged her remark with a polite, "So soon? Very good, but you must excuse me a few more minutes." He went back to the briefs. This rather concerned Alexandrovna, who wondered whether she might have missed something; and nervously she consulted her print-outs. Methuen waited, disciplining himself into steely calm, watching both scientists; they were going to challenge, just out of gamesmanship, and his problem would be to smooth out such challenges and get them both into a mood of cooperation.

Presently Chu looked up: "I think I am ready now." His voice was rather high and clipped, as contrasted with the ponderous contralto of Alexandrovna.

Methuen said: "Then I will begin by formulating our task-force problems as charged by my chief. *One*: what sort of creatures are these? *Two*: on what planet or planets did they originate, and when? *Three*: how did they get themselves entangled in a comet clicking off three percent of light velocity, and without body-damage? *Four*: do the creatures represent any threat to our Erth?" (546!) *"Five,* the problem which is ancillary to all others: how do we analyze their language or languages so that we can get into communication with them for the sake of their experiential testimony? Undoubtedly related problems will emerge, and the chair will welcome any additional formulations now or later."

Chu beat Alexandrovna to the first punch. "As to problem one, I think these medical data take care of it, along with the narrative account of their first confrontation. As to that narrative account, clearly they are hostile to each other; and we note that the humanoid is advanced enough to carry a stone-beaked spear, while the winged creature appears to be a fang-and-claw savage. The medical data show that both creatures are strong and in the prime of their lives, their health seems excellent; although the winged one appears to prefer vegetation including tree-roots, and he has a sub-stomach for storing vegetation and breaking down the cell walls as an ungulate does. As to their intelligences, both have well-developed humanoid brains, although the encephalograph of the humanoid implies left-hemisphere symbolic dominance, while that of the batwing clearly shows right-hemisphere intuitive dominance. Another part of problem one, what sorts of creatures are these, will have to do with their respective cultures;

77

I have a hypothesis or two, but I yield to my colleague from Centralia."

Olga Alexandrovna challenged Methuen, leading to it obliquely but without much delay. "I understand that at least one astronomer will join our task force within the next few days, and that is pertinent to problems two and three. So for now I believe we three can properly concentrate on problems one and five, which fall within our disciplines. Addressing myself immediately to problem five, I would ask Commander Methuen about his thoughts relative to analyzing the languages of the specimens."

The captain bypassed his downgrading, it was merely pardonable ignorance, his print-out hadn't come and he would not assume captain's insignia until it did. "We have made some degree of start on language," he told them. "I have a telepath on our unofficial staff, and she has established communication with the humanoid, whose name is Quarfar. The batwing is Quarfar's possible brother, Narfar. My telepath has already flaked some preliminary exchanges with Quarfar, together with translations; and this morning she is preparing a more detailed flake of further communication. It may make good sense to work first on these flakes."

Alexandrovna bristled, this being her territory. "Until we know the credentials of your telepath, we can give her report no credence."

"The only credentials I can give," Methuen candidly admitted, "are that she correctly read my mind in an intensive test, and that she has been constellation-cleared to handle material of the lowest classification—which applies to these creatures and to this task force, pending disclosure of something which might upgrade the classification. Also, in a few instances where she gave me the meaning of a phrase by Quarfar, I was able to repeat the phrase, and Quarfar evidently understood; twice he obeyed my requests."

"If the woman is a true telepath," snapped the linguist, "these may have tested her telepathy but they did not test her credibility. While you were speaking to this Quarfar, she could have been giving him your meanings. Commander, I am afraid there is no substitute for direct discourse between me and Quarfar, flaking it for linguistic analysis."

Said Methuen: "I could not agree more completely. I should add, though, with respect to problem two, that my telepath elicited from Quarfar, and was able to report to me, a description of the constellation which dominates the skies of the planet from which both creatures may well have come here, together with an account of the relative brightnesses, relative temperatures and physical compositions of nine stars and three nebulae in that constellation. I find this most intriguing, and I have reported it for expert analysis. Now, shall we go?"

"Go where?" demanded Alexandrovna, upset.

"Go to my apartment where my telepath and my lieutenant are guarding Quarfar. You said that you wanted to interview him directly."

"But Mr. Chairman—your apartment—do you consider that secure confinement?"

Responded Methuen, arising, "It is humane confinement, and Quarfar is at least as human as we are, and there is some evidence that he should be accorded high-courtesy status. You may have been informed that the batwing creature, Narfar, has already escaped from stringently secure confinement. If now we lose Quarfar, we would have lost him anyway."

An attendant interrupted: "Captain Methuen, another member of your task force has arrived. She is an astrophysicist from Senevendia."

"Send her in, by all means," Methuen ordered.

Alexandrovna uttered, *"Captain* Methuen?" It was only a one-rank difference; but correctly in her eyes, it was a sort of orbital jump.

At the apartment, Quarfar was displaying acute interest in celestial geography. He and Dorita and Zorbin were gathered close around a card table on which the lieutenant had spread charts pulled out of an attaché case which he regularly carried. For starters, he pointed to a star chart whose right ascensions ranged from zero to twelve o'clock, while the declinations ranged from ninety degrees to zero—a full half of the northern sky.

"This," he explained to Quarfar (with Dorita mind-translating and learning as she went), "is not a technical astrogation chart; that would be too confusing for a beginner at this. You are looking at a chart of the stars and constellations in our sky, prepared for use by amateur and professional astronomers and other star-lovers who study the sky from our planet Erth." He hand-swept the chart, which ranged from Cassiopeia to Ursa Major, from Pegasus to Leo Minor, all the way down to the near-equatorial constellations like Pisces and the top part of Orion and also Canis Minor and Cancer and Leo.

Poring over the chart, with the spear across his lap, Quarfar mumbled, "It is very hard to understand. I see straight lines radiating out from a center at *that* star" (he indicated Polaris); "the lines have markings at the bottom ends" (they were numbered 1h, 2h, and so on up to 12h); "and I also see curved lines crossing the radial lines, and the curved lines have markings at both ends" (80°, 70°, and so on down to 0°). "What *is* all this?"

"Here," said Zorbin on an inspiration, "I can do something which will help you." Pulling a scissors out of his marvelous attaché case, he clipped all the border material off the chart so it became the simple half-circle of the northern sky from east to west looking toward Camelopardalis and Lynx. He then bowed the chart inward so that it became half of a hemisphere with the stars on the inside, and he fastened it that way with a length of tape. Then, tape-fastening the half-hemisphere to the table so that it made half a bowl with Polaris down at its apex, he told Quarfar: "Look down upon that—and it will be rather as the sky would look if you were looking upward."

Peering down, Quarfar murmured, "I begin to see. It is like the sky of Dora, only different stars. Is *your* star on this chart?"

"No, it can't be. The chart shows how this quarter of the heavens looks to us, here on Erth; and we are too close to our sun for the sun to be shown. Let me demonstrate that." Producing a stylus, Zorbin held it erect with its writing point on the celestial north pole, close to Polaris, and its rekamatic eraser end in the air about at the level of the celestial equator. "That," he said, pointing to the eraser, "would be Erth—us—and our sun on this scale would be right next to it."

"Yes, I see!" Quarfar exclaimed; and so did Dorita, who for the first time in her life was beginning to understand star charts. Then Quarfar added, almost plaintively, "Is Dora on that chart?"

"I have no way to know. I do not know which star is Dora's. It could be on this chart, anywhere—or on one of three related charts showing other quarters of the heavens."

Quarfar was taut. "Dorita tells me that I have been fifty thousand years away from Dora, and so has Narfar. Those people must be in terrible trouble without either of us. *I have got to find my way back there*—and back there—then!"

That was when Methuen arrived with his three task-force members.

Methuen presented the guests to Quarfar, then asked through Dorita if Quarfar minded being put on exhibition while they interviewed him. Quarfar said he didn't mind, and he offered to take off his clothes. When this offer was communicated to the committee, the two women were confusedly and diffidently interested; Dr. Chu settled it by remarking, "We have complete medical reports; and in courtesy, if he is to strip, so should we all." The decision was that he should not strip. Quarfar, puzzled by all the fuss about stripping, watched while Dorita seated Methuen at one end of the dining table and arrayed the three committee members and Zorbin along the two sides; and then Quarfar allowed her to place him in an easy chair somewhat back from the other table end. While she took a standing position behind Quarfar, there was a paper-rustling.

Methuen opened it: "Gentlepeople, what is your pleasure?" Methuen, receiving Dorita's mind-translations and understanding that the pleasure of the task force and not his pleasure was momentarily wanted, courteously and attentively waited.

Linguist Alexandrovna opened peremptorily. "I recall *Captain* Methuen's excellent formulation of our five problems: what sort of creatures are these, where and when did they originate, how did they get caught in a comet having velocity .03 C, do they represent any threat to our Erth and how do we crack their language or languages so we can communicate. I wish to address the fifth, which, as the captain said, is ancillary to all the others—"

Crisply inserted Dr. Sita Sari, the Senevendian astrophysicist, a trim, petite, dark-skinned brunette with a faint trace of Hindu twang: "If only those problems have been voiced, I will add one. We must learn everything we can about the comet, including details of its trajectory and reasons why it was traveling so swiftly. I cannot emphasize enough that this is a unique comet. It is indeed unfortunate" (and here she looked fire at Methuen) "that Captain Methuen saw fit to capture it before the trajectory had been adequately tracked."

Methuen responded, "Dr. Sari, desert-thirsty people, including those of your own subcontinent, needed the ice. We do have some good tracking figures for you, extending over a period of more than forty hours, a distance of well over four hundred million kilometers. Over all this distance, the comet's track was a perfectly straight line; and the fact that it was following the five-forty-six gradient leads to the obvious inference that its track would have reached Erth. Nevertheless your formulation of a sixth problem is noted. And now I will add a seventh: to analyze the five-forty-six gradient, which we have now tracked all the way from Erth to four hundred seventy light-years out, which is a first. Committee?"

Brief silence followed; now Astrophysicist Sari, too, knew about their chairman.

Then Alexandrovna came in hard: "I submit that the first problem in time-priority is the languages of this Quarfar and his brother, Narfar, in order to get at the other problems."

Methuen looked around. "Hearing no objection, let Dr. Alexandrovna proceed."

She said, "You have presented Miss Lanceo to us. Is she the telepath who has established communication with Quarfar?" Methuen affirmed. "Then I should like to begin by testing her. Young lady, I am formulating a clear thought in my mind. Can you read it?"

Dorita responded, "Madam, I cannot understand the Moskovian words in your thought, but the thought essence is that the square of the hypotenuse is equal to the sum of the squares of the other two sides—the Pythagorean theorem."

After staring, Alexandrovna snapped: "Correct, but it could be a clever guess at what I might formulate as a test. Will a colleague try?"

"Try me," piped Anthropologist Chu.

Dorita told him, "Your thought is that the appearance of Quarfar, along with his medical records, gives every reason to believe that he is exactly like an Aryan specimen of *Homo sapiens sapiens*." She turned then to Sari: "You are not volunteering, Madam, but you are thinking that if you were to test me, you would ask how the Pythagorean theorem is used in celestial geography. And I'm afraid I do not know."

That made Sari smile, and there were chuckles. Methuen noticed that Sari's face when smile-softened was rather merry, in a tight sort of way.

Alexandrovna went back at it. "Miss Lanceo, you do appear to qualify as an expert telepath, but there remains a question.

82

We have no way to know whether you are translating to and from Quarfar correctly, or instead for some reason falsifying translations."

"Miss Lanceo," the chairman told them, "has made extensive flakes of the information that Quarfar has given her, and in many instances has associated the word-sounds of Quarfar with their mind-meanings. For supplement, we have Dr. Almagor's flakes of the sounds made by both Quarfar and Narfar when they were first unfrozen. Do you wish to listen to playbacks?"

"How long would it take?" the linguist queried.

"At normal speed, approximately seven hours."

"For my linguistic purposes, you could play it at hundred-speed in slightly over four minutes. My recorder-computer here would catch all the word-meaning associations and would create a language pattern, if there is one, a few minutes later. But perhaps others would prefer normal speed for their own purposes?"

"Do speed it up," requested Senevendian Sari. "I'll be flaking it for private playback tonight." Chu affirmed. All three now had recorders on the table; those of Sari and Chu were pocket-size, while Alexandrovna's was more elaborate.

Nodding, Methuen produced apparatus and played back the seven hours of creature-flaking at hundred-speed, while Dorita mind-sketched for Quarfar what was going on. (For a being out of touch with any world since the paleolithic ages, Quarfar was remarkably apt at comprehending modern apparatus and concepts!) There followed several minutes of waiting while Alexandrovna's little computer beep-muttered; whereafter it climaxed by laboriously emitting a long tongue of print-out tape—much more tape than its bowels would seem able to contain, if you didn't understand the principle of reonic expansion out of a condensed hyper-liquid pack. A good deal of suspense generated itself while Alexandrovna was using another three minutes to scan the tape.

Then the linguist asserted: "The language of this departed Narfar, from the brief specimen that we have, appears to be an impoverished version of Quarfar's language. And indeed this language includes distorted elements of pre-Tellene, as Lieutenant Zorbin is said to have intuited, although there are many other sorts of linguistic elements. I have the sense of it now, but I have to gain a preliminary mastery of the enunciation also, otherwise Quarfar and I will not understand each

83

other. Excuse me another few minutes while I study these phonemes—"

A bit of side conversation was beginning to develop between Chu and Zorbin, between Methuen and Sari, between Dorita and Quarfar. . . .

Alexandrovna broke in: "I think I have it near enough now; I can correct myself in the course of conversation. What I wish to do first is to talk directly with Quarfar for the purpose of checking on the accuracy of Miss Lanceo's reporting."

Dorita stiffened; Quarfar stiffened also. Smoothly Methuen intervened: "As to that, I see two little difficulties. First, the speech of Quarfar is so much slower than ours that you must speak to him through a recorder for slowed playback to him, and vice versa."

"No difficulty," announced the linguist, making adjustments to her computer. "My little friend here will do all that automatically."

"And second—in order to test the accuracy of what Miss Lanceo has reported, I think you will have to know what she has reported. And I don't think you have that knowledge from a hundred-speed playback."

In the silence that followed, they all watched embarrassed Alexandrovna. Finally she had the grace to smile faintly. "Former Commander Methuen," she murmured, "you merit your promotion."

She raised her head. "I will merely try a few exchanges with him now, and I will test Miss Lanceo tomorrow. Quarfar—"

"Yes, Madam?"

"I try speak your language. You understand me?"

"With difficulty, Madam. But it will get better."

The exchange had been in Quarfar's tongue; Alexandrovna now translated into Anglian, and there was a little round of applause for her. The linguist accepted it impassively; Quarfar looked pleased.

Alexandrovna (and it may now be easier to call her Olga) rejoined: "Where you come from?"

"I come from Dora."

"Where is Dora?"

"Please help me find out. It is important for me to get back to Dora."

"Why is important?"

"To let out the good evils. I have been away too long. Dora may be dead without the good evils."

"Good evils? What they?"

"It is hard to describe. I do not think I can say." But Dorita was getting a cloudy double image in a dismal contexture.

Olga wet her lips. "Quarfar, you know, maybe we not find where Dora is. Maybe you have to stay here. What then?"

Prolonged thought by Quarfar. Decisively: "Then I have to get into Erth-ice and explode Erth to make a comet. Maybe the comet can take me back to Dora."

Olga froze. Chu demanded: "Translate!" Olga uttered the Anglian. All froze.

Sari expostulated: *"Explode Erth? Can he do that?"*

Before Olga could relay the question to Quarfar, Dorita replied, "Probably he can, you know. I think he is some kind of a god."

Quarfar vanished.

Two minutes later, Quarfar reappeared in the same chair, freezing the task-force arousal which had followed the shock of his disappearance. "You see what I mean,'" he said quietly in his tongue. "You have no control over me. I remain here voluntarily, and only to help you find my Dora. Please forget my threat, I respect your Erth, I will not injure her unless finally I must."

Dorita had to translate; Olga Alexandrovna had swooned.

Chu, dry: "We seem at least to have begun a meeting with problem four: do the comet-creatures present a threat to Erth. In Quarfar's case, it appears that he can, but he doesn't want to, but he reserves the right."

12

The task force had adjourned until 0900 hours tomorrow in order that its members might privately study (at normal speed) their flakings of Dorita's flakes, together with their flakings of today's upsetting conclave, and arrive at some orientation—which, in view of Quarfar's bizarre behavior, would require also a certain amount of quality alcohol and a great deal of good food at Norwestian expense. It is worth remembering that the flakes included the primitive yet surprisingly good astronomical data which Quarfar had given her concerning Dora's prime constellation Mizdorf and the relative brightnesses and chemical compositions of its stars.

Methuen remained in the apartment with Zorbin, Dorita and Quarfar. Reporting by phone to the assistant secretary, he discussed everything, including the semi-threat by Quarfar and his subsequent disappearance and reappearance. His chief, impressed, ordered this material classified SECRET, and promised some sort of an alert. Over a light lunch with the others, Methuen sardonically reflected that his telepath, who was cleared only for CLASSIFIED information, already had hold of some that was SECRET; he would have to do something about this, but he didn't quite know what; he would sleep on it.

Since Quarfar was growing uncommonly nervous in semi-confinement and in his anxiety to get on with Dora-homing, diversion was in order; and the four of them set out on a skimmer tour of Manhattan and its immediate environs. Methuen judged (and Zorbin agreed) that their guest was not likely to try anything rash as long as he could hope for decent progress.

The comet-man showed interest in the sights of Manhattan, which were principally the astonishing buildings. They were beginning to talk together fairly well, more and more often bypassing Dorita's mediation. Neither officer was a fool with languages, and neither was Quarfar (but why?); Dorita had helped them enormously, so that the officers were building their vocabularies in Quarfar's tongue, and he in theirs. They were even learning to surmount the tempo barrier: he was making himself talk fast and high for him, the Erthlings slow and low for them, and words came through, and many were understood and learned. Zorbin kept wondering *why* there were the frequent word-inclusions which seemed to be distorted Tellenic.

They visited the Metropolitan, where in a one-hour quickie visit their guest manifested prime interest in ancient Kamat and in 19th-century landscape painting. "Want more," he remarked, and they promised for another day. (He had shrugged off ancient Tellas!) They hurried him through parts

86

of the Museum of Natural History; in an hour there, he liked the evolutionary exhibit of humanoid-to-human skulls, and he loved the dinosaurs, and he marveled at the whale models. "Want more," he repeated, and they promised.

Then it occurred to Zorbin that the planetarium would be highly in order, but unfortunately it was late in the afternoon. Dorita mourned that they couldn't have a private showing, where they could discuss the stars without troubling the spectators, and perhaps hold and zero in on certain projections. "Good idea," agree Methuen. "Let me try—" He went to a public phone, ranged his last five quarter-credit coins on the rolling ramp at telephone top and called the planetarium. When someone answered, *thoop* went a coin being sucked into the slot. He gave his name, rank and service, and asked to speak with the planetarium director, to whom he said (*thoop*): "Excuse me, sir, but we have a situation here involving an extraplanetary guest. He is being studied by an interconstellational task force of scientists, and I am chairman. Might we possibly" (*thoop*) "arrange a showing after hours—" The male director broke in with enthusiasm: "That would be one of the creatures from the comet? Indeed, Captain. I can arrange it—at 1730 this afternoon, if that" (*thoop*) "will be convenient. We'll use the standard show and the usual voice-flake, but I'll be on hand with the projectionist so that we can" (*thoop*) "freeze scenes or backtrack and enter into two-way discussion—"

Methuen, breaking in: "Done, sir! I'm out of quarters!"

Quarfar watched awed through the early projections, with Dorita mind-translating the narrative: the change from daylight through twilight into starry night, the sun, the solar system with planets wending their ways, the starry processional across the heavens from sunset to sunrise. He leaned back and gazed at the starry dome of the northern sky (that is, the sky north of the celestial equator, which is relatively independent of changing seasons) while the flake went through the customary discussion of constellations and some individual stars, with a glowing arrow pointing to the subject of discussion. In a spectacular rotation of the heavens, the scene shifted to the southern sky. . . .

Dorita became aware of some sort of interest in the mind of Quarfar, a focused interest, a puzzled interest. She spoke to Methuen, who called down to the director in the floor-center projection dome: "Can we go back for a moment to the northern sky?" It was done; and again Quarfar gazed at the 0500 sector in the neighborhood of the celestial equator.

Presently he mindspoke rapidly; Dorita translated to the captain, who inquired of the director: "Sir, is it possible for you to show the celestial hemisphere from plus ninety to minus ninety and from zero hours to 1200?"

"Please give us a couple of minutes," the director responded. And after a brief wait, the overhead dome glowed with *that* night sky. Again, having been told what it was, Quarfar zeroed in on the five o'clock sector around the equator.

He twisted his head around to stare at that area from another angle.

Methuen urged in the alien's tongue: "Tell where you look." Quarfar pointed. Having leaned over to sight along Quarfar's arm, Methuen called to the director: "Can you please point your arrow at Orion?" The arrow whisked across the sky and aimed itself at Orion's belt. "Yes," said Quarfar in Anglian, "but—" He gave up, his thought was too complex for limited words in either language; he mindspoke to Dorita; when she had comprehended, she relayed to Methuen.

The captain called: "Sir, please bring your arrow down to Saiph." That was the star in Orion's right foot, if you assumed that Orion was looking at you. Quarfar barked "Yes!" and rapidly mindspoke to Dorita.

On hearing what he wanted, Methuen swallowed and called: "Sir, this may be most difficult if not impossible. Our guest would like to have most of the sky filled with the constellation Orion *as it would look from Saiph.* Is that a possibility?"

Pause. Then the director, apologetically: "Captain, we must have these data somewhere in our files, but we would have to bring them out, study them, and design a whole new arrangement of projection lenses. If this is important, I can put my staff on it tomorrow, we would hope to be ready by 1730 tomorrow afternoon. Would that work?"

Zorbin whispered, "B.J., remember that Saiph lies exactly on the line of the five-forty-six gradient, and their declinations are the same: minus nine degrees forty-one minutes."

Methuen responded to the director: "Thank you, sir, it will work, and indeed we may be on to something important."

"However," added the director, "we need a stipulation of coordinates—"

88

"Sir," Zorbin suggested, "please assume that the celestial equator is described by a circle whose radius extends from Saiph to Betelgeuse. Call the Betelgeuse direction 0000 hours, and take it from there."

 13

Was Orion in fact the home constellation of Narfar and the conquest-quarry of Quarfar? Was it Saiph that was the sun of Dora? Did the mysterious five-forty-six gradient, which speeded up space ships and even a comet, extend all the way out to Saiph which was 2100 light-years distant from Erth? To express the distance indicated by 2100 light-years required incomprehensible numerals: in kilometers, the number 2 followed by sixteen zeroes: twenty quadrillion kilometers. On Erth in 2464, light which had departed Saiph in the Age of St. Augustinus was only just now arriving.

These questions were playing tag in the Methuen mind all during dinner at an expensive restaurant (a thing which Quarfar needed to experience, at Norwestian expense) with Zorbin and Dorita and their extraterrestrial guest. All other data at the captain's command confirmed the bizarre possibilities. The gradient certainly extended as far out as Bellatrix, which was four hundred seventy light-years from Erth, less than a quarter of the distance to Saiph. (If relatively nearby Bellatrix shared the constellation Orion with Saiph and other more distant stars, it was only because our eyes looking at stars flatten distance-differentials the way Grandma Moses flattened perspectives.) The gradient had speeded up the comet to an inordinate degree; Methuen was eager to get at his calculator in order to figure whether the age of the comet when it reached the neighborhood of Bellatrix corresponded to its velocity assuming an origin near Saiph.

And—how dangerous to Erth was this Quarfar?

It was hard, just now, for Methuen to pursue these ruminatings in a disciplined way. His eyes kept going for the charms of girlish Dorita, whose attraction for him had been many times multiplied by her superb committee-aide operation. He was vexed by the paradox of living semi-intimately with Dorita in the same apartment but chaperoned by two other men—one of whom, Quarfar, was monopolizing her time and attention, for reasons functionally necessary to Methuen, but probably for other reasons also. The captain was even noticing with irritation the occasional murmurings between Dorita and Zorbin: the two evidently liked each other, and he kept wondering how much more there might be.

By the time dinner was over and they departed for the apartment (at perhaps 2100 hours), Methuen had blown all his reserve about Dorita. He knew he was in love with her, that he had to have her permanently. At the same time, he was caught in a functional net: she was absolutely necessary to task-force operations, and therefore she had to maintain her mental intimacy with Quarfar; as to Zorbin, she had to be friendly with him even if this should lead to flirtation and perhaps more.

Methuen found that his intellectual self-containment was dissipating into an emotional quagmire. He fought to keep its head above surface. It kept running through his mind, all the way back to the apartment, that if he should confront Dorita with his love, Dorita might settle everything down. . . .

The following he knew for sure. He did not want to have Dorita on even a semi-permanent basis unless she loved him in such a way that she too wanted permanence. And he was not going to wreck his career for love of Dorita; which meant for immediate purposes that he was not going to blow this assignment. And if Dorita *truly* loved him, she too would value his careeer as high as the love.

If she loved him. And that he had to learn—or had to win.

And so it became a curiously critical night. Imperative for Methuen to find out *tonight* about love with Dorita. Equally imperative for Quarfar to push ahead with his intuition about Orion; and that demanded Dorita's attention to Quarfar and not to Methuen.

In the apartment, Quarfar was moody; and it was a long time before even Dorita could draw him into talking about permanent concerns. Vexed, Methuen had found a moment to tell her that he was eager to talk with her privately; and she had patted his hand and promised some time later on.

The promise had buoyed Methuen; Dorita had hardly noticed it, so deeply was she involved with the Quarfar adventure.

Eventually, though, Quarfar adresssed Zorbin; Dorita, sitting next to Quarfar on the sofa, mind-listened attentively to fill out the chopped words. Said the alien in Anglian: "At—planetarium?—I point to star—you say something to Methuen. What you say?"

Zorbin looked puzzled at Methuen: "Can you help, B.J.?"

Methuen was alert. "The star Quarfar pointed to was Saiph. And you reminded me that Saiph is right on the line of the five-forty-six gradient."

Zorbin said, "I think we need your help, Dorita." She mind-repeated the remark.

Quarfar demanded, "What a five-forty-six gradient?"

Zorbin addressed Dorita: "I want to tell him that it is a rekamatic polarization of a path in space. In this case, the polarity is double, so the gradient speeds travel both ways. Dorita, do you understand that well enough so you can tell him?"

The task of getting her to understand rekamatic double polarization required a ten-minute discussion among her and the two officers; fortunately she brought some knowledge to the question. When she grasped it, she conveyed it.

Instantly Quarfar demanded: "Okay. What *this* gradient?"

It was, they told him, a fiber-thin space-road polarized at one end by Erth and at the other end by some star or planet. And since it appeared that the gradient might possibly extend to Saiph, there was a possibility that Saiph, or one of its planets if it had any, was the other pole.

Quarfar didn't understand polarization, he had no background for that. They worked with him; and Methuen finally tried an analogy with a creek which springs out of a rock (one pole) and runs downhill to a lake (the other pole). Quarfar got that, and then they began to qualify: in this case, the gradient worked both ways: you could run up-gradient, and it would be as though the ground had been tilted so that the lake became the source and the spring the receptacle. . . .

The best part of an hour went by during this mutual working; but Quarfar finally had the picture. He tested: "Gradient go through sky?"

"Right," said Methuen.

"Go from someplace to your Erth?"

91

"Right."

"Someplace maybe Saiph—or Dora?"

"Maybe."

Quarfar ruminated. He demanded then, "What make this gradient?"

"We don't know," Zorbin confessed in the alien's tongue. Then he queried: "Quarfar—you been to Erth before?"

The comet-creature spread hands. "Maybe. Not sure. Tell why you ask."

"You talk like some of our people, a little."

"Oh?"

"What name of your *home* planet, Quarfar? Planet you leave when you go to Dora?"

"No name. Just world."

"Any of our people ever come to your home world?"

"No—but—"

He was deep in thought. Eagerly they waited.

He turned to Dorita and mind-communicated rapidly. She translated with raised eyebrows: "Quarfar noticed in the museums that we have long had a metal culture. He wants to know if there was ever a being on Erth who—stole fire from the sun and gave it to man." Spreading hands, she waited.

Quickly Zorbin responded: "That would have been Karfareon the titan, in a middle-eastern area of Erth. It's a silly legend, of course, but a stirring one. But I am fascinated that you should ask the question." (Jolted, he was thinking: *Karfareon?*)

Hearing this through Dorita, Quarfar leaned forward and replied through her: "That legend may help me to find Dora. Tell me please, what afterward happened to your Karfareon?"

Zorbin was leaning forward. "The god Zeus became angry at Karfareon for resisting an attempt by Zeus to take over the mankind which Karfareon had adopted. Karfareon was bound to a high rock in our Caucasos mountains, and vultures were sent to tear at his liver forevermore.'"

"Vultures," Quarfar meditated aloud. "Tearing at his liver. Well do I remember that aspect of the myth, because what I went through certainly felt like that—" He stopped himself, seeing how the other three were staring: off-guard, he had been speaking Anglian like a native. To cover, he went through Dorita with the next question: "According to the legend, did Karfareon have a brother?"

Zorbin emphatically nodded. "The brother was named Narfareon (*Narfareon?*); and by the way, Karfareon means Forethought or Wisdom while Narfareon means Afterthought or Impulse Action followed by Indecision. One version of the story says that Narfareon created all animals including man, but he liked the other animals better than man and gave the other animals all the strength-attributes like running speed and claws and teeth. But when Narfareon found that man was now disadvantaged and on the verge of extinction, he called for help by Karfareon."

"And this Karfareon did help?"

"Not, I fancy, in a manner appreciated by Narfareon. Falling totally in love with mankind, Karfareon conferred upon man a large number of skills which eventually brought man into dominance over beasts. Chief among these gifts was fire, which Karfareon is said to have wrested from the sun—"

"I *didn't* wrest it from the sun!" Quarfar blazed, again in perfect Anglian. "People already had fire by accident, from forest or brush fires caused by lightning or wind friction. Either they feared it, or they worked up courage to steal burning faggots from accidental fires and use it for warmth and for protection against carnivores. All I did was show them how to make it for themselves and how to use it—"

Mind-silence.

Methuen gently queried: "Apart from your disclosure that you speak Anglian admirably—was it *you*, Quarfar?"

Quarfar dropped his head. "My dear Dorita, your mind-translating has been magnificent, but it wasn't ever really needed. No, I take that back; it was needed, because I was pretending not to understand Anglian, and your mediation permitted us all to communicate before I felt ready to reveal myself. But now that Lieutenant Zorbin has ferreted me out, I may as well drop the mask."

Methuen murmured, "I think that would be fine."

Dorita annotated, "Here is a thing I plucked this morning from the mind of Dr. Alexandrovna, although she didn't voice it. She was comprehending that in Quarfar's language, Quarfar has to mean Forethought, Narfar has to mean Afterthought."

Privately, Methuen marveled at her insouciance in the face of a put-down. In fact, Dorita couldn't care less about her role as a telepathic mediator: that had been a mere means to a long-range end; rather, she was containing euphoria, so much closer to that end she seemed to be coming!

This is how Quarfar told them his version of the real story:

"Pray defer the question, how I so well understand Anglian. Language is merely a knife and fork; what counts is the meat.

"Narfar and I are indeed brothers, and yet our species are different. That is to say, Narfar is a mizdorf, yes; and I was born of his parents who were mizdorfs like Narfar; but I was what they called a funny child, you would say that I was a mutation, shorn of wings as the involuntary price of a greater capacity for creative thought and long-range evaluation.

"Our planet was the one you call Mars, and it was dying of progressive desiccation. Ultimately drought killed our parents; and that was a mighty tragedy, because the longevity of a mizdorf is normally very great indeed—as you are seeing in Narfar and me. What were we two brothers to do then?

"On impulse, Narfar fled the planet: his great wings beating in the thinning atmosphere of Mars drove him up to escape velocity; and once out in space, he folded the wings and coasted, ultimately going into suspended animation as both of us did in the comet. Approximately three years later, like one of your robot-mariners in your late twentieth century, quite by chance he was drawn into a decaying Erth orbit. He might have been burned up in your atmosphere or smashed on your rocks, except that in orbit he awoke just enough to apprehend the danger; and he spread wings and coasted in like your 20th-century space shuttle.

"Once he had collected himself, he cruised Erth, surveying his new early paleolithic world. The year was something like 70,000 BC: the dinosaurs were long perished, and your world teemed with almost all the present animal-species along with some others which men have driven into extinction. Also there was a squat species of human which rather aroused Narfar's jealousy because they were comparatively intelligent and they too-much resembled Narfar without wings; your scientists call these people *Homo neandertalensis*. He resolved to take charge of this world; but he lavished his attention on beasts including those of the microscopic world, and he simply snubbed the humans.

"Man was animal, however, even in Narfar's eyes. And I have always entertained a suspicion that Narfar snubbed humans partly because my brother could not think of a way to give them equality with the beasts. The time came, perhaps ten thousand years after his arrrival on Erth, when Narfar had to face up to the fact that Neanderthal humans were on the verge of extinction; and extinction was not the sort of event that Narfar wanted to see happen to any animal.

"That my brother would ask me for help is the measure of his desperation. Across space, on Mars, I received his mind-call. By then, Mars was about played out: even the vegetation was almost gone; and the few surviving mizdorfs had accepted their doom, there was nothing more I could do for them. So I went to Erth, faced my brother and laid down the condition that if I was to help, he must leave it all to me, sitting back and watching if he chose.

"Your bio-paleontology tells you what I did, although my own existence doesn't appear therein. The humans whom I adopted were the funny children; you know them principally as Cro-Magnon man and his descendants and upward mutations: *Homo sapiens*, and *Homo sapiens sapiens*. I taught them nothing whatsoever, in the sense of face-to-face teaching; I merely soul-dwelt in the minds of their leaders and otherwise invisibly hovered about them, fostering a creative climate, a predisposition to try new things. I did not steal fire from the sun, I did not even teach them to use fire or show them how to mine flint and then metal; they developed all these creations themselves, within my creative climate.

"And, as you know, I chose my children well: it has gone on and on until what you have here now. I thoroughly know your history during most of the past fifty millennia—"

Methuen, intent, interjected: "Tell us how you know."

"What I tell you will also explain how I know your Anglian and a large number of other languages.

"When I was inadvertently caught in my own comet, and as the Kelvin-cold of outer space chilled my blood, it came to me that I was facing a very long cryogenic journey, and there was no point in wasting my time. With Narfar sealed in the same comet, I thought to go back to Dora and nurture its funny children. Extricating myself from my body, I threw myself into the five-forty-six gradient behind the comet and willed *Dora*. Unhappily, the comet-motion had already predisposed the gradient's polarity toward Erth; and back to Erth all unwillingly I came.

"And since I was back here bodiless, I took up my task again, dwelling in the brains of your world's leaders, inspiring them but never telling them anything. Let me hurry to say that the achievements of your leaders like Timurlaine, Alexander, Caesar, Napoleon, or Hitler did *not* derive from my inspiring: their achievements were not truly creative, they were shrewd and determined expansions-and-amalgamations based on old ideas. Rather, I dwelt in the men and women who one after another have brought humane progress to your world: most recently, in that same Thoth Evans who invented and fostered the governmental corporation which now rules Erth world by consent of a republican democracy.

"Well, to put it swiftly, last week I was lurking in the brain of someone whom I will not name, when through his brain I learned about the arrival of your comet containing two extraterrestrials near its center, one with wings. Immediately I reentered my own body in the comet, slept with its sleep, awakened with its awakening. And here I am, confessing everything to you who may not believe me.

"If I have affected ignorance, forcing this charming Dorita to mind-translate, believe that my purpose was not malign. I wanted to see what you, who are at many removes my people, would be intelligently and creatively able to do with a totally inscrutable cryptogram.

"'Oho, but I have been monologuing far too long, I surely must be boring you. Please ask me any questions."

"We need to understand," said Zorbin, "how and why Narfar went to Dora, and how and why you followed him."

Quarfar smiled down at the floor—smiled, but he was frowning, too. "It is a sad complex of stories; but it is also one of the oldest of ironies, far older than mizdorfs.

"Why did Narfar go to Dora? It began on Erth when my wonderful creative men created religions and were so thoroughly motivated by those religions that I became unnecessary to them; so I left them with it and went away to sulk—that was my time of being liver-beaked by vultures. Then Narfar found that in many of those same religions he was included, only he was figured as the spirit of evil; in his heart he could not deal with this, and he came to me for counsel. I advised that he depart Erth for another planet;

96

indeed, I *required* that he do so; but I warned him, that unless he would follow my principles in dealing with highly intelligent creatures on that planet, I would follow and take the planet away from him. He agreed, so I sent him to Dora—"

"*How* did you send him?"

"Well, Narfar selected a certain constellation because to him it looked like a mizdorf, and he chose the star which constituted the mizdorf's head, and I perceived that the star had a planet harboring intelligent life, so I pointed my spear at the planet, and thither I dispatched Narfar instantaneously."

"How nearly instantaneously?"

"Absolutely instantaneously: I pointed, and he was there."

Dorita queried: "Have you then so much magical power in that spear?"

"What you call magic is only higher knowledge. It is not in the spear, it is in me; I use my spear as a talisman, to focus my attention on the object of my power."

"Are you telling us," Methuen demanded, "that your spear-focused power created the five-forty-six gradient?"

"Not at all. My spear-focused power sent Narfar instantaneously to Dora; and it was his instantaneous transit which homogenized the gradient."

Zorbin: "Before we pursue that, let me draw you back to the question, why and how you followed Narfar there."

"I followed him after he had been there five or six or seven thousand years; in those days we were all careless about time-definition. I did this when I had mind-perceived across space that Narfar was not keeping his promise: he was building a social order which made man the peer but not the master of other animals, which exalted tradition and enslaved creativity within the bounds of Narfar-lore; he was perpetuating the situation by being always present before the eyes of his people as their god-king. *How* did I follow him, Zorbin? I just *went*, instantaneously, along the five-forty-six gradient which was the way requiring least effort."

"Thank you," Zorbin acknowledged; "I trust this is not seeming to be a discourteous—grilling, as we say in police dramas."

"Not at all, sir; you are being most courteous, and I want to tell you what I can."

"Then tell me this. You saw the mizdorf constellation and

97

the Dora-star from Erth and you have given Dorita good eyeball-information about the relative brightnesses of the stars in that constellation as seen from Dora. But also, you told Dorita about the relative temperatures and chemical compositions of those stars; and this is not eyeball-information. You must have explored and analyzed those stars; you must know what constellation they compose."

"Truly, I have made no exploration or analysis, I simply intuit such facts, they come into me and I know they are right. And I was not playing a game with you at the planetarium. I suspect, but I do not know, that Mizdorf is the constellation you call Orion, that Saiph is the Dora-star. My remembrance of dispatching Narfar is almost sixty millennia old; and we did not then call constellations by your names or even see them in your configurations, and the whole business is now rather foggy. If, in the planetarium tomorrow, I can look at your constellation Orion as it would appear from Saiph, then perhaps I can reorient my gestalt and tell you for sure. In all candor, it is really like that."

Zorbin nodded and meditated. Methuen took it up: "Our next pressing question would have to be, how you and Narfar were trapped in the comet."

Again Qarfar smile-frowned down. "Narfar's entrapment was on purpose. My own was a little mistake.

"I had been doing a year-long reconnaissance of Dora; and Narfar got wind of my presence, and up went *his* wind. Above Dora's northern ice cap he came out to challenge me. It was final showdown, and I tried to persuade him to go away, but he kept coming, shrieking his intent to kill me, although killing was not what I wanted for either of us.

"The planetary situation inspired me with a tactic. With my spear I distance-drew a broad circle on the ice directly beneath us and called up Dora's vulcanism at that point; as intended, Dora blew off a chunk of ice at escape velocity. My intent was that the ice would entrap Narfar and carry him remotely away from Dora before he would find means of escape; he would never find his way back, so he would alight on some planet and work out his destiny. Unhappily for me, I didn't get away fast enough: the ice caught me and Narfar almost at the same instant; its surface was slushy still from atmospheric friction-heat, we sank into it facing each other, we were caught in the space-freeze. I suppose I was too shaken by the surprise of it to collect my thoughts and use

98

my will and my spear to get myself out; and when I did collect my thoughts, it was too late for changing directions."

He arose with effort, pushing himself erect with his spear-haft. "Forgive me, I am more weary tonight than I ever am normally; perhaps it is from the soul-excitement of the day. May I be excused?"

"Please, one more question first," Methuen urged. "Is it with your spear that you would execute your threat against Erth?"

"What threat against Erth?"

"That if necessary, you would explode Erth to make a comet in the hope of getting back to Dora."

Quarfar hand-wiped his forehead on which a few drops of perspiration glistened. "I am sorry, I gave all of you the wrong impression, I did not sufficiently restrict the meaning of my word 'explode.' I meant only that I would find some unpeopled area in one of your polar ice caps and explode myself outward on *that*."

"Then you mean no harm to Erth?"

"Why should I harm Erth? It is my planet."

He started for his bedroom. He paused, turned, and added with a wan smile, "One urgent caution which is also a request. Do not reveal to anyone, not even to the members of your task force, what I have told you tonight—not any of it, not even my knowledge of Anglian. It is a caution because they would not believe you and so you would be discredited. It is a request because, in questions of factual knowledge, humans must always have free rein to inquire and discover in terms of their own resources; they should never be fettered by supranormal revelation."

He turned toward his bedroom, then turned again. "One more thing since you mentioned threat. On Dora there *is* a potential threat to Erth; but whether and how that threat may be realized will depend on my interplay with a woman named Dorita."

 14

Night deepened in Central Park; it was too late for all except lovers, and even these did not penetrate the lagooned copse where Narfar crouched on a tree-branch. A quarter-moon fully awakened Narfar, creating ages-old stirrings in his groin once aroused by the two small moons of Mars, then successively reinforced by the single splendid moon of that other planet and the single modest moon of Dora. He was aware of his beloved beasts about him: owls and other night birds, incautious nocturnal squirrels, fish in the lagoon. Needing no syrinx, Narfar trilled a complex low whistling, finger-playing on his lips; the beasts gathered below and around him, even the fish poked heads above water in his direction: they communed with him, some of them even answered him.

The Narfarian trilling ceased; the beasts drifted away. Narfar was miserable, the beasts had helped him very little. He was not home; he was so far from home that he did not know where home was, or *when* it was. To make it worse, Quarfar was somewhere about, unless Quarfar had already beaten Narfar back to Dora. Having once found courage to go out and face Quarfar, Narfar did not find it in his guts to try it again; yet sooner or later, Quarfar would find *him*.

Huddling in the crotch where the limb joined the tree-bole, wing-cloaking himself, Narfar squeezed shut his eyes and crowded knuckles against forehead-slope, laboring to think out the problem. But the gift of sustained systematic thought was not one of his gifts. How to learn where home was? how to deal with Quarfar? These two questions were straining his limits of formulation, and they were so different from each other that he could not think about both at once, yet somehow they were so conjunctive that he could not separate them. Eventually he gave it up, shuddered all over, then welcomed the respite of a beautiful impulse: another good night like last night!

Again he bat-flew the city, cruising particularly the residential apartment areas; and it wasn't very long before he was attracted by a frustrated-widow smell on 71st Street between Ninth and Tenth Avenues.

Somewhat later, in a different quarter of the city, he was arrested by quite another sort of smell—the smell of Quarfar. Narfar, shocked and frightened, arrested himself in midflight and located the smell source. It came from down there—that window, on the—what floor? Narfar counted on fingers: one, two, three, four, *five* stories up. The window was dark; indeed, only one window in the building was lighted, and that was remote from this one.

With effort, he brought all his conflicting feelings under control by one immediately dominant feeling: see what the situation is, and go from there. On that basis, he descended to hover near Quarfar's window, smelling and otherwise sensing.

Quarfar it was, and he was asleep in there. But something was wrong. . . .

Molecularizing himself, Narfar passed among the molecules of window-glassoid and stood beside the bed of his brother, seeing and smelling and sensing him clearly in darkness. Quarfar slept like a babe, raw, lying on his right side facing Narfar, legs drawn up, left hand clutching his spear, head pillowed on right hand on pillow. But Quarfar at moments became a restless sleeper, quivering, stiffening, with an abnormal hoarsenesss in his breathing. And there was perspiration on the forehead of Quarfar, although the night was comfortably cool.

Narfar's brother-enemy: defenseless here, and beginning to be sick with something here. With the greatest of ease, Narfar could fang him, and that would be the end of Narfar's troubles forever. On the other hand, Quarfar his brother was sick with something; and Narfar could cure him here and now, being able to charm all beasts visible and invisible.

Which was Quarfar most to Narfar—mostly enemy, or mostly brother? Oh shit, he had to *think* again! He crouched on the floor beside Quarfar, crowding knuckles into forehead—and smelled a new smell.

Well, he couldn't think efficiently until he had found out about *that!*

The new smell was frustrated female, all right, and it was

101

strong and near. But the frustration was not the same sort, not at all; this was *like* rut-urge, but not exactly the same, so it was different, but still most enticing. And the woman was *young*, for a change. And she was just in the next room.

Abandoning the problem of Quarfar, Narfar penetrated the wall. He found Dorita lying supine and uncovered on a sofa, with hands folded behind head and elbows out. As a concession to the cause of good order in an apartment with three men, Dorita, who preferred to sleep raw, was wearing semi-sheer black pajamas. She was, of course, a funny child; on the other hand, the prejudice of Narfar against funny children for pleasure purposes had been somewhat mollified by the experiences of two nights; and this one was a perplexing mixture of funny child and funny mature woman.

The very young woman's eyes were closed, but they were aimed up at Narfar; she was not asleep, only musing on the verge of slumber. He tasted her thought-feelings: they were a delicious pudding, a jungle, with shadowings of mysterious indefinable secrets which were untouchable but perhaps ought to be touched. Her nipples were erect as though she were erotically aroused; but erotic wasn't quite what her arousal was, not quite. . . .

It was worth pursuing. He could tell in her mind that she was eligible for him; that she was none of the sorts of innocence which were tabu for him, nor was she the sort whose extensive experience repelled him.

He went telepathically into his dream-weaving routine: *You asleep, you dreaming. Me a dream, a good dream for you.* . . .

Her eyelids flicked back. She seemed unstartled. She examined him head to toe, wingtip to wingtip; she gave particular attention to that which was imposingly, quiveringly erect. Lazily then she asserted *in his tongue*, not changing her position: "I not asleep, not dreaming. You Narfar, you excited. Answer for now is *no;* maybe later, we see."

She watched his gradual detumescence. "Good," she said. "Now we talk. Here, sit beside me." Stilll supine, she squeezed over against the sofa back to make more room; and she patted the sofa edge, smiling at him.

Obediently Narfar sat facing her face with his wings to-gether-clasped behind him (he didn't quite know what else to do with them). This incredible child—yes, she *was* a child—seemed to be taking charge; and amazingly, he was liking it.

She patted a hairy Narfar-thigh. "Poor Narfar. You far from home. Why you run away from us?" She was talking high-rapidly, he was actually just-understanding her.

From his recent experience with Erth-women, he grasped that they talked lower and slower than he, almost as low-slow as Quarfar; and so he answered slow and low: "You catch me in box, I see out, but it box. I know quick you people here all funny Quarfar-people. I run away." Narfar was not talking down to her, the diction was normal for him.

Slowly she ran a hand over his thigh-crest, barely touching the thigh, touching rather his orange-red hair-tips; it brought on a semi-tumescence, and quickly she drew her hand away. "Poor Narfar. We not your enemy. Quarfar your enemy?"

"Yes."

"You fear Quarfar?"

"Yes."

"Tell why."

"Quarfar want to kill me."

"Tell why." Her voice caressed him, although no longer did she touch him.

It all came out of him in a twitter-blurt, so that she could not catch his rapid words but had to follow his mind-action. "I make world for beasts, somewhere, dunno where, maybe here. Quarfar not like, he change world for funny people. I not like. I go to Dora, make world for men *and* beasts. Quarfar follow me later. I think he want to kill me because he not like new world I make either. I go to fight Quarfar, save my world. Something happen, somehow we both go to sleep, wake up here. Where is *here?*"

Laboriously synchronizing the words and the thought-train, Dorita felt that she had made full-enough sense of it; and certainly in its own crude way it checked with Quarfar's account. She told Narfar then: "*Here is Erth.* Erth is where you first make world for beasts, where Quarfar first come and change to world for funny people. You think I funny person, yes?" He nodded. "I think I just woman, our men just men, not funny—well, some funny, but most not. We masters of beasts; we try to help them, but they die because we so strong. What about your Dora?"

He sat proudly upright, expanding chest, extending arms and wings; in a primitive way, he was really quite splendid; Dorita felt her nippples rehardening; she quelled it. "Dora

103

world for men *and* beasts—for men *and women* and beasts. Not funny people like you, just people—like me, only no wings, and color different. I learn from Quarfar, but I do better. On Dora, masters, servants, beasts, everybody know place, everybody happy. I king!"

Dorita considered him with melancholy. She told him: "You and Quarfar, you caught in comet, brought here to Erth in comet. You gone many *many* years from Dora."

He stared at her. He said, "Shit again, I got to think again." And he bowed head, folded wings, drove knuckles into forehead. Dorita didn't have the word for *shit* from Quarfar, but she caught the mental sense. Holding in a smile, she waited.

Narfar looked up: "How long many many years?"

Going to telepathy, she conveyed the sense of a man being born and growing old and dying, another man the same, and so on, one after another, man after man after man, many many men. She went further: no telling about glaciers on Dora, but Narfar had undoubtedly known glaciers on Erth; and she filled his mind with a picture of a continental glacier laboriously advancing and prolongedly pausing and indolently receding. She said, *"That* long."

He looked at her with new interest. *You mind-talker mind-listener like me?*

"Yes."

He frowned. "But I gone from Dora so long—Dora might even be dead now."

"Yes."

"Nobody there remember me? I not king any more?"

"Maybe."

Seizing her hands, he leaped up and pulled her off the sofa. "Then we have fun here, yes? I fly up to sky with you, we schlurp in sky—yes?"

She held him off, insisting: "No! Not now! Not on Erth, not in sky! *No!*"

He let go one of her hands and stared. "Tell why not?"

Dorita had found the approach to her purpose.

Firmly she told him, flooding his mind with affirmative suggestion: "You go back to Dora. Take me with you. Maybe I be your woman on Dora. Maybe."

He let go her other hand and stared, alternately tumescent

104

and semi-detumescent, while she dropped onto the sofa and ran a hand back through her sweat-wet hair and stared up at him. She was more aroused than he, but in a different way. He was powerful-impulsive enough to rape her at will, to take her up into the sky at will. She could not have resisted and would not have wanted to resist—except that her long-range purpose was beginning to formulate itself, it somehow involved Dora and some Dora-secret that she had sensed in both Quarfar and Narfar without having grasped the nature of the secret. A wild sky-fling now with a bat-flying Neander-thal, appealing as it was from a viewpoint of unprecedented perversity, might drain all the heat from Narfar's arousal, and he might never take her to Dora. And Quarfar, she knew *now from within him,* could *never* be seduced into taking her there. Quarfar was a magnificent loner, in solitude as the Loving Unlovered Allfather he nurtured his humans and fought their enemies; and he was much too wise to be Dor-ita diddled. . . .

Narfar demanded: "But *where* Dora?"

She was improvising rapidly, but with solid background. She went to mind-talk, it was better: *I think I know where Dora is, but I will know for sure when night comes again. When I know, I will tell you. You come again tomorrow night.*

What I do in between?

You'll think of something.

But how I get to Dora even if I know?

How did you get there the first time?

Quarfar send me. I just go.

How long did it take you to go?

No time. I just think go, I there.

Via the five-forty-six gradient, obviously. Whether Narfar could take her to Dora without killing her en route in sub-zero airless interstellar space, gradient or no gradient, was a question which Narfar would be quite incapable of answering.

The thought she now projected was obbligatoed by a rose garden of demure love with endless indefinite promise. *Go your ways now, dear Narfar, go. Do whatever you want to do in between, fly to the moon, charm bats, make love, any-thing at all; but go now. Come back about the same time*

105

when night comes again, and we will see what is next for us together. Will you do that for Dorita?

He gazed at her with rallying tumescence. His mind let out one boiling *YES!* and he turned and crashed outward through a window, having forgotten to demolecularize himself.

Prevoyance Three

Methuen's third prevoyant dream was troublesomely sequential to the prior ones. Its dream-date was 20 January 2465, and he had been assigned as expert consultant to the chief of Norwestian Civil Intelligence Service with full-time duty on the question of the two attacks. At the moment, he was in the chief's office, telling him: "Sir, I really believe that this hunch of mine ought to be explored. I have kept having this feeling of 546 in connection with both prior disasters, and we have just about concluded that they must be extraterrestrial attacks. My point is, that we have recently established the extension of the five-forty-six gradient at least as far out as the star Bellatrix; and this gradient happens to be dead-on with the star Saiph—"

The intercom sounded; the chief took it, allowing Methuen to hear it. Male private secretary's voice: "Sir, I have a call from the Army Chief of Staff. At least five army bases have come up with inactive rekamatic missiles and unexplodable conventional cartridges. He had to cut off for other business, but he wants you to call him back."

"Right, get him now," said the chief. He turned to Methuen. "Even if you are right, Captain, I don't know what we can do about it. Erth has no defense of any kind at all."

"Not *quite* no defense," Methuen countered. "Remember that a number of spaceships were already cruising before ship-inactivation and are still out there. . . . Hey, oh God, Chief, let me preempt your phone!"

He seized it and put in a priority call to the Fleet Admiral. "Sir, Methuen here. I urge that you immediately fire orders to all cruising ships: stay away from the five-forty-six gradient! Repeat—"

Part Three

A MARVELOUS DAY IN SPACETIME

Day Zero

Over breakfast in pajamas and lounging robes—a hearty breakfast, dialed of course by now-lightly-clad Dorita—Methuen complained of a warm draft despite the air-conditioning; and this led him to discover the broken-out window. He hurried to it, studied it, peered out (thrusting head and neck within a rim-border of jagged glassoid more than large enough to pass a man's body), inspected environs up and down and sideways, pulled back in; Dorita and Zorbin were watching him.

"It's new since we went to bed!" the captain exclaimed. "Dorita, what did you hear?"

"What did *you* hear?"

"Nothing," averred both men. Methuen added, "But we were asleep behind closed doors, and you were right in this room!"

Wide-eyed she lied. "I guess I was pretty soundly asleep." An idea for diversion occurred to her, and she was alarmed by the time she announced it: "There is something else that I *do* hear right now, and that is Quarfar's breathing."

The men listened, frowning at each other. "I'd better check," Zorbin volunteered; and he went to Quarfar's door and knocked. No response. Zorbin went in. He reappeared, face grim: "Come here, both of you."

Quarfar lay on his back, eyes open, face and hands and body sweat-wet, breathing a hideous mighty rasping.

Methuen said: "Saul, alert emergency at Astrofleet General Hospital, top government priority, and order an ambulance with oxygen equipment and the rest of it. Then notify Almagor." Dorita had fled to the bathroom; as Methuen bent over sick Quarfar, she returned with a fever thermometer and thrust it into the titan's open mouth under his tongue and closed his lips around it, then departed for the kitchenette. Methuen held Quarfar's lips closed, although this made the

111

patient's breathing more difficult. Dorita returned with ice in a towel and another cold-wet towel, put the ice compress on Quarfar's forehead and bathed his face and body, while Methuen removed the thermometer and whistled, allowing Quarfar again to seek open-mouthed breath.

Zorbin returned: ambulance en route; Almagor notified, he'll be there; then he went into the living room and flung wide the broken window, while Dorita continued her ministrations and Methuen phoned a secretary at Astrofleet: "Emergency with Quarfar, cancel 0900 task-force meeting at apartment, have task force convene at 1000 in Astrofleet Hospital lobby, we'll arrange something." During that call, a solichopper-ambulance drifted to the open window; two medics entered through the window with a stretcher, picked up the patient, took him out the window into the ambulance and whirred away, working on Quarfar.

At 1046, a supervising nurse came into the visitors' lobby, identified the members of the task force (seven of them today), and invited them to follow her. She took them to the executive staff conference room, seated them along two sides of the long table near its head, assured them that the chairman would meet them in a few minutes, and served coffee.

At 1107, Methuen (at last wearing four sleeve-stripes on his jacket) entered with Zorbin, Dorita, Almagor and the assistant secretary of ESC. Methuen offered the head-table seat, first to his chief, then to Almagor; both deferred to the captain, who stood there while the other four seated themselves at his left and right.

Said Methuen calmly: "Gentlepeople, we welcome four new task force members, but their introductions must await more pressing business. As you have been told, our prime subject, Quarfar, is gravely ill, they have him here under intensive care. Dr. Almagor is in close liaison with the hospital director who has kindly allowed us to conduct our morning business here, and if necessary our afternoon business also, permitting us to receive hourly bulletins about Quarfar. I have to say personally that—having known Quarfar, I am personally concerned, and so are Lieutenant Zorbin and Miss Lanceo.

"Before we enter into anything else, I'd like for you to

112

hear some comments, first from Dr. Almagor, then from the assistant secretary." Methuen sat.

Almagor spoke from his seat, looking down, troubled. "I should tell you people that I feel unhappy and personally guilty about this. If you have studied with understanding the reports of our initial medical examinations, you know that among other things we tested Mr. Quarfar for antibodies against the full spectrum of known human diseases, and we found him well defended. Consequently I did not prescribe any special medical precautions when I released him into Captain Methuen's custody.

"It now appears that his lung tubercles have been invaded by some sort of virus growth which is entirely strange to us. We have nothing with which to attack it. He did not contract it inside the comet; this we know because the central comet ice has been exhaustively analyzed.

"I do have a hypothesis, but I do not know how to test it. As you know, viruses mutate, producing new strains; and some very old strains become extinct. Quarfar may have harbored this virus fifty thousand years ago before he was caught by the comet; but at that time, perhaps he had antibodies to keep it under control. During all those millennia of suspended animation, perhaps those particular antibodies died while the virus merely slept; this is far-fetched, I admit, since his other antibodies remained intact. Anyhow, this virus has now awakened and taken control.

"We are working intensively in two directions. This hospital is using every known method of sustaining life in Quarfar; there is some faint hope that his body will develop or re-awaken antibodies to fight off the virus for itself. At the same time, all members of the pertinent research staff at the Science Institute—*all* members—are working at the highest feasible speed to analyze the virus and learn how to attack it.

"I will entertain questions."

But Almagor had answered almost all the questions that anybody could think of, given the uncertainties which he had expressed. Two questions were asked: "Can we see him?" and "Will he live?" The first was answered, "Not for several days, at least"; the second, "I do not know; and if he cannot live, I do not know how soon he will die."

The possibility of cloning Quarfar was not raised; as yet, human beings could not be successfully cloned, their nervous systems were too complex.

Methuen nodded to the assistant secretary, who arose. "Gentlepeople, I will stand because reluctantly I must leave on other business. I appreciate the concerns here, and I want you to know that they are shared by the Norwestian and Erthworld governments all the way up to Chairman Evans. We have placed all our resources at the disposition of Dr. Almagor in the hope that Mr. Quarfar will live and recover, for his sake and for ours.

"My role here is threefold. First, I want to assure all of you that your work is valuable and should continue with top concentration even though you are temporarily or—perhaps permanently deprived of the services of Mr. Quarfar. Second, please be informed that my office has been continually monitoring several local and world-wide services in search of the escaped batwing monster, whose name I now understand to be Narfar; but so far, nothing; we will keep you informed. Finally, I wish to reiterate our confidence in your chairman, Captain B. J. Methuen, and to remind you that neither the disappearance of Narfar nor the illness of Quarfar was within the captain's control to prevent.

"Dr. Almagor, pray proceed with full institute energy. May I depart now—or are there questions?"

There would have been some, undoubtedly; but Methuen, sensing departure-urgency, excused his chief, who left on the nod.

Now Methuen stonily presented the four new arrivals, and presented the prior-arrived members and Zorbin and Dorita to them. He reiterated the charges to the task force and its listing of primary problems as expanded in yesterday morning's meeting.

He turned then to Olga Alexandrovna. "Madam, we agreed that ancillary to all other problems was the question of language. You made some good inroads yesterday; is there any further progress?"

"Only," said Olga, "that I have been able to learn thoroughly the vocabulary already derived, to develop a preliminary form of structure for the language, and to do a little comparative study, which confirms that the structure and even some of the words more closely conform to pre-Tellene than to any other tongue I know. However, there are numerous departures from what we know of the pre-Tellene of ancient Mykenae; at the same time, the language of Quarfar is

114

as complex as high Tellene in its conceptual flow, although it is not at all high Tellene, but fundamentally a different tongue.

"For what my suspicion may be worth, these findings lead me to suspect that this very planet Erth was the one which Quarfar inhabited before he went to Dora. It is a most difficult hypothesis; how would he have crossed space to the other planet, wherever it may be? Our developing findings may easily knock down this guess. Nevertheless, the strong but less than perfect resemblance of Quarfar's tongue to pre-Tellene is as though Quarfar in pre-ancient times had taught primitive pre-Tellenes the rudiments of his language, and they took it their way while he went on with his way. As an analogy, Gallia developed modern Gallic from its own Barbarian roots infused with a number of imported Ramic roots and structures.

She turned to Methuen: "All my studies, Captain, have been based on the notion that they would develop a means of communicating with Quarfar. It is evident that I have a personal and professional stake in his recovery."

Resolutely Methuen was repressing the urge to report what Quarfar had told them privately last night. As Quarfar had observed, solutions ought to come from human inquiry and not from revelation; and certainly the linguist had gone far with her aspect of this process.

He turned to Astrophysicist Sita Sari. "Madam, particularly in your province are two of our problems: the origins of Quarfar and Narfar, and the nature of the five-forty-six gradient. Any progress yet?"

Small Sita Sari looked around at her colleagues with a wry little smile of semi-embarrassment that Methuen found somehow fey-charming. "I do have something," she said, "but I'm afraid it will take me awhile to present, perhaps half an hour or so. Perhaps Dr. Chu or one of our new members would prefer to inject something first."

Chu and the other four negated with head-shakes. The lean black psychobiologist from North Africa, Dr. Harlo Ombasa, remarked in a basso almost as rich as Quarfar's: "I do have a thing, but it can come later. I defer to Dr. Sari."

From having been momentarily feminine-charming, Sari now went precise and crisp: "These two problems—the

115

origins of our aliens and the nature of the five-forty-six gradient—are tightly linked with each other and with the age, velocity, and trajectory of the comet.

"The comet trajectory, as recorded off Bellatrix, appears linear, not curved. In the excellent observations which we have from Mr. Zorbin, I can detect no departure from this perfect linearity over a distance of nearly half a trillion kilometers. And this trajectory, extrapolated in both directions, is perfectly aligned with the five-forty-six gradient. Furthermore, the unusually high velocity of the comet suggests that it may have been accelerated by precisely that gradient.

"Let me give a transient moment to the *nature* of the gradient. Captain Methuen was perceptive enough to take samplings of space along the route. As all of you probably comprehend, space is not a vacuum, but is instead a plenum of little random events the largest of which is much smaller than the smallest subnuclear particle yet identified. Because of their randomness, all proper samples of raw space will contain practically equal event-counts, equally distributed between positive and negative or ingressive and expressive events. Well, along this gradient, while the total number of events in each sample is the usual number, there is an overwhelming preponderance of negative events, and only a small minority of positive events.

"Let me put it less technically. It is as though some mysterious object, traveling at near-instantaneous velocity, had created the gradient as a sort of wake by galvanizing all events in its path into negative expression and driving all positive ingression away from the path. The effect on other objects subsequently falling into this gradient would be to urge them along at heightened velocity in whichever direction they might happen to be traveling when they would enter the gradient.

"I am not ready to guess how long so unique a gradient might persist, or how long ago this particular gradient was created, or what sort of object might have created it. Judging by the age of this comet and the evidence that it may have been traveling in this gradient almost since origin, the longevity of the gradient would seem to be astonishing."

She had her audience, all right!

"As now we return to the question of the comet's probable origin," Sari continued, "I wish to give you a visual." She produced a little projector from her purse; asked for and got room-darkening; and projected on the conference room's parabolic screen a planar view of the northern celestial hemisphere, with all stars and constellations appearing just as they would to a viewer who might be standing at the north pole of Erth. She drew their attention particularly to the constellation Orion spreading in the right ascension range of 0500 to 0600 hours and in the declination range between minus 09°41′ and plus 09°55′; for she had considerably tilted the projection slightly, allowing fifteen degrees negative to show near Orion, at the expense of fifteen degrees positive near Camelopardalis.

"Now," she announced, "I am going to replace this planar projection, which is the way our eyes see the sky, with a holographic projection which takes account of the relative distances of the stars from Erth. You must understand that when we look at the sky with naked eyes, we lose perspective; the sky becomes a primitive inverted bowl, all stars appear equidistant from us, and therefore apparent constellations appear even though they are composed of stars whose distances from Erth vary by hundreds of light years. To illustrate this, as we shift to the holograph which is identically the same hemisphere of sky, I want you particularly to watch what happens to Orion."

They gasped. Orion went into total depth-distortion, its configurations vanished, it was no longer recognizable as a constellation.

Sari proceeded calmly: "On this projection, which is surely familiar to Captain Methuen and Lieutenant Zorbin, it is possible to show the five-forty-six gradient with fair accuracy. Just at the center of this projection and in the near foreground of it, you will have noted a yellow circle: that represents Erth, and Sol also if you will. I am now going to cause a yellow line to go outward from Erth; it will represent the five-forty-six gradient. Understand that the term five-forty-six represents the gradient's *right ascension* of five hours forty-six minutes; but to make sense in the sky or in this holograph, the line must also follow the *declination* of the gradient, and that declination is minus nine degrees forty-one minutes."

They watched the yellow animated line emanate from Erth and move slowly outward to their left. After an appreciable number of seconds, the yellow line stopped near a star. "That star is Bellatrix," she told them; "and although it is only four

117

hundred seventy light-years distant, it is the nearest to us of all the stars in Orion. Let me show you." She flashed back to the planar projection, and she placed a yellow arrow-light on Bellatrix: the left shoulder-star in Orion. "It would be too complicated to show the gradient on this planar projection; but flashing back now to the holograph," (she did so) "we can see that the gradient narrowly misses Bellatrix—by about seventy light-years, in fact, which is just about where the comet passed Bellatrix and was pursued by Captain Methuen."

Several grunts were audible.

"Now," Sari resumed, "let us suppose that the gradient continues for a great distance out beyond Bellatrix, but always with the same right ascension and declination. Let's allow it to grow——" They watched the yellow line move outward, always with its tail connected to yellow Erth: another Bellatrix-distance, and still others. And it stopped, making a direct hit on a star. A yellow circle appeared around that star.

"Let us turn again to the planar sky," Sari purred, "and see what star that may be, and in what constellation." Again Orion leaped into clear view, and already the yellow arrow-light was poised on a star which made the right foot of Orion. "The star, as you see, is Saiph. Its distance from Erth is two thousand one hundred light-years. The five-forty-six gradient makes a direct hit upon Saiph.

"And twenty-one hundred light-years is almost precisely the distance that the comet would have traveled, in the fifty thousand years which are estimated as its age, and at the velocity of .0326 C or 9780 kilometers per second which Lieutenant Zorbin recorded and repeatedly verified."

They were all quick-glancing among Sari and Zorbin and Methuen. . . . There was a little scattering of applause in which Dorita joined; Methuen and Zorbin refrained, sensing that some of it was for them, although mostly it was for Sari.

"Now," the astrophysicist continued, "there remain problems; all is not resolved. I do not know that the gradient does not extend far out beyond even Saiph; it certainly was not created by the comet, since it was observed long before the comet appeared, and the comet does seem on this showing to have originated near Saiph. For that matter, I have not proved that the gradient extends even as far as Saiph; but it seems a good inference from the speed and age of the comet and its linear gradient trajectory where it was plotted. We do seem to have here strong evidence that the two creatures contained in the comet did begin their journey in it near Saiph; but whether Saiph was their origin as creatures, I have no way to judge. I was interested in Dr. Alexandrovna's hypothesis about Quarfar's Erth-origin based on linguistic indications.

"And there is also a report by a subject to be taken into account. The creature called Quarfar has reportedly given to Miss Lanceo an accounting of the nine brightest stars, along with three nebulae, *as seen from the planet Dora.* Incidentally, has Dr. Alexandrovna verified the credibility of Miss Lanceo's reporting?"

"It is credible," Olga affirmed, while Dorita reddened.

"Good," Sari commented. "Well, to make a fully scientific comparison, we need more than we have, but we can start with two assumptions. The first is, that the nine brightest stars as seen from Saiph would all fall within the constellation Orion, which has a number of high-magnitude stars; and the presence of three nebulae, one of which *could* be M-42, is further confirmation. The second starting assumption is this; if we know the distances and magnitudes of those stars and nebulae from Erth, along with their right ascensions and declinations, we can compute the relative magnitudes of those stars and nebulae as seen from Saiph. Want to think about that for a moment?"

They bowed heads in prayerful thought. Presently a majority of heads came up again, some comprehendingly, some willing to be shown.

She queried: "Shall I proceed, Mr. Chairman? or shall we first explore my concepts?"

"Go ahead," said Methuen. "We can take questions later, but some of us do understand the concepts." He now had the measure of Sari, just as she yesterday had learned the measure of Methuen.

"Very well. I will stay with the planar projection to show you my findings, based on a preliminary calculation which remains to be checked.

"Quarfar reported that from Dora, the brightest star was a very hot blue-white star whose dominant element was helium. That corresponds to Hatsya." A yellow arrow appeared pointing to the tip of the Orion-sword.

"The next-brightest was a fairly hot blue-white helium star.

119

That would be Rigel." The arrow darted to Orion's left foot; and thereafter it continued moving to each named star.

"Third was another fairly hot blue-white helium star, hotter than the second but not as hot as the first. It could easily be Alnilam." Middle star in the sword-belt.

"Fourth: another blue-white helium star, about as hot as the third. Alnitak." Belt-star at Orion's right.

"Fifth: still another blue-white helium star, about as hot as the third or fourth. Mintaka." Belt-star at Orion's left.

"Sixth: a different sort of star entirely orange-red, major element titanium, the least-hot star of the lot. Betelgeuse." Orion's right shoulder. "I have to confess that this one almost led me into the error that the planet Dora might be our own Erth; as seen from Erth, Betelgeuse is fourth-brightest, and the small error could be a difference in visual judgments. However, the stars that are brightest to us include several in the yellows, and Quarfar reported only one yellow-white.

"Seventh: again, blue-white helium, just about the hotness of three, four, and five. And that would nicely correspond to that very Bellatrix where the comet was first sighted." Orion's left shoulder.

"Eighth: an extremely hot blue-white helium star, hottest of all except Hatsya. I say, Heka." The head of Orion.

"Ninth: a yellow-white, probably just a bit hotter than our Sol, with a variety of metals. I nominate Tabit." Orion's left forearm.

"Saiph was not named, of course. Saiph would be the sun of Dora, it would not be thought of as a star, and it would not be part of a visible constellation any more than our own sun is.

"Quarfar mentioned also three nebulae. The one of considerable brightness could easily be M-42, the beautiful night-object in the sword, just above Hatsya. The others could be M-43, near M-42, and 2024 between Alnitak and Alnilam.

"Pending more information, Mr. Chairman, I will summarize my views. The five-forty-six gradient extends from Erth to Saiph and possibly beyond. The comet originated near Saiph, somehow picked up the two creatures without damaging them, somehow fell into the gradient, and proceeded with high velocity along the gradient toward Erth.

"I will entertain questions."

Silence.

The presentation had illuminated Dr. Mabel Seal, a cheery plump brown archaeologist from Eskimoland. She breathed: "What magical star names! Erebian, aren't they?"

"Right," Olga grunted.

"I'll bet there's a delicious Erebian myth attached to every name. I wish I knew the stories."

Olga responded, "*Rigel* means right foot; *betelgeuse* means shoulder; and so it goes. Sorry about that."

Then Cathay's Chu, timidly: "It seems to me that Dr. Sari has brilliantly solved all the problems in the astrophysical area confronting this task force. May I ask what remains to be done in this area?"

"At least one thing," Sari responded. "I have not found time to calculate the precise positions of these nine stars and three nebulae as they would be seen from Dora, which is apparently a planet of Saiph. And Quarfar did mention a constellation which to Dorians resembled a—Miss Lanceo, please help me."

"A mizdorf," said Dorita, "or a winged creature like the one in the comet, flung headlong upon the planet. With the flinger watching overhead."

"Very well, a mizdorf. Well, until we can see a projection of these twelve objects *as a constellation seen from Saiph*, we cannot make sure that the constellation would resemble a mizdorf, and therefore we cannot positively nail down the identifications of Orion and of Saiph."

Methuen inserted: "Such a projection is now being arranged by the planetarium director, it will be available to us at 1730—"

A nurse entered and whispered to Almagor. As he listened, he frowned sternly, then he whispered to Dorita. Stricken, she arose and departed with the nurse.

Arising, Almagor told them: "Mr. Quarfar is failing rapidly, he is expected to die within minutes. He has asked to talk privately with Miss Lanceo. We can only wait—and pray excuse me."

In the course of the ensuing hour, reluctantly the task force proceeded with its business.

Psychobiologist Harlo Ombasa had an important contribution to make. "Gentle people, as a newcomer to this task force I speak diffidently; but I have discovered a thing which seems

121

to fit into the developing pattern. It is derived from the medical analyses of Quarfar and Narfar, which I received on my arrival here yesterday afternoon and which I studied thoroughly last night. There is a new technique, which may not have come to your attention, since I have not yet published it, for analysis of the dendrites of neurons in order to establish the age of those neurons. Its use is particularly telling when applied to brain neurons, which are not regenerated and are always as old as the organism. In the cases of both Quarfar and Narfar, their brain neurons appear astonishingly to be eighty thousand years old, give or take ten thousand years. I hasten to add that this is an inference from meager data; it should be reinforced by studies of the subjects deliberately slanted toward this sort of measurement. But I submit it for what it is worth."

Anthropologist Chu Huang was stimulated by Ombasa's remarks. "We seem to be on collision course with common and scientific sense, and creative science is at its best in that sort of situation. I think it is time to start stringing together some of these findings from a viewpoint of prehistorical anthropology. Dr. Alexandrovna has suggested that Quarfar may have taught rudiments of his language to Erth-humans who then went their own way with language. Dr. Sari, with her inferential evidence that Quarfar and Narfar departed Dora in the comet about fifty thousand years ago, establishes that if these two creatures were previously on Erth, it had to be more than fifty thousand years ago. Dr. Ombasa now informs us, subject to further inquiry, that these two creatures may be about eighty thousand years old. And I am reminded that our Neanderthal men, who resembled Narfar only without wings, became extinct when they were replaced by our Cro-Magnon men who resembled Quarfar or indeed any of us. I think the approximate date of Neanderthal disappearance does fall somewhere in that allowable time-range between fifty and eighty thousand years ago—I'm sorry, these datings are not perfectly on target for my own disciplinary area; can anybody help me?"

Archaeologist Mabel Seal smiled at Chu and said softly, "Neanderthal men became extinct approximately sixty thousand years ago. Cro-Magnon man was already very much on the scene."

Chu spread his hands. "There you are. The major difficulty is, though, that the trend of our findings would seem to complicate science by introducing two supra-human creatures as leader-guides in the course of our social evolution. Science, including prehistorical anthropology, rejects such complicating ideas, shaving them away with Occam's razor: pursue the simpler of two competing hypotheses, defer the more complicated until the simpler ceases to work. So far, the simpler hypothesis of social evolution without supra-human aid has worked very nicely indeed. And yet here we all are, face-to-face with what seems hard evidence that there *may have been*, after all, supra-normal intervention by Narfar and Quarfar—"

It all broke into agitated discussion, with all seven scientists actively into it, while Methuen and Zorbin listened with absorption. . . .

Dejected Dorita reentered the conference room on an arm of Dr. Almagor.

Having assisted Dorita into a chair, Almagor, standing, addressed the task force. "With profound regret I must report that Mr. Quarfar died a few minutes ago. There was, to put it in lay terms, an irreversible clogging of the lungs. We attempted a hydrolytic lung-bypass, but without success. He is dead."

The task force mood was just as dead. Zorbin remarked, "The death of Karfareon." Several nodded. Silence.

Methuen muttered (546!): "Doctor, you know, I haven't given any thought to the question of body disposition, our task force here really ought to discuss the question and make a recommendation to our chief—"

"This I anticipated, Captain. The body will be placed in deep freeze pending a decision." Almagor inhibited an allusion to appropriateness. "I should advise you, however, that word of his illness has leaked, the newskenner people are waiting in another conference room. Your thoughts?"

Methuen looked up at him. "I think we need to meet this head-on." He turned to his committee: "Would you people be agreeable if Dr. Almagor and I should meet with the press immediately and give them a full account of Quarfar's illness and death and of our deliberations?"

"It hardly seems necessary," Olga rumbled. "This is entirely an intergovernmental affair."

Countered Chu: "My dear Dr. Alexandrovna, obviously you do not understand the Norwestian free press. You and I could get by with brushing off the newskenners, but here it cannot be done. I support the captain's proposal."

Surveying them, Methuen saw a preponderance of nods, with one abstention, and with a vigorous negation from Olga. He remarked, "I see majority agreement with my proposal, and this will be done—"

An intercom-buzz interrupted him. Almagor took it. With his back to them, his shoulders were doing odd things. They heard him demand low: "Beyond doubt? Absolutely beyond doubt?" Squawking. He said low: "All concerned are to give full time to verifying this and picking up what cues you can find. I will be with you soon. Out."

He came to Methuen and bent to whisper. Methuen's brows elevated, and he murmured, "Please repeat that, Doctor." Almagor whispered further. Then Almagor sat, watching Methuen.

The captain, addressing a stylus held in both his hands, told his task force: "The body is gone. Vanished. Right off the deathbed, with an orderly watching. Leaving all tubes hanging there."

While stupefied, they consulted their scientific wits about this—a reprise of what three members had witnessed yesterday morning, but this time post mortem. Dorita arose, saying wanly to Methuen, "Please excuse me, Captain. I really feel—I should go home now and rest—"

He jumped up and drew her to him; the other men arose also. He whispered: "Of course, dear, of course. Are you sure you'll be all right? Maybe Saul should go with you—"

She looked up at him, managed a smile, kissed his cheek, patted it, told him: "No, really, I'm all right alone, I'm not faint or anything, Saul should stay with the meeting. It's just that—you know—as a telepath I felt so close to Quarfar—I have to rest and meditate—"

Chu said with crisp appreciation, "You are an excellent consultant, Miss Lanceo. Pray rest well, and we will be needing you tomorrow."

After the Methuen-Almagor meeting with the newskenners (taxing, taxing, especially for Almagor), the men had a quick lunch at the hospital snack bar and returned to the conference room. Members of the task force were already straggling in after *their* leisurely luncheons. Methuen whispered to

124

Almagor, who nodded and ducked out; he had pressing business with respect to Quarfar's gone body.

When all were seated, Methuen said, "Gentlepeople?"

Dr. Mabel Seal, the buoyant brown archaeologist from Eskimoland, asked for recognition. "Captain, I have read the prior proceedings, as I am sure have the other new members, and I have been a most interested listener and spectator this morning. We who are present represent various disciplines— astrophysics, linguistics, anthropology, psychobiology, glaciology, stratogeology, archaeology—but only one of our several disciplines can well be brought to bear in the absence of either comet-subject, except by visiting this planet Dora whose location we only surmise. It seems to me that the only discipline pursuable at present is the astrophysical discipline so ably represented by our colleague from Senevendia, Dr. Sari. I think our next order of business would be to view the planetarium's projection of Orion as it would be seen from Saiph."

Tartly interposed Harlo Ombasa: "My distinguished colleague from Eskimoland has noted my prime discipline, which is psychobiology, but she has omitted mention of my related interest, which is paranormal research. We had two creature-specimens, and both have mysteriously vanished, one from a confinement capsule, the other from a hospital bed after death. I respectfully suggest that these two vanishings constitute our immediate order of business."

Olga snarled: "Why don't you stay here and investigate the paranormal while we go see about Orion?"

Methuen stylus-rapped. "It may be desirable at this point to break into subcommittees. Before we decide, let me check one point. Excuse me."

He went to the intercom, asked for a connection, got it, spoke softly. At the end of it: "Thank you, sir, we will be there within the hour." Returning to the table and sitting: "That was the planetarium director. He has already worked out the desired projection, and he has a small planetarium room for staff purposes where he can show it to us. I suggest that all who wish to accompany me there raise hands, and then we will work out something for the others."

All but Ombasa raised hands; the psychobiologist stayed taut-tart.

"Very good," said Methuen. "I'll arrange transportation.

As for you, Dr. Ombasa, I take it you wish to study the disappearances?"

"Those and relata—including the evidence I cited showing abnormal ages."

"Then I will put you in immediate touch with Dr. Almagor. I suggest that we all meet tomorrow at 0900 in the Science Center—"

In the small planetarium room there were in-the-round seats for about fifty people; the center-located planetarium (the instrument) was so small as to be practically invisible on the operator's console. The director, who was operating, sat entirely in the open for easy cross-conversation. Rather fussily he spent a few moments reviewing the problems of obtaining the sort of projection which he was about to offer; Sari cut him short by saying, "Thank you, Doctor, I hadn't found time to do it myself. May we see the projection?"

"I am going to do it," said the unflapped director, "in a series of projections. The first is Orion in concave planar projection as our eyes view it from Erth." The dome was filled with a replica of Sari's projection. "Now, Orion in holographic projection from the viewpoint of Erth, but showing depth perspectives and relative distances of stars." Orion came unstrung in three-dimensional distortion, this time neatly labeled with star names, distances, right ascensions, and declinations. Through these two projections Sita Sari silently suffered, having done it all for the task force this morning.

"Now," announced the director with a certain dramatic flair, "here is the constellation Orion, in planar concave projection, as it would be seen by an observer on some planet near Saiph."

All the stars appeared to be rearranging themselves. Then in the dome-sky they assumed a configuration which bafflingly suggested a constellation, although no pattern formed in any watcher's mind. So it must have been for naïve prehistoric sky-watchers, feeling somehow that there must be patterns but having no important legendary shapes to impose on the stars. (Was it like that for us when we were untaught children?)

Sari crisped: "It might help if you could interpose the Orion-lines between stars, to show how Orion is distorted here."

"This request I anticipated," the director crowed. Interstellar lines and star names leaped into light-being on the dome: now it all looked like an Orion mashed into shapelessness by some cosmic juggernaut-car.

They gazed at the weirdity. . . .

"Please remove the lines." It was the voice of Lieutenant Zorbin. All turned to him as the lines vanished.

Zorbin added: "Doctor, this may be too much to ask—but would it be possible for you to introduce new stellar lines as I may direct?"

"Quite feasible," the director answered. "But it would help, sir, if you would join me at the console here and show me where you want the connections placed."

Zorbin went down. With absorption the task force watched the small dome as, one by one, pairs of stars were joined by lines. And presently, all stars were line-linked. . . .

Someone ejaculated, "Well!" It *was* a constellation, certainly; but what sort of thing the figure might represent, only Zorbin and Methuen, having seen Dorita's drawing, had the experience to comprehend.

Zorbin told them, manipulating the arrow: "If Dora is a planet of the star Saiph, then you are seeing what people on Dora would see as their brightest stars. Quarfar said that the Dorians saw this constellation as a mizdorf plunging headlong upon Dora, flung out of the sky by a demon. A mizdorf is a batwinged humanoid like Narfar of the comet; all of you have seen photos of him. I have a feeling that Narfar himself may have given this legend to his people, and that the demon is supposed to be Quarfar.

"Bright Hatsya is the burning demon, watching the fall from above; Hatsya is the brightest of all stars from the Dorian viewpoint.

"Fancy that we are looking at the back of the falling mizdorf. Betelgeuse, here, is the orange-red head, aimed at Saiph or Dora, which do not appear. The right wing is Bellatrix, M-43, M-42, Rigel and small stars; the left is Heka, 2024 and small stars. The arms are neglected, constellations do get simplified. We then trace the body upward to the crotch, a small star, from which extend two legs: the right leg marked by Tabit and a small star, the left composed of Alnilam, Alnitak, and Mintaka. In my own mind, without question this constellation could be understood by primitive

127

people on Dora as a semi-divine creature whom they well knew: namely, a mizdorf—like Narfar, their king-god.

"I want to show you some independent support; please wait a moment." Zorbin spoke with the director, and the stars changed to become once more Orion in planar projection as seen from Erth.

"Quarfar told us that Narfar chose to go to Dora from Erth because its sun was the head of a constellation which reminded Narfar of a mizdorf. Sir, will you please kill the Orion star-connections?" The lines vanished; only stars remained.

Said Zorbin: "Regard this configuration, but alter your thought of it. Imagine that what we see as arms, Narfar saw as legs; and Saiph as head, not foot; and what we see as a head, gender-proud Narfar saw as a phallus. Watch." New connecting lines produced a new pattern.

"Mr. Chairman," said Zorbin, "if I as a consultant may presume on the patience of this task force, it is my opinion that the projections we have here strengthen enormously, indeed almost definitively, the hypothetical web of Dr. Sari. The home constellation of the planet Dora is, I believe, the one called by us Orion, and by the Dorians called Mizdorf. And Dora is a planet of the star which does not appear in the Dorian constellation, and through which the five-forty-six gradient passes directly: the hot blue-white helium star which we call Saiph.

"And if we assume that the planet Dora is an Erth-like planet with a mean temperature about like that of Erth, remembering the high heat of the star Saiph, then we can provisionally expect to find Dora on a mean orbit of something like two billion, nine hundred million kilometers out from Saiph—which is about like the mean distance of Uranus from Sol."

The task force, and very particularly Sita Sari, now had also the measure of Zorbin.

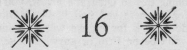

16

The captain and the lieutenant arrived home just before 0800, both men meditative and weary, saddened by the death of Quarfar (it was particularly poignant that the titan could not be with them at the planetarium to recognize the Dora-constellation Mizdorf); tending to be elated by the successful locating of Dora; frustrated because the death of Quarfar and the earlier loss of Narfar prevented the task force from moving effectively into the other aspects of its mission. Methuen felt somehow comfortable about the performance of that always sharp and sometimes charming Sita Sari; but just now he wanted to share his feelings with Dorita, to be comforted by her, to comfort *her* (since Quarfar's loss was most hurtful to her). Paradoxically, before the brooding night would be out, he and Dorita might have love, and they might prove to be *in* love. Zorbin, too, looked forward to being with Dorita, although he did not love her; and he wondered whether tonight Dorita would quit the sofa and claim the bedroom vacated by Quarfar—with or without B.J.

They found the salon unoccupied. Methuen, feeling delicate about calling out for her, went looking for her, while Zorbin hit the kitchenette to make drinks. Methuen began by stealing silently into Quarfar's bedroom, suspecting that Dora out of sentiment might be resting on the titan's bed. . . .

He was in there for a while, presumably having found her. Zorbin finished making two strong bourbons with water and one whiskey sour, brought them into the salon on a little tray, set the tray on a large circular coffee table strategically grouped with the sofa and two easy chairs, took his own drink to one of the chairs, sat sipping and meditating.

Methuen stood before him, frowning profoundly, offering him a note. Setting down his drink, Zorbin took it and read it. Dorita's handwritten scrawl:

Good friend B. J.,

I'm pinning this to Quarfar's pillow, you're sure to look for me here and find it. I'm leaving with Narfar; don't look for us, we will be unfindable, and we won't be on Erth or anywhere else in this time-slot. This could be the grand goal of my life. You're a good guy, B. J., and a wonderful Astrofleet captain. And it was great with you, first night and everything else. My kind regards to that good Lieutenant Zorbin. Maybe you'll want to give this apartment back to the family I conned out of it; the landlady can help.

D.

P. S.: The window was broken out by Narfar, last night; I had him aroused, a little.

Zorbin looked up; Methuen, still standing, had picked up his bourbon, ignoring the sour which had been for Dorita. He glugged about a third of the drink and queried: "What proportions?"

"Two bourbon, one water, lots of ice."

"Right now, I think it ought to be stronger—" Zorbin twisted around to watch while Methuen went to the kitchen, poured off half the remaining two-thirds of his drink, filled the glass with bourbon without adding ice, meticulously stirred with a swizzle-stick cadged from a posh restaurant on the planet Vash, returned, sat, sipped.

Silently Zorbin returned the note. Methuen, now jacketless with tie removed and collar open, took the note without looking at it, folded it crudely with one hand, thrust it into his shirt pocket, sipped.

Zorbin waited.

Having sipped some more, Methuen queried: "How many drinks can you handle before dinner?"

"As many as you, I imagine. Maybe more, if you stay with that strength."

"What sort of dinner is best for a drunken sailor?"

"A very large very hot pizza with everything imaginable."

"Please be sure to dial it when your imagination hits maximum and before it fades. But put a hold on the pizza. 'Scuse, I want to make a call while I'm sober—"

The only visiphone was at the little desk; this apartment

was not perfectly modern. Methuen punched a number with a private associated code. Meanwhile Zorbin, using a check-off list, dialed two pizzas; his imagination was never all that great, but in the course of pizza-years he had developed a system: one of the ingredients was kosher pastrami. He put the order on will-call. When he turned to the desk, the face of short-blond-haired Rear Admiral Manx filled the visiscreen, collar open; and Methuen was saying, "Sorry to ring you at home, Dave, but this is rather peremptory."

"Go ahead, B. J.," said Manx. They were old friends in Astrofleet.

"You're familiar with my task force."

"Of course."

"Did you know that our prime subject Quarfar died today?"

"I caught it on the 0700 kenner. Bad luck, my friend."

"Well, Dave: the thing is, that today the task force identified the planet Dora, the home planet which Narfar was defending against Quarfar, as an unknown satellite of the star Saiph in the constellation Orion."

"No!"

"No question at all, Dave, the evidence is beautiful. Well, as you know, my task force is interdisciplinary. And with Quarfar no longer available for information about the planet, I am betting twelve to seven or higher that tomorrow they will want to go to Dora and investigate."

The eyes of Admiral Manx went toward his own ceiling.

"There is also," Methuen added, "a potential threat to Erth, of some sort." Inhibiting reference to the prevoyant dreams, he explained: "Quarfar's words about that were, quote: 'Whether and how that threat may be realized will depend on—factors which I am not ready to disclose.' End quote." The captain was falsifying the end of the quote: for the admiral, mention of Dorita would be a red herring, as the dreams would have been.

Said Manx thoughtfully. "Twenty-one hundred light years."

"Right."

"Would a frigate do it?"

"I think so, suitably fitted out."

"With VIP accommodations and some technical stuff."

"Right. I had seven members today, and the total potential is ten plus myself."

"You'd be commanding?"

131

"I think that might be best."

"Who pays the bill?"

"Either Norwestia or Erthworld, that will have to be worked out."

"Any preferences as your exec?"

"Zorbin, but promote him." Zorbin re-hit the dinner dial, having thought of a new ingredient for the pizzas.

"That part sounds feasible. Any other crew preferences?"

"Not off the *Ventura,* they aren't used to hot ships. Give me an experienced frigate crew."

"Then why Zorbin?"

"Believe me, he's ready."

"B.J., you know I can't promise anything, I'll have to wait for orders from somebody."

"Right, but I thought you might want to know, so you can be readying a frigate just in case."

"You are a bastard."

"You are an admiral. It takes one to know one."

Over the masterful pizzas, which were being washed down with bourbon-laced Chianti:

"B.J.—"

"Saul?"

"You going to lead the task force that way?"

"I don't think I'll have to."

"But one way or another, it's going to go that way."

"Yo."

"Jealousy?"

"Mm?"

"You in love with Dorita?"

"Ouch. Wait till I rip off a juicy slice."

"B.J.—"

"Saul?"

"She said, don't follow."

"She doesn't command me."

"She said you'd never find her. She'd be in a different time-slot, she said."

"That's a problem."

"You can navigate in time?"

"Can *you,* Saul?"

"Of course not."

"Neither can I. But I get a strong impression that Dorita can."

132

"With Narfar."

"Yo."

"Think she loves him, B.J.?"

"Not a chance. Fascination, not love."

"Think she loves you?"

"I think she used me. I think she's using this Narfar."

"What for?"

"God knows."

"You want to solve the problem of Dorita."

"At least that. There's more, believe me, but don't ask. Hit me with the spiked Chianti, I need to dip my fingers in it."

"Do you think she plans taking him back fifty thousand years to his own era?"

"Could be."

"If you can't follow her back there, what's the value for you of visiting the planet?"

Methuen gazed at Zorbin; Methuen's mouth was twisted, and his eyes glittered. "Maybe I just want to inspect the late-on remains of the mess that I think she will have made, back there in the old time."

At Quarfar's hospital bedside:

Quarfar—

Dorita!

That's right, Quarfar, do not speak, just think at me, I'm entirely with you, talking would weaken you—

The body is already weakened beyond use, Dorita; but the mindsoul is unimpaired, which means that I am unimpaired. But I have to think talk quickly with you now, because afterward I will not be able to get through to you.

Go ahead, dear Quarfar.

First, I want to say that you have been good for me.

And you have been good for me.

Good, now to the business. I was not entirely asleep last

night. I knew when Narfar was standing beside me, trying to decide whether he should kill me. And I mind-heard you and Narfar afterward.

Oboy.

And I know your mind rather well, Dorita. I know what you want. You want whatever anybody else has not done and could not do and should not do.

Ah.

That is why you involved yourself with Methuen to help investigate us two unprecedented space-time-comet creatures. And that is why you want to go to Dora with Narfar. Partly why; because in one way you would prefer to go with me, but there is a certain primitive charisma about Narfar. Besides, him you can control.

Quafar, you are wearing yourself—

Quiet, Dorita, listen: I am my own best judge. And I wish it were possible for me to believe that my brother Narfar is his own best judge; but Narfar is—limited.

True.

It was I who made it possible for him to go to Dora.

You mean the five-forty-six gradient?

Exactly. His transmission to Dora was instantaneous, and that created the space-trail. And I did not erase the trail afterward; still it lingers; but for a bulky thing like a star-ship or a comet, it will only accelerate the thing, it will not provide anything like instantaneous transmission.

But Quafar, that was much more than fifty thousand years ago; all the positions of the stars have changed. How would it continue to link Dora with Erth?

It is a question of relative positions, Dorita. Saiph and Sol inhabit the same armtip of our spiral galaxy, their distance apart is a small fraction of our galaxy's diameter. Within our sector, the relative positions of most stars have not changed significantly. The main thing that changes is our seasonal and equatorial view of the stars; and that is merely because Erth wobbles on its axis, it is called precession; every twenty-five thousand years, one precession is completed, and the stars are all back where they were before. But even if Erth did not precess, our end of the gradient would vary diurnally. Right now, this end of the gradient is describing a wave-girdle around Erth; it has kept right on linking Erth with Dora, except when the sun or some planet has cut it.

You are telling me that I can find the gradient?

I only need to know when you will be starting out for it and how long it will take you to get there.

How fast can Narfar fly?

At full speed, probably a thousand kilometers per hour.

Quarfar, would a calculation be too much for you?

I still can hack it, Dorita.

Suppose I were to depart Manhattan on Narfar wings at 1500 this afternoon. From what you have told me, at his full speed it would take us twenty hours to go halfway around Erth. When would we pick up the gradient?

You would not have to depart Manhattan. Actually the gradient swept through our apartment yesterday afternoon, I smelled its traces when we returned, it passed through my bedroom. I would expect it to pass through the salon today at 1500, right across your sofa. You and Narfar could simply sit there; let him do the activation.

Right through the ceiling—and two ceilings above it?

No problem for Narfar; but if it is a problem for you, Dorita, why then, simply go to the roof and stand directly about your sofa. Can you get to the roof?

Yes; but once up there, can I locate the sofa position?

That I leave to you; but a small error won't matter if you let Narfar know what you are doing, he'll be on the smell for the gradient, he'll catch it and wing with it—holding you, I'd imagine. And if you miss today, you can easily con Methuen into calculating tomorrow's position.

I won't miss today. Do I hold my breath in outer space, or what?

You'll be on Dora in a breath, Narfar will keep you from smashing down. Dorita, I have to leave this now, there's another thing—

Quarfar?

I respect my brother Narfar. We've had no reason for love, but I respect him. But only for what he is; and what he is is limited.

I know.

He messed up humans here on Erth, he gave too much power to beasts. I had to come to the rescue. He was doing better on Dora, but finally I could see that he had dangerously drained off one essential ingredient from the souls of his humans. The drain-off has helped Narfar to generate a splendid soft docile culture which had beasts at a friendly

135

stand-off. But without that special ingredient, if his people should lose Narfar, their culture would quickly perish, they would become inferior beasts.

And what is this ingredient?

He seemed to be ignoring her question. *When I saw this, I used the gradient and followed Narfar to Dora, intending to enter into friendly partnership with him and free that ingredient and show him how to let it deploy itself. But Narfar, sensing my arrival, went defensive and met me aggressively off Dora. You know the rest.*

Why weren't you smashed when the comet hit you?

We don't smash easily.

Why then are you dying now—oh, I didn't mean that—

I am dying now, or my body is, because I am allowing it. I have done my work on Erth, and I find it good; and I have been driven away from Dora. There are other planets, and I will find one for my work, but I will not be operating in my own body.

I want to assimilate that. I can't do it in a hurry.

Of course you can't, but now there is no time. Listen to me, Dorita, my body is weakening fast—

I am listening, Quarfar.

Not far below the north pole on Dora, there is a certain crater like a circular box. It contains something of great value. Knowing you, I am sure that you will find it. Dorita— you must not open it! Under no circumstances may you open it. Do you understand, Dorita? Do not open that box!

But why may I not open it?

Because you must not! I enjoin you!

She was ready with another eager question. Then her mind sensed that Quarfar was dead.

136

 18

At home, Dorita mind-called Narfar. Awakening (in a Central Park tree again), he came to her quickly and easily, flying rather low in his haste, so that a number of people saw him and swore off pot.

While waiting, she used a measuring tape and a compass (both luckily in that serendipitous desk) to get distance and azimuth from the center of her sofa to the foot of the up-ward stairs which happened to be on a direct line from the sofa through the open apartment door. Hearing a wing-clatter in the apartment, she hurried back to find Narfar standing with outstretched arms and wings (necessarily equidistant from both side walls, his wingspread being four meters). "Stay here," she commanded. "I'm doing something impor-tant for both of us," and she closed the door from the out-side.

Up the zigzag stairs she prowled to the sixth floor, and sighted down the stairwell to assure herself that the stair-foot on her fifth floor was in line with the head-and-foot on this sixth; then up another flight, and another down-sighting; then up the final flight to the roof-door at its head, and a sighting. Passing through, she hooked the end of her tape to a latch-lever on the door, walked a catwalk out and over and back, paused when she thought her position was about right and checked her tape and compass. She was off a meter over and a meter back, she would have to leave the catwalk and tread the graveled roof-surface; would she break through? Remov-ing her shoes, cautiously she stepped off (the roof held), and found the position which had to be exactly over the center of the sofa. This she marked in the gravel with a finger; and she hurried back to Narfar—who, at her entry, again extended arms and wings, grinning like a coal scuttle and not in any way drooping.

The time was 1441.

She approached the eager one cautiously, pausing a meter and a half from him and extending her hands, saying, "Take my hands, no more." He seized them and started to draw her to him, but she fired a peremptory mental negative, at the same time frowning; he released her hands and began to droop everywhere. She warmed him with tentative encouragement; he brightened a little.

She mindspoke; this was too important to risk bad speech. *Now listen, Narfar, I know how to get us to your world, but it has to be done right now. Do you know what the five-forty-six gradient is?*

No—

It is the space-trail you took when you first went to Dora. Now do you know?

Trail still there?

It is. Do you remember how it smells?

Oh, sure! Where trail?

Come! she ordered. Taking one of his hands, she led him to the apartment door, opened it, peered out: nobody; she'd have to take a chance on the upper floors, but maybe it didn't matter anyhow. She led him up the three flights of stairs on a run and checked her watch: 1452, time tightening. Around the catwalks she led him, and paused in front of the mark in the gravel. *Now listen carefully, Narfar. Pick me up, but don't fool around with my little body. I want you to hover— hover, get it?*

Hover, yes—

Hover just above that cross-mark you see there in the gravel, maybe yea far above it, almost touching it; but you must not touch down upon it. Got it? Her concern was that his weight, or anyway their combined weight, would break through the roof.

For answer, he wrapped both arms around her waist, held her midriff tight against his own, grinned down upon her, and lofted. An instant later, they hovered at the right position; her cutichron told her that they had no more than two minutes to wait, and a good thing in view of what she was sensing low.

Hugging him, she mindbreathed: *Smell the air, Narfar! Smell for that gradient, that space-trail to Dora! When you smell it coming, leap into it!*

Oboy! Back to my Dora—

138

She clutched him, fearful of space-death. Twenty-one hundred airless frigid light-years. . . .

An instant later, they stood in knee-deep rank grass on a world strange to Dorita. The heat hit her like a suddenly opened furnace door. But the mind of Narfar was exulting: *Home!*

She felt his exultation die. He almost whimpered: *But Dorita, this right where my great king-city is, I know smell—but where city?* She had stepped away from him, looking about, already beginning to be heat-weak. In every direction, long grass grace-noted by occasional trees and a pond or two; then, in every direction, jungle. . . .

Minute by minute she was more heat-oppressed, more clothing-wet; and insects were droning malevolently about her. Nevertheless, she tried to reassure him. *Narfar, believe me, this has to be your Dora. Right place. But wrong time.*

Wrong time? What you mean?

You were away from Dora for a long time, Narfar; I told you that. Looks like things happened while you were gone. Like maybe all your people got sick and died.

My people would never all get sick and die! I fixed them up so they could not!

Then where are they?

He looked about, frowning, wing-drooping.

Narfar, this is not the time you knew. This is many many years later, many many lives later, generations later. Nothing now is the same as you knew—

Unexpectedly, he seized her and winged aloft with her. The jungle had crashed open; the meadow was filled with stampeding horned four-legged beasts, something between bison and moose. Their dust and their hoof-thunder went on for many minutes, they were trampling each other, there was no evidence that there was any end to them. . . .

They maniu, they my friends, my creatures, mind-snarled Narfar, *but they stupid, now they crazy, they not know me, they trample us. We stay up here till they go by. Must be you right, Dorita; my men keep maniu down, they not grow too many; now they too many, must be no men any more.*

Ultimately their noise died; the maniu vanished into far jungle, smashing through trees and into trees. Many of their bodies lay mangle-scattered in their wake.

Now we go down? suggested the batman.

Dorita's big means-moment had come: not the biggest of all moments, but the one which had to lead to that. On this one, it was do or die again. Only, right now, the tropical humidity was improving the attractiveness of *die.* . . . .

What you thinking, do or die? he demanded, clutching her to him, afraid that she might fall.

Her mindthrust was urgent. *Narfar, you say this is where your city was. Can you smell out your great house?*

Oh sure, but it not there—

Take us down, and find where it was.

Swinging himself around into swan-dive position, Narfar swooped and head-down cruised the broad meadow, his nose inches from the grass except when he had to loft over a maniu carcass; thoughtfully he had transferred his Dorita-burden to his back, and there she clung terrified, head between his pumping wings and agitated by those wings, clutching his chest with her arms, clutching his pelvis with her legs. . . .

He stopped in midair so abruptly that she was nearly catapulted over his head. *This it,* he announced with satisfaction; and turning in the air, he dropped softly into the grass, on his feet. Dorita let go and fell into the grass; she got herself cat-seated erect and looked up at him.

From triumph, again he had gone disconsolate. *This where it was,* he asserted, *but it gone. Where is?*

Are we inside where your great house was?

Yes.

What room are we in?

Great room where I meet with my leaders.

Did you have a throne?

What?

Did you have a big seat where you sat to meet your leaders?

Oh yes. Wait, I find. Right here, but no seat now.

You are standing in front of a little mound in the grass. Why don't you dig into it? Here, let's find something to dig with—

Not need; strong smell, I dig fast! He mole-burrowed into the mound, and rapidly he unerthed a little stone throne with a narrow curly-edged back and no arms, rather like the throne of Minos at Knossos. Dorita repressed a giggle: she'd always wondered why the throne of Minos was so silly-looking; but she saw the reason for the structure of this one, Nar-

140

far had to curl his wings around the seatback. Had there been wings on Minos? Cut it: there was serious-dangerous work to be done.

Good, she told him. *You found your throne, your great seat. Now sit on it.*

I sit. He did so, with considerable dignity.

Now, she announced, *I sit on your lap.*

That nice!

But let my bod alone, she cautioned, positioning herself crosswise on his thighs below his genitals. *Now listen closely, Narfar. You and I are going back in time.*

That mean what?

We are going to move from today into yesterday, and then another yesterday, and then many more yesterdays. We are going back as far as it took the comet to bring you from Dora to Erth. Do you get it?

Maybe, a little. Like I remember what I do long ago, and all of a sudden I doing it again. Like that?

Like that. But I need your help.

All right. How?

I do all the moving in time. I move both of us. But I have to stop once in a while. Every time I stop, you tell me if we there yet.

There? Where?

Where you were before you went out to fight Quarfar.

I up north, in ice.

I not mean that. I mean, where you were before you go north and meet Quarfar.

Before, I here in my great house.

I know, but . . . I mean where in time. Narfar, before you go north to fight Quarfar, you maybe meet with your leaders?

Sure. Right here. I sit on throne.

You know all the leaders?

Sure.

They know you?

Sure.

All right. Now, when we go back in time, every time I stop, you tell me if you see your leaders that you know.

Oh, that good, Dorita! Now I get it, all of it! Do time-stuff! Go!

She clung to his neck, frowned with intense mind-body concentration, and did what she had done when she had gone

141

into day before yesterday to inspect her stolen money. But now, perilously, she made the time-journey open-ended.

The savannah vanished, and there was a mighty giddiness and a rushing blur, like running at high speed an elevator with no walls and having no indicator to number the floors swishing past. She had no *business* doing this unprecedented thing, no mortal *business*; and never in her life had her euphoria boiled higher.

19

She switched it on. After an indefinite while of disorientation, arbitrarily she cut. Same broad hot savannah surrounded by jungle, but being drenched now by soaking rain. Far in the future of *then* yet; she did another time-dive of longer duration. . . .

Savannah again, but sere under hot sun, obviously during a long drought: her wet clothes were steaming, and so was Narfar's wet body. Still not *then* by a long time, but she would linger here to dry; and she departed his lap and moved about in order to do it more efficiently, while Narfar circled in low air for the same reason. . . .

He yelled: "Hey!"

"What?"

Dropping to the grass beside her, he grabbed her hand and pulled her to a nearby place where two rotted posts were sticking out of the ground; they hadn't been here before—or later? He gabbled in his tongue, she lost it and mind-begged for thoughts; aroused, he told her, *Those wall posts of my great house, still a withe hanging to one!* He dragged her back to the throne: *Sit on me, Dorita, we do more time-stuff!*

Knowing little about rotting-speed for wood and withes, at a broad guess she estimated that they had back-timed to an era only a few generations later than Narfar's. Already so deeply into the past! On Erth now, men had perhaps ad-

vanced to the point of rough-chipping crude stone tools. . . .
Well, now she would have to bring off some very delicate further increment.

She therefore now held them in rushing limbo while she counted from one thousand to one thousand ten; and she cut; and she and Narfar fell to the ground, for the throne had vanished; the savannah too had vanished; they were crowded in by trees and vines in dark jungle—and in a tree just overhead, a red-and-white-banded snake the size of a full-grown anaconda hissed down at them and writhingly prepared to drop and attack. . . .

Releasing Dorita, Narfar lofted to an air-position level with the tree-branch; eying the serpent's eyes, he commenced a chittering; the serpent began to weave with its head, mouth closed, tongue flickering. Presently Narfar extended his long arms and began to stroke the neck-back of the snake with one hand while he caressed its neck-underside with the other. The snake raised its head high in sensuous ecstasy; presently, flowing off the limb, it coiled itself gently about the body of Narfar and peered with contentment into his eyes while he continued his stroking.

Serpent-cloaked, Narfar dropped to the ground in front of ground-sitting amazed Dorita. *This one of my friends,* he told her; *almost all beasts my friends. But you go too far back with time-stuff. This what my city-place and my great-house-place look like when I first come to Dora. I scout it first, find it like this; I bring my people here, we chop down trees and grub roots and make place for city, I eat a lot of the roots, I charm so trees never come again in city-place, I tell all beasts we need space, they say okay and go deep into jungle and leave space to us. Can you go more forward with time-stuff?*

Who'd know? Dorita mused, watching the snake. *Do we take him or her with us?*

For answer, Narfar chittered lovingly at the snake; it tongued his nose, then uncoiled from him and vanished into jungle. Narfar then sat on the ground with legs extended together and stretched his arms toward her: *Come, we go.*

She objected: *You are sitting in the throne-place. We must not be where the throne will be, or we will end up inside it.*

He hunched-over a meter to his right.

She demanded: *Will anything hard be there?*

Think not, he replied; *maybe, but think not. Come, we go.*

143

She tried six seconds forward. She was relieved to see that they had come out of transition beside the stone throne, not inside it; but Narfar, peering about, leaped horrified to his feet, dropping her. They were in a rotting palace built of wood and withes and thatched with grass; there were many holes in the walls, and much of the roof was gone.

He ran out through the single door, and she heard the heavy wing-beat of his departure aloft. She followed outside: he was gone, but she knew what he must be doing. The scene was painful. She stood beside the palace (it was big, all right) in a great city of huts like something out of ancient Africa—only, it was no longer a vital city, it was a sprawling graveyard of desuetude.

Intrigued by the ruins, Dorita began to prowl streets of high rank grass, entering a few huts. In one, she found a child somewhere between two and five, a naked bluish-green male, emaciated, crying with the pain of his hunger and his bloated belly. She shrank back: it was her first confrontation with utter misery. Panting, she ran out of the hut; she could not help the child, she had no food to give him. Food? She saw rank abandoned gardens; she peered at the bordering jungle and thought of weird edible tropical fruits: there was food aplenty for a million children, but this little kid alone had no way to get it. . . . She didn't dare harvest wild stuff in an old garden or go to the jungle for tree-fruit: in either case, she wouldn't know what was poison and what not; in the jungle-case, there were surely lurking carnivores. Where were the child's parents? For that matter, where were all the other children?

Narfar alit beside her, panting, not fatigued but anguished. He seized and hugged her, pressing his forehead to her chest with his nose between her breasts, not in lust but in misery-needing-woman-comfort. *It can not be!* he mind-blurted. *I fly everywhere, over whole city: all ruins, no people! I make forever-city here: can not be it ever go to ruin!*

Above his mighty hairy shoulder, above one shriveled wing, Dorita saw something. Holding Narfar, she peered at the something. It was a most ancient blue-green man emerging naked from a nearby hut, emerging in a laborious hands-and-knees crawl with head low. He got about body-length out of the hut and paused, exhausted, breathing hard, swollen belly nearly touching ground, ribs threatening to break through dry skin.

144

Having got his head up with difficulty, he stared at Dorita and Narfar, stared prolongedly as though with bleared eyes he sought to see clearly. His head, face, and body were Neanderthaloid, like Narfar's; only the skin-color and the winglessness were different.

He opened his mouth, and coughed, and coughed again, and swallowed, and swallowed again; then he managed to eject a feeble short chitter; then he dropped his head, and panted, and coughed, and panted. Dorita was electrified: distinctly she had heard the old man say, "Narfar!"

And Narfar had heard! Narfar raised his head away from Dorita, then released her and sprang to his feet; he whirled, stared, and ran to the old man; kneeling beside him, Narfar raised the ancient to his knees and peered into his face. He demanded: "Who you?"

The feeble one managed to utter: "I Glans."

"You? *Glans?*"

The old man nodded.

Narfar's head turned to Dorita: "He my best young leader—" He turned back to Glans: *You too weak to talk. You mindspeak to me. What happen to you? What happen to city?*

You went away, Narfar. Long time ago. We not know what to do without you. You give us laws, but laws not work without you.

Laws not work without me? Can not be, Glans!

The ancient nodded apathetically. *So we think too, but not so. You teach us, everybody follow leader, leader follow his leader, and so on. You teach us, not think up new things, just make things better the way they are. When you go, we keep on doing that. For a time it work. But leaders all have to follow leaders, and top leaders have to follow you, and you not there. Top leaders not know what to do, so bottom leaders not know what to do, so nobody know what to do.*

Glans was interrupted by a fit of coughing and breath-gasping as though he had been talking aloud. Then he went on: *So then one top leader say, I be king now. That Herdu, remember him? Other top leaders say no, Narfar is only king. I one of other top leaders, I say no too. Herdu say, I king now, you not like, you fight me. That start a lot of fighting, all top leaders fight with all, I stay out. When all top leaders fight, bottom leaders begin fighting too, some bottom leaders fight top leaders, all men in city get fighting, women get fight-*

ing, children get fighting. First thing I know, most people in city dead and nobody alive know what to do any more. City go to hell. People die. I alive, last except one—

Fiercely Narfar demanded: *What one besides you still alive?*

Dorita intervened: *The child I saw in that hut over there.*

Glans nodded once. And then he fell, dead of thought-exhaustion.

Narfar stood, frowning down at the Glans-corpse. He said aloud: "We bury Glans. We take child."

Neither is necessary, she responded. *If we get you back to your people before all this trouble starts, it will never happen.*

How that be? It happen already!

But you said it could not happen.

That right. Could not. But it happen, somehow.

Maybe you having bad dream. When I get you back, it will be all right, it will never happen.

He straightened, stretching his wings. *That sound all right. I make dreams for people, you make dreams for me. Okay. Come, we go sit on my throne and do time-stuff.*

Narsua gazed upward at the towering walls of her world. She had eaten many, she had survived, she had learned much. Coming into her was a potent sense that something arousingly important was happening out there. But the feeling of it was rock-wall-clogged, she could not discern the nature of it.

Perhaps it was important enough to report to the god whom they all nurtured. . . .

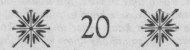

20

Only for an instant did Dorita backtime, a spare two generations deeper into past. . . .

She came into orientation in Narfar's lap on the throne in

the throne room (fresh withe-walls, fresh thatch, green, *alive*) confronted by a group of randomly positioned, naked blue-green Neanderthaloid men who were gaping their amazement at the abrupt reoccupation of the throne. Somebody gasped: "Narfar!" and somebody else shouted, "With goddess in his lap!" and they all prostrated themselves on the fresh-reeded dirt floor.

Narfar arose with dignity, clasping Dorita around the waist with one arm so that she hung dangling; so hanging, she continued to appraise the men, recognizing a young version of Glans among them. Narfar addressed them; and by now her ear was well synched to the tempo of his gibber, so that she understood most of what followed.

The winged king-god demanded: "Why all this falling down? Get up!" Their heads came off the floor. Slowly Glans got to his feet, then another, then two others, then all of them. And they stood shocked-staring.

A heavy-set, powerful fortyish man advanced and exclaimed as though badly upset and even somewhat put out: "Narfar! You back!"

"You think I not come back, Herdu? You be king then, maybe?" Herdu edged backward until he was partly behind another man. (Dorita was appreciating the spring green hue of the Narfar-skin, with its orange-red fire-hair, among the general blue-green of his minions.) These were obviously the top leaders, since they had dared congregate in the throne room without their king.

Glans cried out: "But you gone many suns! We not know what to do without you! We *glad* you back—*glad!* Who woman?"

"Woman?" Suddenly Narfar remembered Dorita; he set her gently on her feet and hugged her with a big arm, spreading wings a little. "I god, this my goddess. I bring her from another world far away in sky. Name Dorita, good name for Dora! She rule all Dora with me! You all fall down now, like you do to me!"

All of them hit dirt—except Herdu, who stood glowering at Dorita. She scented a developing emergency: cloudily she saw what it was. . . .

Narfar demanded. "What trouble, Herdu? Why you not fall down to Dorita?"

Said Herdu stolidly, "She funny woman." Heads were leaving the floor.

Narfar grew terrible. "So?"

"You tell us funny people no good. You send them all away. Why you now bring funny woman for goddess?"

Several men were up on their knees, evidently of two minds about this rebellion. Dorita was soul-chilled. But then Narfar rebutted with surprising patience. "She look like funny woman, but she not funny inside. Inside is where counts. She mindspeak to me, I mindspeak to her; funny people not mindspeak, just talk funny. You not know that, Herdu?"

From everywhere in the room she was getting bad thoughts. If the people of Narfar should revolt against their god-king because of her, where would that leave her? What would it do to realization of her ultimate objective? Would Narfar stand up to them for her? Which side would he choose?

He surveyed them for a moment or two. Then he turned to her, his face very stern, and he clasped both of her shoulders and mindspoke, *Dorita, you like me?*

Sure.

You like to stay here with me, be goddess of Dora?

Sure, but—

These guys, they no understand not funny woman inside, all they see is funny woman outside. I can fix that, but it hurt a little. You decide, Dorita. You hurt a little and let me make you not-funny outside? Or you go away? I want you here, but these my people, they need me; if you stay funny outside, you have to go away. Whay you say, Dorita?

In panic, she comprehended what was in his mind for her. Hurt a little? Why, it might kill her in slow agony! And even if she should survive—what of her woman's pride? Among her own kind, she would be forever a monster. . . .

Dorita, what you say?

On the other hand, who gave a damn about people? The quest was the thing . . . But could she stand the physical anguish?

She temporized: *How much it hurt?*

Not much. Maybe not any. Here, I fix. I make it like dream for you, you watch what I do to you, you not feel it, just see it happen. Yes or no?

Suicidally she yelled: "DO IT! MAKE DREAM!"

Abruptly she was hovering invisible somewhere above all the people, watching herself with interest as Narfar, in front of all his leaders, laid hands upon her, twisted her legs so they bowed, thumb-pressed her chin until plastically it receded, molded her forehead until it too receded while bone-ridge bulged above her eyes. . . .

The woman named Dorita fell unconscious to the floor. Just for an instant longer, the scene was visible to Dorita above: Narfar turning in triumph to his leaders; Herdu and all the rest falling prone to the reeds. . . .

Part Four

INTERTIME FUGUE

*Days One through Thirty
(following Day Zero marvelous
in spacetime)*

21

Day One through Day Eleven

Methuen faced the full ten members of his task force in a conference room at the Science Center. Other than those previously vocal, the yesterday-arrivals were a glaciologist from Antarctica and a stratogeologist from Bolivaria; today appeared also a zoologist from Sudafrika, a botanist from the Fertile Crescent, and a microbiologist from Polymicronesia.

Their chairman told them flatly: "We are in pretty bad trouble as an investing group. We have lost our two prime subjects from the comet, and also our telepathic interpreter. Quarfar died yesterday; while the batman called Narfar appears to have departed to his home world of Dora—taking with him our telepath, Miss Lanceo." (A woman murmured, "Fascinating.")

"We have, however, made some progress on some fronts. We know a good deal about the language of Quarfar, which appears to be an enrichment of Narfar's language. Through our absconding interpreter—she absconded with Narfar—we have a good deal from Quarfar about the relationships between the two comet-creatures and about the planet Dora. And through Dr. Sari here, working partly with information from Quarfar, we have established that Dora is a planet of the star Saiph in Orion, and that the five-forty-six gradient extends at least to Saiph; and finally, that the comet called Gladys originated near Saiph and was accelerated by the gradient. Dr. Sari, do you wish to correct my remarks?"

She negated with a headshake, then uttered softly, "All will understand that these conclusions are theoretical and do require some sort of empirical confirmation."

"So," Methuen acknowledged. "Now, your chairman confesses that he is at a bit of a loss as to how this task force can proceed with its charge. I await your thoughts." (*Masterful*, Zorbin reflected, frowning to avoid smiling.)

Dr. Llana Green, the trim café-au-lait glaciologist from

Antarctica, decided to assert herself. "Mr. Chairman, I have read the record; and because of my own peculiar discipline, I was interested indeed in Quarfar's account of Dora as a planet extensively capped by ice at and far below both poles and with a relatively narrow tropical equator zone. Such a phenomenon could only occur if the planet's axis were vertical, that is, tangential to its sun all year round, instead of being tipped with respect to the sun as with Erth. On Dora there would be no rotation of seasons: all year round the sun's rays would fall directly on the equator; whereas at the poles the rays would always come in at acute angles to the surface, having to work their way through much more atmosphere, losing much of their heat. Expressing personal and professional interest, I would like nothing better than to visit this Dora and study its icecaps. And I suspect that my colleagues here would find various other sorts of interest in such an expedition."

Sari nodded vigorous assent. Olga rumbled: "Perhaps I could pick up the existing language or languages and make some backward inferences." Others were eager to make their own insertions. . . .

Methuen interrupted with a dampening comment. "Please recall that Quarfar and Narfar have not seen Dora during the fifty thousand years of their comet-transit to Erth. This task force was convened, not to study the planetary system of Saiph, but to arrive at conclusions directly related to the comet and its humanoid inclusions and to the five-forty-six gradient. A study in situ of the planet Dora merely as of now would come under some different jurisdiction in which, to be sure, some or all of you might be involved. This task force, of course, can make recommendations beyond the immediate scope of its charge—"

That made Chu furious; he rose to his feet, although he was so short that many did not notice this. Controlling his anger, he asserted with icy precision: "Captain, I fully respect your own discipline, and indeed I respect you personally as a man and as a mind. But in this case, conceive that you may have underrated the capabilities of the various disciplines represented here. Visiting Dora now, I as an anthropologist can make many useful inferences about Dora's ancient cultures from evidence presently available there; and so can Dr. Seal as an archaeologist. You yourself, I am sure, will admit that Dr. Sari can make better computations of past astrophysical facts on a basis of present observations; and that Dr. Green not only can make valid inferences about past ice fields from present observations, but may even be able to throw considerable light on the origin of Comet Gladys. Similar observations apply to Linguist Alexandrovna, Psychobiologist Ombasa, Stratogeologist Peranza, Zoologist Hoek, Botanist Farouki, and Microbiologist Manumuko. Also, sir, there is the little matter of empirically verifying that the five-forty-six gradient extends at least from here to Saiph and determining whether it may extend even farther. Oh, Captain, such an expedition by this task force *would* be pertinent to our charge, even necessary to it!" He nodded once. He sat, trembling a little.

Olga Alexandrovna moved that such an expedition be requested. Chu Huang seconded.

Mabel Seal suggested, "By way of discussing the motion, I wonder whether time-length of the expedition should be decided and costs projected before we vote."

Zorbin raised a timid hand; the chair recognized him. Zorbin told them studiously: "I can perhaps help you on the question of costs. The ship would have to be a frigate which could perhaps be taken out of mothballs and refitted; no charge for the frigate; for refitting, it would depend on what you would want, but we'll mention a working figure of 100,-000 world credits as recently revalued. The frigate could make the trip to Saiph in about two weeks, which is incidentally the same length of time it took our little spacedragger to travel a quarter of the distance; round trip, four weeks; average pay per crewperson of 1,000 credits per week for a crew of forty-two comes to 168,000 credits during four weeks; add rations for all, fifty-two people at 140 credits per week, subtotal for rations roughly 30,000; add ship maintenance, about 100,000; fuel is free, it is raw space. This makes a subtotal of 398,000 credits to resurrect and refit the ship and travel two ways between Erth and Saiph.

"Now, costs of remaining on Dora for X length of time. We will assume that the ship itself is inactive during such a period; but the crew must be paid, and there will be fuel costs for utilization of land, water, and atmospheric vehicles which the ship will bring along; we'll minimize the food costs, assuming that suitable food can be found on Dora, since Quarfar could eat our food with ease, and presumably Narfar also ate here somehow. As an example, assume that the expedition remains ten weeks on Dora: crew pay, 420,000; cargo food, 30,000; maintenance, 50,000; subtotal for the stay on Dora, 500,000 credits.

"To this, of course, we have to add the government's part in your own salaries. The government costs are difficult to estimate here, because your various institutions would be negotiating varying arrangements, ranging all the way from full pay by the institution to full pay by the government. Let's assume, excuse me, that the government share would average 1,500 per each of you per week, subject to negotiations. For ten of you, this would be 60,000 in salary costs for the round trip, plus 150,000 during the ten weeks on Dora: subtotal government-paid scientific salaries, 210,000.

"I will summarize. Cost of refitting a frigate and making round trip to Dora, excluding your salaries, 398,000 credits. Added costs for a ten-week stay on Dora, excluding your salaries, 500,000 credits. Government costs for your salaries, 210,000 credits. My total estimate for such an expedition is 1,108,000 credits, subject to adjustments of my averaging, and subject also to pro-rata adjustments for a different length of time on Dora.

"It is worth noticing that this amount is only about four times the cost of sending the *Ventura* out to bring back a single comet. On the other hand, the recovered comet, purged of dross, has provided about five trillion kilos of ice for water or refrigeration in dry-belt countries. Funding this expedition might directly or indirectly have to be taken in part from funds for comet-dragging. I do not know this, I merely mention the possibility.

"I hope these estimates may prove helpful. Thank you, Mr. Chairman."

Afterward, Methuen inquired: "Saul, in view of your final comments—are you with me or against me?"

"With you," Zorbin asserted, "but only in terms of full understanding by all concerned."

"Then," declared Methuen, "you are with me indeed."

Immediately calling the assistant secretary for ESC, Methuen arrange a meeting of the entire task force with the ESC Secretary for the same afternoon; and he asked and secured permission to invite his friend Astrofleet/Rear Admiral Manx. Him Methuen then called to report developments.

"All I need this afternoon," snorted Manx, "is another

156

committee. Okay, B. J., I know what you'll be wanting—and we *have* located a frigate for you, she's the *Farragut*, remember her?" The captain did, and most favorably, having served aboard her as an ensign; but seeing a cunning related angle, he praised Manx as follows: "Fred, you're no run-of-the-mine bastard, you're a bastard's bastard!"

ESC Secretary Naomi Farragut (small, spare, gray, studious) listened with care to her assistant secretary's report. She turned then to Methuen: "Anything to add, Captain?"

Said Methuen, "Only my full support, madam." The Secretary panned the task force faces; all responded "Support" or "Urgent support," and several nodded vigorously.

She invited a word from Manx. Said the admiral, "I may remark that Lieutenant Saul Zorbin, who prepared the preliminary cost estimates, is up for promotion on merit. I consider his estimates reasonably accurate. The *Farragut*, a frigate which we can release out of mothballs for the expedition, was only recently placed in reserve, and is in fine shape, requiring little refurbishing. That is, of course, if no great amount of special equipment needs to be installed for scientific purposes."

The Secretary queried softly, "What did you say her name is?"

"The *Farragut*, madam. Rather a nice coincidence."

Naomi Farragut smiled tightly, raising an eyebrow at Manx—who deadpanned. She inquired, "Admiral, what is your time estimate for releasing the ship to Captain Methuen?"

"If this is approved, madam, I will immediately release the ship to the captain who will supervise her preparation and will depart when he and his task force are ready. We think we can rather quickly scrape up a competent crew most of whom have *Farragut* experience in deep space, with Lieutenant-Commander Zorbin as executive officer." All looked at Zorbin, who soberly examined a small section of carpet, unaware that he was fingering the soon-to-be-occupied space between the two gold stripes on his cuff.

At a sign from Farragut, Methuen asked his committee, "Does anybody need any special equipment other than what you can get released from your own laboratories?"

Glaciologist Green said, "Let me answer later"; but the others all negated, being eager to get started.

"Then," Methuen told them, "I will ask each of you, be-

157

tween now and tomorrow morning, to list the items that you will bring aboard, and to make arrangements with your institutions for immediate shipment by the fastest safe method." He followed by securing permission from the admiral for the task force to visit the ship next day in order to make space dispositions and discuss installations. Whereafter they all looked at Farragut.

Said the Secretary, "I'm for it in principle. A major question will be, where in the budget we can find one or two million credits without going to Erthworld Council for a special appropriation. I'll bring this to the Norwestian President this afternoon, with a favorable recommendation and a request for speed; and I'll remind him that Erthworld Chairman Evans has expressed her interest in this project.

"Gentlepeople, I thank you."

Standing quickly, Methuen responded, "And we thank you, madam Secretary."

A great variety of scientific instrumentation would be needed; but as it turned out, most of the equipment already on hand in the institution labs of the individual scientists was portable (some massively portable despite pattern-laser microcircuitry) and adaptable to self-contained nuclear-pellet power. Llana Green specified the only exception: she claimed to need some systems whose roots were firmly embedded in Antarctic glacial ice or in sub-ice bedrock. Methuen headed off a delay of many months by pointing out that similar anchorages could hardly be attained on Dora in time to pay off during a hundred-day stay (the revised figure). After some consultation with her stratogeologist colleague and with the ESC chief of interplanetary geology, she huffily compromised on substitute nuclear-powered and portable systems which operated on the sonar principle and were locally available.

The frigate Farragut was lean-mean impressive, torpedo-shaped to get her through atmospheres in a hurry en route to and from space; length half a kilometer, beam behind her nose eighty meters tapering back to ten. Preliminary exploration revealed a disappointing paucity of private cabins, and they were tiny; but the storage space was beautiful, and the engines and differential mass frightening.

At the end of a tour, they met in the captain's mess over cocktails; there the task force members, carefully avoiding the subject of their personal discomfort, complained bitterly

158

about having to deploy their instruments along with their bodies in such cubicles. Methuen inquired which ones among them would need to use their instruments while in space-transit. It developed that the only one was Astrophysicist Sari. The captain then observed that there was excellent storage space for instruments which would not be in space use; and he added that a special lab for Dr. Sari could be set aside within the storage area. That silenced the task force; and Methuen wickedly drove home the needle by remarking that the officers who normally would enjoy single privacy in these cubicles would have to double up to make room for the scientists.

At that, Olga surprisingly moved (a) that Captain Methuen and Executive Officer Zorbin should not be displaced from the cabins they would normally occupy, and (b) that Captain Methuen be authorized to make all cabin assignments subject to appeal only to himself. Sari seconded.

Methuen as chairman asked and secured permission to introduce an amendment, namely, that he and Zorbin would co-bunk in the captain's cabin, thus releasing an additional cabin for assignment. Olga seconded, hoping for assignment with her instruments to the slightly enlarged space of the executive officer's cabin.

The motion as amended passed. "Thank you," Methuen remarked; "the amendment will allow me to assign the executive officer's cabin to my second and third officers who together will find the space barely adequate for their operational needs." Olga knew better than to comment.

The urgency within Methuen was close to frantic; objectively, though, he seemed a systematic iceberg as, during ten hectic days, he drove to completion the complex preparations for departure. . . .

On the evening before take off, weary Methuen looked about him for dinner companions and did not immediately find any; Zorbin was away overnight, and various scientists were beginning to pair a bit. While he considered the question, he felt a female hand on his shoulder and heard the voice of Sita Sari: "If the captain has no other plans, I would love to buy both of us a good dinner."

Gratefully he reached back and patted the hand, gazing

159

into her face, whose look was mischievous. He told her firmly: "*I* buy."

"Compromise? Dutch treat?"

He picked a little-known small-great place; and during more than two hours they wallowed in goodies the best of which was rich conversation—no, that was second-best; the best was camaraderie. He was more than half inclined to suggest that they make a night of it; but over after-dinner liqueur she remarked: "This has been very good, B.J. And now I think we both need to sleep-up our energies for takeoff tomorrow. And I stipulate that we are to part now and sleep separately."

He let her have a gentle grin. "You are psychic, Sita?"

"I am female. You are male. But I eschew that. Even if I were otherwise inclined, I am too full of tomorrow's departure to be distracted by my senses."

He leaned forward. "You are enthusiastic, Sita?"

Her low voice told the ceiling: " 'Him the Almighty Power hurled headlong flaming down from th'ethereal sky, with hideous ruin and combustion—' "

Methuen soberly responded. "Milton, *Paradise Lost*, Book One. God hurling Lucifer out of Heaven."

"Right," she told table-knife. "Do you catch my reference, B.J.?"

"The overhead star-demon, with the mizdorf hurtling down. Only, you are converting the demon to God and the mizdorf to Lucifer."

She looked up, sparkling with mischief. "Let me lead up to this by pairing Milton with a modern poet who shall be nameless. We spent an early spring in northern Italy, basing ourselves in Strese on Lake Maggiore; and one day we drove to the Italian side of the Matterhorn. Afterward, he uncorked this:

> " 'Go penetrate the country, alternating
> toy village streets thick-lined by grocery shops
> with paddies worked by peasants rice-awaiting,
> or feudal castles haunting mountaintops.
> In cosmic wonder, we two pilgrims eyed,
> breathless, the snowbound heights of Matterhorn's
> backside.'

160

"Well, Captain? Do you see the composite picture?"

He regarded her with new interest. Almost in a breath, four personal revelations: Milton, mythology, quasi-Byronic whimsy, and just an ankle-flash of personal history. . . .

He inquired, "Doctor, is it not that you are burning with eagerness to see the backside of Lucifer?"

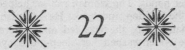

22

Day Two through Day Eleven

Dorita, coming partially out of fiendish and prolonged delirium, opened her eyes and recoiled from the hideous face that bent over her. The face chittered and patted her gently; at length she calmed and drowsed.

Again she awakened: same face, but it smiled and offered her a gourd filled with liquid. Laboriously she managed to sip a little: water. She lay back and appraised the face, thrusting herself into orientation: it was that of a mature big-breasted plump woman, Neanderthaloid and blue-green of course. With the recognition, Dorita stiffened back on the cot, clenching eyes and fists and jaws, beginning to comprehend that her nightmare had been no dream.

She roused: now the one bending over her was Narfar. He chittered soothingly, but neither her comprehension of his language nor her telepathy had returned yet. Apathetically she examined him, wanting to hate him, not quite succeeding.

Narfar reached out to somewhere and brought back something like a banana which he peeled and offered to her. She negated. Delicately he bit off a piece with his front teeth and brought it to her mouth with his fingers. Surrendering, she took it and laboriously toothed it like an old woman gumming with arthritic jaws. She felt no pain, but her lower jawbone simply was not operating right.

He gave her another morsel, then coaxed her to sip from the gourd. Standing, he chittered something and vanished. The woman came back into view, offering the food and drink; Dorita refused, but she felt an urge and pointed to her

161

crotch. The woman lifted her and carried her outside to a midden where Dorita relieved herself quickly, repelled by the potent odors; then she was returned to the cot, and she fell asleep immediately.

Awakening next morning, she felt barely strong enough to get her legs off the cot and sit on its edge, giddily supporting herself with her hands. The woman ran in, helped her up, assisted her to the midden and back. Having resumed the cot with the woman's help, she was fed and watered; clutching the gourd, she water-washed her sleep-glued eyes, then felt for something to dry them with—and noticed for the first time that she was naked. The woman, equally naked, did not seem to understand Dorita's need; so Dorita semi-dried herself with her own long tangled hair and examined her nurse.

The point of the examination was, not so much to know the nurse, as to comprehend how she herself must appear, having no mirror. The woman was a female version of Narfar, only sloppy rather than muscular-lean; she was all-over black-hairy, her legs were bowed, her jaw was heavy, her nose was flat, her chin and forehead receded, her post-orbital ridge was massive. No need to be delicate in front of her: Dorita went about checking herself—her own bowed legs (but her body still was relatively hairless except as to scalp and armpits and pubis), the feel of her nose (flattened so that she would have to get used to a new breathing-feel), the slope of her forehead (receding and heavily eye-ridged), the form of her lower jaw (not heavy, but with chin receding). It was a done thing, then; she scarcely needed a mirror.

She surveyed the hut-interior: thatched roof, withe-walls, doorless door, no windows; two other cots, no other furniture. A few pertinent words of the local tongue returned to her, and she inquired, "How long I here?" Even her voice was deformed, a sinus-resonant nasal.

The woman held up three fingers: "That many suns."

Holding up three fingers of her own, Dorita tested, touching fingers: "One sun—two suns—this third sun now?"

"Yes."

"I Dorita. Who you?"

"I Merli. Woman to Narfar. He put me here for you."

"You here all time, Merli?"

"No. Yesterday my afternoon, last night my night, today my morning. This afternoon come other woman to Narfar,

162

name Lari; tomorrow other woman, name Kosa; next day I come again."

"You good, Merli. Narfar have three women?"

"Now he have four women."

Dorita grimaced, then queried: "I see Narfar here yesterday?"

"Yes. He come every morning and evening to see you. He like you very much. He sorry for you."

As always, she was catching meanings by telepathy when she did not understand some words; recognition of this talent-in-progress reminded her that she had it.

She said, "You nice, Merli. You have things to do, maybe?"

"Yes, but I watch you—"

"I all right. You go do things. Go now, good Merli. Come back when your next turn come."

The woman shrugged, smiled, and departed—leaving Dorita to the solitude she needed so that she could meditate the meanings of her misery.

Narfar exploded into the hut. "Hi, Dorita! Up! Up! We go flying, I show you city—"

He paused as, with a wan smile, she raised a restraining hand. "Narfar, I weak, I no fly, I fall off your back."

His jaw dropped, his head went down. "You mad at me because I do this to you."

Having worked out that emotive issue within herself, she patted the side of her cot. "Come sit here." She felt him go faint inside, he was remembering their first meeting.

He sat beside her, stroked her forehead with a finger, stroked her nose and chin, saying, "You pretty now, Dorita. You always pretty inside, but now you pretty outside too. You glad?"

Smiling broadly because it was so comical-ironic, she struggled up to a sitting position (she wasn't pushing very expertly with her new-bent legs) and clutched his shoulders with both hands, looking into his face. With severity: *Narfar, I said I would let you do this so I could stay with you—but I didn't know you had three other women.*

He pressed one of her hands on a shoulder. *You be queen of all three, now. They be just extras. You my goddess. Tomorrow we go to bed.*

Perhaps the other three would accept her preeminence,

163

perhaps not; she anticipated problems, but they weren't important in view of the secret transience of her stay here. Once back on Erth, plastic surgery would quickly rearrange her. But she did have to get her special status defined.

Forlorn she looked up at him, her still-blue eyes pleading. *But Narfar, first we have to get married.*

Married? What that?

It is Erth custom, it has to happen first. We have big ceremony, all leaders there, many other people there. Holy man say words over us, make us man and wife. Then we go to bed. Not before.

He barked aloud: "We get married then! How do?"

She told him sweetly, "You my god. You say how marriage will go. I help you plan. But I have to get strong for marriage."

Narfar hugged her tightly to him, exclaiming: "Marriage new thing, but Narfar say *good* new thing. Maybe good just for us, maybe good for all. I dunno, we see. I gotta go now, but Lari come soon, Kosa tomorrow; both young and strong, you work hard with them, you be strong real quick. Dorita, you do!"

This time, when he vanished, it was the natural way: walking out through the door. Presumably he had gone the same way yesterday.

Lari who was young-rangy and Kosa who was young-petite-strong were distant at first; but Dorita turned on everything she had including affirmative suggestion; and they became such great pals that one or the other of the young women would come every day to the hut to help their patient get quickly strong for Narfar. Dorita had a feeling that none of these three had ever looked upon herself as more than a concubine; so that if this Dorita was to become his queen-goddess and rule over them, the best thing to do was to win Dorita's favor—and quite without jealousy.

She went walking with Lari the same afternoon; and while mastery of her new-bowed legs came slowly, fatigue diminished as mastery progressed.

Regularly during their probings of the hut-city, Lari or Kosa would pause to yatter with townsfolk, first presenting them to Dorita. Because Narfar's leaders had passed the word, the opening routine was always the same: both men and women would drop to their knees and bow their heads;

164

Dorita would encourage them with a few words; immediately they would resume their feet, lose stiffness, and gossip with her in quite an ordinary way. Leadership-followership went easily in Narfar City.

The women were invariably naked, except for instances when the time of month made a breechclout needful: a bulky affair of long leaves interwoven with vines and stuffed with moss. Men, to her surprise, were *not* ordinarily naked entirely; rather, they wore slim breechclouts (perhaps mainly for self-support) in any situation outside the throne room; and whenever she saw a man who wore some additional garment, usually the pelt of some animal, she came to recognize him as a leader. Only Narfar among men went always god-naked. Family arrangements appeared roughly patriarchal: men seemed clearly in the ascendancy; the same woman was usually with the same man, but this was not always the case, and Dorita suspected that roving diversion was easy for both sexes.

After three days of in-city activity, she invaded jungle edge with Kosa; and over a period of days, regularly she jungle-roved with one or the other of the young women. It was more than a matter of strength-gaining: Dorita felt a practical need to learn jungle ways, and both her teachers were excellent at this. They showed her which snakes were venomous and which weren't; which vines were toxic or even aggressively carnivorous; which beasts were docile and which dangerous; which insects were noxious and which merely friendly-annoying; how to distinguish edible fruits and berries and fungi.

At the first pond they encountered, Lari gave instruction about dangerous reptilian swimmers and about quicksand. But after a little of that, it penetrated Lari's awareness that kneeling Dorita was staring at the water surface without paying much attention to her tutor. "What matter?" Lari wanted to know. Laughing a little, Dorita stood quite easily; her strength was returning, her legs were behaving well. "I look at my new face," she told Lari.

"You like?" her friend asked.

Dorita spread her hands. "It a face." Her new appearance had not shocked her as much as she had anticipated; she had formed a pretty good idea of it from self-touching.

She learned that the hut where she was staying had been

commandeered for her by Narfar. It was adjacent to the palace, and he had been keeping his other three women there; but them he had relocated by bumping a family in the next hut farther downstreet to a hut recently vacated by old-age death. It was a signal to Dorita that she was indeed his favorite; and since it had been equally a signal to the other women long before her awakening, she understood that they were prepared to accept her, that their friendliness was genuine. She thought a lot about that: she hadn't really felt friendship before.

One day when she and Narfar were alone in the hut, he sat on her cot (withes woven on a rude wood-frame and raised half a meter off the floor on two pyramid-piles of cross-branches withe-tied), pulled her onto his lap and demanded: *What this marriage thing? You mindspeak so I get it for sure.*

She wriggled herself into a comfortable position, reflecting that this lap-sitting would be a ball, indeed a highball, when the right moment would come to let him turn loose. But that moment hadn't come yet. . . .

Hard to explain marriage, she told him. *I say it this way. We two agree that we will be the most important people to each other, all our lives.*

That mean you be more important to me than leaders?

Not what I say. What I say mean, I be more important to you than any one leader, or any one man or woman. And you be more important to me than anybody.

We not need marriage for that!

No; but in marriage, we say it to each other in front of other people, we give our word, it is a promise, it is a bond.

But I god, I not like bonds. You not saying I not schlurp you without marriage?

Yes. I am saying that.

But that silly, Dorita! I want you, I schlurp you when I want!

But don't you want me to want it?

Well, sure, you no special fun if you not want it—

All right. I not want it without marriage. With marriage I I want it. That good enough?

He shrugged. *I guess so.* He was no longer holding her on his lap, but she stayed aboard by hooking an arm around his thick neck.

He said presently, looking somewhere-nowhere: *That mean I can't schlurp anybody else?*

I didn't say that. I wouldn't stop you, I couldn't. But if we get married, I come first. If I need you more than she does, you come to me. Always.

He slipped an arm about her, mind-murmuring: *Well, that better. I can live with that. . . .* He gripped her, eye-confronting her: *Marriage mean you can't schlurp anybody else?*

She answered demurely: *As long as you with me, you plenty for me. And you always come first.*

His arm-grip tightened about her waist, and she sensed a beginning of Narfar-arousal. He said aloud, "So far, that sound okay. You tell me how do marriage thing."

On another day, she mounted his back; he caught her up into the sky and overflew the city with her in leisurely-intricate flight-patterns, now soaring high, now low; so that Dorita, enthralled as much by the experience as by the spectacle below, could comprehend the living city in detail and in fullness. "This my city," he kept reminding her. "I make."

To her it resembled nothing so much as a congeries of African cities in various nations when pre-white Africa had been black-culture high. She had seen pictures. And she had picked up enough about cultural anthropology to be amazed that Narfar had been able to bring his biologically primitive people to so high a level during the few thousand years of his reign—and all without any sort of fire!

It also served to remind her of her utter isolation from Erth and indeed from humans who were biologically full-developed. And briefly, in midair, she regretted B. J. Methuen. He was sweet, he was potent, he was humanly patient and professionally competent, he was all a woman would want for a husband, and he had wanted her. Had she been on Erth with her own face and legs, would she have accepted him? No, sardonically she reflected; for despite her marriage plans, a husband was not what Dorita wanted.

Departing the city, they were overflying lush jungle; there was a distinct possibility that he would continue straight ahead, possibly setting her down for jungle bivouac a night or two or three en route, until they had girdled his world.

A question was nagging her; and his wingbeat-wind, cooling even in tropical heat, brought the question to imperative. She mind-inquired: *Is it true that there is glacial ice above and below this middle belt of Dora?*

Is so.

Does anybody live up there, or down there?

The question troubled Narfar, he thought about it soberly during an appreciable time of flying. Then he evaded: *I bring them all to warm country. Colder country not good for living. Need fire. I not like fire.*

Because of Quarfar?

I not like fire.

She kept thinking, she always kept thinking about the dying words of Quarfar: *Not far below the north pole on Dora, there is a certain crater like a circular box. It contains something of great value. Knowing you, I am sure that you will find it. Dorita—you must not open it! Under no circumstances may you open it. Do you understand, Dorita? Do not open that box!*

And of course, out of respect for Quarfar, she would *not* open that box. But she did intend to find it—had not Quarfar expressed confidence that she would? She wanted to know, among other things, what sort of box it might be—and what sorts of things it might contain, what essential ingredient that Narfar had somehow drained away from the people on Dora. And it surely wouldn't hurt if she should discover *how* to open it, even if she would leave it unopened. Finding a secret box containing world-tabu material, and learning *how* to open it and release the contents, would be fulfilling triumph—the greatest of her life! She would be total mistress of a planet's ultimate secret!

Now she mind-coaxed: *I would like very much to see that polar ice.*

Eagerly Narfar returned: *Goddess want to see polar ice? I show from here!* And he began to ascend rapidly aloft, perhaps five kilometers per minute. . . .

After less than two minutes, Dorita, freezing cold and choking for air, mind-pleaded: *Down, Narfar, down! I am dying up here—*

Abandoning his impulse to take her up about a thousand kilometers, Narfar power-dived for planetary surface. Just short of crash-down, Dorita lost consciousness in a fifteen-*G* pull-out.

She awakened on her cot in her hut. Five heads bent over her: Narfar's concerned face; the worried faces of Merli and

Lari and Kosa; and a grinning skull. She jerked herself up and around to stare at the skull: it was a wooden mask on a witch-doctor who was doing droning-swishing things with a string-swung gourd containing dried beans.

Narfar voice-gentled her, timidly finger-touching her. "Be quiet, Dorita. We be married soon. Then I take you to ice."

23

Day Twelve through Day Twenty-Four

Methuen-driven, the frigate *Farragut*, crewed and task-forced and intricately equipped, departed Erth lazily on stubby retractable wings until she was five hundred kilometers aloft; orbited into position; then catapulted herself into an arrow-shot directly at Saiph. Some maneuvering was needed around a couple of solar planets which were currently eclipsing Saiph, and it was always a good idea to pick one's way carefully through the asteroid belt between Mars and Jupiter. Nevertheless, when after twelve hours *Farragut* passed Pluto-orbit nearly six billion kilometers out, she was already thrusting more than six hundred *G*'s, although (behind her battleship-grade 1:1,500,000 inertial shield) passengers and crew were noticing little if any acceleration.

But then the frigate leaped again. By the end of twenty-four hours, she was maintaining a steady acceleration of 5,600,000 *G*'s, which seemed a continually oppressive four *G*'s to the passengers—they felt as though they were in a jet plane which accelerated in ten seconds from zero to 1,500 kilometers per hour and then maintained this takeoff burst endlessly undiminished. This *G*-thrust would get the *Farragut* up to 109,500 times the velocity of light at mid-course; whereafter she would rotate and brake the rest of the way, reaching Saiph-orbit in a neat fourteen days. In 2464, they straightened out space-curvature with repulsor-drive which fed on raw space.

Farragut, like all trans-light ships of the era, was able to exceed light-velocity (and higher velocities are limited only by thrust) with the aid of its differential mass. This mass was a mighty sphere in ship bowels which had the property of becoming geometrically more massive as velocity increased. Thus, as the speed of light was approached, the mass of the ship became greater than the distance-relative mass of any star they might pass; and since (by relativistic convention) the motion of a less-massive body is relative to the position of the largest mass in the vicinity, it worked out (relatively speaking) that the *Farragut* was motionless, and it was the star that moved. Nobody had ever worked out the math of what this did to the entire cosmic system of motions when many ships using differential masses were moving in different directions at the same time.

Before departure, Methuen had anticipated the tensions which could arise among his scientific passengers, who were unaccustomed to interstellar voyaging over a period of many days, and who certainly would be dangerously oppressed by a sustained thrust which would appear to them like four *G*'s. He had convened the task force to discuss this hazard, which, as he pointed out, could disable them for useful work either during the voyage or afterward on Dora, and which might even incapacitate some of them for life. Most of the scientists were inclined to downgrade the hazard, pointing to the cases of interstellar crew members who made voyage after voyage like this (Methuen himself, for instance), and citing their own experiences in high-*G* joy-park centrifuges. But some of them, notably Psychobiologist Ombasa, comprehended the hazard more soberly and shepherded the committee into a more usefully serious mood.

At a suitable moment, Zorbin, having discussed the matter last night with Methuen, proposed a two-part solution. First, the crew program director would be instructed to devise diversionary programs for passengers at numerous times during each day, and these could be attended optionally by scientists who desired or needed psychic relief. Second, the standard complement of three cryogenic capsules for crew-member emergencies would be increased to thirteen; and a passenger might at any time be deep-frozen in a capsule, either voluntarily, or by direction of the ship surgeon or Zorbin or Methuen.

The second part of this proposal came under sharply argumentative criticism, the most acerbic critics being Olga

Alexandrovna and Sita Sari. Each insisted that she was the best judge of her own condition and would tolerate no freezing by direction. Ready for this type of objection, Methuen amended the proposal: non-voluntary freezing would be done only by concurrence of any two among the three mentioned by Zorbin; and he made it plain that in any case, unfreezing would start as soon as *G*-pressure would cease in freefall around Saiph, so that the scientist would be ready for action immediately at touchdown on Dora. Sari claimed an exception: if by some unfair decision she should be forced into a tank, she must be already operational again when Saiph orbit would be achieved; and Glaciologist Llana Green seconded this for herself, observing that she should be able to make glacial observations from aloft coming in on Dora. Methuen said that as chairman he could accept these exceptions in the case of these two if the committee could. Sudafrikan Geologist Hoek moved acceptance of Zorbin's proposal as amended by Methuen, Sari, and Green. Eskimo Mabel Seal seconded. Carried, seven to two with Olga abstaining.

In the space-outcome, Olga experienced a nervous breakdown on the fourth day and was tank-committed by concurrence of Methuen, Zorbin, and the surgeon; while Sari, on the fifth day, stalked coolly onto the bridge, reported to the captain that she had placed all her instruments under computerized control for star-observations in transit, and requested that she be frozen forthwith. Microbiologist Manumuko capitulated on the sixth day. By the eighth day, either voluntarily or by direction, all scientists were frozen except three: Seal, Green, and Ombasa; even these three were internalized, remaining in their cabins or talking moodily in twos and threes, unresponsive to the diversions provided by the program director.

All these personal dynamics were discussed at length, offwatch after offwatch, among Methuen and Zorbin and the surgeon, sometimes with Ombasa present (it was his bag, but he listened apathetically). The surgeon had read a great deal of very early archival space-age literature filled with dire 20th-century predictions about the emotional effects of long periods in space under tight confinement. Few of those predictions had come to pass—yet now, after nearly five centuries of space travel, here they all were, abruptly, with this group: *why?* Zorbin reminded the surgeon that, from the very beginning, astrocrews had been intensively trained to head off emotional trauma. True, said the surgeon, but how about lay passengers? Well, reflected Methuen aloud, as the interplanetary and interstellar services had developed, they had never been activated until all passengers could be suitably coddled. This was perhaps the first time in history when ten passengers, all amateurs in space and some first-timers, had driven themselves through the cosmos for days at a sustained apparent thrust of four G's. Here, the others agreed, must lie the explanation.

Privately, Zorbin judged, and Methuen had to admit to himself, that the fault really lay in the lap of Captain Methuen, who had dynamized the fourteen-day trip to Dora without adequate prior training for the lay passengers (all scientists, but nevertheless laypeople in space), because of Methuen's private passion to pursue Dorita. Otherwise, the expedition might easily have been delayed at least six months for personnel preparation and trip-time could have been extended to (say) thirty days for thrust-reduction, while Dora would have stayed there patiently awaiting the arrival of Dora's investigators. (Zorbin knew nothing of Methuen's dreams.)

And Methuen felt guilt: lacerated himself with guilt, having to exercise rigorous self-discipline in order to husband his guilt and stay captain-operational. Many times he seriously considered resigning from Astrofleet after this trip; and the question remained active in his mind.

Zorbin, however, concluded to exonerate his captain. Was it not Methuen who had thought up the cryogenic capsule gambit which would almost surely head off lasting trauma for any member of the task force?

Then, too, there was Quarfar's ambiguous warning about a possible threat from Dora.

After one late watch, Methuen encountered Dr. Harlo Ombasa just off the bridge; and on an impulse he inveigled the psychobiologist (with an interest in the paranormal) into the captain's mess for a nightcap. Ombasa, less apathetic than usual for him lately, offered to fix the captain an Afrikan drink that Methuen would long remember; and at the bar, he came up with a long quick-frosted glass filled with a mélange of vodka and fruit juices, altogether tangy. The vodka, he explained, substituted for the natural ferment of the fruits. As

172

for Ombasa, he stayed with icewater, his religion being Erebian.

Neither was much for small talk, so Methuen went casually pro. "Dr. Ombasa, you never told us whether you got anything out of your look-see at paranormality in connection with the Quarfar and Narfar disappearances."

Ombasa consulted his ice water. "Nothing," he responded in his purling basso. "There has to be something, but there was no evidence to indicate what."

"Will you pursue it?"

"How can I?"

Methuen was on the edge of extremely deep water, and he wanted to broach the topic to this scientist in some way that would not make the captain seem nuts. While he hesitated over this, Ombasa leaned forward. "Captain, I have seriously studied many aspects of paranormal phenomena, and I exclude no competent testimony. I think you want to give me some."

Having strengthened himself with the drink, Methuen looked straight at Harlo's eyes. "There are some things that I am not ready to tell you, but I would like to hit you with a few hypothetical questions."

"Pray do."

"Have you ever studied the old old fictional stories about time travel?"

"Of course."

"And have you theorized about the possibility?"

"Of course."

"Can you brief your thoughts?"

"Concerning time travel by spirits, I have nothing to say. Concerning time travel by physical animal bodies, I do have a few theory-grounded ideas."

"Please push them at me."

"You have what you consider to be a practical interest?"

"Perhaps."

"Then, Captain, it would be best for you to ask questions—the topic is far too complex for me to attempt a quick briefing."

"All right." Methuen felt more confident. "First, do you think it theoretically possible for a bodied human to invade the past? Never mind how it would be done."

"Yes, I think it might be possible."

"Might it be done without some kind of time-machine?"

"If it can be done at all, most likely a machine would be useless; it would have to be brought-off psychobiologically."

"Might a time-invader bring another body along with him?"

"If they were in physical contact, it might be done, if the act can be done at all."

Methuen breathed and drank deeply, then inquired: "If a person should enter the past, how could he possibly influence the past, all of which is all over and done with?"

Ombasa drank, then addressed the tabletop: "I think you understand how complex your question is. Let me remark that there are two main parts to it. The first part is, how could a person go into the past and change the behavior of what is already past? The second is, if such change could be effected, would it change the entire course of subsequent history? You are perhaps thinking about time paradoxes, of which I will mention a classic: a man goes into the past and kills his own grandfather before his father is conceived, thus cancelling his own existence so that he could not have killed his grandfather."

"Something like that," Methuen agreed, finishing his drink and holding out the glass.

Taking it and standing, Ombasa remarked, "There were three ounces of vodka in the drink, and the fruit juices reinforced it."

"Fine," declared Methuen. "Thank you."

Ombasa made him a new drink, reflected, made himself a drink, brought them back, sat and sipped, remarking, "On occasions such as this one, when the thinking is almost mystical, the ethics of my religion can be superseded by the recommendations of Lao Tse."

"Acknowledged," said Methuen, awaiting the answer which Ombasa must have been formulating at the bar.

"I theorize," began Ombasa, "that the answer to the first part of your question is, Yes: a person can enter the past and change it. I will simplify the explanation. Every living thing—and that includes every atom of everything organic or inorganic—leaves the track of its past existence in the past. That is what the continuing past is—those tracks; and every track is unchangeable and imperishable. But along each track is an indefinite series of what I call if-nodes: it is a place where the person or the atom might have done one thing but

174

instead did another thing. Do you follow me so far, Captain?"

"Possibly. Go on."

"All right. If the person invading the past should stimulate an if-node, this might start germinating a whole new course of history parallel with the still-unchangeable old course."

"Doctor, I have a feeling from what you say that the man who entered the past and killed his own grandfather would *not* thereby eliminate either his father or himself."

"Beautifully deduced!" cried Ombasa with admiration. "There is, however, a catch to it; and now as you see we are already into the second part of your question.

"To avoid absurdity, let's forget the grandfather murder. Say that a man goes into the past and, by his presence, stimulates new directional growth at a number of if-nodes. He does not thereby change what is past; but he starts the growth of a parallel past."

"Would it grow at the same rate of speed as the old past?"

"Again, aha! I have contorted myself over exactly that question. It is a most significant question, because on it depends the further question whether this newborn past could change the present. Do you see that, Captain?"

"I do. Where are you with it?"

"Only as far as logical hypotheticals. The new track could develop slower than the old one, or at the same rate, or faster. In the first two instances, it could never affect the present, because the present would keep on moving away from it on the basis of the old track. But in the third instance, the new track might burst into the present, and something would have to give."

"Pray pursue that possibility."

"In that case, if nothing gave, the same world would contain two parallel sets of mutually exclusive conditions, which is absurd. The absurdity might be eliminated if the two sets of conditions immediately made war on each other, until one annihilated the other—or, if the two were to merge, so that out of the merger a single course of novel history would proceed."

"I see. Do you prefer one or the other possibility?"

"Captain, obviously I have no way to determine a preference."

"But you do think it not impossible that a person might enter the past and stimulate development of a new past parallel

175

to the old—and that the new past might develop faster than the old had developed, so that the new might break into the present?"

"I think it not impossible."

"How much faster than the old past would such a new past develop? I mean, if the past were changed, say, fifty thousand years ago, would it take fifty thousand years for the new past to catch up with us?"

"Obviously not, Captain; for if the new past took fifty thousand years to develop its own fifty thousand years, at the end of that time the present would still be fifty thousand years ahead of it."

"Okay, Doctor: faster, then. How much faster?"

"Who can measure that, Captain, in the absence of known cases? The new track might develop one-third faster than the old, or two-thirds faster; or different changes might futurize at different rates, one twice as fast as the old, another five times as fast. I simply don't know."

"But still we are talking about what seems not impossible?"

"That is right." Ombasa was engrossed: the captain obviously had something definite on his mind.

Methuen breathed and demanded: "Might a new-burgeoning past traverse fifty thousand years in five days? or even in one day?"

"Within my theory, possibly; or one new track in one day and another in five days—I have not yet developed any basis for rules."

Methuen pondered; Ombasa waited.

Methuen plunged. "Doctor—scientifically, *can* there be any such thing as prevoyance of the future?"

"That is an abrupt switch," Ombasa averred, "and the rules are different. The future is a cloud of yet-unrealized potentials gradually coming into concrescence as our present behavior narrows the scope of future probabilities. Are you following me?"

"Yes—"

"In other words, Captain, *trends* can develop among concrescing potentials; and, as you well know, some minds are more sensitive than others to developing trends. Such trend-detection can be called prevoyance; but careful prophets hedge their predictions, because some new event in the present can destroy any trend."

"You have been talking in terms of intelligent wide-awake foresight."

"Yes."

"What about prevoyant dreams? I mean, dreams that seem to preview the future quite independently of any wide-awake foresight?"

Ombasa sipped and sighed. "Such dreams have occurred; they have been extensively documented along with outcomes. Some are truly prevoyant, some are not, some may have been prevoyant before events changed trends."

"Then a prevoyant dream does not forecast with certainty?"

"If a dream is truly prevoyant, it forecasts what is certain to happen unless something intervenes to change the trend which the dreamer is subconsciously detecting. Given an appointment in Samara, one need not always meet it."

"How can one tell whether a dream about some future is prevoyant?"

"The quality of the dream will be circumstantial and convincing. However, many non-prevoyant dreams are also circumstantial and convincing. So circumstantiality and conviction are necessary to, but do not denote, prevoyancy."

Methuen wet his lips. "What if there is a series of *three* apparently prevoyant dreams, all sequential and consistent, with the succession of acts and dates being logical in terms of what is dreamed?"

Ombasa hesitated. "I know that your questions are hypothetical, but—would you mind hypothesizing how far in advance the predicted events are previewed?"

"Let us say—less than a year in advance."

"I think then," ventured Ombasa, "that there might be reason to enter into tentative action anticipating the happenings—but always with careful guards, until something in waking life strongly supports the probability."

Sipping brood.

Draining his drink, Methuen said with a slight fuzziness: "You know, Doctor, those drinks *were* strong, and I do have duty tomorrow morning—"

"Of course," Ombasa acknowledged, rising; and he departed leaving half his own drink and knowing that Methuen was not drunk but wanted to meditate.

24

Day Twenty

The marriage of Dorita to Narfar, of an Erth-human woman to a winged god-man, was the most dramatic event that had ever transpired in anybody's memory or in the legends—or, for that matter, in the life of Dorita *up to that point*.

It took place two days after the Dora-bound *Farragut*, a thousand light-years from Dora out in deep space, reached its velocity peak, rotated, and began its stern-first braking approach to Saiph orbit. Two days later—yet fifty thousand years earlier.

Fiendishly Dorita had planned the wedding, and joyous Narfar had built it up with extra-fiendish touches. They staged it outdoors so all the townsfolk could turn out to watch. In the event, it took place during a two-hour drenching gulleywasher; everybody, including the ceremoniously unclouted men, being naked or the next thing to it, nobody cared.

The witch doctor (let's call him simply *witch*), wearing a wooden joy-mask which he had carved for the occasion, awaited them outside the palace door, flanked by senior leaders Herdu and Glans. Arrayed behind the three men were Narfar's other three women, with Merli in the middle; Kosa was an exception to the general nakedness, it was a bad day for her, she wore a stuffed breechclout. The masks of the witch were an interesting example of Narfar's delimited creativity, being at least ten millennia ahead of his era in Erth terms.

The parade formed at city outskirts, with hard rain wetting the celebrants while churning up dust and plastering it on their bodies. Ahead marched half of the town's music group, seven men and six women chanting offbeat and hip-wriggling in counter-time; the men were beating together hollow sticks for tympani. Behind them strutted five senior leaders other than Herdu and Glans. Behind *them*, riding in a chair-car carried by four young blue-green bucks, gay Dorita, naked except for a rain-bedraggled flower wreath in her hair and a flower lei around her neck, threw kisses left and right; above her, totally naked unbedecked body-dripping Narfar flew slow-low, grinning left and right and shaking his wet-clasped hands. After the bridal couple danced five more senior leaders, then the twenty-four younger sub-leaders, then the final thirteen members of the chorale, all flower-lei naked. And thousands cheered.

In front of the witch and his flankers drew up the procession, and broke. Ranging themselves in semicircles, the ten marching senior leaders joined Herdu and Glans, the twenty-four junior leaders crude-straggled into formation behind the seniors, the twenty-six musicians scurried into rank behind the juniors without missing more than two dozen beats—leaving alone, precisely in front of the witch, the four young bucks with the chair-car and Dorita and over-hovering Narfar. Thronging spectators handclap doubled the music's rhythm.

Narfar now drifted downward with stately deliberation, clasped Dorita from behind (one carrying arm about her waist, one symbolic arm about her breasts) and lifted her above the chair; whereat the four carriers hastened off to set down their chair and kneel at one flank of the wedding assembly. Acting on Dorita's prior suggestion and Narfar's direction, five musicians parted from their line and arrayed themselves on the other flank for aesthetic balance: four kneeling like the chair-carriers, the fifth on hands and knees to simulate a duplicate of the recumbent chair.

Silence fell.

While Narfar holding submissive Dorita floated two meters in the air in front of the witch, that official (pre-schooled but not dictated-to by Dorita) commenced his leadership of the utterly new sacrament of marriage.

Witch: "Why you come here?'"

Narfar: "We get married."

Witch: "What that mean?"

Narfar: "You tell us, you the witch."

Witch (as coached by Dorita): "That mean, you always first with Dorita, she always first with you. Okay?"

Narfar: "Okay. Make us married quick."

Witch to Dorita: "You too?"

Dorita, feebly: "Yes."

Witch: "Hold still, I marry you now." He went into a hellish dance around them, noisily brandishing his bean-gourds; Narfar held stolidly stationary, but Dorita's head swiveled after the witch until it strained her neck and dizzied her. . . .

Coming in front of them, the witch leaped high in the air with legs in an open scissors and yelled "YOW!" He dropped to the ground still open-scissored; Narfar winced. From the ground groaned the witch: "I guess you married now. I all through."

The crowd went into hysteria as Narfar embraced his bride: embraced her with arms and wings, clasping her high and low against himself. Dorita, hugging him necessarily, surmounted her own arousal for an instant and whispered into the spread of his hairy ear: "Not now—they all watching—we go inside!" Maybe in the palace she could head him off, although at the moment she didn't particularly want to head him off: her garbled thought was that she should withhold his reward until after he would take her to see the secret north-pole box. But panting Narfar mind-informed her: *They have to see the schlurping, it make the corn grow.*

That was too much even for Dorita: she didn't care for exhibitionism even when it suited her purpose, which now it didn't. Gathering her forces, she pierced him with a negative imperative. Wilting then rallying, he roared at the people: "All done now for you guys! You all go home, the rest for me alone, I do it up high over the corn!" Catching up his quivering bride from the grass, he flew her into sky so high that nobody on the ground could see them as more than a double speck; and lofty over the corn, he visited upon Dorita the most ecstatic anguish she had ever known. It crescendoed while he flew her over jungle, while the afternoon passed and the evening waned and one by one stars appeared: Hatsya, Rigel, Alnilam, Alnitak, Mintaka, Betelgeuse, Bellatrix, Heka, Tabit, three nebulae. . . .

It was perhaps midnight when he held her passively, idly overflying jungle, gazing down upon her eyes-closed mouth-opened face with ultimate devotion, totally satisfied for now, loving her supremely forever. Inert in his arms, exhausted, ultra-replete, Dorita let her eyes come part-open and watched stars past his shoulder for a long time with no thoughts at all.

25

Day Twenty-One

Dorita awoke struggling with semi-smotheration as though bedcovers had worked up over her face. Convulsively freeing her face, she discovered the real trouble: she lay nude on her back in a woodland bower; and Narfar snored prone beside her, an arm over her chest and a wing (until she had thrust it away) over her face. She lay there for awhile, pleasantly achy, lethargically replete: it had been *quite* a night!

Presently with gentleness she removed the arm from her body (Narfar merely grunted), sat up, got herself oriented, inspected the back and bottom of her new husband. He was quite a specimen, enormously powerful, skull broad and squat, neck broad and squat, shoulders and back bulging under their natural mandarin hair-blanket (she enjoyed a little whorl in the small of his back), buttocks broad and hard, thigh-backs heavy-muscular, calves back-bulging, feet flat and huge. And well she knew about the power now hidden beneath all that!

Yet, god or no god, wings or no wings, he was a primitive. A full modern Erth-human would call him somewhat mentally retarded, on the borderline between moronic and slow-normal—not in brain-power, but at the level of intellectual use. He did have intelligence, he had as much language as any man in his city, he could conceptualize to a limited degree (but so could a chimpanzee), he had memory and foresight and could distinguish between them and present perception. And did he have force and tenacity of will! But Narfar was fundamentally a child-god, so near to being purely passional that he never used intelligence more than enough to serve his momentary whim.

Well, perhaps that was in part unjust. From Narfar's thoughts and Quarfar's reporting, she knew that Narfar had, during thousands of previous years, held to the complex task of creating and organizing the city after his own desires carried out in terms of earlier positive and negative inspirations from Quarfar. After all, did even a weak-minded god go through some eons of life without learning *some* tenacity, without forming *some* plan and holding to it until it was done? Erth had seen morons with interest and self-discipline acquiring in their later years considerable verbal fluidity and a noticeable amount of fundamental human wisdom.

Her contemplation turned from her husband to herself; and she became aware of a physical state of affairs, unrelated to her bladder, which caused her to smile with amused rue. Being messy-dirty-sticky didn't bother any brittle nicety in Dorita, but she did hate to be uncomfortable.

Noiselessly she stole off a little way to a nearby hummock; atop it, she surveyed the surrounding jungle (they were in a relatively sparse area) and saw water gleaming in early sunlight a little distance away. She went there slowly, exercising tutored jungle caution. Having eliminated the probability of nearby serpents or crocodiles or piranha (or their Dorian equivalents), she plunged, luxuriated, then emerged and by turns stood or squatted in sunlight allowing herself to dry and to think. (She knew better than to *sit* on the ground or on a fallen log without first finding out about the neighborhood insects.)

And what did Dorita think about?

Some, but not much, about the driving sexuality of Narfar, its wild ecstasies and its ultimate torments; for last night, that was done, she was sated; it would probably pick up again some time this morning, and she would enjoy it, but she wasn't longing for it. At best, lying with a hungry batman had been an along-the-way box to be opened, but not at all an ultimate goal.

She did not meditate on her stupidity, if it was that, in getting herself trapped as the wife of this brute-god: she didn't feel trapped. Her attitude about marriage was the attitude of Erth in her day: you can get out of it easily if you like, or you may want to stay permanently with the guy even without marriage (although there may be civil advantages in having the union registered, and the occurrence of children always puts a different face on the matter). Nor did the aspect of having children occur to her: the concept of being fertile with a bat-winged Neanderthal was bizarre beyond her imaginings.

182

She did not consider herself excessively rash in getting herself marooned on a primitive planet—nearly seven hundred parsecs from Erth. It had been risky, yes; but not foolhardy, she was fairly sure. Just about now or very soon, she imagined, Methuen would be arriving here in the future-distant 25th century: if he didn't drive himself into coming here, his task force would; and a stay of a month or two or three by the task force could be envisioned, with continual wide exploration. This meant escape for Dorita, if at any time within the next limited number of weeks she would resolve to chuck it all and foretime into Methuen's present.

What Dorita thought about primarily, beside the pond after her swim, was her *ultimate objective* in coming here and instrumentally getting herself married to Narfar. And she worried a bit that since he had stripped down her defenses and consummated and reconsummated their marriage, she may have lost an incentive-hold which she had maintained upon him in order to get him to take her to that ultimate objective.

Also she considered the difficulties of that goal, that frigid North Pole goal! She was on a planet which had no man-husbanded fire, no source of warmth other than the sun. She had almost frozen when Narfar had flown her up high right here in the tropics! She thought she knew how to "invent" fire, but she also knew that Narfar would not take kindly to this— would, indeed, violently kill this. He had his own personal tabus. She had to think carefully about preparing herself for such an expedition, since assuredly Narfar wouldn't be thinking about it without her prompting: he needed no protection, she needed much. Systematically she thought in terms of fur layers along with a high-caloric diet; and even then, she frowned as she confronted the difficulties of athletic maneuvering as a befurred cocoon.

With all that thinking-solving behind her in a preliminary way, she surrendered to rapt contemplation of the ultimate goal itself. Such contemplation elated her as the conquest of Everest must have elated Hillary. The highest climax of last night paled before this body-soul-pervasive glow which had so much more *meaning* than copulation. . . .

Awakening, Narfar missed her, smelled, found her quickly. Standing behind her, he demanded, "What is?"

Unsurprised Dorita had little need now to mindspeak with

him. She had, during these weeks, learned his language well: this tongue was limited enough, except for the inflections which you had to master—for instance, the word for a stick being used for beating had a different ending from the word for a stick that you tripped over. She maintained some mind-contact with him, mainly to sample the tenor of his thoughts and feelings; but she gave him none of her own, and they conversed in words only.

She answered: "I swim. I think."

"Thinking easy for you?"

"Not easy, but I can do it."

"Thinking hard for me. I just swim now."

From a standing start behind her, spreading wings but not beating them, he dove in a ten-meter arch, folded wings, and went under like a grebe. He surfaced after a bit, in surprise-company with a five-meter crocodilian whose presence now-unnerved Dorita hadn't noticed. The two played for a while; then Narfar gave its snout a mock slap equivalent to a blow from its own death-dealing tail, and shouted, "Go!" and the croc gently tail-whipped Narfar's rump and went.

Narfar came out of the water in a motion and stood before her, dripping. He demanded, as though there had been no hiatus: "What you think about."

"I think about wedding trip."

"What that?"

"That trip for husband and wife alone after wedding."

"We do that last night."

"Last night we not go far enough."

"You want *more* schlurp? I think we did that pretty good—"

"Not what I mean. I mean, we not go far enough away from city."

"Then I take you halfway around Dora. That as far as you can go. Go farther, you coming back."

"I told you, Narfar. I want to see the polar ice."

Frowning, he sat on the ground beside squatting Dorita; no insect would harm him. "That cold, up there. That cold cold. You nearly die when we fly up *there*." He pointed aloft.

"You give me furs and bring a lot of sugar. I not die.

"Furs? What kind?"

"What kind you got?"

He wrinkled. "Shit, I got to think—" He brightened. "I know. Gadzyook furs."

"What gadyzook?"

"Gadzyook big animal, bigger than me, live in polar ice, have thick white fur, eat anything, eat even people. I think one gadzyook pelt be enough for you, you get lost in it, but I go up and bring back two so you have a change."

"How you get pelt?"

"Easy. I find two gadzyook, say to them, I Narfar, I need your coats. They say, Okay Narfar, please kill quick so we not hurt. I say, You good gadzyook, after I take your coats I do good thing for you. They say, Thank you, Narfar. So I kill quick and take two coats, then I do the good thing for them, I give what left of them to other gadzyook, they eat and get souls of gadzyook I kill. Then I bring back coats, tan with herbs to be soft. One day fly up, one day find and kill gadzyook, one day fly back, two days tanning: we tan real quick. That makes—what?" He counted fingers. "Five days. Next day we leave on wedding trip to polar ice."

It was one of the longest speeches he had ever emitted.

26

Day Twenty-Five and Twenty-Six

At Sari's direction, the *Farragut* warped into a close-in Saiph orbit: close enough in, that is, to circumnavigate the blazing blue-white star in a reasonably short period of time, yet not close enough to accelerate the ship.

Sol, a 5,000° yellow star (photospheric temperature Kelvin, rather than coronal temperature, which is enormously higher), sheds upon Mercury, nearly fifty-eight million kilometers away, heat amounting only to less than one degree per point-instant; but this continuous heat, cumulatively retained, builds up to 446° mean temperature of the planet. Were the *Farragut* orbiting 25,000° Saiph at Mercury's distance, the heat hitting the ship per point-instant would be as high as three degrees; but the reflecting surface of the ship would prevent much accumulation.

Methuen felt fairly safe at an orbital distance of merely

ten million kilometers where the star heat per point-instant was way up to eight degrees; it would have to rise within the ship to more than 300° Kelvin before passengers would begin to feel noticeably uncomfortable. On this orbit, the sixty-three million kilometer course around Saiph could occur once in a bit over six hours, coasting at the million kilometers per hour with occasional inward acceleration for course correction. This satisfied Astrophysicist Sari, who had all instruments wide open and wanted to circumnavigate the star at least four times, once on the belt where they happened to hit it and three more times at progressive 45° declinations, holographing and spectrographing and otherwise instrumenting all the way, before abandoning the star for its planet. Impatient, Methuen could make do with this; it would lose him only a day.

By now all ten scientists were about: Sari most active, having been awakened earlier; the just-unfrozen six beginning to stretch limbs and work out cramps; and the hitherto lethargic unfrozen three attentive to the star and to what Sari was doing.

They had not, however, found the planet Dora. And, assuming that she was Erthlike with a point-instant temperature of about 0.4° Kelvin off a 25,000° parent star, Dora could be anywhere at all, in any direction, on a theoretical sphereshell whose surface was in the neighborhood of seventy-six octillion square kilometers: 76 followed by twenty-seven zeroes.

Luckily there were shorter ways to go. While they revolved around Saiph, while Sari was going crazy with all her instruments trained on the star, Methuen and Zorbin and a couple of aides were using ship's instruments for sky-sweeping, seeking planets as once they had been seeking comets. They could locate only two planets for sure, and these the innermost; but these two planets established the plane of the planetary system (if, as usual, it was planar) and reduced the possible locations of Dora to a circle-perimeter of about eighteen billion kilometers.

At high acceleration, the *Farragut* took off on a broad outbound spiral which would pass near the second planet after one revolution of Saiph. Her instruments, beefed up by those of the astrophysicist, continually reconnoitered space.

186

Halfway around Saiph for the second time since departing Saiph, they located Dora.

Five hundred kilometers off Dora, the *Farragut* circumnavigated her ten times at eighteen-degree declinations, photographing and otherwise instrumenting; the photography was the usual reconnaissance-spread of cinematography, holographic and at three simultaneous focal lengths: wide-angle, telescopic and normal. After the tenth revolution, Methuen assembled the task force for a showing of samples. They reviewed each sixteenth exposure of the normal, then each thirty-second exposure of the wide-angle; at each of these projection-passes, one or another scientist would ask to review the corresponding telephotos, and the operator would oblige them instantly with a flick of the switch. The ten ship-orbits had required nine hours; the projections used up another two hours.

At the end of it all, the lights came on, and the eleven task force members and their consultant Zorbin brooded.

After a bit, Methuen said, "I assume that many or all of us will wish to see more later, but not right now. Then our immediate problem is a good place to set down. Before attacking that, I raise the question: Did any of you see any signs of creatures having advanced intelligence?"

Zoologist Hoek contributed: "We saw a number of mammalian life-forms, and quite a few birds; but none of these animals was humanoid. Of course, a non-humanoid life form might develop a culture equivalent to that of advanced human intelligence. You might instead ask whether any of us saw signs of current advanced culture."

"All right," Methuen agreed. "Well, did you?"

"No," replied Archaeologist Seal. And when Methuen looked at Anthropologist Chu, the Cathayan's head negated.

"Then," asserted the captain, his hopes for Erth rising while his Dorita-heart was dying, "it appears that we have been orbiting a planet having broad ice caps at and far below its poles, and lush with vegetable and animal life in its broad equatorial belt, but devoid of humanoids and of any sort of advanced culture. None of you needs the caution that our experiences on the surface may turn out differently. Again: our immediate problem is, the best place to set down. I know that our Antarctic friend Dr. Green would want to be situated on a polar cap; but for obvious reasons this would be

187

impractical, and our atmospheric vehicles can fly her there whenever she may choose. It seems to me, subject to your correction, that our first concern is to discover whether there *has been* life of humanoid intelligence here; and so I would think that our friends in archaeology and anthropology would call our first landing site, subject to my correction in terms of what is practical for the ship."

Chu, who had been whispering with Seal, spoke up immediately. "My colleague here spotted a large clear space in the jungle, located at approximately ten degrees thirty-two minutes north latitude, eighty-three degrees forty-one minutes longitude, using Dr. Sari's arbitrary coordinates. Dr. Seal saw there a hummock which seemed unnatural in such a location, and she thinks a dig might be suitable."

It happened to be exactly the place where Dorita had touched down with Narfar. It was the site of what once had been Narfar City.

Most obviously, Dora was not the planet which would launch attacks upon Erth next January, if Methuen's dreamings had been truly prevoyant.

Unless. . . .

They landed at a just-past-dawn hour which Sari, after a bit of work with an ordinary sextant, identified as approximately 0600 Dora Central, subject to later correction. Methuen occupied an hour with the customary atmospheric tests; whereafter he announced that the atmosphere was breathable with ease, not much different from Erth's; and he deployed outdoors all members of the task force, most of his officers and such other crew members as could be spared from a skeleton watch. He assigned one or two crew members to shepherd each scientist, carrying side arms or ray-muskets and watching out particularly for wild animals. He told all of them: "I suggest that you spread out in your own directions exploring this clearing for an hour or two; but I must enjoin all of you not to enter the jungle just yet." That was all right; the great clearing was enough for now.

Sari went a little distance away from the ship and squinted through dark glasses at the sun called Saiph; presently she was using a small instrument with a black disk in order to eclipse the body of the sun and eyeball the corona, incidentally picking up a screening analysis of spectrum and temperature. Geologist Peranza moved in a zigzag semi-pattern

188

holding in front of her an instrument resembling a forked water-dowser but which was in fact a device for locating near-surface bedrock strata with an additional goodie of detecting radioactivity. And so on.

Methuen and Zorbin stayed with the ship, checking her inside and out. Methuen ached, and Zorbin knew it, to be out there looking for traces of Dorita; but the captain believed her note-hint that she and Narfar had gone into the past, and he saw no way to trace *that*; he could only hope that his scientists would uncover something pertinent.

As for his lost Dorita-love, intellectually Methuen had checked that off, however his passions might continue to quiver. It was perfectly clear that she had preferred Narfar; and from his comprehension of Dorita's thrill-readiness, the captain could partially understand that. So far, so human: you won some, you lost some; and Methuen had reached the point of love-generosity where he blessed whatever would make his love happy. The trouble was, that he could not *entirely* understand her preference for Narfar, whose limitations beyond the physical were so evident. And remembering how he had been used by her on the night of their first meeting, Methuen had a strong belief that Dorita was using Narfar for something. *What* something? He had no notion—but the difficulty for his intellect, as it defended him against his emotions, was that if Dorita was using Narfar for *anything*, then Dorita did not wholly love Narfar, which left the possibilty. . . .

Besides, Dorita might be in serious trouble, somewhen in the past. But since Methuen knew nothing about backtiming, he was helpless in that direction.

Being helpless, he prayed a lot. Some of his praying had to do with a "potential threat to Erth" which, Quarfar had specified, "will depend on my interplay with a woman named Dorita."

Archaeologist Mabel Seal headed immediately for the curiously unnatural hummock, and Anthropologist Chu Huang followed her. When he came up with her, she was excitedly examining a small chair—or throne?—which, from above, had been hidden by the dirt mounds around it.

As he approached, she glanced at him, uttered "Look!" and clambered down into the shallow hole where the throne was; and she began talking rapidly, running her hands over throne contours as she spoke, "It is stone, you see?—something like alabaster—and the marks indicate that it was carved with stone tools, probably something hard like obsidian. Tell me, Huang, what do the scalloped sides of the back remind you of?"

Chu promptly responded, "The throne of Minos, Mabel."

"Precisely," the Eskimo agreed. "I can't wait to get at this chemically. Now let me show you something else, and this is weird." She pointed to a dirt pile. "What do you notice about *that?*"

With arousal, the Cathayan noticed it instantly. "That is dirt from a *new* digging!"

"That it is!" Seal gazed triumphantly up at him from down in the hole. "Something or somebody has *recently* tossed up that dirt—in fact, here way underneath is some that is still damp!"

Chu looked about him with apprehension. "It has to mean that there are humanoids hereabouts—or bear, or some other animal that can scoop-dig—"

She clambered up and stood beside him. Now they were about of a size. She announced: "Huang, we are on to something big. If there was a throne as sophisticated as this, there was a civilization. Probably the house or palace was made of wood, so it would be long gone; but if we can work out a plan for careful digging, I can detect the remnants of post holes for uprights; and there are sure to be some remaining shards of something or other, broken tools or potsherds—"

"I hate to keep mentioning this, Mabel, but we may also be on to something big *now*, not only then. What about the recent digger? First off, we have got to warn the captain."

But Seal poofed it. "Look around you, Huang! We two people have four armed guards watching in all directions! Simmer down, my boy; let's go back to the ship and get a flock of my chemistry; and *then* we'll warn the captain."

Even Ombasa was finding the humid heat operationally uncomfortable; Chu guessed that it hovered around thirty-five degrees Celsius or higher, and he imagined that Eskimo Seal along with Antarctic Green must find it intolerable. The heat did not, however, inhibit Seal's bustling; and Chu, equally curious, went along. He followed her closely as she jogged the three hundred meters back to the ship; she entered, he followed (both of them blessing the air-conditioning); rummaging in her equipment, she produced two armloads of apparatus; he collected more than half of it, recognizing some of it; she clutched the remainder and they returned outdoors (cursing the air-conditioning for the contrast it created) and jogged back to the throne-hole.

Methodically Seal applied her instrumentation, not only to the throne itself, but also to the dirt around it. Chu was able to help her a little; his anthropological discipline was necessarily allied with hers.

When all was done, Seal, still in the hole, leaned back against dirt, closed her eyes and meditated. Above, Chu squatted at hole-rim, gazing down upon her.

Said Seal, after a bit, "I'm sure you know that our latest radiocarbon techniques reduce probable time-error to one percent and permit immediate read-out of the measurements."

"Of course. But do they take account of era-to-era differences in accumulations of radiocarbon?"

"They do for Erth, but we have no data on Dora. However, making an assumption that on Dora the era variations will statistically come out like those on Erth—"

"Well?"

"My friend, the age of this throne is fifty-one thousand years, give or take five hundred or so."

"This I would have imagined."

"Further, of the dirt around the throne, the oldest layer of dirt, which had drifted up as high as the seat of the throne, is about forty-nine thousand years old."

"All right."

"But—"

"Well, Mabel?"

"Within no more than twenty-seven days of now, this throne has been sat upon by bare humanoid buttocks!"

Nocturnally patrolling the campsite, Methuen and Zorbin spied the silhouette of a seated sky-watcher. Approaching, they found without surprise that it was Sari. Inviting them to sit with her, she remarked, "Well, gentlemen—there it is." And she swept the sky with a wide-arm gesture.

There indeed it was, filling a very large space of sky: the down-tumbling mizdorf, his head burning orange-red; and above him balefully glowered blue-white Hatsya the Star of God.

Methuen murmured, "The backside of Lucifer."

Reverently she returned, "Tomorrow I will be cruising up there, out there. But tonight, here on the ground—oh, fellas, just *look!*"

27

Day Twenty-Seven

The wedding trip began in high style. The entire city, with the leaders forming the inner circle, gathered around Narfar and his bride in the central square before the palace: he naked as usual, she dressed in the togs she'd arrived here in (she'd found them and pond-washed them), a costuming which on Erth would be sturdy-utilitarian but which the Dorians regarded as goddess-festive.

Narfar and Dorita stood there in circle-center holding hands and slowly wheeling to bid *au revoir* to this quarter and that; flower petals rained upon them amid enthusiastic screaming; quite a few women fainted, and there were a number of male and female orgasms-without-contact. From the free hand of Narfar dangled two harnesses: one carried the two gadzyook pelts for Dorita, the other bore a large bag of coarse-woven vines containing relatively nonperishable rations. ("No sweat about sugar," he had advised her. "In ice country we eat plenty nael blubber.") Still another harness tightly clasped his pectorals, leaving free play for arms and wings; from this harness dangled a short rein.

When flight-moment came, Narfar raised a hand high, hushing the crowd. He went down on all fours and hung the harnesses about his neck. Dorita, who'd had some practice with this, straddled the high of his rump and bent forward to grip his shoulder-harness under his arms, hooking her feet around his thighs near the knees. Narfar stood; her hooking feet slid down to his upper calves. Narfar waved at the crowd with both arms, bawled, "We come back!" and took off into the sky.

Would they come back?

Sensitive to the limitations of his bride, Narfar selected an altitude which would give him optimum wing efficiency while not chilling his back-passenger too much. This turned out to be five hundred meters aloft, and with her clothes on she tolerated it quite well here in tropical warmth. At first she clung tightly along his back, until she began to notice that he was no longer accelerating: he had settled down to a steady wingbeat which drove them northward at a speed something like five hundred kilometers per hour. Cautiously she raised her head a little, then ducked as the headwind caught it. Speaking or even screaming to Narfar and being heard was out of the question; she mind-urged, *Can you slow way down so I can get control of this?*

Cupping wings forward, he braked too suddenly for her safety. *How this?*

Slower, please—but don't throw me.

He eased off to something like a hundred. *How this?*

Hold it there, let me try— She raised her head: not bad; about like stunt-flying an archaic open-cockpit airplane (she'd done it, too). Gradually, gripping the rein, she semi-erected herself, then fell back; she didn't dare release foot-grip on his knees; she should have designed in stirrups. . . . *Narfar, can you pull in your legs, like kneeling?* He did so, and it drew her up to a full sitting position; she dared lean back on the rein, breasting the wind. *That very good,* she told him.

He responded testily: *This too slow. You have to stop for sleep some time. Take us many days, we run out of food.*

All right. Try speeding it up, very slowly.

How speed slow? Speed quick!

I mean, like flying a little quicker, then a little quicker, then—

That enough; I got. You tell when too quick. You maybe fall off, you mind-shout, I zip down and catch.

He accelerated gradually until she felt that she had reached her speed of maximum tolerance. *That it, Narfar! Stay there!*

That better, he mind-sighed, relieved. *Now we go almost as quick as before. We get there in three days now, if you not tired.*

By degrees, she grew accustomed to the steady headwind; he was not accelerating, but winging at an invariant speed a bit over three hundred. Calculation told her his plan: ten flying hours per day for three days, giving her plenty of resting time. This would allow them to make stops; and they would be needed, if only because of leg-and-foot cramps.

Could she ease the progress of that cramping? With care, she tried a few ploys: released one foot, let it hang (it was blown backward); reclaimed his leg with that foot, released the other; clung with both feet and released a hand, letting it swing; switched to the other hand. All went well: this was beginning to be high fun! Recalling his promise to catch her if she fell, she mind-shouted: *Look, Narfar! no hands!* and released the rein entirely, clinging with feet only, swaying like a bareback horsewoman at gallop.

You getting good, he told her laconically. *But watch out. Might not hear mind-scream.*

She was more prudent after that; nevertheless she found many ways of resting herself in flight. Perhaps tomorrow she would urge him into some aerobatics.

The new ease allowed her to take interest in the swift-passing below-scenery. They had been a couple of hours en route, and still the terrain was generally flat and bejungled. Weird carnivores and herbivores burst out of jungle and vanished behind them, often the one chasing the other. It was positively criminal for them to move so rapidly when instead they could be exploring; but when she tested Narfar's mind on this, responded: *We come back slower, but right now we have place to go. Wedding trip, remember?* Her husband's mind might not be diversified, but it was strong all right: it locked onto whatever occupied it at the moment, and for that time there was nothing else for him.

And just now, that was a good thing for Dorita. The route was beguiling—but the biggest thing in her life was *that goal*.

Actually it was five hours before she had to call for a rest stop. Her muscles might have held out longer; her bladder could not. Her steed spied a good place and spiraled downward; fifty meters above grass, he came to a dead halt in midair and helicoptered them to the ground, landing on hands and knees for their convenience. She dismounted. He commanded: "Wait there!" and went over to the bushes and vanished therein. He returned almost immediately: "That okay for your private place, no snakes."

She queried: "How about—" She wanted to ask "—spiders?" but it came over her that she had never heard the

194

word in his tongue—nor, for that matter, had she seen a spider on Dora. Her urgency was too great for playing with this idea: she retired into the copse. Narfar had always respected her wish for privacy with nature's urgings; and she had found that this custom was general among Dorians, except for her at first when her companions had taken her to the midden because of her weakness. She hadn't learned whether it was a matter of nicety or a question of magic. For primitives, an enemy who found your leavings could use them to work magical injury upon you.

When she returned to the clearing, Narfar was returning also, from another copse, both hands loaded with bananas. He queried: "We eat now?"

Over lunch, he reminded her: "Where we stop tonight, a lot cooler, maybe no food; we save food we brought for that. Next night, cold; I catch birds, we eat while they still warm. Next night, very cold, deep ice country; I catch nael, we eat blubber while it still warm. Dorita, you warm while we fly? You want one gadzyook pelt now?"

Having munched and swallowed a juicy mouthful of banana, she told him that if she should grow too cold, they could stop while she got out a fur from the pouch. Then she mind-said, quite casually: *Lots of snakes and bugs on Dora. No spiders on Dora?*

It did something quite terrible to Narfar. He quivered all over, dropped his banana, leaped to his feet with face contorted in the fury of hatred, taut-stretched both arms and wings, menaced her with clawed hands. She crouched away from him. His menace eased off, he stood trembling, he commanded in a mind-quaver: *Dorita you not say that word again you not say that word—*

Quickly she said, "Be easy, Narfar, I not say that word."

The transition from tropical to temperate was rather abrupt; and the effect on Dorita, high-speed-flying at five hundred meters, was swift-chilling. *Need fur*, she mind-gasped. Narfar landed as quickly as he could without endangering her, and tenderly wrapped her in one of the gadzyook pelts; the legs remained on the pelts, and the paws had been adapted as hand and foot mittens. Then they lofted and went back at it. The pelt's warmth was almost absolute, She discovered that in this latitude it was too much, so she freed hands and feet from the mittens; thanks to a couple of clever little bone safety pins, she was able to wear the fur as a flamboyant flying cloak, with her arms and legs bare of it (although she wore long trousers), and yet with comfort across her chest and over her shoulders.

By late afternoon, the rolling landscape below so much resembled the forests and meadows of her homeland that it almost made her homesick. They landed beside a tree-and-meadow-bordered lakelet with no sign of habitation anywhere. Narfar took off into sky after food, while Dorita discarded the fur and went to work weaving a bower for rain-shelter (the sky threatened) or anyhow against dew. Narfar returned with five wild ducks, their necks already wrung; she assumed that he had asked them and they had given adoring permission.

Selecting one for herself, she began plucking it (not easy when raw and unsinged), while Narfar tore into his unplucked four and devoured them spitting-out feathers. Even Dorita didn't pluck thoroughly, there was no time, the birds would be no good eaten cold; she too had some feathers to spit, but she ate well, having grown used to raw meat. Narfar offered her what was left of his last duck, and she accepted and finished it while he cracked and sucked bones. Watching each other eat raw meat aroused them sexually; and soon they were at it, grease and all.

A couple of hours later, with the sun already set, they skinny-dipped in the shallow cold pond and dried each other with her fur coat. "You wear tomorrow morning," he suggested. "It get dry in sky real quick."

They lay in their bower, he cradling her head on his chest. He had ripped up two rich turfs for pillows (luckily they contained no ants); and they pillow-talked with their minds, for it didn't seem a time to make noises.

After a while he brought the talking around to spiders. She could tell that he had resolved the matter in his mind, he had simply conquered it, and now he wanted to talk about it—but not too much.

He told her: *When I first come to Erth, I make good world for all beasts. All but spiders. I not like spiders, they got eight legs and eight eyes, that bad number, I like two and four and six better. They always hurting nice beasts, especially bugs. I like all bugs, they nice and funny, but spiders make web traps for bugs and suck out juices, it not fair.*

*Some spiders worse, kill mice, hide in bananas, bite monkeys
and people. Besides, spiders not do what I tell them, they not
like me. I decide I better get rid of all spiders.*

*But Quarfar stop me, he a big nuisance, he say spiders as
good as bugs, keep spiders but just make people stronger. I
let him have his way because he smarter. So he go get fire
and bring it to people, and everything go wrong after that.*

*Then I leave Erth and come to Dora. I find two evils here:
spiders and funny children. I decide I have to make Dora
good for people and beasts too, not just for beasts. But I keep
out fire, because Quarfar ruin Erth with fire. I keep out
metal, because Quarfar ruin Erth with metal. And I get rid of
the two evils—spiders and funny children. So no spiders here.
And when a funny child show up, I get rid of that one too.*

She did not have to ask what he meant by funny children:
he meant people like herself, before he had fixed her. Instead
she queried, feeling that she was close to the major secret of
Dora: *How you get rid of spiders and funny children?*

She could feel his mind stiffen. He told her peremptorily:
You keep away from that question.

But then, feeling guilty, he took the edge off his sharpness
with body-love—and during lulls she reflected that she didn't
really need his answer, she thought she knew what it was. But
the now-suspected coupling of funny children with spiders *in
that box* introduced a new hazard into her grand adventure.

28

Day Twenty-Seven and Twenty-Eight

The equatorial site, despite the humid heat, was as good as
any for most of the task force. Stratogeologist Peranza was
making test borings and sonar seismic analyses; Zoologist
Hoek, Botanist Farouki and Microbiologist Manumuko
prowled, with guards, the nearby jungle; Linguist Alexandrovna grumped and theorized.

For Archaeologist Seal, Anthropologist Chu and Psychobiologist Ombasa, it was the best of all possible sites. They

knew from Dorita's reporting of Quarfar that Narfar's culture had been sited in this tropical belt; and right at this fortuitous place, already they had found Narfar's throne and were (with crew-aid and Seal's archaeo-sensitive rekamatic equipment) cautiously extending the scope of the dig.

Those who found the site unfruitful could rove as they might in high-speed vehicles. Astrophysicist Sari was provided with an aerospace scouter in which she could take microsensors above the atmosphere. Glaciologist Green had an aeroscouter and was off reconnoitering southern ice.

Methuen and Zorbin had little to do; and that was particularly bad for Methuen, as Zorbin understood. The exec could almost read his captain's thoughts: *Right here is where Narfar would have brought her . . . She wouldn't have moved spatially from this area, she'd have moved temporally only . . . How far back? Obviously as far back as the origin of Comet Gladys . . . Narfar is reassuming rule of his people, perhaps he is festively marrying Dorita* (acute jealousy twinge, quickly fought down because it was selfish) *. . . Right here! but not here-now, rather here-then . . . Inaccessible, with all the modernities of advanced science: intangible, untouchable, but right here somewhen . . .* Just as galling as his ultimately frustrated Dorita-urge was his inability to really comprehend the time-cause of his frustration, despite Ombasa's theorizing; and the human *coup de laideur* was the impossibility of *doing* anything about it.

Compounding the irony: if Dorita had been here, *she* could have helped him—but if she had been here, he would not have been needing her help.

Abandoning that line of thought, he turned to present practicalities—and hazards, acutely remembering his conversation with Ombasa.

After outdoor camp-supper, those who were on hand met for conference aboard ship. (They weren't sleeping outdoors in the tents they'd brought, because of problems with insects and snakes.) Absent were star-scouting Sari and glacier-scouting Green. Of the eight present, all were enthusiastic about beginning progress, with the exception of Olga who was morose because she had found nothing resembling language to work on.

Seal bubbled about more discoveries in chemical analysis of the throne. Then she sprang her surprise bomb. The extended excavations had already uncovered three post-holes in a beginning arc which might indicate the walls of a palace; the dirt in one of these post-holes contained molecules which, judging by their species distribution, had once been wood; while another hole—this was the grisly part of her bomb—contained a few bones which definitely had to be those of a small humanoid infant. On this revelation, she passed the ball to the anthropologist.

Chu responded with studious graveness; and he specified that his comments were inductive hypotheses, not deductive theorems. First, the combination of a throne and post-holes did in his opinion suggest a palace, especially since the theoretically extended circle of the already-discovered arc would be quite large, say thirty meters in diameter, and the throne would constitute roughly circle-center. It was impossible yet to infer the construction of the palace in a positive way, but a preliminary guess might be that the walls were woven withes and the roof, if any, was thatch. Here Seal interposed that the sizes of the post-holes indicated tall heavy posts, which seemed to mean outer walls and not room-dividers. Chu agreed, but added that because of the sophisticated throne and the size of the outer walls, there probably had been rooms for one or another purpose of privacy or storage or other convenience, with the throne centered in the largest room. He pointed out that even in Achaean times on Erth, the central hall of a king's palace had not often exceeded two hundred square meters, and there would be plenty of room for such a hall in a palace whose area would have exceeded seven hundred square meters.

Chu now commented on the evidence of infant burial beneath a post. "The practice of sacrificing an infant to the god or gods by placing him dead or alive beneath a temple post is well known on Erth, an instance being on primitive Tahiti. But one does not normally find thrones in temples. One has to judge, in a preliminary way, that this structure was *both* a palace *and* a temple, and that the god was the king. This king presided over a culture which was full of anomalies from our point of view, being primitive enough to build even its temple-palace of forest materials, yet sophisticated enough to design a stone throne of considerable artistry, yet primitive enough to carve the throne with hard stone tools and not with metal, yet sophisticated enough to carve so intricate a throne with stone tools.

199

"And my colleague from Eskimoland has pointed out to me a remarkable absence which she did not mention; she will forgive me for introducing it. So far in the dig, we have discovered *no evidence of fire!* Now this is a total anomaly, in terms of what we know not only from Erth but also from other planets. It is almost perfectly safe to say, that if there is a palace, then there is a hearth; or if there is a temple, then there is a ceremonial hearth; or, for that matter, if there is a once-inhabited paleolithic cave, there are fire-chars—even in the tropics, at least for cooking purposes, with any creature much later than Australopithecus. But we have excavated this palace from the throne to the outer wall in an area equal to a radian, roughly sixteen percent of the total palace area; and we have found no ashes, no chars. Mabel Seal assures me that even wood ashes have an enormous life, that they have been discovered from eras far older than this one. So then— unless further excavation proves us wrong—we are talking about an anomalous pre-civilization which had, not only no metal, but also *no fire!*

"I yield to others."

Olga was displaying mild interest for the first time in two days. "There is a faint possibility," she growled, "that the designs on the throne could constitute a primitive form of writing." Seal cordially invited her to the dig at her convenience. "Tomorrow," asserted Olga, and she finger-drummed the table, frowning ferociously.

Methuen had been looking from one speaker to another, courteously attentive always; but Zorbin could see that the captain was worried. Everyone was in silent thought after Olga's insertion; presently they were all looking at their chairman. It was Chu who apprehended what Zorbin sensed; and he remarked, "I suspect that the captain has something to contribute." Zorbin looked at Chu with gratitude; Chu caught the look and nodded.

Said Methuen, talking slowly, "Your chairman has been delinquent, in that he did not report to you a piece of information which our telepathic interpreter Dorita Lanceo elicited from Quarfar. Independently, you have now confirmed this information. Quarfar said that Narfar had excluded fire from his Dora culture—and that he had also excluded metals."

Silence again. Then Seal, quietly: "Oboy."

"Right," Methuen agreed. "But there is more on my mind;

and please be advised that your chairman knows he is going way out.

"I am facing a group of scientists who are eminent in eight disciplines. The following is a sober question. Other than Dr. Ombasa—what does any of you know about *time-paradox*?"

The silence that followed Methuen's question was a jolted one. All these scientists had learned to respect their chairman as a realistic pro in his own field which happened to make sophisticated applied use of several of their disciplines. When such a man hit them with a query about time-paradox, he just possibly might be mad, but he certainly wasn't joking, and they'd better explore the matter seriously pending establishment of unexpected insanity. Further, seven of the eight were drawing inferences from the discussion-exclusion of Ombasa who had adopted an attitude of close attention.

Chu was the one who responded first. "I don't know of any actual time-invasions, but I happen to like a select group of science fictioneers, and many of them write about such invasions. A time-paradox is a situation in which a person from the present invades the past, changes something in the past, and thereby alters the entire course of temporal evolution, so that the present suddenly becomes different from what it has been. Is that how you understand it, Mr. Chairman?"

"Precisely," said Methuen, and reflected. They waited, glancing at Ombasa's poker face.

The captain said, very low, "When Dorita departed, she left me a note stating that she was leaving with Narfar, and that they would not be on Erth or, as she stated, quote, 'anywhere else in this time-slot,' unquote.

"We know from Quarfar that this very planet Dora was Narfar's home, that Narfar was in some sense king of it. Dr. Sari confirmed that Saiph, the sun of this planet, was the sun of Quarfar's Dora; and she established also that Saiph lies directly on the five-forty-six gradient. This gradient could conceivably have been established by Narfar on his first flight from Erth to Dora much more than fifty thousand years ago—long before the origin of Comet Gladys.

"Let me put this all together. I think—and I believe that I think with good reason—that Dorita and Narfar followed the five-forty-six gradient to Dora. And I think that Dorita somehow took Narfar time-traveling back to the era when he de-

201

parted Dora on the comet. If time-travel is a possibility, I would not put this ability past Dorita."

He paused for a look-around. All were staring at him; Olga was gaping; Chu was quizzical; Ombasa seemed faintly alarmed—possibly because he now understood that the captain had questioned him for practical reasons.

Methuen put it to them. "Tell me, gentlepeople of science—*if* time travel is a possibility, and *if* Dorita and Narfar did indeed bring it off—*could they possibly* have discovered Narfar's old era still alive and able to respond again to his renewed leadership?"

Now all of them were frowning down.

Chu said presently, "It does not seem to me a possibility. Either past eras no longer exist except in their present vestiges, or else they exist perpetually frozen as they were and incapable of being revitalized. That is what my logic tells me. But I do regret the absence of Dr. Sari from this discussion." Some of the others nodded.

"Unfortunately," Methuen rejoined, "she is not here. And—I have to tell you this—I am seeing a possibility of hazard for us, a hazard which may materialize before Dr. Sari returns for consultation."

Chu anticipated him with silky precision. "Perhaps I see this hazard. We are camped here on a Dora which has moved along through time many millennia since the comet-departure of Narfar; and obviously civilization and perhaps all human life has ceased to exist here. But if you are right, Captain, and if Narfar with Dorita *has* returned to his era, why then his germinal civilization *did* or *now will have* continued to flourish in its era, and—" he paused, raised eyebrows, waved a hand, "—somebody please take it from there."

Blandly Ombasa reentered: "In such a case, perhaps, the culture which *had* died will now *not* have died. Captain, I see your premonition of hazard. You are thinking that perhaps we will go to sleep tonight in this jungle desolation, and will awaken tomorrow suddenly surrounded by Narfar's people, his cultural descendants and perhaps his blood descendants, all abruptly entering into life tomorrow as a chain consequence of the time-paradox precipitated by Dorita and Narfar."

Agitated, Peranza broke in. "If that is the form of your problem, Captain, how can it possibly be a problem for us today? Even granting the proposition, if Narfar's era were fifty thousand years back, wouldn't it take fifty thousand years for the consequences of such a paradox to reach the present?"

Methuen demanded, "Would it, Doctor? You tell me."

Olga snarled. "Peranza, Peranza, where did you study logic? That's an infinite regression! If it takes x years for Narfar's culture to progress from x years ago to today, then today will no longer be in the present, but the present will have gone on another x years meanwhile, and the culture will still be x years in the past! That would create problems only for archaeologists and not for any then-current culture—and certainly not for us here now! Captain Methuen, I'm not competent to say whether your fear has any substance, but I will say this: in my opinion, *if* such a time-paradox can occur and has occurred, and *if* it has the potential of creating consequences which will indeed break through eventually to change some present, then I do not know how to calculate the velocity of such changes, and I would imagine that they could make themselves manifest just any time at all."

Methuen said, "Thank you, Doctor. You have expressed the basis of my apprehension, and you echo certain speculations by Dr. Ombasa. My position is, that the situation may not create a problem for us, but then again it may; and we need to be on the lookout."

Manumuto queried: "As our leader, Captain, do you have any suggestions, recommendations or orders?"

"Commander Zorbin has the security con," Methuen asserted. "May we hear from you, Commander?"

Zorbin said promptly, "First, I have extended ship-security sensors to a range of five hundred kilometers in every direction. They are programmed to warn us of any creature having humanoid cephalic rhythms, even if such rhythms are drastically different from our own.

"Second, I recommend that all of us enter the ship daily at sunset, or on sunless days when the ship sounds a siren indicating that light has dropped below sunset level. The siren might also be an emergency return signal. This recommendation adds that none of us should leave the ship until a suitable bell signals that outside light has risen above sunrise level.

"Third, I recommend that we immediately make radio contact with Dr. Sari and Dr. Green, who are distant on detached duty. We should advise them to be on the lookout for humanoids, to alert us when humanoids are first observed, and to drop everything else in order to observe such humanoids from the air and report continuously. When they return to the ship, they are to exercise caution, signaling all the way, and waiting for our reentry instructions. Finally, we should advise them to run for the ship at the first sign of aircraft; we will have to deal with that sort of problem from here.

"Fourth, I recommend that the entire crew be placed on standby security duty. And this will mean, of course, that crew assistance for your projects will become somewhat limited and conditional, subject to the orders of myself or the captain.

"I await your instructions."

Profound mood of brown.

Said Chu, with unusual heaviness: "Captain Methuen, you are the captain. I regret such measures, but I see the point. Let me be the one to mention to my colleagues that as captain you have authority to override us on this matter anyway. After that remark, I for one give you my vote of confidence."

Sensors, detecting above-sunrise light-level outdoors, automatically tripped the sunrise bell aboard ship. The bell was virtually unheard, however, because a dozen other sensors had triggered an alarm-horn warning that humanoid creatures were present close to the ship. And two startled human sentries, mounting duty on a small external submarine-type deck atop the broadest beam of the ship (which lay horizontally on the grass) realized simultaneously with the warning horn and the sunrise bell that a city had materialized all around them.

The entire crew, male and female, many still in pajamas or undershorts, burst like startled hornets from their cabins and barracks and moved swiftly to beef up the second watch at action stations. Uniformed Zorbin, currently pulling duty in command of the second watch, hurried up to the sentry deck; pajama'd Methuen almost immediately joined him, followed by muumuu'd Olga and kimona'd Chu and pajama'd Seal and the other scientists on board.

It was a city of adobe houses having thatched roofs right out of modern Anglia or Norska. It extended as far as they could see in every direction—except in one direction, the quarter where the throne had been discovered; and there the city beyond was hidden by the mighty bulk of a circular adobe palace which rose in stepped-back tier upon tier to a height of seven stories and whose ground-diameter must have been at least a hundred meters.

Chu murmured, low but clearly audible in the hush: "Captain, you were right again. Madam Archaeologist, pray consider the modern outcome of the rooted-out vestiges which you exposed there only two days ago." Ombasa was reflecting that if this paradox had first been generated on the day when Dorita disappeared, he had his first verifiable measure of chain-consequence velocity: fifty thousand years in a mere twenty-eight days.

Methuen snapped, "Mr. Zorbin, our alarm horns will have aroused the people in that city. Kindly activate measures of passive defense, but do not attempt any aggressive activity until one of us two is certain that we are under attack which can do damage."

Spear-armed men were appearing in the city streets. . . .

29

Day Twenty-Eight

The humanoids were clustering round the *Farragut*, peering upward toward the people atop her on the observation deck. Someone handed Methuen his holographic binoculars (ten-power, self-focusing); he studied man after man, all breechclouted and otherwise naked; then he whistled and passed the glasses to Olga to his left. She examined two or three men, whistled low, passed the glasses along, and observed to the captain, "It's remarkable how much they resemble the holographs I saw of that Narfar creature, except for their winglessness and their blue-green skin color. I would call them splendid living examples of Homo neanderthalensis, except that the species pooped-out on Erth about sixty millennia ago."

Chu, who was next to her and had just relinquished the glasses to Seal, added, "Also, except that their city is more sophisticated than anything Neanderthal could have built."

"Not necessarily," Olga countered. "I've gathered that Neanderthal may have been natively as intelligent as Homo sapiens, just constructed differently and perhaps lacking our ambition and imagination. Captain, if you let me go down, I can learn to speak with them, but I do have to hear and record their talking—"

"You may have that learning already," suggested Methuen.

"I may? How? Oh—you mean, if they speak the language of Quarfar and Narfar? But that's impossible!"

"Why?"

Seal contributed: "I know of a modern Tellene who went on a dig as a laborer. He happened to be the one to unerth a tablet dating from the tenth century BC; and although he was ill-educated, he was able to read the most ancient Tellene inscription quite easily."

Olga expostulated: "But that was written language! Without writing, or even *with* writing, language evolves, is distorted, pronunciations change—" She fisted her forehead: "Now why am I talking like this? It might be basically the same language, and I can cut through the evolved variations—"

Methuen told her, "If you will go to the bridge and see Zorbin, you'll find that he has a crew watching and listening and reporting from a level near the ground, using viewports and receptors, of course. See what you can do with what you hear; the crew chief may even be able to select a particular man for you to hear while fading out the other voices."

And as Olga disappeared below, he turned to the others on deck. "Gentlepeople, pray excuse me. All of you are enjoined to remain aboard ship for the time being. As soon as Dr. Alexandrovna succeeds or fails, I will try to communicate with these people."

Methuen went to the observation room which was located deep amidships, not at either ship-flank, but centrally. Viewscreens were arrayed to simulate ship-shape; they worked rekamatically like picture windows, revealing all that was occurring on the ground forward, aft and on both flanks. The intricate sound-pickups caused the small room to reverberate with noisy babel which had been tuned down somewhat so the crew would not go mad.

Olga entered, squired by the crew-chief whom Zorbin had summoned to the bridge as her attendant; she carried the little apparatus that she had used with Quarfar. After one

206

cool nod at Methuen, she stationed herself at room-center and peered first at one quarter and then at another. She had a way of peering with concentration for several seconds in one tight direction, then shifting her head and eyes a bit to peer for several seconds at a nearby quarter; Methuen suspected that she was picking out individuals, trying to read lips while ear-filtering each person's contribution to the sound-confusion.

Presently she selected one group of three men who stood talking intently to each other, glancing frequently at the ship but (unlike most others) not shouting at the ship; these three men wore animal-pelt cloaks. She said to the chief: "I think those are leaders. Can you give me a tight sound-focus on that one group and fade the others down?"

The chief nodded and issued an order, pointing. The general babel quieted, and three easily discriminable voices came in loud and clear. As anticipated, it was a high-pitched twittering.

Olga was recording the voices; without replaying the flake, her face transmuted itself into an attitude of astonishment. She looked at Methuen: "Captain, I *can* understand them, it *is* the language of Quarfar and Narfar! And you know, it isn't so terribly distorted, at that!"

Methuen queried: "So what are they saying?"

"One of them thinks they ought to attack our ship. Another is counseling patience, he says let's wait and see what the beings inside will do. The third is reminding them that the god has been advised and will be coming, the god should make the decision."

"That would be the king," remarked Chu, who had followed Methuen. "Do you suppose those three men are his top-kicks?"

"I think so," Methuen commented, gazing at them. "Their authority and self-control are certainly the highest among that crowd . . . Look there!"

A crowd-jostling had commenced in a quarter behind the three leaders; it developed into a thrusting-through and a making-way; and gradually the babel died into silence. Those immediately behind the leaders parted; two men appeared thrusting them apart with spears which appeared to be stone-beaked. Behind them, with dignity, walked up to the three leaders a man who was the tallest among them—and he was

207

not blue-green, but yellow-green—and his head-and-body hair was orange-red—and folded on his back were batwings!

Somebody yelled: "NARFAR!" The yell was taken up, the multitudinously repeated name reverberated in the chamber, while all the men including the three leaders fell to their knees. Narfar stood beaming, slowly rotating to wave at all the men; and as hush returned, he folded arms and stared up at the bulk of the *Farragut*.

Methuen ejaculated: "The original Narfar, I am certain! Well, I'll be—"

Narfar was conversing earnestly with his three leaders, now on their feet. Two finally nodded; a third spread hands. Turning to the ship-flank, Narfar spread wings wide, cupped hands around mouth, and bawled: "You guys come out! We talk! You not hurt us, we not hurt you!"

All members of the task force were now aboard ship, Sari and Green having caused some native consternation by homing-in this morning; they had been pre-briefed by radio.

Methuen called a conference for the purpose of designating membership of the first party to visit King or God Narfar in his palace. Zorbin spoke up more quickly than his wont, remarking that a representative of ship's command would have to be protocol leader of the visitation party; the hazard of the assignment was obvious, and he felt strongly that he (Zorbin) should lead the party, leaving the captain aboard ship to deal with whatever might arise. Methuen responded, "Commander Zorbin might perhaps prove a better leader than I will be, but leadership of this party is my job. The executive officer will remain aboard ship to deal with whatever may arise." That settled that.

In the end, it was agreed that Methuen should be accompanied by Alexandrovna for language, Chu for anthropological appraisal, and Seal for her own archaeological edification. By now, Olga was able to offer each member of the party a brand new goodie: a portable two-way translator, to be hung about the neck so that it would dangle on the chest with leads to the ears and throat; the translators, programmed in terms of the word-and-phrase correspondences elicited by Olga and her computer with Quarfar and modulated this morning, would make communication two-ways direct, and would continuously improve their services by what they would be learning as communication proceeded.

208

The party, Methuen insisted, must have no visible guards: hat would only inflame their hosts, and the party could be :ept under protective surveillance by ship's instruments.

Emerging from the ship's portside crewdeck hatch onto the op platform of a ship-activated transparent airlift shaft ten neters high, the party found themselves awaited at airlift-foot y a raggedly drawn up honor group consisting of the three officers, a number of breechclouted men, and a number of aked women. Methuen and his three colleagues dropped in he shaft; and instantly upon their emergence from its foot, he native women produced an assortment of musical instruments, drums and rattles and pipes, and set up a caterwauling hat troubled the Erth folk because they could discern no hythmic or harmonic system in it. Nevertheless, it was obviously a welcome.

The leaders came forward to greet them. The number-one eader, who was grizzzled, asserted (and it came through in hopped Anglian via the chest-interpreters): "My name 3rozny. Welcome. You come with me to Narfar." Methuen eplied in his normal Anglian, having been assured by Olga hat his interpreter was programmed to trim off decoration nd color words which would confuse the natives: "My name s Methuen. We are pleased by your welcome. We come eace. Pray take us to Narfar."

The god-king, naked and unadorned as usual, sat upon his hrone, to receive them; but these were unusual visitors, and e made no effort to impress them with his great dignity or to umble them. Instead, he stood with extended arms and vings as soon as they entered his hall (which was larger in his modern palace, although the throne was the same hrone). Brozny, arraying the four visitors before the god, vhispered to Methuen, "Be yourself with Narfar."

Standing at officer-loose ease, Methuen addressed the king. Great Narfar, my name is Methuen, I represent the planet Erth. These are my friends Alexandrovna, Seal, and Chu. We re proud to be received by you."

Broad-grinning, Narfar yipped: "Welcome!" He advanced pon Methuen, whom he overtowered by quite a few centimeters, clasped the captain in both arms, and kissed juicy macks upon both Methuen's cheeks. He then did the same to

Olga, Chu and Seal. Olga took it grudgingly, Huang stoically
Mabel with wide eyes.

Stepping back, Narfar told the four of them: "Erth grea
planet. We glad you come. We drink big now. Then we ea
big. Then we talk big."

They managed to get back to the ship by 1900 dinner time
It hadn't been easy to break from ultra-hospitable Narfar. A
lunch (if you could call it that), their winged host ha
poured some kind of sweet ferment out of gourds down thei
gullets until they were bug-eyed (was it mixed juices o
pineapple and banana?); whereafter he had stuffed them wit
course after course of fruit and fish and vegetables and pork
meat and sweets, until, eating everything out of politeness
their bug-eyes were glazed. Narfar then took them on a walk
ing tour of the city, fully two miles of it, difficult even fo
these exercise-hardened people with their bellies the way the
were. As a grand finale, somewhere near the outskirts, Narfa
had seized Methuen under one arm and Olga under the othe
and wing-flown them back to the palace, returning to taxi i
Chu and Seal.

By then it was 1700; and Narfar, squinting at the wester
ing sun, declared that it was happy hour. They lounged on
palace patio, sipping an entirely different sort of fermente
drink (dark unstrained, uncooked barley-beer?) and talking
talking.

Narfar urged them to stay overnight in his palace
Methuen, seeing desperation in his companions' eyes, tol
Narfar that the night air of Dora was poisonous to them, tha
as a matter of health they must always pass nights aboar
their ship.

Narfar looked puzzled. "That funny. Night air on Dor
not poison to Dorita."

Inwardly agitated, Methuen leaned forward: "What abou
Dorita? Is she alive?"

"Oh, no. Dorita die many many lifetimes ago. But she no
die of night air. She die old woman. Narfar never get old
that bad some ways, good some ways. Know many men an
women, all die, hate that, but good when they bad. But neve
any woman like Dorita! Anyhow, you see, night air not poi
son. So why you not stay here tonight?"

Leaning back, Methuen closed his eyes. "We have impo
tant business on the ship tonight."

210

"Oh, well. Why you not say that first time? You better not drink any more, bad for business. You better go to ship now. You welcome here, you go where you want, do your what-you-call study stuff."

It was precious little dinner that was eaten by the four members of the diplomatic mission, while the other scientists and ship's officers were poking down great hot gobbets of steak sliced off some sort of wild ungulate shot two days before. And when after-dinner drinks were passed, the four diplomats limited themselves to rehydrated small beer or Vichy fizz. (Between stars, some of the raw space for fuel could be diverted to synthesize hydrogen and oxygen and from them water.)

The after-dinner conference was prolonged. Its first two hours were devoted to the diplomatic mission. Methuen gave them an overview of the experience and drew some chuckles with his description of Narfar's potlatch-type hospitality, and it went into open laughter as he described the two-by-two flight back to the palace (Olga was grinning small, Chu was grinning large, Seal was convulsed). It quieted some when Methuen assured them: "I see every reason to believe that we can move along peaceably with our mission. Narfar has given us carte blanche, and I trust him—except that he is impulsive and could change quickly. It behooves all of us to be most courteous to all his people. Dr. Alexandrovna, are there any more of those chest interpreter gadgets?"

She replied: "I have eleven, and I have already programmed six."

"Can our technicians make more?"

"I can give them specs and diagrams."

"Please push ahead with that. I desire that as soon as possible, every scientist or crew-leader who works outside on the ground will be wearing one at all times and will make full use of it for friendly communication. Let me insert here warm commendation for the services of our linguist who perhaps will have some comments later. Just now I would like Dr. Chu and Dr. Seal to share with us their anthropological-archaeological impressions—"

It went on like that. After Olga had finished the diplomatic team report with some comments on the entailed linguistics, the captain turned to others. There were openly ecstatic comments from Llana Green, who had been touring the south po-

211

lar ice fields and was eager to survey the northern ones
before zeroing in on detail work; conservatively sub-ecstatic
remarks from Sita Sari whose astronomical experiences aloft
had been mostly as predicted but with some remarkable surprises awaiting study; laconic impressions from Hoek who, in
his jungle-prowling, had narrowly evaded a carnivore which
looked like a cross between a bear and a werewolf; and so
on. . . .

The conference broke at 2311; and all of them went to
their rooms to taper off and sleep, with the exception of the
captain and the exec who visited the bridge first. Tonight,
Zorbin was off duty from 2400 until noon, with a trusted
lieutenant having the con during those watches. The two top
officers exchanged a few words with the lieutenant who had
already appeared on the bridge; then Methuen and Zorbin
visited a little bar behind the bridge, a sanctum consecrated
to officers going off bridge duty. Methuen had a sipping
whiskey; Zorbin, being on duty another half-hour, a Coke (he
would cognac-sweeten another Coke at 0000.1 before sacking
out.)

Toward the end of it, as Methuen was preparing to go to
their joint cabin, Zorbin remarked, "At least, B.J., we've had
our time-paradox. So I guess now we can rest easy on that
score."

Frowning, Methuen stood; frowning, he moved to the
hatch; there he turned and said, "I wouldn't be too sure
about that, Friend Saul. Keep your security alert undiminished."

30

Days Twenty-Nine to Thirty

Swaddled in both gadzyook furs, Dorita clung tight to the
reins and leg-hugged the naked flanks of Narfar, who seemed
impervious to cold. They were north of the arctic circle. There
would be no midnight sun, since the north-south axis of Dora
kept itself erected tangentially to the arc of the Saiph star

surface; nevertheless, northern lights played even by daylight. Narfar was flying slowly at an altitude no higher than five hundred meters, which kept them far below most of the snow-capped peaks, many of which reared their bulks three or four thousand meters aloft.

It was a fair day. They flew in full sunlight (although the sun stayed far below zenith southward) except when white clouds shadowed them; sky blue matched sea blue, with scattered white cloud-flecks counterpointing tiny ice floes in the sea beneath. Her face was cold, particularly her nose-tip, and the cold started tears which froze quickly; she did not care, so exalted she was; holding the rein with one mittened hand, she pressed the other mittened hand over her nose and mouth and peered above it at sublime frozen eternity.

Narfar thoughtspoke: *We go high now, you see big glacier, then we come down.* Up he went indeed, climbing another two thousand meters where the air was so thin that she breath-gasped; although an occasional pinnacle still sneered down upon them, Dorita could now look down and survey a solid ice field four thousand kilometers wide in all directions, breaking into ice-fingers which probed downward from the main mass through mountain valleys until they thrust themselves into the sea, the fingertips of ice flaking off into iceberg calves. Narfar had no detectable thoughts about the ice, except that it was there, a fundamental condition of the northland. Dorita knew from high-school geology that the ice could easily be five kilometers deep at ice-field center; and she strongly suspected that a volcanic eruption beneath the ice field might well have been the origin of Comet Gladys which had brought Quarfar and Narfar to Erth.

More importantly, the mental sensors of Dorita, telekinetically sweeping the ice, told her more and more strongly that indeed the object of her highest desire was here somewhere. . . .

We go down now, thought-gruffed Narfar; *too cold for you up here. Hang on.* And he downswooped.

Nearly at water-surface, they came in on a mighty glacial face; and here Narfar hovered, drifting back and forth for his ride's pleasure. With the headwind gone, she could unmask her face and shed her mittens; and after awhile she was able to unclasp the front of her outer pelt, so temperate the sunny weather seemed when the wind was still.

She brooded before the glacier, almost worshipful, under-going an experience entirely new for Dorita: pure apprecia-tion of natural magnificence unrelated to any goal that she might be pursuing. And for this while, astonishingly, it was enough! The hard face of the glacier rose more than thirty meters above the water; or perhaps, rather than a face, it should be called a forehead, with all the rest of the face from the eyes down to the chin submerged. Two widely spaced apart ice caverns at water level might be brows for sub-merged eyes; above them, the forehead was randomly smooth-ly incised as though by a dull flintstone chisel where great masses of ice had yielded to gravity and broken away smash-ing down into the water to become icebergs. Such calves were being born while she watched—calves, indeed! They were rather goddesses being spawned out of the forehead of the glacial Zeus! And as though he were gelid-horrified at his own forehead-calving, the hair of this god stood atop the forehead in erect ice gouts which were the fore-edges of sur-face-crevassing. Narfar rose a bit higher to show her the top surface of the glacier winding back into mountains: if this was the cranium of the ice god, it was hoar except for three streaks of black, two at the sides and one in the middle; and these were moraines of rock dust which the ice had ground out of the mountains.

It was coming into Dorita that Narfar was doing this lei-surely glacier-cruising for her pleasure. *For her pleasure* Narfar was being *generous*—he was *giving!* And what was Dorita giving to Narfar? Nothing but her body, which was little enough for a god who could enjoy any body he might choose. And what was Dorita *going* to give to Narfar, in the process of using him for her highest desire? *Trouble!*

Momentarily guilt-anguished, she made such restitution as she could: it was a small price for what he was doing for her. She made herself brood upon the magnificence purely, she re-quired her heart to leap at the magnificence purely, and she conveyed her brooding and heart-leaping into the mind of Narfar.

She felt his warm heart-filling gratitude. And it compound-ed her guilt. Angrily she trampled her guilt, it was a deter-rent to achievement of her grand goal—compared to which, insistently she told herself, Narfar was nothing.

When he gathered that Dorita had been sated by the gran-leur of the glacial face, Narfar cruised leisurely elsewhere in his glacier bay, spreading its delights before her. Whales played: two allegretto killers, two largo baleens. A pair of seal streaked for an iceberg, churning white wakes in blue water. An eagle perched indolently on the pinnacle of a small berg; a pestiferous gull nuisanced him; the eagle took off after the scared-running gull, overtook him, swooped down upon him with talons extended for the kill, barely missed the gull (an obviously intentional miss), and having made his point with the gull, lazed back to a still taller berg, found *its* pinnacle, and lazed there for as long as Dorita could see him from the back of outflying Narfar. . . .

Thought-said her husband: *You see land of ice now. You like?*

Fervently she affirmed.

Good wedding trip, eh?

Marvelous, Narfar. Full of wonders.

Wedding trip over now? We go home now?

"NO!" she shouted aloud, and her thought also was a shout.

Hearing the shout, feeling the powerful mind-negation, Narfar braked so suddenly in midair that he threw his bride over his head; luckily there was catching room, they were a hundred meters up, and he caught her just above water and lofted cradling her in his great arms. "Sorry," he crooned to her. "Narfar do bad, I not do again."

" 'Sall right," she managed feebly. "You good, Narfar. You good."

"You want wedding trip go on? Where we go now?"

She caught her breath and put it to him. "Remember when we were up high, looking at the whole ice field?"

"Right. You like?"

"Very much indeed, my husband. But—now listen. Way far away, I saw a place where there was a long line of rocks sticking up out of the ice. They were slanty rocks. They looked like teeth of great fish who eat people and other fish." She was thinking of shark's teeth, she mind-conveyed the image of *shark*; and Dora evidently had that sort of animal, since Narfar instantly comprehended. Said Dorita: "I want to go there."

In the mind of Narfar, she felt a great shriveling.

Presently Narfar said curtly, "You get back on my back." He placed her there. He hovered, meditating.

She mind-quavered: *You not want to take me there?*

Why Dorita want to go there?

No reason. Just look interesting.

That not so, Dorita. You talk straight to Narfar. I feel your big interest. You got special reason to go there. What?

Damn this guy, he was so *honest,* so *dear.* . . . She decided to make a sort of semi-clean breast of it. *I know you got secret up here somewhere. I your wife now, husband no keep secret from wife. I think that where your secret is. Is it, Narfar?*

Bertrand Russell once made the shrewd point that it takes a certain minimum of intelligence and sophistication to lie: you have to suppress the truth and substitute a non-truth, and this is not animal-natural. Below an early age (three, maybe?) children can't do that. Narfar had the intelligence for clumsy lying, but not the sophistication to do it readily. He could, however, refuse to talk. Mind-sulking, he said: *I no tell.*

You would not keep a secret from your wife? she wheedled.

He grew huffy. *That my business. Not business of wife.*

She hit him with all the affirmative suggestion-strength that she could muster, saying within this compelling cloak: *If you love me, you not keep secret from me. If you not love me, then I go home.*

It was grossly unfair, and she knew it. In the first place, he *did* love her; in the second place, he hadn't the wit to deny her consequent; in the third place, he did not think to wonder how she would go about getting home without his help.

And he told her, after a deal of misery: *I take you to see line of rocks. They make circle, I fly you all around circle. You not go inside circle of rocks. You not ask questions. We fly around circle, we go home: end of good wedding trip. Okay?*

Let's try it, she evaded. And now she knew for certain that she was on target.

During many hours he flew reluctantly, sluggishly, and at low level above the table ice, while the sun reached noon and waned into afternoon. The chill grew by perceptible degree drops; Dorita had her second fur coat tightly pinned about

216

her; and she lay close against the back of Narfar for protection against the wind-ice of his wings. Bye and bye she was continuously shivering, but blessing her tremors for keeping her blood flowing lukewarm. And always they were homing on the shark-rock circle, the glowing center of her intangible dream.

Already far back, near the glacier bay, they had overflown what looked like a similar crater of jag-rocks, much smaller than their target: it seemed to be a crater; and within it, accumulating snow-ice lay massive-inert while the glacier ice flowed around it. Dorita had queried: *What that?* Narfar, curt: *That where comet start.* Dorita: *Comet that bring you to Erth? It blow-off here?* Surely affirmative. I confirmed the Quarfar story, increasing her respect for Quarfar, who had with his spear evoked vulcanism violent enough to fire a huge chunk of ice into air at the forty thousand kilometers per hour velocity necessary to clear Dora's gravitational field. Also, the knowledge unclouded a question: the larger crater which was their goal was *not* the source of Quarfar-Narfar's Comet Gladys, although it may have originated some earlier comet; and therefore that larger crater had existed before Narfar's departure from Dora and could in fact have been there when Narfar had sought and found a box for his world-secret.

Long before they came to her target-crater, the height of its walling, in the perspective of Narfar's low flying, eliminated any possibility of seeing its interior. As the sun sank late in the west and darkness followed quickly, already the image of circularity had been lost and the shark-tooth walling loomed like a continuous linear barrier quickly lost in darkness except as its top-silhouette vagued against stars.

Narfar dropped to the ice and made camp at ridge-foot. His own body needed no shelter; but he clawed up ice and formed a tight-packed igloo into which he and Dorita crawled, a lightless dungeon not two meters in diameter and no more than a meter in central height, but a dungeon which sealed in his own body warmth so that it radiated without heat loss to warm the body of his bride. There they broke out the bag of rations; it now included a huge slab of nael blubber which had held nicely in flight-refrigeration; he tore away a chunk for Dorita, and she gnawed at the cold stuff hungrily, chewing it with enormous difficulty, but relishing

217

the oily juices which gradually began to trickle down her gullet. After a while, the warmth from Narfar caused her to shed her outer pelt; the inner fur followed as inward warmth began to pervade her from the blubber; and before long she lay comfortable, entirely naked like Narfar, on the double blanket of the gadzyook furs.

She lay inert now, weary-indolent, yet intensely conscious that she lay just beneath the walling of her dream. She could only surmise, from Narfar's hints, what might be contained within that walling; but once within, she would know what it was, and then she would decide what to do about it.

Then slowly the inner misery of Narfar percolated into her.

She mind-said presently, not daring to speak aloud to him: *What the trouble, Narfar?*

His mind spoke to her stumblingly, she could not see him, probably he was not looking her way. *This deep. This bad. This worst of all for me. I bring you to what I should not bring you to.*

His inward anguish was heart-piercing. For the first time in her very young life, Dorita found herself up against an honest emotional conflict between a desire that was supreme to her and a creature she loved—*loved?*

But how could she love Batwing Neanderthal Narfar?

—Except that she did, in dismay she comprehended.

Narfar had oriented the doorway of their igloo to the east; both of them awoke almost simultaneously when the pre-sunrise dawn was snow-reflected in. Dorita was outdoors at once, clutching one fur about her, hands and feet thrust into the paw-mittens, zeal-gazing up at the shark-tooth rocks. Narfar crawled out behind her like a piteous wingwet moth working its way out of its chrysalis; he came up behind her, arm-enfolded her shoulders, and stared where she stared.

She said blunt: "Take me up. I go down in."

He said stolid: "Dorita not go down in."

She stamped a paw-mittened foot: "This I have to do. You let me go."

Pause. Then: "Narfar go down in with you."

"No. Narfar stay out. I go in alone."

"They kill you in there."

"Who they?"

"Never mind."

218

"They not kill Dorita. I know what to do. I show you what I do. Narfar, you think this: *I kill you, Dorita.* Think it honest, get real mad, try to grab my throat."

"I not do that to Dorita—"

Do, Narfar, do! Her affirmative was overpowering.

"Okay," he said. "Watch out!" His upper lip curled, showing fangs; he panted, he sweated in the frigidity, he roared: "I KILL YOU DORITA!" He lunged at her throat—and was brought up short by a negative suggestion so powerful that it paralyzed him.

She went to her frozen batman, smiled at him, kissed him. It released him from the paralysis and the trumped-up rage; he stood panting, weak.

"You see," she told him, "they not kill me, I know what to do."

He fly-carried her to the top of the ridge. He alit atop a tooth and set her gently down. The tooth actually was not all that sharp, once you were up there. They stood on an irregular rock-top having a surface of several square meters; even alone, she could have stood there with reasonable safety, except that stiff winds gusted and were hard to predict. At this altitude, she could see the pale horizon-sun of early morning.

Fur-bundled over her Erth clothes, she stared around and down in. The crater's diameter might have been five kilometers, it was enormous; and all around it jagged the unbroken wall. Down to the outside ice, the altitude was a dizzying three kilometers vertical; down to the inside crater-bottom, it might have been deeper yet; the sun was too low to shine into the crater, she could not see the bottom.

She turned to Narfar. "What it like in there, down there?"

"Warm. Trees. Grass."

"Why green in there? We in ice!"

"I put roof on, keep bads in. That keep warm in too, make rain. Here, I show you." With folded wings he stepped out into space over the crater, teetering slightly because he could not see the floor that he was walking on—a floor that was a ceiling and a sealing for the crater. How had he done it? Had he in his godhead commanded the lighting to form a force-field roof?

Dorita could infer what she could not see. Because of the

219

invisible roof, the crater was a gigantic herbarium which had established its own ecological balance. Carbon-dioxide exhalations from the creatures imprisoned here had collected near the transparent ceiling, transmuted sunlight into diffuse warmth, melted the imprisoned snow-ice which had run down into rock-holes and ravines to form ponds and lakes. Plant cysts, ever present even in ice, had germinated, grown, generated oxygen, proliferated into jungle . . .

Returning, Narfar stood again on the crag, looking down at her.

She asserted with total decision: "I go down in."

"Dorita—"

"Open place in roof for me, I go down in. After that, close place if you want to, I get out again anyhow."

"I go down in with you!"

"No!" The force of her negation nearly threw him off the pinnacle; had it done so, it is a question whether he would have tried to save himself by flying.

He capitulated. "Place is open now, I just think *open*, it open. You be careful. You come back. I wait here for you."

"Narfar, you shouldn't wait up here, might be long time. You go home, I come back to you there."

He asserted with dignity: "I wait here." Her mind felt his mind: it had an irrevocable decision-force of its own.

She inspected the nearly sheer inwardness of the walling, as far down as she could see it before it was lost in shadow; inspected it with the amateur expertise gained during summers in childhood and youth scaling difficult heights with her father. There were plenty of crevasses and crannies; she felt that she could make it.

She looked at Narfar. He had turned his back on her and had folded arms and wings, standing spread-legged, facing outward; the hairy-massive shoulders, back buttocks, thigh-backs, and calf-backs would have inspired Auguste Rodin beyond all his monumental inspirations. They might have inspired Gustave Doré, too: was Narfar the devil, the worldly ruler of worlds, in perpetual combat with sky-focusing Quarfar?

Then she saw those shoulders convulse in one paroxysmic heave, and quiet again. Her gorge filled, tears burst; she clutched his shoulders and pressed herself against him, mind-urging: *Narfar, you good, I love you, I come back to you, I have to do this thing but I come back, after this thing I be good always.*

He mind-uttered: *You do bad for me. But I know you have to do it. And I have to let you. Now you go down, Dorita.*

Prevoyance Four

"We believe," Methuen told the Council Chairman, Erth's pro-tem top executive, while the chief of Norwestian CIS sat nodding approbation, "that an enemy planet somewhere along the five-forty-six gradient is using the gradient with intelligent precision to knock out our political and military potential. The planet could be as far away as Saiph. I have no idea of their motive unless it is to invade us and acquire our resources. And I do not know who they are." It seemed to be 26 January 2465.

The Chairman countered: "But Saiph is very remote. Even if they have singled us out for some reason, how could they bring off these precision attacks?"

Methuen spoke with great difficulty. "Sir, there is a planet of Saiph called Dora; it has a very high civilization. I was there last year with a party of scientists, and some of us were psychoprobed, and those who were subjected to this probing are now useless vegetables. The Dorians may well have acquired detailed knowledge of our political and military structure and of our resources. They may also have learned about the gradient. Along the gradient, they could transmit programmed rekamatic impulses at nearly instantaneous velocity, and such impulses could have incinerated Nereid and knocked out our grounded spaceships and our army ammo. I regret, sir, that I did not pattern on this possibility last summer; I might have used the gradient for near-instantaneous communication."

"So they knock out our political organization and our defenses. What then can they do?"

"Sir, we were able to travel along the gradient from Erth to Saiph and back in three weeks each way. And they can do the same sort of thing with attack ships, perhaps just as fast. I beg you to remember that the first attack upon us came sixteen days ago; within days, their invasion may be upon us—"

A phone ring interrupted; taking it, the Chairman remarked, "My calls are screened, this is situationally important or it would not come through, I want you to hear it."

A male voice filled the room. "Sir, this is the Fleet Admiral. At the time when our spaceships were grounded, we had about a hundred out in space. Despite Captain Methuen's warning, they keep blundering into the five-forty-six gradient and perishing. Our surviving force numbers one battleship, three frigates, and seven destroyers—"

Awakening, Methuen mulled this fourth dream in the prevoyant series. The logic of developing events were continuing impeccably. But a new factor had entered: Methuen's dream-report of a high civilization on this Dora which had nothing more advanced than the friendly fireless barbarians of Narfar.

A remark by Quarfar came back to Methuen: "On Dora there is a potential threat to Erth; but whether and how that threat may be realized will depend on my interplay with a woman named Dorita."

Part Five

DORITA'S CRATER

Days Thirty through Thirty-Six

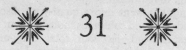

31

Day Thirty

Wearing only her Erth clothes, shoes soled with rubberoid, Dorita maneuvered cautiously down the nearly sheer inner face of the crater wall, making a very great point of not looking back up toward abandoned Narfar.

She was wiry; and even though she had never attempted a descent of this magnitude, she knew that a twenty-meter fall can kill you as surely as two thousand meters. She had watched cinemas of highly experienced climbers in action on formidable steeps (but how about the nobody who perched perilously apart taking the pictures, when all the mountaineers in the party were on camera?). She knew the fundamentals: find a solid hand-and-foot perch; plan out the course of your downward progress as far as you can see it clearly, looking for continuous faults along which you can move, but watching out also for rock-decay along the route; project your next few moves in detail, making sure that if you err, you can get back up to your prior position; execute the moves with great care, never being afraid, but never being overconfident either; and so on. Above all, don't overtax your strength: be on the lookout for resting places, and use them. Prior climbs and descents had taught her about the inexorable body-drag of gravity, including the relative weights of her slight body's parts; for instance, on a precipice she ceased to pride herself on the slimness of her hips, and instead used every opportunity to keep them tucked in and minimize their drag.

Before she had descended a hundred meters, a tiny fraction of the whole altitude, all critical muscles, long disused, ached almost beyond the point of tolerance; particularly, there were shrill complaints from her back. That was when she sought the first resting place. She found one in a semi-horizontal crevasse which was practically a shallow ledge; and there she huddled for minutes, stretching this and that muscle cautiously in minimal ways so that she would not lose grip or balance and roll to her death.

While resting, she went into a quasi-yoga discipline which she had learned: suspend conscious thought about down-climbing techniques; instead, let your total body-mind subconsciously integrate all that it has experience-learned about the kinesthetics of the business.

After a half-hour, she thought she was ready. And it went more smoothly and therefore faster after that, although never did she relax caution.

Before noon, she was well into the crater shadow; outside, the dividing line would have been sharp, but in this tropical interior humidity it was diffuse. Now she was working in the day-long twilight of the pit, and the paucity of light trebled the hazard. When you are young, though, the irises adapt quickly, and so do the brain's optic centers, and so do all cerebral sub-centers involved with correcting raw visual impressions—and so does the mind. This twilight was the governing condition of her down-climbing; down-climb she would, so she made do with it—slip-sliding a couple of times, recovering both times, remembering more lore (for instance, don't trust those little dwarf shrubs which cling to rock-crannies).

At a rest stop, she studied what lay below, able now to see the spread of thick jungle. And now she could also see a foot-feature of this inner mountain wall, a feature which could give her trouble. The finale of her descent was going to be like the inside of a smooth bowl: no foothold or handhold crannies, just a swift crippling or killing down-slide. Now how would she negotiate *that?* But the concept of giving up never entered her mind; there had to be a way. She pondered, letting her mind loose-fish for inspiration. Presently she thought of an untried backtiming technique which might help her. She resumed the descent, thinking about the new time-trick along the rugged way, but never losing her concentration on the opportunities and perils of the pit.

The dilute sun reached shallow zenith, overpassed zenith began to decline: it made no temperature difference, the upper carbon-dioxide layer moderated all changes; only one factor affected temperature, and that was altitude, for the lower she descended the hotter it grew.

She clung now to a ledgelet which was not fifty meter above the final hundred of smoothery. And smoothery it wa

ndeed: gazing downward, she marveled at it: surely the
power of Narfar had mind-polished it, heat-treating the rock,
perhaps, to keep in what he wanted to keep in; for the bowl-
interior was vitreous, in sunlight it would have mirror-shone,
there was no foothold for anything at all. In the uncertain
light, was she deceived by the appearance of smoothness?
Could she *really* feel safe in sliding down? And once down,
with the momentum of a hundred-meter sliding, could she
surely brake herself to safety with psychokinetic thrust?

You never learn your own powers until you think of trying
something. It hit Dorita: if she could project thoughts and
imperatives, if she could move objects in spacetime and herself in time, if she could psychokinetically brake herself—
could she perhaps mindfinger the rock-surface and *feel* how
smooth it really was? She tried: nothing; the clear mind-sense
was that she simply couldn't reach it from here. As a control,
she tried mindfingering the roughnesses just below her feet: to
her amazement, the mind-image superimposed itself upon her
visual image in perfect register, with the addition that her
mind could feel depths and even toughnesses. Aa! she
grinned, wishing she could release a hand to slap her own
forehead: *now* she'd learned about the ability—and she
could have been using it all the way down here!

Bit by bit she tested, mindreaching farther and farther
down, until she lost range fifty meters below, just at the top
edge of the smoothery. So it was a question of descending a
bit farther, in order to mindtouch the smoothery for testing;
and further descent was necessary anyhow, before she could
body-reach it.

Vaguely now she sensed animal motion at crater-bottom.
Was something awaiting her down there? It was a new hazard, one not anticipated: her notion had been that she would
get to the bottom, hide, and by stealth size up the nature of
the imprisoned evils before acting with respect to them; but
now she wondered if something might pounce upon her when
helpless she slid to bottom. If the thing had a mind, perhaps
even at this distance she could detect its field. Putting out
sensors, faintly she encountered an inferior mind of puzzling
form and great ferocity. Not encouraging, not encouraging at
all.

She beamed an impression at it: *I friend.*

The response seemed non-sequitur: *You food?*

She replied: *No food. Friend.*

229

After a moment of perceptible confusion, it answered: *You not food, you not friend.*

Well, it had to be done. Utilizing her eyes and her new-found mind-touch faculty, she charted a somewhat zigzag course down the fifty meters to smoothery's edge. Then she began to work her way downward along that course, always making sure before committing herself to a descent-step that she could if necessary reascend. All went well; and perhaps twenty meters short of the smoothery, she paused four-limb-clinging to rock projections, meaning again to mind-test the final surface below. . . .

A foothold and a handhold crumbled, and the startlement caused her to release hold with the remaining hand and begin to fall backward. Instantly she backtimed a fraction . . . and found herself crouching again on the higher ledgelet exchanging puzzling mind-signals with the creature below: *I friend . . . You food? . . . Not food. Friend . . . You not food, you not friend.*

And if by backtiming, returning to the earlier perch *at the earlier time,* she had lost thirty meters of descent work, nevertheless she had saved her own life, and she had learned an astonishing thing which now needed codification in order to be used. She got it systematized this way. When long ago she had hidden her bank-stolen treasure in her apartment of two days before, she had backtimed the treasure *in situ:* she had moved it in time without changing its spatial position. And again, when she and Narfar had backtimed to the vitality of his city, they had backtimed *in situ.* But this new application was different: just now, she had back-*space*timed; that is, if all her moves were plotted on a diagonally linear course on spacetime chart, then she had moved diagonally backward along that line. She had gone back, not only to *when* she had been, but to *where* she had been.

And there she crouched, thinking it over, trying to introspect how the feelings of backtiming *in situ* and back-*space*timing were different, so that she could in the future control them to obtain one or the other. While she ruminated, passively she was creating a very small time-paradox, crouching here on the ledgelet far past the moment when actually she had been down below losing her grip on rock-crumbles. . . .

Ping! The upshot web-line hit her.

230

32

Still Day Thirty

Narsua had defeated and devoured so many adults of her
species, ingesting with each body all its experience including
the experiences of all whom the devoured body had ingested,
that she was undisputed queen of the spider people in the
crater (and that was all the world any of them knew). She
attacked only adults, of course. To attack an infant, apart
from interfering with species proliferation, was in the first
place not sporting, and in the second place was folly because
the child could give the adult no experience worth mentioning.

Her royal status gave her no immunity at hunting times;
rather, she was now prize prey, for to defeat and devour Narsua would give the victor all Narsua's knowledge along with
queenhood. On the other hand, few sought Narsua nowadays,
she was too likely to win; her only rivals were those who felt
sure that they had very good chances to win, and all others
avoided her on the hunt—creating food difficulties for Narsua, who frequently had to chase and challenge. But at times
other than hunting periods, Narsua ruled without question
and was admired, envied, imitated, and fawned over.

With all this knowledge and status, Narsua nevertheless felt
profound frustration. Still she could not solve the problem
of getting out of the crater, still she had no handle on the
other-side mystery; and her growing obsession with finding a
way out was as potent as Dorita's obsession with getting in.

Prowling the foot of the crater wall late one afternoon,
peering up the shaded hundred meters of concave unnegotia-
ble bottom-bowl and on up the surmounting roughness to the
inaccessible heights, light-luminous (she had never seen the
sun), Narsua froze at the sight of up-high motion. It wasn't
much motion; she stared at it: a creature of some sort clinging to cliff-roughness, moving a little and breathing a little and

that was all. Narsua's mind labored to bring into clear singleness the eight eye-images. (Her eyes were not compound.)

Unexpectedly she felt a message from the creature: *friend.* That was what she always felt when a competitor approached her for combat, but there was something dangerously alien about the quality of this message. She flung back a query: *You food?* She apperceived counter-puzzlement in the aloft-creature, and presently it responded with an absurd distinction: *Not food. Friend.* Having mulled that over, Narsua formulated and telecast her bafflement as follows: *You not food, you not friend.*

It terminated the dialogue, if that was what it was. The aloft-creature began to move cautiously downward. Eagerly Narsua watched its down-climbing technique: this Narsua too could do, upward, if she could only surmount the slippery polished bottom bowl which even the smallest spiders could not conquer.

Then Narsua went into confusion, because abruptly the creature was back where Narsua had first seen her, and the queer dialogue about friend and food repeated itself whereafter the creature clung to the rock. . . .

Shaking herself out of the confusion during which she had seemed forced to hear and respond what she had already heard and responded, Narsua studied what she could see of the creature. It might know something that Narsua needed to know. Maybe it *was* food, despite its denial; it had called itself friend, which *meant* food. . . .

On an impulse (she wouldn't have tried it had she thought first), Narsua swung her abdomen between her legs upward and fired a web-shot.

And she hit! the creature was web-stuck to the rock!

All that way up, even above the smooth to the rough! Narsua felt a bit dizzy: she'd had no idea that she could shoot so high, it hadn't occurred to her to try, that shot had been easily five times as long as any she'd ever attempted. Also she felt physically depleted, as though she had unwebbed herself totally; had some of her insides followed the web-thread? While introspecting this, she was fastening her end of the cord to a rock at her feet and biting it off; then she moved back to comprehend what she had done.

She had, for the first time ever, established a straight diagonal webcord-road across and above the smooth to the rough.

And if the creature had climbed down the rough, surely Narsua could climb up. But there must be special tricks to such climbing—which Narsua would know, of course, as soon as she had devoured the creature.

Leaping onto her web-line, she ran up it, never doubting her balance. When she came to the entangled creature, she clung to her web-line, inspecting.

The creature looked out at Narsua, it was obviously terrified, it was little larger than the spider. But then, from the creature, an insistent thought-throw pervaded Narsua: *You not eat me. I friend. I not food-friend, I friend-friend.*

It was the sort of weird nonsense distinction that her own masters might have made. And it came into Narsua that this creature was human like the masters—and female, too! And that made her as food-tabu as any infant spider!

Narsua challenged: *I not kill you, you not kill me?*

Quick response: *You not kill me, I not kill you.* Although, now that the spider thought about it, how this woman would go about killing Narsua wasn't at all clear; she seemed as helpless as the masters who ruled Narsua only because of their god-superior authority. Did this woman have equal god-superiority?

Every queen knows that it never hurts to be tentatively respectful to an alien who may prove a more potent queen—or may not. Narsua conveyed her respect: *You hang on to rock, I cut you loose; then you hang on my back, I take you to ground.*

Obviously the woman was gaining confidence. She inquired: *I get on your back, what I hang on to, not to get poison?*

Hang on anywhere except my head, Narsua instructed, beginning to bite away the entangling strands.

On the ground, the spider told the woman to stand free; then Narsua turned to examine the web-line. Some rival might find it and use it, and that would never do. The question was, how to get rid of the line, which was anchored aloft: If Narsua should run up to it and cut the upper anchorage free, Narsua would have no way down except rolling to her death.

Reading her thought, Dorita suggested: *You run up and cut it loose. I stop you from falling.*

How?

For answer, Dorita picked up a small rock and chucked it

upward about twenty meters; as it began to roll down the bowl, she mind-braked it; sedately the pebble slid down the smoothery. Twice Dorita stopped it dead on its way down, to make her point; then she allowed it to ease on downward, much slower than normal falling, and come to indolent rest at the bottom. (Ruefully Dorita was reflecting that she might have done the same for herself.)

Narsua asked no further questions: this *was* a human with god-authority. Running up the webcord, the spider cut it loose; then, clinging to the end, she committed herself to the downslide. Dorita eased her in. Narsua coiled the web-line and hid it at jungle's edge.

She turned to the woman: *I Narsua, queen of spiders.*

The woman replied: *I Dorita, queen to Narfar.*

Instant mutual respect, even tentative liking. Narsua knew *Narfar* only through human lore, as Evil King of the Outside; if this woman was his queen, she must have every courtesy—and be guarded against.

If you like, Narsua suggested, *I take you to king of humans. You like?*

I like.

Follow me then. Not fear other spiders, we not kill humans, you human. Nothing else to fear in jungle.

33

Days Thirty to Thirty-One

As they entered the tropical forest, Narsua broadcast a mind-command which Dorita picked up: *Hunting time over now, special thing, I bring human from outside to Medzok, you come and follow.* During all the subsequent trek, Dorita was conscious of accompanying spiders in growing numbers: big hairy brown ones like Narsua, smaller varicolored ones like overgrown garden spiders, still smaller rat-sized black ones; and there were myriad other tiny ones. There was no communication, mental or otherwise, only the quiet sound of multitudinous foot-flittering. No feeling of spider-enmity

234

came into Dorita, only an awareness of many-minded curiosity.

During the trek, light dimmed to a point where Dorita was sure that outside the sun must be setting. Up to then she had been routinely cautious, as she followed Narsua, in terms of her jungle training: above might hang a predatory snake, on the ground might lurk a carnivore; yet Narsua had assured her, *Nothing else to fear in jungle;* and one had to infer from Narfar that he had immured no evils here except spiders and funny children. Anyhow, in this twilight murk, it was no longer possible for her to see danger; even Narsua ahead was growing dim. Dorita appealed: *I not see to follow you.* Narsua invited: *Come ride on my back again.* So Dorita rode the rest of the way, mentally apologizing to Narsua for being a burden, receiving courteous mind-reassurances.

They came to a place where fires augmented the deep twilight: fire, Narfar's bane, a third evil probably generated by the funny children here. It was a wide clearing, and the firelit silhouettes affected Dorita profoundly. The least of her surprises was the bordering circle of woven-twig huts thatched with something indiscernible: so far, it was a village which was a small-scale version of Narfar City, circular rather than rectangular in plan. What got to Dorita was the relatively stupendous works in the center. Both her minds went into simultaneous action—one trying to comprehend the figure 8 arrangement of upright rocks, each taller than a man, which occupied the foreground; the other mind studying the rock-heap beyond the 8, a heap whose irregular rocks were obviously in process of being systematically piled in ever-diminishing circles, a heap whose diameter was easily thirty meters at the base and which had already risen to some ten meters in height, with a flat top-area a good twenty meters wide suggesting that the intent was to build a very high conical tower. . . .

Narsua stood motionless, appreciating Dorita's impressions, allowing her to watch five Narsua-size spiders wrestling still another rock upward toward tower-top while several human men at the base craned upward watching. *Humans get ideas like this,* Narsua remarked; *spiders like to help, men pleased, they pet us for it, we feel good about it. They got some kind of feelings about these things, like circle bigger than humans, the rock pile bigger than humans; they bow down, we get big*

235

feeling from them, Narsua not able to tell. Now you see. You get off my back, Dorita; wait here with other spiders; I go see King Medzok.

Dorita dismounted: why not? Narsua skittered away and vanished into a quite ordinary hut. Spiders clustered around her, big browns and medium varicolors and semi-small blacks; a few courageous tiny ones mounted Dorita's legs, a very few extra-heroic ones went on up to her arms and shoulders but stopped short of her neck; almost panicking, Dorita held steady, requiring herself to think of the little ones aboard her as curious children.

Narsua emerged from the hut, and behind her walked a human male: not naked but wearing a diminutive leaf-skirt; not winged, simply a round-headed brunet human; no excessive hair, no overhanging brow, no bowed legs, but erect as an athlete. As he approached, Dorita felt her shoulders squaring themselves; her belly was always flat, but now her buttocks pulled themselves in, and she tried to straighten her Narfar-bowed legs—though there was nothing she could do about her Narfar-distorted face.

The man stopped in front of Dorita, inspecting her with deliberation; Narsua slid out of the way. The man was as tall as Methuen. While he studied her surgically Neanderthal face for a few seconds, presently she was aware that he was bypassing the face as such, and focusing on her eyes.

He said in a pleasant baritone, using a refinement of the language of Narfar (how had he learned it?): "Dorita, you welcome here. I Medzok. You understand me?"

"I understand you. Medzok, you king of crater?"

"I king of world," he said simply. "I stuck here in crater, but I king of world. Some day I go out to claim world. Never mind that, you important visitor; you hungry now, maybe? Thirsty?"

He led her near the fire centered in the larger circle of rocks. Five meters away from this fire, she found its heat uncomfortable, for the jungle warmth had diminished very little since sundown. She stood it, though, since he was standing it. They continued to talk; but because Medzok used many words of which Narfar had never thought, Dorita was mind-sounding him as he spoke, and she was replying with mind-reinforcement of her limited speech. She was marveling at the relative sophistication of his concepts; and he, in turn,

236

was marveling at the ready receptivity of this primitive-looking outsider-woman who was Narfar's wife, her quick comprehension of his ideas, her countertalk which enriched his ideas. . . .

"This a holy fire," he told her; *holy* she mind-apprehended, his word was strange to her; the feeling of his word was that he knelt in submission to a fearsome yet beloved master. "This fire do no work, it mean the god we worship" (another new word). "We not know the god, but we know there is one. Maybe fire *is* god, maybe not. We put rocks around fire at just right distance so firelight dance on every rock, make more holy.

"Those other rocks there"—he indicated the smaller circle completing the 8—"they built around village oven; that fire do work. *These* rocks pick up magic of holy fire; *those* rocks give magic to oven. Oven bake bread, heat up some fruits which we like hot. We sit here, Dorita, it supper time. Pretty soon men bring us drink, we drink, those guys sit down with us and drink. Then pretty soon women bring us hot bread and hot fruit from oven, we eat, they stand around behind us to keep flies away, they eat later." (Flies here too? Narfar never put them here, but they do get around. . . .) "Me, I much ready to drink now. Hey guys, bring drinks!"

Two dozen men came bearing gourds in each hand. They bent, giving two gourds each to Medzok and to Dorita; then they squatted cross-legged nearby, each sipping the drink in his left hand. Medzok drank off the liquor in his right-hand gourd, then worked on the left while holding out the right; instantly a man arose and ran to him with a refill, and so it went. The liquor, Dorita found, was high ferment; she sipped cautiously, enjoying the belly-warming, having no intention of calling for a refill—two of these drinks would seem to be more than a sufficiency.

Narsua, privileged to hover behind them, drank no drink, but listened.

Medzok said, "Hot stuff come soon. Start telling me why you come here."

Brought up short, Dorita accepted the challenge. "I very funny woman. What not right, I want to do, if nobody hurt bad from it."

So interested was Medzok that he stopped drinking. "You funny woman, we funny people, that why Narfar put us here. What you want to do that not right?"

She told him candidly half of it. "This crater is tabu, that what Narfar tell me. He say nobody can ever enter it. So I enter it. And I get him to help me."

Medzok spilled some of his drink. "Narfar—*help* you?"

"He fly me to top of crater. He open ceiling a little so I can come in. He wait for me up there now."

Women danced in, bearing hot bread and hot fruit. Medzok stayed them while he pressed Dorita: "He let you in—he wait for you—then maybe Narfar sorry, want us to come out now?"

That she flatly negated. "He love me, so when I want to come in, he let me in. He want to come with me, but I not let him. When I ready to go out, he let me out. But he not let *you* out."

King Medzok brooded upon her. He said softly, "Narsua tell me you help *her* find a way to get out."

Firmly Dorita shook her head. "I not help Narsua. Narsua use me to help herself. And Narsua not get out that way. She get up, maybe, but not out. Ceiling stop her."

Absently Medzok reached for bread, it was given; he offered some to Dorita, she took. he ate, she ate; he was engrossed in her. He demanded: "*Can* you get us out?"

Daringly, she nodded.

He pressed: "*Will* you get us out?"

She demurred: "Why I get you out?"

He bent a ferocious glare upon her. "You no get us out, I make spiders bite you and eat you, they learn from eating you how to get out."

She smiled small, swallowed bread (first in a month, best she'd ever eaten), sipped liquor, and countered: "You no get spiders to kill me. I human, they not kill humans."

"I *make* them kill you!"

"Maybe I ask Narsua, *can* you make her kill me?"

He arrested her with an upraised hand. "No ask Narsua, she say no. Spiders do anything for me, but they not break tabu even for me. I try this another way. You get us out, that be thing you like. Is not right, nobody hurt bad for it, that what you like."

Thoughtfully she munched. "That sound interesting. I think about it."

"Give me hot fruit!" he commanded the women. He held some out to her in both his hands: "This very good, you eat!"

She queried: "No meat here?"

"What is meat? Oh, you mean spiders. Tabu for humans to eat spiders, they tough anyway. Only spiders eat spiders."

"Humans eat humans?"

"No. That tabu. Human not learn anything from eat human. Just get bellyache and hate self."

Quarfar meant Fore-Thought; *Narfar* meant After-Thought; *Narsua*, Dorita gathered, meant After-Learning, or maybe After-Dinner—the two meanings blurred into each other.

Medzok left her alone that night. She'd half-expected to be seduced or even raped, but he made the matter plain to her before bedtime: "I like you, but you woman to Narfar, so I not take you now, first I have to see Narfar and tell him I take you, *then* I take you." He quartered her in the house for his favorite four women; they treated her as an honored guest and were most chic with her. She slept decently well, although more than once that night she dreamed about Narfar sitting cold sentinel up there.

Next morning they got her up for breakfast at an hour which must have been very early, although the degree of light suggested that the sun (which they never saw in here) may have just risen outside. She breakfasted with the four favorite women on more hot bread and fruit baked in the central oven by today's duty-women. Then Medzok quite informally came over, followed by Narsua, and invited Dorita to go up the tower; and the four women looked and felt scared, as though this were a most magical honor to which they didn't dare aspire.

The king ran up the rocks ahead of her; she clambered up, aware that Narsua behind her was ready to help. At the ten-meters-high flat top, she found Medzok in a prayer-attitude facing across the rocky figure 8; that was when she comprehended, from relative brightnesses of overhead diffuse daylight, that the 8 was oriented east of the tower, presumably signifying what eastward religious orientation has always signified, but meaning also that these people, who since infancy had never seen the sun, had formed some dim concept of its rising.

If these were the funny children abhorred by Narfar, they were funny indeed: mutants of smoothed appearance, much like Erth's Caucasians; not necessarily of higher intelligence than the Neanderthaloids, but more keenly motivated to

239

make something good of every chance; not tradition-inclined toward the setting sun, but ambition-attentive to the new sun's rising. A school-day memory bobbed into her foremind, a text which had told her that Neanderthal man, while uglier and clumsier than Cro-Magnon man, may have been equal to Homo sapiens as to brain power; only, for some reason not understood by the anthropologists of paleontology, the new-appearing Cro-Magnon had rather swiftly crowded Neanderthal out of the living Erth.

Maybe in Eden there had been Neanderthal first? Maybe Edom and Avé were merely the first mutant Cro-Magnon pair—and maybe no Neanderthal woman would have dreamed of taking the forbidden apple?

Done with his devotions, Medzok turned to Dorita, seizing both her hands, and began to talk rapidly, frequently freeing a hand for a broad gesture. "We make double stone circle first, for the god; then we think of tower, to stand on and gaze across double circle in direction of god who give us fire. We find places in crater where stones are heaped up, we not know why but there they are, we think maybe god left stones for us to use, we have to think how to use. We try to move stones, but it very hard; then spiders try, and big spiders can do it. Spiders always want to help us, I not know why, but we thank them always, we pet them. Spiders pull away big stones the way we say, put them in double circle the way we say. Then we think of tower, and spiders help again. They lay first circle of stones, then try to pile stones on top, not work so good. Then we think of making bottom stones flat on top and top stones flat on bottom. How to do? We find out you can do this with fire, you heat stone and throw cold water on it, piece break off, leave stone flat. So that what we do, and you see how tower go. We got one guy, he notice when we heat some stones, dark stuff in stones flow out like water and get harder than stone when cool; he think he find a way to flatten stones even better with hard stuff, he not know how yet but he working on it.

"Anyhow, we start with little tower, just high enough to see over double circle. Then we think, hey, maybe if tower high enough, we use it to touch sky. If tower touch sky, we get out of crater, see world—"

"How you know," Dorita demanded, "that there is a world outside?"

"We think about it a lot. Here this little world, what we all crater, walls all around it, Narfar put us in here, walls must be to keep us in or keep something else out—why else? We have stories about Narfar, old men say *their* old men big boys when Narfar put them here, so they know Narfar, he bad god with wings. Narfar not here, must be outside—where else? Then we see sky, sometimes light over *there*, sometimes light up *there*, sometimes light over *there*, then dark: must be some light outside, going across once every day, maybe big fire—what else? We want to go outside and see. Very dangerous, but it *there*—we want to see it!"

These were humans, all right; Dorita was thinking pre-rocket moon-aspiration. She queried: "If god Narfar put you here, he not god you pray to. Who god you pray to?"

"To god who give us fire."

"Who that god?"

"We not know, but *some* god."

So the name and being of Quarfar was not known to these people who had been immured here as children, or whose ancestors had been. It was long ago indeed that people on Dora had used fire, and Quarfar had nothing to do with it because he hadn't then reached Dora. But Narfar had made fire tabu here. Nevertheless, doubtless the old tradition had been secretly handed down, particularly among the funny people; and the child-ancestors of these crater-folk had picked up the story about the dangerous flaming stuff before Narfar had put them away. These endlessly curious people had played with the story, and ultimately had begun playing with something like the reality: rain clouds in the crater could be capricious, perhaps they had stayed away from some outer quarter during a long drought period, perhaps trees and vegetation had dangerously dried, perhaps there had been a wind and a dangerous rubbing-together of dry branches, perhaps even within-the-crater lightning. These people had caught on to it, they had learned to tame fire and use it for holy god-stuff and for cooking. . . . Good God, if those long-ago children and some not so long ago) had learned how to make babies, why not fire?

"Well," Medzok was continuing, "we figure, to make tower higher, it has to be wider. So spiders bring more rocks and we make big bottom, and we come up from there, you see how high we come, you here. But we know now, not reach sky with this tower, not big enough at bottom. We think later

241

we try bigger, taller tower right beside wall. But we keep on
with this one, for good magic. We make good tall tower here
that tell taller tower how to be good. Then we get out o
here! No?"

She tested: "It might be bad outside. You might fall of
world, outside, fall through sky forever."

"So," agreed Medzok with composure. "That why I be firs
to go up big tower, see what outside; and Narsua here g
with me. If we not come back, then another man and anothe
spider try—they picked already, and so on. If nobody com
back, I guess maybe the ones still here will quit trying. Bu
maybe they won't. *I* won't!"

Nor I! Narsua echoed.

Then—as they overviewed the village and surveyed, be
yond and above the surrounding jungle, the jagged rock-wall
of their crater-prison—Medzok (which meant, she compre
hended, *Eldest Son*) put it to her directly. "You decided
Dorita? You get us out of here?"

No, she had *not* decided. The concept of getting them ou
no longer held the allure that it had exercised upon her be
fore she had come in. *Then*, the combined impossible project
the deliciously *wrong* project, of getting in herself and gettin
out with them had been the ultimate goal of her life. But sh
had now brought off the first part, and she *knew how t*
bring off the second part: that was enough, wasn't it? Wher
now was the motive to go through the motions of *doing* it
She might as well drop the whole idea and save Narfar a lo
of headaches. . . .

An enormous amount of future, clear up to Erth's yea
2464 and beyond, would depend on this decision. But Dorit
had no concept of this, it was remote from her concern, he
concern was herself.

He repeated, urgently insistent: "You get us out of her
now?"

Perhaps she should temporize, rather than saying a flat no
she had a feeling that these Medzok-humans, under duress t
realize some dream, would be capable of anything, even pro
longed torture. She might get by for now by promising to d
it, might even get Narsua to conduct her back to her point o
arrival under pretext of studying ways and means; might the
use the back-spacetiming technique to escape alone, havin

242

made her supreme point with herself; and afterward she could decide what greater coup might come *next*. . . .

Too late she remembered that Narsua could read her thoughts. To Narsua they were incomprehensible, but they were mighty suspicious. Narsua demanded of Medzok: *Dorita human?*

"Yes," Medzok told her. "Dorita human."

Human get us out of here if human can?

"Yes, Narsua. She get us out if she can."

Dorita was hideously apprehensive. Remorselessly the spider was building up a logic, and Dorita anticipated where it was going. . . .

Narsua drove right at target. *She not get us out, she not human?*

Medzok stared at Narsua.

The spider insisted: *You king, you say what is human. She human, she get us out of here if she can. And she can. She not get us out, she not human?*

Medzok knelt to scratch the great spider's ruff, meanwhile looking speculatively up at Dorita. "Good Narsua. I not think of that. Human get us out if she can. And Dorita can. If she not get us out—she not human."

Narsua in one hop did an eight-stiff-legged turn and eight-eye stared at Dorita and launched a malevolent challenge: *You not get us out, you not human, tabu gone, Narsua eat you and learn all you know. Then* Narsua *get us out!*

She swung her body between her legs, aiming her tailgun at Dorita.

Dorita flung a defensive negative. No effect on Narsua: the tail-gun quivered. . . .

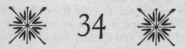

34

Days Thirty-One to Thirty-Six

So well disciplined were the crater-folk that only five days and nights were required to prepare the entire Medzokian-Narsuan symbiosis for the outmoving. Gone was Medzok's boast that he and Narsua would be first and alone to try it: his enthusiasm for the venture had swept through the human and spider tribes—they were all going at once, to escape or to die.

As for humans: the men would carry some firewood, the women some utensils and some bread and an occasional papoose, the walking kids would make it or die on their own legs, and that was nearly it. At Dorita's insistence, ill comprehended but obeyed, the women worked hard stitching big leaves together with spider-thread for clothing, including unheard-of shoes.

As for the spiders, they would have no food or furniture to carry. They were all adult females, the males having copulated and been eaten earlier in the year. Each spider would carry her own egg sac, which naturally would include some male eggs, and nothing else.

During prolonged conferences with Medzok and Narsua, Dorita had warned about the ice-field peril, abandoning words for telepathy in order to convey richer meanings, although Medzok stuck to words. . . .

Dorita: *We travel many days on top of ice, you not know about ice, it cold hard stuff.*

Medzok: What *cold* mean?"

Dorita: *Cold like* . . . She paused, seeking a simile understandable by these denizens of quasi-equatorial heat. *You never get sick so sometimes you feel like fire but sometimes you shiver and wish you could be in fire?* Medzok nodded, Narsua stared. *Well, then: imagine you very sick, shivering, wish you could be in fire. That what cold mean. Then imagine colder, colder, colder than you ever been. That how ice is.*

"Tell again—what *ice* mean?"

Ice is water, water got so cold it get hard like rock. Ice make you cold like worst sick you ever got, and much worse. You get so cold maybe you die first day. All of you.

"We have to go across that?"

For days and nights and days and nights.

"Then maybe we better stay here?"

Dorita felt a warm spot of hope. Diffidently she responded in speech: "Maybe you better stay here."

Ten eyes consulted each other: Medzok's and Narsua's. Then Medzok: "After we get across ice—what?"

Dorita was not a liar. "*If* you get across ice, then more and

244

more trees, more and more food, still cold at night but not so cold—*if* you get across ice. Then, after many many days, you reach place just like here, only bigger, much bigger."

"But first we have to cross cold ice?"

"That right. For days and nights and days and nights. So cold you all die before you get across, maybe first day. How you get across?"

After thought, Medzok said: "Got answer. We bring along firewood and fire-sticks, we make big hut of some firewood and all gather inside, we burn fire in middle, all warm. When firewood get low, we burn walls of big hut; by that time maybe we nearly to end of ice. You think, Dorita?"

"If I not think that, what I do?"

Narsua, fiercely: *You not think that, you stand still, I kill and eat you; you not stand still, you run, I kill and eat you anyway. Then I know what you know. So you better tell.*

Dorita was trapped, and she hated that; on the other hand, they were really *asking* to be used, forcing her to test her escape plan—and that was good, really, it would complete her triumph. Once outside, they would all perish, so it wouldn't really hurt Narfar. But she would not be with them.

They began the escape from the crater at what passed for sunrise in a land without sun. Led by Narsua—who this time was not back-ridden by Dorita, for Narsua had a huge egg sac to carry, but instead was followed immediately by Medzok and Dorita—the procession of heavily laden men and women and children and assorted spiders departed the village, entered jungle, and headed for a wall-base point diametrically opposite the place where Narsua had brought Dorita down. Here they would not hazard meeting Narfar at the top. Medzok had suggested: "Narfar might foresee that we would escape at the other side, might be waiting; or he might be watching and see us across crater and fly to kill us." Dorita reassured him: *You are giving Narfar your own thinking ability, he does not have it; he promised he would wait there for me, and he will wait there, and he will not be suspicious.*

Clearing the jungle-edge, they approached the wall-base with its ubiquitous polished hundred-meter bowl-inside. Narsua swung body and shot, achieving a higher anchorage than before; she called upon her sisters to try the same thing, and all the big spiders tried, and about ten more shots hit rough rock although none as loftily as Narsua's. It was enough.

245

In the first operation, all the big spiders ran up the eleven strands and bound their egg sacs to the rocks. They returned to ground, took men and women upon their backs, ran up the strands and scrambled on up the rough rock four kilometers aloft just below the Narfar-roof; here they bound the people to rough rocks and returned to ground for more people including children. Once these were safely bound on high, the spiders ran down to their egg sacs, returned aloft and secured those. Meanwhile the smaller spiders, carrying their eggs, did the uprunning without any problem, and waited.

Now Narsua bit-free Medzok and Dorita, positioning each of them on a ledge to which they could cling securely. And Narsua launched a command, in Dorita's mind it felt like a hissing: *You do that thing now!*

It was the pre-escape instant, the box-opening instant, the ultima of Dorita's victory. Just for a hesitant moment before bringing it off, incautiously Dorita allowed her own private escape plan to well into consciousness out of her subconscious where she had kept it hidden from Narsua. Once having brought off the ceiling-cut—*if* she could bring it off—she would back-spacetime, replacing herself on the far side of the rim with Narfar *before* her descent. She would arm-hook his neck, smiling into his face, and tell him: "Good Narfar, change mind, I not go down. You take me home now. Don't forget to close hole in ceiling."

She would vault aboard him, and he would fly her homeward over the ice—for his city *was* home. Perhaps, in some other dimension of this intertiming, she would already have released the Medzok-people and the spiders; but it would be useless to look below for their trekking, they would all have died before the end of the first day, freezing on the ice, and first of all the spiders. Perhaps she felt worst about the spiders. . . .

Dorita! you do that thing! It was a snarl from Narsua.

Obediently, Dorita energized her mind-thrust into a sort of psycho-kinetic laser and cut a hole thirty meters wide in the Narfar-ceiling just at crater's edge. Cold outside air rushed in rolling back tropical inside heat. Sensing high hazard, Narsua sent her sisters a-scurry to cut loose and send up all the other humans; while the smaller spiders ran at high speed over the crest and down the outer slope ahead of the others, because their instincts assured them that they were in frigid trouble.

246

Atop the whistling rim, Medzok blinked in clear blinding low-sunlight; Narsua was totally blinded, but her cold-weak-ned sense of smell held true. Medzok declared: "This awful! What that bright fire in sky?"

"That sun," Dorita explained. "That what give you light down there, only you can't see it down there because of walls. That give you heat, too."

Goose-pimpled Medzok objected: "Not feel any heat out here—"

"Can't explain," said Dorita curtly. "Anyhow, sun your guide to warm country. Follow sun at noon, it noon right now, follow where it is. Sun rise over there, set over there; when halfway between, like right now, that where you go."

"Not understand," Medzok protested, "but okay because you lead us—yes?"

"I lead you—no," she asserted. "Cheers, Medzok, Narsua. Good luck—"

Not waiting to fire her tail-gun, Narsua leaped and clung and fanged the neck-back of Dorita.

35

Day Thirty-Six

By sunset on the first day all the smaller spiders were dead, either having expired on the slope and rolled and lodged frozen in crannies, or having made it down-crater to fairly level ice before their terminal shriveling.

The big Narsua-type spiders were hardier. They suffered dangerously, but they could see that their masters and mistresses and their human young were suffering at least as badly. Probably the Narsua breed saved itself, for that day anyhow, by their self-awakening body-heating efforts to hurry the humans down. They downshot web-rope after web-rope a hundred or more meters at a time; they showed the humans how to rub snow on their hands to keep those hands from sticking to the ropes, allowing the humans to swing or slide themselves down rather than having to ride on enfeebled spider backs. It was a hand-lacerating business, although the sticky spider-goo on the ropes when clutched by wet hand formed a lubricant to reduce slide-friction. Humans male and female and their young tumbled off ropes and killed themselves bouncing down the rocks; and it happened to a number of spiders.

Two-thirds of the way down, with the sun as enfeebled as the trekkers, Medzok and Narsua and the double burden she carried bumbled into a col and discovered that the surrounding walls of rock and snow were sheltering them from the wind. Narsua issued a call to her sisters: *Bring the human here!* In col-center, Medzok required his chilled limbs to group a few sticks of his wood-burden and operate a fire-stick with recalcitrant hands having three frozen fingers. Wood was added as humans struggled in; they discovered a new property of snow; that fire turned it to water which wanted to flood the fire as it sank; luckily, Medzok had picked a place where only a few inches of snow covered bedrock, and the sputtering fire survived. People and spiders huddled round the fire; the col-walls concentrated heat inward; melted snow obligingly trickled away from the bedrock center; some of the women, once they were warm enough to think and act, got little pots off their backs and collected the water for drinking. The blessing of the col had rescued them from vainly trying Medzok's ill-conceived plan to build an overnight hut with the scant wood they carried; had all of them survived with their burdens, what they carried would not nearly have done it—and only half had survived with their burdens.

Women began to produce bread from their pouches, sharing it first with the surviving children and then with men and then with spiders—who rejected it and went hungry. Today there had been no time for the spiders to hunt each other; tonight there was no energy; when other hunting-meat would eventually be found, there would be no more inclination, except at ritual times when the queen must be challenged.

Medzok began lethargically to count human noses, doing it by finger-fives on one hand and then by fives of fives on the other. He seemed to have remaining nineteen male adults, a few more than twenty-five female adults, a few more than twenty-five children and infants who seemed to be mostly girls. (Once twenty-five was reached, both hands were used up and that ended counting.) He sighed heavily: they numbered few more than half the ones he had led away from the village. He didn't think to count spiders, nor did these count themselves; but the big spiders were certainly decimated, and the smallers ones were not there any more.

Medzok went into full lethargy, warming himself, slowly masticating a bread morsel.

A young man muttered, "Better we went back down into crater when Narsua killed Dorita."

Aroused a little, Medzok answered, "Too late for that. Crater cold now, got cold when Dorita open sky. All trees in crater dead, ice coming into it. We have to keep moving toward midday sun—or die on ice."

Another youth strongly asserted: "Medzok right. Not our way to quit. We keep on moving toward sun. If we die on ice, we die on ice *trying!*"

Amid scattered sounds of feeble agreement, Medzok turned to Narsua: "Why you bite Dorita?"

She going to leave us, go back to Narfar, not lead us. That make her not human. I bite.

"Then why you not eat her? Why you bring her?"

I not kill her. I think maybe we use her.

Medzok gazed at Narsua's two temporarily discarded burdens: her huge egg sac, and the web-mummified inert Dorita-body. He sighed. He started to say something. . . .

He interrupted himself. "I got thing coming into me. I confused. Wait now—" He appeared to be in some sort of physical-mental turmoil; feeling it, Narsua was tempted to shrivel.

At length Medzok struggled to bring out the following: "Something to eat, around here. Something to make us warm. not know what. Something to hunt—not spiders. I all confused—"

Medzok gazed with concentration into nowhere; his entire body was trembling. . . .

"Men. Take long sticks. Make sharp at one end. Go hunting. Find moving thing to eat, not spider, kill with stick; put stick inside thing, it die. Spiders hunt other moving things, do same with web-cords and biting. Not human, not tabu. I show you when I see and know what."

Narsua demanded: *Maybe that help us eat—but how that make humans warm?*

Don't know yet. Something about skin. We see tomorrow. Men, go sharpen long sticks. We see tomorrow."

Acquiescing without knowing why, to her sisters Narsua said: *Medzok say important thing, I feel this for sure. To-*

249

morrow, hunting time all day. You catch and kill anything moving, not human or spider, bring to all of us, Medzok say, who get what. And another thing. You keep eyes out for egg sacs, big spiders, little spiders, any egg sacs. You see one, you pick it up and bring it in. Tomorrow night we share the load. That way we live even if we all die.

Part Six

———•◦◆◦•———

THE FINAL TIME-PARADOX?

Days One Hundred Twenty-Three through One Hundred Twenty-Five

✳ 36 ✳

Days One Hundred Twenty-Three to One Twenty-Four

At the late-night end of their ninety-eighth day on Dora, Methuen bedded with a bunk-mate: his professional satisfaction. Their expedition had been a stunning success—astonishingly, successful even for Olga, by reason of the time-paradox. The scientists had spent the day stowing all the equipment which they would take back to Erth. Some equipment deep-planted in bedrock by Peranza or in polar ice by Green or in animals or plants by Hoek, Farouki, or Ombasa, and some orbited off Dora and off Saiph by Sari, would remain here flaking data which could be picked up by a later expedition. (No point in sending telemetry which wouldn't reach Erth for twenty-one centuries.) Tomorrow would be a day of relaxed festivities with the natives; on their hundredth day here, the party and crew would sleep it off aboard ship and depart for Erth late in the afternoon.

Best of all for Methuen: his apparently prevoyant dreams had been negated. Nothing discoverable on Dora could mount any kind of attack on Erth, sophisticated or otherwise. And Sari had established that no other Saiph-planet bore life. If 546 meant anything, it meant Saiph; if Saiph offered no threat, the dreams were nothing. Methuen had tested to the extent of sending a message to Erth along the gradient, requesting immediate reply; nothing had been received; either that intuition had been mere brainwork, or else he didn't know how to use it.

A prolonged after-dinner conference had established the professional delight of everyone. This didn't mean that they had learned everything there was to know about Dora and its sun; they would need time on Erth to digest and publish their hundred-day findings; whereafter, in due course, there could be a more leisurely expedition, possibly including some diplomats. Their rapport with Narfar and the natives was superb;

tomorrow's festivities would take place in and around the palace and would involve the whole city. Narfar had ever reacted well to the suggestion of inter-world trade, once he in his one-city insular world had semi-grasped the idea. Remembering Erth, he had proposed quite seriously: "Women maybe—some of yours for some of ours. Okay to do, can't have babies, we too different." Methuen had glided past the proposal.

There had been no more time-paradoxes. The captain concluded that Dorita may have shot her trouble-wad, fifty thousand years ago, when she had revitalized Narfar City. Yielding to pressures from his stricture-discontented task force, Methuen two months ago had terminated the curfew and allowed all crewmembers except those on skeleton watch to aid the scientists. Subsequent tranquillity seemed to justify the decision. He had, however, maintained ship's alert on yellow; and occasionally he called an alert drill in which everybody fretfully participated.

As he drowsed now in his bunk, he took special satisfaction in his serenity about the loss of Dorita. She had gone her way, and it was different from his way, and that was that.

He awoke traumatically out of a dream that a ray-cannon had shot him skyward; he awoke on the hard cabin floor rolling; he kept rolling as though the ship had hit a space storm, while the horning of the humanoid alert filled his head; he got himself into some sort of orientation, worked himself erect with the aid of a stanchion, flipped on the intercom, demanded of the bridge: "This is the captain. What the hell?"

The duty-lieutenant answered: "Captain, we don't know what the hell, the ship has been somehow lofted by something coming up under it, we are teetering on top of something, we are using stabilizers and getting damage reports, we are in no position to take off. Sir, we need you and Mr. Zorbin on the bridge."

Zorbin was now under self-control and listening. Neither he nor Methuen waited to dress: pajama'd, they staggered to the bridge. The *Farragut* had floodlights sweeping around and down, and the situation revealed by the lights was upsetting in every imaginable way.

Methuen, personally taking the con, assigned Zorbin to the intercom which was already lighting up with calls from scienists. Zorbin took none of these calls; instead, he went on general broadcast: "All scientists hear this, Commander Zorbin speaking for Captain Methuen who is here on duty. We have an emergency, we are dealing with it, we cannot accommodate you on the bridge. Repeat: we cannot accommodate scientists on the bridge. I will now note two exceptions. Because of certain anthropological and communicative entailments, Dr. Chu and Dr. Alexandrovna are needed on the bridge; repeat, urgently request that Drs. Chu and Alexandrovna come now to the bridge. The remaining scientists are requested to dress, keep cool, watch your viewports and keep your intercoms open. That is all."

Using all bridge viewports—front, sides, rear, top and bottom—Methuen got some sort of grasp of the precarious and weird situation. It appeared that the *Farragut* was teetering atop a skyscraper building which must be at least a hundred meters high. The roof on which they were perched was never meant for any sort of perch, particularly not for a space-frigate; they were holding balance only because of their stabilizers, which the duty lieutenant had intelligently activated. Still it was deep night at 0331 hours; but the ship's floods gave a clear all-around picture over a diameter of two kilometers. It was not nearly enough diameter to reveal the full size of the city below. It was an Erth-modern city with bizarre modifications, displaying a dozen skyscrapers of assorted sizes and shapes arrayed around a spreading park nearby: this park was positioned where Narfar's palace had been located, only now the park fielded half a dozen spacious buildings, among which the central structure was a sort of cross between Buckingham Palace and the Taj Mahal. The city was virtually deserted at this early hour; but night stragglers and a couple of police-persons had spotted the weirdity of a spaceship tower-teetering, and they were gawking upward; more were gathering, and now appeared two ground vehicles which could well be police cars.

A trio of small wingless aircraft was moving in on the *Farragut*, their markings resembling those of the police cars; around the nose of each craft, eight tubes which could be ray or rocket guns were moving differentially to train themselves on the intruder. From one of the craft, a female voice bullhorned a question in an incomprehensible tongue. Now, how would one go about communicating? One might of course run out a white flag to indicate peaceful intent, but would a white flag mean peace *to them?*

Olga said immediately, "It is basically the language of Quarfar and of Narfar, but badly distorted and adulterated. Try your translators."

Again the female bull-horn was challenging. Zorbin negated the lieutenant's question as to whether he should train guns on the aircraft.

Donning his translator, while Zorbin donned his, Methuen called through the exterior transmitter: "We are peaceful. Please repeat your question." Pause; then he said it again.

Long pause. Then a reply, most difficult to understand: "We hear. You hard to understand. You understand me?"

"Not very well," said Methuen, "but some. You understand we are peaceful?"

"Understand that. What you do on top of building?"

Olga intervened: "Captain, I've already done a provisional reprogramming of my translator. Would you like for me to talk with them?"

"Well done," Methuen acknowledged, "but let me have your translator." They traded instruments.

To the aircraft Methuen responded: "Hard to explain what we are doing up here. Surprise to us. Understand?"

The reply was clearer than before: "Now we understand you quite well. Go on."

Despite the stabilizers, instruments were telling Zorbin that ship's weight was beginning to crumple the building's roof. He didn't dare activate downward repulsors for fear of doing hideous damage below. From Methuen he requested and received permission to send out two tenders which could loft the ship temporarily.

Methuen called to the aircraft: "We are sending out two small boats. They will attach lines to our ship and pull her up a little, to ease weight on the roof of your building."

"Go ahead and execute."

The three police aircraft were now being joined by larger and differently marked craft which could well be military. There was all-around silence for several minutes; then the *Farragut*'s radio operator announced, "Sir, I have their wave length." A buzz of conversation among the aircraft filled the *Farragut*'s bridge, and her officers through their translator could semi-understand much of it. Meanwhile Olga made more adjustments to her translator on the captain's chest.

256

The frigate vibrated, lifted perhaps a meter, steadied. Methuen this time spoke into the radio transmitter: "This is Captain Methuen of the frigate *Farragut*, the ship that is on top of your building. Will the individual in command of your group please come in."

After a pause, a crisp alto: "This is Commander Varji, in charge of this group. Over."

"Let me clarify, Commander, for my understanding. How does the title *commander* rank in your service?"

"Second to captain, and captain is the senior rank below flag rank. How does *captain* rank in yours?"

"Senior below flag rank. However, Commander, it appears that we are intruders, and I accept your command."

"Very good, Captain. Over."

"Commander Varji, as you see, we have our ship lofted minimally above the building roof. But our boats cannot hold us up very long. We cannot use ship's power because of hazard to what is below. Can you help us?"

"Tell me why we should not destroy you."

"Because if you destroy us, your superiors will never know anything about us. Commander, please expedite your decision. Can you help us?"

Long pause; then: "I see your point, sir. I have called for two large freighters to loft you. Will your ringbolts hold?"

"They will support our weight for a long time, but not forever."

"We will loft you and convey you to our spaceport and set you down there. Then we will take you into protective custody."

"Commander, why do I understand you so well?"

"Captain, I presume you have programmed a translator; we have done the same; our translators are translating each other."

"Beautiful!"

"That is as it may be. Here come our freighters."

257

✸ 37 ✸

Day One Twenty-Four

During the thirty-minute convoy, with Olga working to program into her own translator all the richness of the new language which her dandy little computer had acquired (whereafter it was a mere quick detail to replicate the revised program into the other translators), Methuen took the intercom and delivered the following general message:

"Now hear this. This is the captain. I am addressing all scientists, officers and crew.

"We have been caught in a new time-paradox. If some of you do not understand that term, it is enough for now to know what has happened. As a result of unknown events during some period far in the past, the Narfar-people with whom we have been dealing have been replaced; and after millennia of social evolution, the new people have established a great civilization which includes a mighty city right here. Our ship was on the ground last night; during the night, a tall building of the city materialized right at our ship-site, lofting us a hundred meters. But everyone must closely notice the following: as far as these people are concerned, their civilization has existed during many centuries, and this great city is not at all new. For them, the appearance of our ship atop their building has been a shocking anomaly.

"All officers and crew are urgently requested, in any contacts with natives, to accept without question their assumption that we are the weird interlopers, not they. Apart from specific orders which the commander or I may issue, please avoid any and all references to time-paradox. Leave such references to the scientists and myself in our contacts with leaders. And even the scientists are not to mention time-paradox before consulting with me.

"Our new hosts are now ferrying our ship to their spaceport. I do not now what will follow. References have been made to protective custody. We may be regarded as en-

258

emies, or we may become friends; the latter is obviously preferable. Remember that our purpose now is to smooth over matters and depart for Erth as soon as possible.

"Continue to await orders from the executive officer or myself. In the event that separate action must be taken by some isolated unit of our crew, follow ship discipline and let the senior among you command. Separated groups of scientists will know how to work out their own programs by mutual agreement. Should one or more scientists be isolated with one or more crew members, the senior crew member is enjoined to consult with the scientists before taking action, and the scientists in turn are enjoined to respect the commands of the crew commander.

"All scientists are now requested to join me in the ward room. That is all for now."

At 0531, the two native jumbo solichopper-freighters set down the *Farragut* at approximate center of the local spaceport—above whose major building a fluorescent sign advertised a name which Olga (somehow intuiting their alphabet) translated MEDZOK SPACEPORT. The scientists, after an all-too-brief ward-room colloquy, were ready for anything to happen.

Methuen and Zorbin, wearing dress uniforms, emerged from the landing hatch onto its exterior platform meters above ground and, in the tropical heat, looked down to see whether disembarkation gear would be brought up. It was brought: not merely a portable stairway, not even merely a portable escalator, but actually an airshaft like the *Farragut's* own, with its top door fronting the two command officers directly.

Within this top hole appeared, air-suspended, a man-sized brown spider. Behind it, two more gigantic hairy brown spiders were poised on six legs each, while two legs each, performing as arms, trained upon Methuen and Zorbin carbines which were probably ray-guns.

Both Erth officers had repressed gasps, but their foreheads were wet.

The fore-spider, which wore a thorax-apparatus resembling the translators worn by Methuen and Zorbin, said in a human alto: "Gentlemen, I am Commander Varji. Please do not try anything rash."

"We do not plan rashness," Methuen responded. "I am

259

Captain Methuen. This is my aide Commander Zorbin. We wish to talk with your ruler."

The spider named Varji asserted: "First you must tell me why and how your ship got on top of one of our buildings. Please also declare whether you are ready to pay for the damage."

Said Methuen, patiently: "Commander, I have already presented Commander Zorbin here, his rank is equal to yours. And he is my aide. I repeat: we wish to talk with your ruler."

"And why should our ruler receive you?"

"Commander, I strongly suggest that someone ranking you would more properly hear my answer. I do not mean any disrespect—is it madam?—but let us all be realists."

Varji considered; her co-spiders were tight on their guns. Varji said: "Sir, my commander, who is an admiral, stands ready to receive you—but while I conduct you to him, I need to have some sort of security guarantee with respect to your ship, which is dangerous."

"What do you suggest?"

"You must permit my two officers here to take charge of your ship, bringing with them a double squad of nervoi."

"Nervoi?"

"I comprehend, sir; you see us as merely large spiders. Indeed we are of that breed; but we largest ones are nervoi, we are rather more advanced."

"Nervoi, then; I respect that. Nevertheless, I am afraid that my crew would regard this as dangerously provocative. We have nothing against spiders of any sort, but we have not learned to understand them, and we have never before encountered you nervoi."

Varji nodded to one of her officers. Methuen and Zorbin heard within their minds the following pleasant soprano assertion: *Gentlemen, we nervoi respect humans, it is a tabu built into us, we will never harm humans except in self-defense. And we do not yet know that you are enemies.*

Varji added: "We have no voice-ability, except through voders like the one I carry. We mind-communicate directly, it is at once an advantage and a disadvantage. I assure you that you can trust us."

Shaken, Methuen responded: "Excuse me while I talk privately with my executive officer." The men deactivated translators, and Methuen queried: "What do you think, Saul?"

"I think we have no choice, B.J. But the scientists should move out with us."

Reactivating translator, Methuen told Varji: "Commander, have ten people who are scientists, they must come with me."

Varji: "Accepted, but your party must be accompanied by an equal number of armed nervoi."

Methuen and Zorbin and the task force were arrayed before a grave aging man, Caucasoid-black and entirely human, who sat behind a desk in an ornate office. Varji stood at his left; behind the Erth-people, armed spiders were on guard. The building and office were air-conditioned at about 24° Celsius.

Said Varji to the graying man: "Admiral Merdo, I have the duty to present Captain Methuen and Commander Zorbin, who say that they come from some planet called Erth. I rather that Commander Zorbin's rank is the same as mine, and that Captain Methuen ranks him, but that you rank Captain Methuen. These other ten people are civilian scientists in Captain Methuen's party." She bobbed her head and six-leg-skittered back.

Merdo stood, partly in courtesy to Methuen, mainly in courtesy to the scientists, who as civilians had no rank or all rank. "You are welcome to Dora," he said, "provisionally. You could be friends, you could be enemies. This we will have to determine."

Methuen asserted: "Sir, it is true that Commander Zorbin and I are military men; but also I am chairman of a scientific task force, and you see our ten other members with me. My chairmanship comes from the chairman of my planet, and this gives me the status of a civilian political legate. On this basis, sir, I request and require that I or we speak directly with your ruler."

The admiral, standing, gave it thought. He said presently: "Before I decide, it is proper that you explain to me what you are doing on our planet and how you happened to beach your ship atop one of our buildings."

"Oh, crap!" Ogla snorted. "We were here already, and our damned building just rose up under us—"

Methuen swung on her: "Madam, I require that you be silent."

She snarled: "But you have no authority—"

"I do have authority. I require your silence."

261

She had her mouth open to argue—and then, at an arm touch from Chu, she subsided.

Methuen turned to the disconcerted admiral. "Sir, I ar sure that you have had your own problems with your own c vilian scientists; luckily for science and for all of us, they ar an independent breed. Well, I have to say, sir, that there ar some extremely complicated factors involved in our ship presence atop your building. It was unintentional, and for u it was nearly disaster. Any further remarks should properl be made to your ruler, and I say this with the authority c *our* ruler for whom I am spokesman here; but of course would be delighted to have you present, sir."

The admiral sank into his chair, considered, activated voice-private intercom, spoke inaudibly into it, listened to a inaudible response, inaudibly counter-responded; the convers tion continued during minutes, and one long pause in it sug gested that the person at the other end was placing a furthe call. . . .

The admiral looked up. "Captain, I congratulate you an your colleagues. The Chancellor of Medzok, our ruler, ha consented to receive you at 0930 this morning, a bit unde two hours from now; and I have been asked to be preser with Commander Varji. Until that time comes, you are cord ally invited to entertain yourselves in my recreation cente Unfortunately, Varji and I have other duties; but I am abou to present to you my chief of staff, Captain Norda—"

Most courteously, Norda (who was human) did courtesie to all the Erth-people, his courtesies consisting of placin hands palms-together in the oriental fashion and bowing each of them; all twelve had the wit to respond in kind. Wit the translator on his chest, he invited them to follow hin and he led them into an informal, comfortably furnishe room whose walls were perhaps ten meters long on a sid having a soda-and-liquor bar and bizarre gaming tables and number of couches and easy chairs. The room was crewed b three white-jacketed nervoi, one behind the bar, two cruisin All the Erthlings were privately forming the same hypothes about a human/arachnid caste system, with humans on to but with spiders penetrating the order all the way up to con mander level; were any nervoi higher?

Having ascertained that alcoholic drinks were acceptabl Norda via the spider-stewards provided each of them with

ool-tasty-light drink called Vesti. Seating himself in a chair
which was undistinguished yet well located to field general dis-
ussion, Norda made an overture: "I am sure that many or
all of you have questions about our city and nation of Medzok
nd our planet Dora. What can I say to help you?"

Zorbin came in fast. "Sir, I think it important that we not
aise any issues which might prove mutually embarrassing. I
think we should not make any statements, except to answer
any questions about our Erth. I think we should confine ourselves to questions about the organization of your Dora." On
his cue, Methuen glared around at the scientists: all of them
got it.

Anthropologist Chu established tone with his opener. "Cap-
ain Norda, I should appreciate answers to the following
questions. First, is this city the only city on Dora, or are
here others? Second, is there just one government on the
planet, or are there several? Third, what is the political sys-
em, or what are the systems?"

"Excellent questions," Norda purred. "I will take them
seriatim. First, there are thirty-nine major cities and many
owns and villages on Dora. Second, there are five nations on
Dora; our nation Medzok is the strongest, but others are con-
inually challenging us, which accounts for our military force
and expertise; however, there is no open warfare at present.
Third, Medzok, whose capital, Medzok City, you are now vis-
ting, is a pluralistic political entity whose rulers are chosen
by popular vote. I hope I have adequately answered these
questions. Next question?"

Chu subsided, unconvinced by the third answer. Hoek
arged in: "Sir, please explain the status of spiders—ner-
oi—in Medzok, and tell us whether their status is the same in
he other nations."

Norda whirled on Hoek, saying too hastily: "I assure you,
sir, there is no prejudice against nervoi in Medzok, although I
cannot speak for other nations. We are an equal-opportunity
commonwealth."

Hurriedly Methuen injected: "Sir, I am enchanted by the
diversified patterns on the surfaces of those tables. They are
ames, are they not?"

That warmed Norda. "Indeed they are, and marvelous
ames! Do you people enjoy games? Would you like to learn
ome of ours?"

"Oh, yeah," exclaimed Sari, startling grateful Methuen.

"We would indeed!" Zorbin echoed. And however the various scientists might variously have felt about it, they were all herded around two tables, while the two spider-waiters brought out two sets of appropriate gaming pieces; and Norda, moving from table to table, explained two sets of rules and got them started playing while another round of drinks was served. . . .

Soon after the third drink-round (Methuen and Zorbin had refused the second and third), a rather ornately jacketed spider appeared at the main doorway and voder-announced "Gentlepeople, the Chancellor is ready."

38

Still Day One Twenty-Four

The chancellor was a slight, middle-aged, brown-skinned man; Merdo was Caucasoid black, Norda somewhere between Merdo and the chancellor; Chu was sure that their natural race-complexion and feature-cast were brown and Caucasoid, the blackening of Merdo resulting from outdoor work in tropical sunlight. Methuen guessed that the chancellor's clothing was not especially formal, might even be casual. The situation was a spacious sitting room-office, air-conditioned, having a mighty desk behind which the chancellor sat semi-slouched; seated flanking him were a young brown man and a darker middle-aged woman.

As the twelve Erth-representatives were courteously herded in by Merdo and Varji and the ubiquitous guard-nervoi, the chancellor (whose name they knew was Medzok 4829) stood smiling and awaited presentations. Gravely the admiral presented Methuen and Zorbin and the others seriatim; the chancellor, who wore a translator as did his two flankers and all the Erth-people, acknowledged each introduction by repeating the name. Then, with a sweeping gesture, Medzok invited them to sit; and, catching his nod, Varji sent the guards outside.

They heard words of courtesy from the now-seated

chancellor. Knowing that his courtesy could be misleading, Methuen responded: "Mr. Chancellor, we are pleased indeed to be here, and we want for nothing to stand in the way of complete mutual understanding."

Leaning back in his rocker-swivel-chair, fingers interfolded behind his head, Medzok told the ceiling: "Gentlepeople, I am going to go right to the point. How did you get here—what are you up to—and what was your spaceship doing atop our building?"

"The intricate story begins," Methuen told him, "with an ice-comet." And he called on Zorbin to relate their early experiences with Quarfar and Narfar. When those names were mentioned, the chancellor sat up straight and stayed alert.

When Zorbin concluded, the chancellor leaned forward and demanded: "Did you say Quarfar and Narfar?"

"He did," Methuen affirmed; and he asked Olga to tell about their interviews with Quarfar. Methuen then briefed their decision to visit Dora, and made it sharp that when they landed, this area was an uninhabited clearing in jungle. By now, Medzok was frowning down, playing with a stylus. Methuen invited Seal to tell about her discovery.

Said Mabel: "Sir, we found a soft-rock throne which presumably was the throne of Narfar—"

"Of *Narfar?*" confusedly echoed the chancellor.

"Of Narfar. And further excavations revealed post-holes which seemed to mark the periphery of a primitive palace—"

"Where were this throne and this palace?"

"Sir, I do not know just where we are now; but with respect to the building which rose up under our spaceship, this dig was no more than half a kilometer away to the northwest—"

"The building *rose up under* your spaceship?"

Methuen intervened. "Mr. Chancellor, already you have enough to realize that we have a mutual mystery here. Let me brief you.

"When we first arrived at the spot where you found us, only ninety-nine days ago, that spot was a clearing in jungle, with no sign of humans anywhere in our widespread scouting of the planet. Three days later, abruptly a primitive city materialized all around us; its ruler was named Narfar, and he had wings, and he appeared to be the same Narfar who had come to Erth in the ice-comet. We worked with Narfar's cooperation during ninety-six more days. Early this morning,

265

your building seemed to rise up under us, and we found ourselves in the sudden presence of *your* highly advanced civilization. Sir, all of us will welcome your thoughts on this series of weirdities."

"My first thought, Captain, would be to inquire whether you are a responsible commanding officer. Mentally responsible, I mean, sir."

"Sir, if these are mad fantasies, then my executive officer and all ten of these scientists and all of my crew are sharing them with me." The other eleven nodded, a few vigorously.

The chancellor now casually alluded to the young man and the middle-aged woman who sat flanking him. "Through negligence, I did not present my two colleagues here. The lady is Manya Keria Léta; her specialty is anthropology. The man is Manya Kandis Poré; his field is astrophysics." Olga's translators couldn't handle *manya*, but probably it meant doctor or something of the sort. Continued the chancellor: "Manya Léta, may we hear from you first?"

Remaining seated, Léta stated as crisply as Sari might have done: "The myth of Quarfar and Narfar is ancient in our world. In one form of it, Narfar loved animals and inferior pre-humans; but hating spiders and fully evolved humans, he confined them in a cold box. Quarfar loved every living being including full humans and spiders, but especially he loved full humans. So Quarfar played a trick on Narfar by sending him a beautiful woman named Dorita, a name obviously derived from Dora and therefore purely mythopoeic. Narfar fell in love with Dorita, married her, and gave the box into her safe-keeping. Out of curiosity, she opened the box, and thereby let-out the full humans and the spiders. And that was the beginning of human progress.

"There is usually some truth in a myth, but truth is buried and distorted by varying traditional incrustations and omissions. Sir, as you well know, our culture semi-deifies Quarfar as the patron of creative humans and our faithful servants the nervoi spiders; meanwhile we respect Narfar, and therefore we have innumerable animal pets, and we take good care of wild animals in zoos and sanctuaries, and we say grace before meat. However, sir, most of us acknowlege that a particular Quarfar and a particular Narfar, if they ever existed, existed only as transient leaders around whom a multitude of legends have accumulated. These legends probably

266

encapsule developmental events around the time when the old stone age was moving into the middle stone age, when the species of full humans that is ancestral to ourselves began to conquer and finally extinguished an earlier pre-human species.

"I find it, if our our guests will forgive me, most difficult to attach any credence to their story, although I do find it interesting that they have learned so much of our mythology. I will inform our guests that there has been some sort of civilization-continuity on Dora during at least five millennia, and that our Medzok City has grown on this site during several millennia and has been a city in the modern sense during five or six centuries.

"And that, Mr. Chancellor, is about as far as anthropology can go in this area. Perhaps my colleague Manya Poré will have some comments."

The chancellor twisted around: "Manya Poré?"

Asserted Poré, whose voice was jerky and somewhat high-pitched: "Mr. Chancellor, my comments have to be sketchy and uncertain, pending detailed sessions with these guests. I have no idea where their planet Erth may be; they have not even described their star. As you know, we have explored by ship or by probe not only the entire Narfar constellation, excluding one of its stars which is for now impossibly distant, but also neighboring stars as far away as" (number and unit incomprehensible), "and we have encountered no planet having life of the human or even the mammalian order of intelligence—indeed, only a few planets have even simple life-forms.

"My preliminary hypothesis would be the following. These people are spies from some other nation on Dora, and that would explain why they pre-knew our conditions. I will not name the nation, but you know the one I have in mind. This nation has built a star-ship of entirely new design, and with it they intended to destroy Medzok City, planning thereafter to destroy our other cities and take command of our nation. The ploy of sending scientists as spies is an old one. Unfortunately for them, there was a miscalculation as they came in upon us, and they got themselves snagged by the summit of that building. They are disguising their purpose and origin by pretending to have come here from some fictitious planet—"

During the increasingly agitated tirade, with its unastronomical chop-logic about spies aboard a ship meant to destroy,

267

the other eleven Erthlings were leaning toward Methuen signaling demands that he interrupt. Shrugging them off, the captain studiously listened. When Poré reached the words "fictitious planet", the chancellor interrupted smoothly: "Excuse me, Manya Poré, but our time is limited, and I do think we have your message."

He turned to Methuen: "Captain, we thank you for the time of your colleagues and yourself. Please return now to your ship; and if our guards accompany you there, please believe that this is only for your own protection. We will deliberate this, and you will hear from us." He stood. "Again, thank you."

The armed spiders were waiting.

Nobody had mentioned time-paradox. Methuen would have bet that such a notion had never crossed the minds of these Medzok people. Instead, surely these people were convinced (and were they wrong?) that during untold millennia they had driven themselves upward and onward until now they were masters of their planet and commanders of the highest technology ever known.

These people and their nervoi were ready to conquer new worlds; not as villians, no, it was simply their manifest destiny.

And into their alert-readiness had now blundered Methuen and his Erthlings: Methuen, inadvertent agent for actualizing his own prevoyant dreams. By accident, he had met his own appointment in Samara.

39

Still Day One Twenty-Four

They half-expected to find a superspider crouching in every compartment of the ship. Instead, when they boarded, no spiders at all were in evidence. Greeting them, the duty lieutenant reported: "The filthy things know their place, they asked for privacy, we put them all in the storage space but we weren't allowed to bar the hatch." Zorbin told him curt:

'Watch your opinions, Lieutenant. They read minds—can you do that?"

Hard-faced, Methuen directed the lieutenant to summon all officers to the ward-room immediately; and he led his task force there. When the complement was complete, the captain personally locked both doors and activated the scrambler shield, remarking as he went to his seat: "Let us hope that it scrambles also brain-waves—"

He paused; raucous music was penetrating the room through the closed main door: rekamatic guitars and a wild male chorus in acid-hard beat. The lieutenant whom Zorbin had reproved spoke up: "Sir, I've organized a crew jam session out there, it ought to scramble anything we say for any mental eavesdropping. Is it satisfactory, or—"

"Well done," Methuen acknowledged. He proceeded with self-contained urgency. "Also it was well done today by you scientists; and I am confident that my officers would likewise have done well had they been present at the conference.

"Now. Our situation is extremely precarious. These people have space capability; and I suspect that if we should try to take off, they could blast us out of space. Their servants, the nervoi spiders, are aboard ship, tracking every move of every person aboard by extra-sensory means; one false move by us, and they could come boiling out of there.

"What I am about to say is addressed to all of you, but I have Dr. Sari particularly in mind. Under no circumstances may any of us mention the five-forty-six gradient. Once again: we must not, repeat *not*, mention or even indirectly refer to the gradient. Need I explain why?" No response; a few head-negations, one from Sari. He pressed: "I urge; if any of you does not understand why we may not mention the gradient, please confess your ignorance; my responding explanation may enlighten somebody else who won't admit ignorance."

That drew some chuckles. A smiling lieutenant said, "Captain, I'm awful dumb; please explain." Heartened, Seal chipped in: "I'm that dumb too. Who else is that dumb? Raise your hands." Seven hands uncertainly went up; and Chu murmured, "We have now defeated pluralistic ignorance in the only possible way."

Sari's hand had not gone up. Methuen challenged her: "Dr. Sari, can you explain?"

Said Sita: "If these people learn about the gradient's existence, they can find it; with it, they can determine where our Erth is located, and they can save energy reaching Erth." She added small: "You think we are facing that sort of menace?"

"Frankly, I don't know," Methuen admitted, "but I want to find out before we reveal too much. We did have a warning from Quarfar." (He omitted mention of his private warnings.)

"I anticipate that an early ploy on their part will be to learn where Erth is located; and, Dr. Sari, I expect that you will be the main target of such inquiry, after myself and Zorbin perhaps. If I am asked about this, I plan to raise technical difficulties involving translation of systems and coordinates; I don't know how long this can be spun out, but I would hope that anyone so questioned would follow that general line."

Ombasa cleared his throat and suggested with difficulty, "Might there be torture? Perhaps even psychoprobing?"

"There might. The outcome would have to be left to the physical and moral strength of each subject."

Long dismal silence, into which Methuen injected: "But I may be sizing up the situation altogether wrong. If these people are creative, they may turn out to be the greatest friends we have ever met. There will necessarily be a period of mutual distrust and probing, after which we will see on both sides."

"That astrophysicist Poré," Sari commented, "is a paranoid ass."

"This the chancellor recognized, I'm sure. But on the other hand, the chancellor may be considering that even a paranoid may recognize real enemies. Or, the chancellor may be seeing real opportunities."

Llana Green grated: "I hate those damned spiders!" Peranza backed her with a shudder.

"Cheer up," Olga commented; "they may prove to be the nicest people here."

Hoek remarked: "As you might expect, I don't hate the spiders, quite the contrary. How often does a zoologist meet-up with a man-sized tarantula who can communicate with the zoologist? The opportunities, Captain! Anatomical study in large scale, probing of behavioral motives . . . Ombasa, how can a spider-brain become so complex?"

"I have no idea," Ombasa rumbled, "and I wish I had one.

270

Captain, do you suppose an interview could be arranged with at least one specimen?"

"I'll check it with their officers," Methuen promised. "But please bear in mind that they are remarkably advanced spiders called nervoi. The singular is nervo. It may pay us to use his label. Anything else before we adjourn for now?"

Sari muttered, "Maybe—"

"Dr. Sari?"

She looked at the captain directly. "Maybe we should erase the five-forty-six gradient."

"Do you know how to do that, Doctor?"

She looked down, giving her head a little shake. "Not exactly, but something about it is bugging me. I know this much: we would have to retrace the gradient to Erth, doing something to it along the way; but I don't know what that something is, I want to think about it."

"Do that," said Methuen gently. "If it will help you to think, please imagine that we will really be able to return to Erth, by that path or any other."

Methuen and Zorbin, passing among the outside crew-distractors, went aft to the storage area and belled the hatch. They were soprano-welcomed from within: "Come in, Captain, Commander." Entering, they found two nervoi in the van to greet them, and the one more in the van wore a voder; probably two dozen others lurked behind in congestion, some roosting on stowage. The two greeters were presumably Commander Varji's officers whom they had met at the top of the airlift; they bore no rank insignia or any other distinguishing marks; presumably other nervoi knew their ranks intuitively, but he wondered how their human masters made such discriminations.

Methuen said through his translator, "Sir—or is it madam?"

The lead nervo returned, "All of us here are female. Our males do only one kind of work. I am Lieutenant Milji."

"Very well, Lieutenant Milji. At least two of our scientists, a zoologist and a psychobiologist, are intensely interested in spiders generally and in you Dorian nervoi particularly. With full respect, madam, I wonder whether one of your group could be detailed or would volunteer to meet with these scientists."

"While your scientists are studying our volunteer, can sh study your scientists?"

"She would be doing that anyhow, wouldn't she?"

"Of course. Please excuse us a moment or two." The sp der-officers went into deep abstraction.

They came alert, and in his mind Methuen heard the Mil voice: *Forgive me if I mindspeak, Captain, Commander what I must convey is too private for the voder. Yes, I wil deliver a volunteer from among this crew to your scientist for study; but there is more. I am to extend to you an un precedented invitation for this afternoon; and after the occa sion, one of two who are highest among spiders will visit yo privately. Is this feasible?*

"Lieutenant, I do not how to mindspeak—"

Speak aloud, then; we will catch the mind-drift; it is hov we have been hearing you anyway.

"As to the volunteer for study and the later private visit b one of two, a wholehearted yes. As for the unprecedented in vitation, I'm sure you want to tell me about it before I an swer."

In two hours there will be a signal international even which is private to nervoi, humans are awlays excluded. have been given authority to invite you and Commander Zor bin and Dr. Sari to witness this event.

The thing about a mindspeak is that you feel the emotiv overtones. Stirred, Methuen hesitantly responded: "I compre hend the honor, madam, without necessarily understanding i unless it is because we are not Dorian humans."

That is indeed part of it. Of course, we will have to hav your word that even the fact of the visit will be kept totall confidential, even from your scientists.

"But why Dr. Sari? She is an astrophysicist, whereas th scientists most interested in you Dorian nervoi are a zoologis and a psychobiologist and probably also an anthropologist—"

I will explain, sir. We invite the commander and yoursel because I am given to understand that, for reasons unknow to me, you two have especially good reasons for interest. W invite Dr. Sari because one of your party should be female and she is the only woman aboard your ship who has abso lutely no negative feelings about nervoi or any other spiders other than a natural wariness.

If it was some sort of trap, it was a devious one. Methuen personally was willing to risk walking into it; but he ought t

272

ave his second-in-command aboard ship, and he said so, eeling Zorbin's disappointment as he said it.

The response seemed almost eager, yet not in a threatening ay. *We see your point, and we concur. How about Dr. Sari?*

"She must speak for herself."

She will have to be present if you are to be present, to take he curse off your maleness, if you will excuse me sir, in the yes of the rank and file.

Methuen smiled. "I understand perfectly—but she must ay."

Behind him, Sari: "Forgive me for eavesdropping. My an-wer is yes, with my respectful thanks."

40

Still Day One Twenty-Four

A small nervo-driven skimmer (predictably having eight ts, six for lift and two for thrust) awaited them at the foot f the airshaft. Nervoi vehicles had a way of appearing from where on immediate call, Methuen reflected as he followed ari aboard; perhaps their drivers were mind-alerted by de-eloping situations and were halfway there when summoned. wo seats rose out of the bare floor for the two humans; ieutenant Milji and a crew-nervo, who had followed the hu-ans aboard, stood on the floor. The driver in a forward bicle, a booth like the head of a spider-body, was com-rtably body-slung in netting. She used all eight jets to anipulate controls all around her; semi-surrounding her was transparent windshield, so that she never needed to move r head for side vision.

At a speed of perhaps a hundred kph, the skimmer sped em across the enormous spaceport to a broad, squat, blue me at the edge nearest the city. Bivalve doors at ground-vel parted to receive the skimmer, which entered and was rked at one segment of the circular interior. The entire me seemed to be dark-blue glassoid, conferring submarine umination upon the interior; other skimmers of diversified sizes were parked elsewhere, seemingly at random; while the watched, a skimmer rose out of the floor and another va ished into the floor. Milji was telling the humans: *We pau here to adapt our eyes in the direction of darkness when w go in, and toward light when we come out. The nervo-city underground, and it is larger than Medzok City; but yo won't be able to see much of it . . . Here we go.*

The skimmer dropped beneath the floor; through transparent roof they could see a rectangle of dome-blu diminishing above them; then the skimmer darted forwar rushing at indeterminate speed through absolute darkness. (was it absolute? As their eyes adapted, a hint of pervasiv blue lumen was emerging, barely penetrating their optic thres olds; the body of the driver was now descriable as a vagu black silhouette, and beyond her into uncertain distance seeming of a horizontal tube hurtled toward and past them.

Sari said conversationally: "I'm remembering that mar Erth-spiders are burrowers and nocturnal hunters. I imagi the driver can see perfectly; at this velocity, it's a reassurir thought."

To us, Milji remarked, *the tube is as clear as dayligl That faint blue glow is a flourescent fungus-growth; prim tively we did not need it, but at these high speeds it is usef to us; we are traveling double our speed on the surface . We're slowing, we're nearly there.*

When they stepped down from the skimmer, they seem in the spectral blue-dark to be in a fairly high hall made gr tesquely irregular by black shapishness. Milji directed: *Ca tain, please climb onto my back and grip my body tight wi arms and legs, but do not touch my head. Doctor, do t same with my aide. We have a spiral ramp to mount.* Bo humans obeyed, and the uprun was rapid and dizzying.

At ramp-top, they paused on an erthen platform in fro of what may have been a portal. *Please dismount,* Milji structed; they did so. Milji stood on all eight before the po tal, her forelegs not elevated; she was probably in the act bowing. Their minds entertained small static; there was inte spider communication in progress, beyond the grasp of a h man mind.

Milji turned to the humans. *You are in the presence Narsua Number 6261. She is our queen. She will recei*

ou. *Enter, stand erect, hear her greeting, respond; then await
hat she may say or do.*

Their eye-adaptation had advanced to a level where they
ould clearly make out a black spider silhouette squatting on
ome kind of raised place, but they could distinguish no de-
ails.

Methuen, standing at attention with Sari equally erect
side him, felt compelled by the noble antiquity of Narsua.
e tried to convey his admiration in waves of mental over-
nes for his words of courtesy.

The queen-spider's response was upsetting. Leaping from
er perch, she came down upon Sari, bearing Sari to the
ound with fangs at her throat.

Sari did not struggle. Taut, Methuen asserted: "Madam, if
ou kill her, I will tear your head from your body while your
rvoi are killing me. But I think your intent is not that. I
ink you are testing us."

Tableau.

Departing Sari, Narsua returned to her high place and
quatted watching. Sari arose and composed herself.

The humans waited.

Into their minds came the Narsua comment. *I am aware
at when I attacked, neither of you received it as a bestial
ack; you took it as a testing by a respected equal. You
mmented on my antiquity: I as an individual am twenty-
ne years old, and that is indeed ancient for a single nervo.
s the collectivity of our species, I am more than fifty thou-
nd years old since we attained self-awareness under the first
edzok. But as the persona of our worldwide species, I am
ung, for we are species-young. We thank you two for com-
g to see my death.*

It was wheels within wheels, and Sari stared at Methuen,
t the captain gazed directly at the queen. "Madam, we un-
rstand very little; we would like to understand more."

The spider shadow appeared to be shuddering, and there
as melancholy in her thought-wave. *Tonight you will indeed
ow more, and Narsua will be your teacher. For me, regret-
bly it is almost time for my individual termination; and so
dividually I must bid you farewell, for this while, or for-
er.*

The totality of her thought ended, as though a door had
sed in their faces. It was replaced by a peremptory from

behind: *We must leave her, now. Pray mount our back*
again.

They sat in an isolated stadium-box bounded by knee-hig
adobe walls in all but total darkness relieved only by the blu
fluorescence. Spiders clustered near them and above-behin
them, their massed numbers extending right and left in grea
depth until their shapes were dark-obscured. It was a vast u
derground arena, its broad lofty dome pallidly blue-luminou
but all forms beneath it dissolved in murk.

Even the thought of Milji was diminuendo as she to
them: *It is the greatest of all events in our nervo world: t*
annual testing of Narsua. Your presence as a male, Captai
is unprecedented; your presences as humans, Captain an
Doctor, are unprecedented; you are here by special di
pensation of Narsua herself, a dispensation endorsed by h
challenger; this dispensation has been enjoined upon all ne
voi in the world, you are respected, you will not be harmed.

Sari responded, "We recognize, and we are grateful."

I need hardly repeat, Milji added, *that you are expected*
keep this visit a secret. It would be blasphemy if Dorian h
mans were to get wind of it. Even your scientists will n
need to know: one of our most intelligent security nerv
aboard your ship is now allowing herself to be interviewed l
your Doctors Hoek, Ombasa, and Chu; she will doubtless te
them something about this annual custom, but the fact th
you are witnessing it can remain a matter of secrecy.

Without hesitation, Methuen said: "This has been accepte
by both of us. It will remain our secret."

Thank you.

"Now be good enough to brief us about what we w
witness."

Our traditions insist that in the very old days, while Narf
held us captive in a cold box along with the Medzok peop
we nervoi hunted each other, having no other suitably lar
food because we would not eat humans. Whenever one of
ate another, the victor thereby learned everything that t
victim had known. By this process, in several human gene
ations and many of our generations, a few of us knew a ve
great deal at the time when we were released from our b
by Dorita; and the one who knew by far the most was o
Queen Narsua the First.

The custom of hunting each other died out when we we

276

ree to attack outside creatures such as insects and mammals
nd birds. At the same time, we acquired new natural ene-
ies such as insects and mammals and birds, and so we did
ot over-proliferate. But we retained, in a way which you
ould call religious, the annual festival of the Narsua-testing.

Queen Narsua is always the nervo who at once knows
ore than all the others and can defeat any of the others in
ombat. Each year at this time, a challenger comes forth: she
chosen by mental consensus among potential challengers.
he has proved her wisdom with leadership; she has proved
er combat ability in the hunt. Now she contests the suprem-
y of the queen; and representatives of all the nervoi in all
e nations on Dora are here around you to see it happen;
d every nervo on Dora, present or absent, will simulta-
ously witness it through our mind-communion. . . .

Look: they are coming forth!

Startled Methuen and electrified Sari saw two great spiders
ming from opposite quarters toward arena center: saw
em clearly in full detail, as though two blue spotlights had
cused upon them. The one at the right was actually grizzled,
e moved somewhat arthritically: the one at the left was
ung and agile.

You alone are seeing them in enhanced illumination, Milji
d them; for the rest of us, all is taking place in bright day-
ht; but we honor your limitations, and so we confer upon
u these special lightings which are entirely mental.

The nervo at the right is Narsua 6261, the personification
d collective memory of all past Narsuas, our queen. The
e at the left is her challenger, and you have met her; you
ow her as Commander Varji.

I will be silent now. Watch; and if you concentrate, you
n mind-hear the intercourse of the protagonist and the an-
gonist.

It was more than a combat theater, it was a spectacle of
t religion. The ambience was more than the blue-glowing
ark, it was Methuen-Sari pervasion by all the intent-devout
elings of ten thousand nervoi here and a million nervoi else-
ere all interacting in one-spider identity. There was no
vision in this feeling, no partisanship; no spiders were back-
either combatant especially: for all of them, both com-
ants were participating in a drama of species-devotion.
n the all-enfolding surplice of spiritual unity, indeed the

277

humans were able, faintly but clearly, to mind-hear the preliminary exchange between queen and challenger.

Narsua: *Who approaches, and for what purpose?*

Varji: *I am Varji, and I challenge you to hunt me while I hunt you.*

Narsua: *In the old days, in jungle, you would have tried to surprise me; and I would have been wary not to be surprised, or, if surprised, to shoot first and better.*

Varji: *No nervo, revered Madam, comprehends as well as you the decadence of our old hunting habits and skills. But I think we agree that it has been well bought: in exchange for the mutual enmity which brought us knowledge-growth, we have turned our knowledge-growth to the advancement of humans and ourselves. Would you go back to the old, madam?*

Narsua: *I would not go back, although it is good some-times to remember and relive the old.*

Varji: *That is why I come and challenge: that all nervo here and everywhere may relive the old in us. Madam, I wish to fight you fairly, without surprise.*

Narsua: *To the death?*

Varji: *To the death. You are friend; therefore you are food.*

Narsua: *You are friend, therefore you are food. Begin, friend.*

Instantly Varji swung abdomen between legs and fired a tail-shot at Narsua who was easily thirty meters away. Antici-pating the shot, Narsua leaped to the left; but Varji, who had learned about Narsua's characteristic left-leap, had led her with the shot, and it caught one of her legs. Falling, Narsua swung tail and shot back, correctly judging that Varji would be running in along the web-line; she entangled Varji's ab-domen, bit-away her own entangled leg (it would regenerate if she survived), and ran in to finish off her antagonist. Varji, unable to bite herself loose from her own abdomen, was chew-ing at the web-rope with calm precision; Narsua's aim slowed her death-run; Varji rolled free, at the same time closer-range firing, and practically swaddled Narsua.

Varji, dragging the coils of web-cord, stood over the helpless queen. *Madam, last year I could not have won. Despicable age has sapped your vigor, but it has sapped nei-ther your courage nor your cunning.*

Cocooned on the ground, Narsua responded feebly: *Even five years ago, Varji, had you challenged, you might have*

278

on. *You were cunning enough to perceive that nowadays I*
ive to move toward my left.

Varji: *Five years ago, I was not so cunning; and five years*
o, you were not physically limited to leftward evasion. I
ld with what I said, revered Madam.

Narsua: *Bless you, Varji. Have done with it.*

Varji: *As with thee, some day with me also. Meanwhile, I*
t thy knowledge. May all our eggs be blessed.

Responded her prey Narsua 6261: *As with me, some day*
th thee also. Meanwhile, eat my knowledge. May all our
gs be blessed.

Varji fanged. Then Varji activated her mouth-parts.

As he watched the devouring, Methuen felt chill spread
om his heart outward. Suddenly Sita Sari turned to press
r forehead against his upper arm, and he felt her repressing
etch.

Milji quietly entered their minds. *Be calm and sympathetic;*
is our way. Narsua is the soul of us, containing all our
ecies memories, deploying all of us as her intellect and her
nbs; she is our will directing us, our meaning available al-
ys to us. When Varji will have completed the eating and
similating of Narsua 6261, Varji will cease to be Varji,
e will be Narsua 6262, the identity of her food, who had
en in turn the identity of her food and the food of her food
back to the beginning of our time.

Now I will take you back to your ship. We promised you
t one of two-high-placed nervoi had volunteered to be in-
viewed by you two privately, beyond the interview of one
our crew-people by your scientists. Now I inform you that
e was to be one or the other Narsua: today's victor. In ei-
r case, it would come to the same meaning. You will be
erviewing Queen Narsua, who will come to you with all
r racial memories, intelligence, and will.

Deal with her gracefully, for Narsua will be graceful.

At nearly the same moment, aboard the *Farragut*, Ombasa
quired of the specimen crew-spider, while Hoek and Chu
tched and listened with absorption: "Do you have any idea
w the brain of a spider, even a large one like yourself, can
member and learn and reason at human level?"

The nervo, who had been provided with a voder, answered
halting alto: "Your question is beyond my scope, but I
member something about it in my schooling. I speak not of

spiders generally, but of us nervoi generally. One nervo ca remember a little and learn a little all by herself. If I have remember a lot and learn a lot and reason a little, I just sta doing it, and I know that all other nervoi are helping me. M officers can do this even better. The one who can do it be of all is Narsua."

Turning to his colleagues, Ombasa said with something lil awe: "It crosses my mind that the shapes of brain-neuro are spidery, and their interplay creating intelligence could b called a sort of telepathy. You know, I really believe we ha run upon that long-theorized thing: a collective brain which each individual is a single neuron or ganglion. And am beginning to suspect that this collective brain has a so whose name is Narsua."

41

Still Day One Twenty-Four

On boarding the ship, Methuen was handed the text of communiqué from the chancellor, pre-translated by Olga:

> Captain Methuen, Sir: We have digested the tran-
> script of your audience with us this morning, and
> we find that a great many questions remain. Conse-
> quently, at 0800 hours tomorrow morning, you are
> directed to emerge from your ship with your execu-
> tive officer and your ten scientists, and to place
> yourselves in the custody of the spider-squad which
> will receive you, under the command of Captain
> Norda. During your absence, temporary command
> of your ship will be assumed by the spiders already
> aboard, under Lieutenant Milji; you are enjoined to
> instruct your officers and crew to accept their direc-
> tions and to offer no obstacle. I am, sir, your obedi-
> ent servant, *Medzok*, Chancellor.

He told the ensign: "Summon all scientists and officers

he ward room immediately, no exceptions; I know it's nearly
appy hour, but they can drink later. Make photocopies of
his for all persons aboard, and bring them personally to the
vard room. Do both at once."

Sari, seated at the conference table, watched Methuen's
neticulous personal checking to be sure that all scramblers
vere up and that the room was sealed off from bugging and
nind-listening. Several had already arrived when the captain
ook his seat. Guitar banging and singing started just outside:
hat lieutenant had remembered to set it up again. The cap-
ain would not begin until all were present, and he sent out a
eneral call to bring in tardies.

When the complement was full, he said in a low intent
oice: "Gentlepeople, it is always good to be with you. I do
ot know what is ahead for any of us. I want each of you to
now that my experience with you has been a valuable one,
nd I want each officer to pass on to his crew that I feel the
ame way about each of them.

"Ensign, be good enough to pass out the copies of the
hancellor's communiqué. Each officer is to take enough cop-
es for all under his command. Read it immediately, and with
are."

He allowed two minutes for the distribution and reading.
le resumed:

"First, all of us will comply with this communiqué to the
tter. Officers, instruct your crews to obey the nervoi in ev-
ry respect and to extend them every courtesy: consider them
uman, which in a larger sense they certainly are. I cannot
ufficiently emphasize that we are totally in the power of
1edzok. Remember that any mayday call even to the nearest
lanet in the Sol/Centauri League could not reach its destina-
on in fewer than twenty-one centuries; and I do not know
f any of our ships cruising within a thousand light-years of
)ora.

"Second, specifically to my officers, I envision the possibil-
y that the chancellor will want to acquire our ship, or at
ny rate to learn the secrets of our long-distance high-velocity
ace capability. Should this occur, all of you are to remain
assive for a period of twenty-four hours after I depart the
ip; during that period, we may be able to accomplish some-
ing with the chancellor. After twenty-four hours without
ord, the senior among you is to fire a robot carrier to Erth

with the message that I am about to dictate. You are then to take off at peak thrust, firing defensively as may be necessary, and maintain peak thrust along the five-forty-six gradient. Arriving on Erth, you will confirm my message to top authorities.

"Here is the message: all of you take it down, to be sure that it will exist. Quote: Anticipate attack upon Erth by sophisticated invaders from Saiph III no later than 10 January 2465 and possibly sooner. Initial attacks will probably be rekamatic along five-forty-six gradient. First strike may be destruction of Nereid; second, inactivation of all grounded spaceships; third, inactivation of all army ammo including missiles; fourth, destruction of remaining ships in space. Invasive conquest will follow. Strongly urge first protective measure be rekamatic blockade of gradient as far out as Bellatrix, followed by temporary evacuation of Nereid to Erth; take back-up measures at your discretion. Signed: B.J. Methuen, Captain Astrofleet, now on Saiph III. End message. Got it?"

They nodded.

He added, "Of course, your escape may fail, and some of you may be captured alive. If this happens, those who can do so will try to sabotage the ship. Above all, once again, none of you is to reveal any information about the location of Erth or about the five-forty-six gradient."

A lieutenant raised a finger: "Sir, what if we are tortured?"

Methuen snapped: "That circumstance always has to be handled by each person alone with his pain-threshold and his conscience. Next question?"

Chu queried: "Sir, if there are no further questions from your officers, can you offer anything for us scientists?"

The captain smiled gently, appreciating the Cathayan for his wisdom and his self-discipline. "Dr. Chu, sir, I am sure that we of the task force will be questioned insistently, perhaps psychoprobed or otherwise tortured, in order to yield the following sorts of information for the chancellor: whether we are really enemies or really friends; whether we really come from some planet Erth or are instead Dorian enemies; whether we really believe the story we told him about Quarfar and Narfar and about a building rising up under us. So far, no problem except pain; but then there will be more searching questions, assuming a finding that indeed we are from Erth. They will want to know where Erth is; and for a

282

third or fourth time I enjoin all of you, if you can possibly resist blabbing it out, to withhold information about the locus of Erth and about the gradient. I think that questions like this should be asked in good faith under friendly conditions; our hosts must know that they must prove their friendliness before they expect voluntary answers. And I think that any such question asked under duress is prima facie evidence of an intention to harm Erth."

Thoughtful silence.

Arising, Methuen with difficulty attempted lightness. "It seems to be 1722 hours; I'll have the bar opened. Before dinner, I suggest that you have your usual two or three drinks, or your usual no drinks if you are abstinent; and that you eat well at dinner. After dinner, the bar will remain open; and don't forget that our supply of restorative pills is plentiful. I propose a toast which Dr. Chu well knows, the wisdom of Lao Tse: may we wine ourselves just well enough so that we walk a tightrope between heaven and hell, but let us not tipple enough to topple."

While the others were heading for the bar, he bent over Sari who lingered in her seat. "Will you be eating dinner?"

"Not after the eating we watched this afternoon. Will you?"

"In view of the visit we two expect, something tells me that we should fast. Would you like a drink, though?"

"If we are fasting, should we drink?"

"Why don't you come with me now to the bridge? Just behind it, there's a little bar with drinks, dinner pills, and restorative pills. What do you think?"

"I think I could drink and pop pills, maybe. Natural dinner, no."

The bridge and the bar-cubicle behind it were a single unit in the nose, separated from the remainder of the ship by a bulkhead. Having dismissed the two duty officers, Methuen seated Sari in the co-pilot's chair, went to the little room, returned with two drinks and two pill bottles, sat beside her.

He started talking immediately, somewhat apprehensive about silence with Sari. "We'd better stay here, since Narsua to appear on the bridge at some time during the next hour or so. I have no idea how she'll arrive, but presumably the ervoi aboard will know when she comes, and someone will call me here. Since the visit is to be confidential, I haven't

283

dared issue reception orders. I haven't set up scramblers here on the bridge, the nervoi will know about Narsua anyway."

"Captain—do set up scramblers."

After eyeing her hesitantly, he arose and obeyed. When he returned, he invited for a second time: "Call me B.J. here."

"Call me Sita anywhere," she repeated. "Well, B.J.—"

"Sita?"

"I think I've made some progress on that business of erasing the gradient."

"Tell me, and don't spare the technicalities."

"It is really quite simple, but I think a trifle impossible. The gradient was created by a body, presumably that of Narfar, traveling instantaneously from Erth to the vicinity o Saiph. It would be erased if our ship should get herself on i and then backtrack instantaneously from Saiph to Erth."

"That *is* a trifle impossible. Any substitutions allowed o the menu?"

"Yes. If we could do it *half*-instantaneously while blowing repuslor-static in all directions, it should scramble the gradient."

"How fast is half-instantaneous?"

"No math for that. But if we arbitrarily define an instan as one quadrillionth of a second, which is generous, it woul come out half-instantaneous if we should cover the twenty one hundred light-years to Erth in one billionth of a second."

"I think you know how much you are helping, Sita."

"I do, B.J. But I am thinking of still another impossibl ploy—"

Her solution reflected her usual blend of brilliance with de tail-elegance. Unhappily, as she freely admitted, there was prerequisite such that she hadn't the faintest idea how t bring it off.

He ruminated: "I know someone who might be able to d it."

"Who?"

"Our departed telepath."

"Dorita Lanceo?"

"Yes."

"You loved her, didn't you."

"Yes."

"But she is departed."

"Precisely. Nevertheless, admit that this conversation abou erasing the gradient is theoretically interesting."

284

"This I do admit, B.J., with enthusiasm."

"Shall we pursue it a bit, on the impossible assumption that our prerequisite can be met?"

"Let's do."

"The first problem that I see is fuel. In backtime, obviously raw space cannot any longer be alive. How would we feed our repulsor engines?"

"If all backtime were perished matter, then time-paradoxes would be impossible. I too had supposed that the idea of a time-paradox was nonsense; and yet within a few days we have experienced two socially and technologically complex time-paradoxes—and the present one is pretty grim."

"Tell me explicitly what you are saying about backtime fuel."

"Perhaps what I am guessing relates equally to backtime fuel and to time-paradoxes. Begin with the hypothesis that every atom of germinal matter, once it is post-germinal, once it sinks into backtime, is frozen, perished. But raw space is pre-atomic, its random thrust-lure events probably should not count as matter. Raw space may be eternally raw; and so no matter how far back into time one may go, raw space is just as alive then as it is now. Perhaps."

"Sita, if your hypothesis is wrong, we could get into backtime and discover that its raw space could not fuel us."

"We could. But also, we might discover that it *could* fuel us."

"Equal chances either way, Doctor?"

"A horse race, Captain, between two unknown horses. But of course, we can bet all night, but we will never see that race—because we cannot backtime."

Both of them were penetrated by a mind-voice: *Bet on a horse, Captain—we* can *backtime.*

They spun in their swivel-chairs. Behind them stood two giant brown spiders.

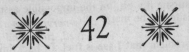

42

Evening, Day One Twenty-Four

Methuen and Sari came to their feet. Methuen demanded: "Narsua?"

The reply in his mind: *Probably you cannot tell one of us from another. I am Narsua, the one slightly in front. The other is my aide and my guard, and she has another useful capability.*

"We are honored, madam. You were Varji?"

I am Narsua.

"My first thought, madam, is to worry about your security. What would become of all your racial memories if you were to be slain with no challenger to eat you?"

That is a kind first thought, Captain; it justifies my judgment of you, the judgment that admitted you to our high festival. Not to worry. The first act of a new Narsua is to select ten nervoi as alternate memory repositories, and to pour into them all her memories including the memories of all prior Narsuas; after which the ten spiders are spirited into ten diverse locations under continual guard. Should the Narsua die undevoured, the new Narsua is selected by combat between two champions, and she eats one of the ten. For me, it was quick to do: all ten alternates for my predecessor survive, and I had only to give them my personal memories. Shall we move on to present business? Pray be seated, Captain, Doctor; you have done your courtesies. Her transmission had required three seconds.

He said as he and Sari reseated themselves, "You are graceful, madam, as they said you would be, as I knew you would be. Please interview us, rather than the other way."

Captain, I applaud your own grace; Doctor, I read in your mindsoul that you are equally graceful. Let me start by saying, Captain: there is no need to send a warning to Ertê. There was a need, but now there is not.

"How did you know about my plan to do that?"

It was clever of you to activate your scramblers, and more clever still to have the singers outside your ward room; the combination quite baffled the crew-nervoi aboard. However, they transmitted all that they received, static and all; and collectively we have ways of filtering.

"Very well, madam; I acknowledge your mind-invincibility. Tell me why I need not send a warning."

Your previsions were correct, Captain: the chancellor would indeed have concluded to invade your Erth. But now he will not do so.

"Now, you are predicting. Can you mind-read the future?"

Only to the extent that I know what I intend to do, having met you. We nervoi are dedicated to serving the purposes of humans on Dora; but part of our service is interpretation and consequent moderation. Oho, you are thinking bureaucracy, *I know your meaning: yes indeed, we are a dedicated bureaucracy. And the chancellor cannot hold you on Dora—because you are going to depart almost immediately.*

"How can we depart? Your ships are capable of shooting us out of the sky. . . . Eh, I think I see: your ships are crewed by spiders, and you will prevent them."

Not exactly that: without preparation, too many of them would be confused by the weird of such an order from Narsa. I am asking you to trust me, I am here as your voluntary hostage. Captain, I do hate to interrupt dinner for your crew—but pray immediately order takeoff.

Sari sat admiring the instant response of the captain: no further discussion, just action. He took the intercom: "Now hear this, this is the captain. With regret, I must interrupt crew dinners; the scientists are invited to linger over their food, they are not needed at the moment. All officers and crew members are to take immediate stations for departure. We will take off in ten minutes, repeat, we will take off in ten minutes. The take off will be easy, no need for hurry: we will do it at ten *G*." He turned to Narsua: "May I have one officer on the bridge here?" She affirmed. He added over the intercom: "Commander Zorbin, please report immediately to the bridge for supervision of takeoff and other instrumental duties. That is all."

Taking Narsua at her word, Methuen activated the *Fargut* in a laze-off from Dora: forty-nine meters in the first second, a hundred ninety-five after another, four hundred

thirty-nine after another; and in sixty-four seconds she wa
climbing at an altitude of two hundred kilometers and an ac
celerating velocity of six kilometers per second. Through he
mighty inertial shield, felt thrust was negligible; the spider
were taking it easily, leg-bracing only a little.

Zorbin, eyeballing the rear viewscreen, reported just au
dibly: "Five Dora killer ships pursuing and gaining on u
Shall I gun it?"

"Will they attack us?" Methuen asked Narsua.

That is their intent, responded the queen; *they do n*
know I am aboard. But there is no need to accelerate. Pleas
take your ship into the shadow of Dora, we need tot
darkness. How far out are we now?

"Over three hundred kilometers, and the Dorians are n
more than fifty kilometers back and gaining. What is the
gun-range?"

Immaterial. Watch them.

The stomachs of Methuen and Zorbin turned upside dow
then righted themselves. No pursuers were now visible.

What I did, said Narsua, *was to shift the* Farragut *in*
backtime by two days; it is the most that I can manage wi
a bulk such as your ship, but it is enough. It is a trick
learned from your old friend Quarfar. So here we all are, o
in shallow space, on the day before you awoke to fir
Medzok City all around you; and yet I am with you, havir
telekinized myself aboard your ship two days in the futur
Shall we call it a third time-paradox?

They had maneuvered so that the Dora-planet eclips
Saiph, and external darkness was as total as darkness ever b
comes under clear but pinpoint-remote stars. Methu
queried: "Madam, did you want our ship to pause here in t
Dora-shadow?"

Precisely that.

Methuen nodded to Zorbin, who rotated the ship and i
creased repulsor-thrust to a hundred *G*, braking the ship to
standstill in space before inertia carried her past the planeta
shadow, then starting her drifting back; now he cut thrust t
tally, the ship was in freefall at a minimal velocity under o
kilometer per minute, she would remain indefinitely in t
shadow.

Perfect! Narsua commented. *Now, Captain, here it is; a*
your friends Commander Zorbin and Dr. Sari will share

e good enough to face away from the stars; look in the
rection of the planet where it is darkest. My aide, here, is
bout to display the major talent that she has: she can pro-
ct my memories visually into the sky.

Captain, you are about to watch events of fifty millennia
o, centering on the person who concerns you most: your
st Dorita. Some of these pictures, the later ones, will be my
ersonal memories; the earlier ones will be out of Dorita her-
lf, whose memories I drew out of her when I fanged her
to paralysis. Dr. Sari, Mr. Zorbin, pray share this revelation
ith the captain: you are the two aboard ship whom he
lues most.

It was a series of still-shots that they watched with absorp-
on and with varying qualities of emotion: still-shots project-
into black space in holographic light-and-color fullness.
arsua was sampling the memory-events rapidly in series,
ey saw no motion, they saw representative stillnesses.

Dorita and Narfar new-arrived on Dora (the watchers felt
e tropically humid heat). Narfar hovering with Dorita, hav-
g snatched her up above the maniac maniu (the watchers
ard the hooves). Narfar on the throne with Dorita on his
p; Dorita backtiming them (the watchers felt the gid-
ness). Narfar before his leaders proclaiming Dorita; then
arfar, in a series of takes, deforming the body and face of
orita to accord with the figures of his people (and some of
ethuen's groan escaped from his chest and was audible to
ri).

But, look: has not this Dorita *accepted* her fate and her
stortion? The wedding procession; the marriage ceremony;
arfar mounting her, then flying her aloft for more consum-
ation (Sari and Narsua saw Methuen's pallor, but he made
sound).

Then the wedding trip: a series of breathtaking shots over
e bay of glaciers; then an aloft-shot as they came in on the
eat crater, and a shot of Narfar and Dorita the next morn-
g looking up at the outer walling of shark's teeth. . . .

It cut, and Narsua came in subdued. *It was Dorita's plan*
enter this crater where Narfar had walled away spiders
d full humans, in order to discover the secret and to prove
herself that she could release us, but not actually to release
Leaving Narfar squatting as faithful guardian with a bro-

ken heart at the peak of the crater wall, Dorita enter
Watch:

Dorita clambering down the inner wall. Narsua hitting I
with a web-rope. Narsua carrying her down the rope to t
interior. Dorita riding through jungle on the back of Nars
with a myriad spiders of many sizes in train (the watche
heard the flittering). Dorita with Medzok and Narsua at t
top of the tower overlooking magical Figure 8; Dor
recoiling, under challenge by crouching Narsua. . . .

I was comprehending that this Dorita did not really inter
to release us, although she had assured us that she knew ho
So I forced her to go through with it. A few days later. . . .

Medzok and Narsua and Dorita leading all the people a
spiders out to scale the crater wall. The web-rope operation
The pause at the summit just beneath the ceiling. Dor
opening the ceiling (the watchers felt the glacial wind rushi
in). . . .

Appallingly, the cynical intent of Dorita was comi
through to the watchers, coming directly through to them
Dorita's musing in Dorita's own voice: *I'll back-spacetim*
replacing myself on the far side of the rim with Narfar b
fore my descent. I'll arm-hook his neck, I'll smile into I
dear face, I'll tell him: "Good Narfar, I change mind, I n
go down. You take me home now. Don't forget to close h
in ceiling." Then I'll vault aboard him, and he'll fly me hom
ward—for his city is my home, now. And back the
emerging from the crater, all the men and women and ch
dren and spiders will die on the first day, freezing on the ic
because of me, and so they will never give Narfar any tro
ble. Oh, this is the capstone of all my triumphs! If it were
for those poor spiders. . . .

While the projection lingered on the multiple image
hideously startled people and spiders at open rim-top faci
into sub-zero gusting, Sari saw Methuen sitting as stiff a
cold and pale as though he were Narfar frozen there.

The image changed: it was Narsua fanging the neck
Dorita.

There were pictures to come, shots of the tragic-heroic tr
of people and spiders across ice; their partly successful hur
ing, their ingenious-desperate efforts to survive; the ultima
attainment of ice-edge by a quarter of the humans and

th of the spiders who had started. Then the prolonged
aggling across the temperate zone southward, filled with
situde and discouragement. Then, gradually, spirits picking
 as the climate grew warmer and the feeding more plenti-
l. And at last, in some mysterious way, their discovery of
arfar City; and their decision to make camp some distance
ay from the city while, on the following day, Medzok
uld enter the city with two or three human companions to
rn what might be learned about their probable fu-
re....

The pictures terminated. Outside the ship now, there was
ly blackness.

Narsua said: *We entered Narfar City one year and eighty-*
e days after departing the crater, which made it one year
d one hundred twenty-one days after Dorita's arrival on
ora. I will spare you my memory-pictures of what followed.
arfar still was away, and the people were demoralized, fac-
ns were rife, there were contestings for leadership. Those
ho became aware of Medzok and his companions remem-
red the old tabu against funny people, and they drove the
ll humans away. This hardened the heart of Medzok, and
organized his surviving handful of male hunters for battle.
ey were outnumbered a hundred to one; but that night
ey fell upon the people of Narfar City and slaughtered
ost of the people and took full possession. I have to confess,
my shame, that we spiders joined in the rape of the city.
edzok said they weren't human.

So, Captain, if you are looking for time-paradox velocities,
appears that the inevitability of the current Medzok su-
emacy was established by the following morning; which
eans that 49,999 years of social evolution have been accom-
ished between Day One Hundred Twenty-Two and Day
ne Hundred Twenty-Three since the arrival of Dorita on
is planet. And yet, I assure you, we who lived through all
ose centuries did live through them, and I remember every
y of them.

Prolonged silence on the bridge. Methuen, rigid, was lean-
g back gazing at the stars above the transparent ceiling. Far
ck in his mind was an awareness that Sita was gripping his
nd on his chair-arm; but other concerns, some of them cos-
c, were in his mental foreground.

He said, tightly disciplining the order of his topics: "I have

two major questions and one secondary question. How cou[ld]
Medzok possibly have taken all of you across a thousand k[i]
lometers of glacial ice without any prior experience of an[y]
thing but your tropical crater? Next: awhile ago, y[ou]
mentioned Quarfar: what about him? And then, the secon[d]
ary question: what finally happened to Dorita? If you li[ke]
we can take those questions one by one."

The answers to all three questions will blend, asserted N[ar]
sua, *in the new projection which my colleague is about [to]
give you, out there on the sky-darkness* . . .

A jungle encampment at twilight. At the forward edge [of]
the campsite, women and children gathering, peering towa[rd]
Methuen; among them, wan deformed Dorita. Behi[nd]
Methuen, wild hoarse zany shouting. . . .

Swing camera: what the watchers were seeing: Medzok a[nd]
his small, triumphant, bloodstained band of men and spid[ers]
returning victorious from sacked Narfar City to their cam[p]
Medzok in the van, wildest and loudest, leaping in Dionysi[ac]
frenzy; beside Medzok, a spider who could only be Narsu[a]
exuding shame from every hair follicle.

Medzok pauses and sets foot on a small rock-outcrop a[nd]
raises clenched fists and declaims: "I WIN! I YOUR KIN[G!]
I MEDZOK! I *MORE* THAN MEDZOK! I *GOD!* G[OD]
NAMED QUARFAR COME INTO ME WHEN [I]
LEAVE CRATER, HE SHOW ME HOW TO BRING [US]
HERE, HE SHOW ME HOW TO WIN TODAY! QUA[R]
FAR COME INTO ME! I QUARFAR! I QUARFA[R!]
MEDZOK! I *GOD!*"

Loft camera, taking in the whole scene, while minor lens[es]
close in on small groups. . . .

Dorita moves laboriously forward and comes to a halt b[e]
fore Medzok and Narsua. Dorita gazes at Medzok; he wilts [a]
little. Dorita gazes at Narsua; the spider wilts massively.

Ignoring Medzok, Dorita levels a demand at Narsua: *W[hat]
happen?*

Narsua, humiliated and therefore terse: *We kill m[en,]
everybody.*

Dorita: *Narfar there?*

Narsua: *Narfar not there.*

Dorita, stern: *Medzok make you all do this?*

Narsua in confessional: *We follow Medzok, we all do this*

292

Dorita: *You proud, Narsua?*

Narsua: *I full of shame.*

Dorita aloud: "You proud, Medzok?"

Medzok, re-stiffening himself into the victory pose: "You call me Medzok! You call me Quarfar-Medzok! I proud! n! I god!"

Dorita to Narsua: *You hear him, Narsua. He not Medzok, Quarfar-Medzok. He not human, he god. He god, he not an. You understand, Narsua?*

The spider eight-eye stares at Dorita. With a sudden spring, -sua turns ninety degrees to stare up at Medzok.

Narsua swings her abdomen between her legs, web-shoots rfar-Medzok, leaps upon him for the kill. . . .

The sky-scene faded out. Absorbed, Methuen apprehended laconic mind-voice of Narsua: *There are two of your an-rs. How he could lead us across the ice, it was that the Quarfar had traveled to Dora in the body of Dorita and subsequently entered into Medzok. Quarfar gave Medzok ative knowledge to lead us through and go on from there. Medzok was inflamed by his own godhead; he became a ocidal maniac. So I ate him.*

She waited while the humans comprehended the last four ught-words and, in varying degrees of trouble, contem-ted the bathos of God-Hero Quarfar's ending.

Then Zorbin wrily queried: "Did this make you creative, sua, and the humans not?"

On the contrary, sir, there was no such effect. Humans re-ined creative, nervoi remained logical; it is what is in the ed. But I did acquire Quarfar's knowledge and skills and spectives, and these we use logically to bridle human esses and improve human applications. For example, when humans chose a Medzok Two, I will not say that we did inwardly influence their choice.

But as to Dorita, Captain. She begged leave to return -thward in search of Narfar. My sting had terminated her e-capability and blunted her telekinesis; I warned her that could die en route. She insisted, pointing out that she had rned some skills during our year-long trek. Medzok Two e her a bag of provisions, a fire-stick and tinder, and a ar, and we blessed her, and she departed. She was a devil, she had brought us our deliverance.

Methuen, dull: "Do you know whether she made it?"

If this interests you, Captain, it will be worth your while
visit the rim of that polar crater before you depart for Er
Can you take us there please?

43

Night of Day One Twenty-Four

The *Farragut* went into rapidly decaying Dora-orbit a
was down to a hundred kilometers altitude when the pla
tary limn began to appear above darkside. The eyes
Methuen and Sari panned planetary surface; Zorbin was tig
on his instruments, locating and heading for the north po
Narsua and her aide watched them passively.

"I have it," Zorbin announced; "approximately 1,620 ki
at azimuth 249°41′22″; I am making for there slowing fro
120 kps. Are we low enough?"

"We are looking," said Methuen, "for a crater at latitu
87°2′18″ north, longitude 18°39′5″, diameter approximate
two kilometers, walled by a circle of shark-tooth pinnacl
How distant is that?"

"We are on the wrong side of Dora, unless we want
cross the pole and come down on the crater from the north
would ask Queen Narsua whether it would be more advan
geous to approach from north or south."

Commander, what you are looking for is on the south ri
if you come in from the north, you will first see it acro
crater, and that will be advantageous.

"Confirm, Captain?"

"Confirm. How distant, then?"

"It will be 787 kilometers beyond the pole on this cour
meaning that we are now about a hundred kilometers sou
of the pole at 25 kps and slowing; at this velocity, we'll
there in—thirty-two seconds if I hold it."

"Keep slowing, Mr. Zorbin, I want to be drifting at
more than a kilometer per minute when we come in on t
crater."

"Will do, sir; a full minute then, averaging 750 per minu

have crossed the pole, our heading is southward at longi-
e 18-39-5."

ari stared at Methuen's face, which was rigid and heavily
d with mouth corners drawn far down toward knotted
n as he fixated the ice-field waste beneath. He said taut:
rop her to three kilometers above the table-ice, Mr. Zor-
. And be good enough to ask the scientists to gather in the
ervation room, I want them all to see the crater where
met Gladys originated—and whatever else we are going to
there."

Having sent the word on intercom, Zorbin consulted his
ichron and reported: "Crater in fourteen seconds, sir; I
nk I see the—yes, shark-tooth ridges dead ahead, north
a. We'll clear them at less than thirty meters; shall I loft us
it?"

"Too late," Methuen snapped. "We're there. What's our
ed?"

"One per minute."

"Brake to dead stall!"

At this nearly motionless drift, they didn't have to rotate
ship: a short blast from three nose-nozzles did it. They
re just past the north rim, gazing down into the great hole
ich by now was snow-filled so that, from the interior view,
ly the very tallest teeth were visible, while glacial motion
wed snow-ice over the buried teeth and on down-
rd. . . .

When we were there, remarked Narsua, *it was jungle way
wn in, because of a transparent sealant which Narfar had
fed us with. After Dorita penetrated the ceiling, she had
downclimb four kilometers of steep cliffs; when we de-
ted, we had to reverse the process.*

"Madam, is this what you wanted me to see?"

*Only in part; remember that what you are mainly to see is
the south rim almost two kilometers distant.*

His voice was dead. "Mr. Zorbin, kindly pass me the tele-
nner." He lifted the twenty-power binocular instrument to
eyes and peered far across the crater.

He said, "Oh, my, God." Handing the telescanner to Sari,
ordered Zorbin to move due south at a kilometer per
nute and to give the con to the captain as they approached
rim. Then he almost snatched the telescanner from intent
i and gave it to Zorbin.

Said the commander, after inspection: "Indeed, B.J., o
my God."

Narsua was mind-silent.

Feathering the ship to a midair standstill a hundred meter
short of the south rim, Zorbin murmured, "Take her, Cap
tain." Personally assuming the controls, Methuen lowered th
ship as though in an airshaft until they were almost exactl
on a level with the sharktooth-peak on which was raised th
ice-mummification of Narfar and Dorita.

They contemplated the statue. Narfar sat frozen into th
gloomy Thinker attitude, chin supported on knuckles, wing
drooping behind him. Kneeling on his hunkered-up knees, a
emaciated and facially deformed Dorita arm-clutched h
neck with her cheek pressed against his cheek; and horro
was frozen on her face.

Had been frozen there during fifty millennia.

Narsua, behind them: *I am sorry, Captain, truly sorry.
know how you feel, and in a blunted way I feel how yo
feel: the emotions of nervoi are flatter than those of human
but we do have them. I hope you will come to see it all
terms of larger purposes. It is regrettable that Narfar and h
co-humans could not survive to work out their co-destin
with Quarfar's Medzok-humans and with us; but Narfar an
his people are gone, and perhaps in the eyes of some god it
just as well so, because Narfar's people could never ha
competed with the Medzok line, they would always have be
second-rate humans in the Medzok scale of values.*

"However," Methuen swiftly rebutted, "there are oth
scales of values."

*This I do not deny, sir; indeed, I affirm it; and perhaps,
due course and with our help, the Medzokians will begin
see this.*

*Meanwhile I say to you, Methuen, Zorbin, Sari—belie
Narsua in every respect; trust me, trust my nervoi. Since yo
three have come into our ken, the modulating interest of ne
voi in humans has come to transcend humans on Dora. Yo
Farragut people are the first extra-planetary humans we ha
encountered since Dorita; you meet us as equals, no
scratching our ruffs as the Medzokians do.*

*Perhaps we have been servant modulators long enoug
That is, continuing as servants, perhaps we need to exerc*

me degree of leadership *by influencing humans toward new
~ys of looking at aliens and aspirations.*

"Then," Zorbin suggested, "you are after all now un-
~eative."

*However that may be, sir, we respect you, and we will not
~ermit the Dorian humans to do evil to your Erth. Neverthe-
~ss, to avoid some mishap, you would be wise to proceed
~ith your plan of erasing the five-forty-six gradient.*

Sari interpolated: "Regrettably, Madam, there is no way
~r us to destroy the gradient. You have been able to back-
~me us only by two days. But, as I have advised the captain,
~e only way for us to kill the gradient would be to start for
~rth from a backtime position of two weeks in the past of
~rminality; and then, taking two weeks for the trip at top
~rive along the gradient, we could by careful timing touch
~own on Erth at the same instant when we departed Dora.
~hus we would have made an instantaneous passage; it would
~e a specious simultaneity, but it would have satisfied the
~hysical requirements to erase the gradient. However, as I
~id, we are only two days back—"

*We are deeper than that. I was able to backtime only two
~ays on the first take; but since then, in a series of passes,
~ have indeed brought your ship back just two weeks. Captain,
~ do suggest that you pour on the coal.*

"You surely do not plan to come with us, Narsua?"

But the two nervoi were no longer there. Neither, as later
~spection revealed, were the guardian spiders.

44

Into Day One Twenty-Five

Yet another two hours drifted the *Farragut* near the eter-
~lly frozen couple, while Methuen brooded, always with Sari
~ncernedly hovering. Zorbin was on the controls again: sym-
~thetic with his captain, almost telereceptive, he saw to the
~nguid purposiveness of the ship-drifting.

Methuen uttered, "I think I want to touch them. Sita, w
you join me?" She nodded. "Saul?"

"I'd better stay here," said Zorbin. "Apart from holding tl
ship in position, I'm doing some internal scanning."

Clad in warmsuits, Methuen and Sari emerged from tl
entry-exit hatch and, using shoulder thrusters, wavered twen
meters to shark-tooth tip. Considerately Sari stood apa
while Methuen went to the statue of paleolithic ice. He stoc
in front of it, peering into the melancholy flattened face
Narfar whose eyes were glazed-open as though he were co:
templating the crater; dwelt on the flattened profile of Dori
who timelessly clutched her Narfar gazing into the god's ui
responsive face.

Going close to them, Methuen removed a warmglov
touched Narfar's cheek, lingered on a frigid Dorita cheek. I
stepped back, replacing the glove. He contemplated them.

Abruptly he lofted toward the ship-hatch. Shrugging, Si
lofted after him. He paused outside the hatch, looked dow
radio-spoke: "I didn't mean to abandon you, Sita—"

Tenderly she replied, "I know that, you need no excuses
He hovered while she preceded him into the frigate.

Out of warmsuit and onto bridge, with Sari silently follov
ing, he demanded of Zorbin: "Saul, are they genuine?"

Zorbin replied: "They are long-frozen organic; I car
imagine why their shapes have stayed so clear so long, the
should be encrusted with ice accretions."

"But, Saul," Methuen murmured, "you forget that the
fifty thousand years here have passed in a matter of days."

And, picking up an intercom transmitter, placidly he sai
"Now hear this, Captain Methuen speaking. The scienti:
aboard will surely wish to disembark long enough to inspe
this double ice-statue which has turned out to be the tr
frozen selves of Narfar and Dorita Lanceo. There are sut
cient warmsuits with shoulder-thrust near the entry e:
hatch. I regret that my officers and crew must confine ther
selves to viewports. Scientists, it is now 2301 ship's time;
depart Dora at 2400 hours, be sure you are aboard. Do n
collect specimens; repeat, do not collect specimens. That
all."

During their hundred days here, happily Dora had :
mained on Erthside of Saiph. They picked up the gradie
and launched themselves along it at a thrust calculated

298

ing them just inside Pluto-orbit in a bit over twelve days,
suming no delaying accidents; that would leave them nearly
o days to pick their way through the complexities of Sol
stem and touch down on Erth at precisely the same date-
oment when they had departed Medzok City. The pseudo-
stantaneous trip in backtime (where in fact raw space *was*
eling them normally) would presumably erase the five-
rty-six gradient; and should there be a delaying accident en
ute, the gradient at least would have been erased to that
int.

When they had it all under control and rolling, it was after
00 hours; Methuen and Zorbin had been up since 0600 the
ior day. Zorbin turned to Methuen with a wan grin: "I'm
r sacking-out, B.J. What do you think?"

Methuen was bone-weary; but also, he was puzzled about
s own mental-emotional apathy. He waved a languid hand:
was affirmation. Zorbin, via intercom, summoned the duty-
utenant. When the officer arrived, Zorbin arose and worked
s way off the bridge.

Methuen turned to Sari, who sat watching him. "Sack-time
r you, too, Sita. Want a drink first?"

She suggested, "We might have one in your cabin."

"We would disturb Zorbin. How about one in *your* cabin?"

"Zorbin is in my cabin."

He stared at her. She spread hands. He worked his way to
s feet and plodded on ahead of her.

Over her drink, she watched Methuen in another chair.
ill he was apathetic.

She told her drink: "Obviously I am available, but I don't
t aroused until something is begun. And I don't get mad if
thing is begun. I just sort of thought you might need a
man around tonight, although I have to admit that as a
man I'm no Semiramis. Well, we can just talk business or
ything else, if you like, just so tonight you have a female
the premises, because—well, you know."

He considered her; until recently, he had thought of her
ly as a crisp scientist. Had she thought of him only as a
isp captain? He acknowledged to himself that her presence
s some kind of gift, no strings; perhaps his most graceful
sponse would be the response that he wanted to give—
accept with relaxed pleasure, to let her ease him
ysically . . .

He blurted: "B.J. means Barathra Jeroboam." And seethe(

She considered him, feeling somehow semi-wifely in comfortable way. "Thank you, B.J., that was generous. Plea lead—or do nothing."

"I'm trying to get my head on straight."

"Say what you like. I will listen."

"I've been trying to decide which one of the brothe Quarfar or Narfar, was more nearly in the soul-image of L cifer."

"Ah."

"And I think I have that one straight now, Sita—"

"My way?"

"Probably. But there's more. I thought I was in love wi Dorita. No: flatly, I *was* in love with her. But when she to off with Narfar, I guess my subconscious accepted what r conscious wouldn't."

"That is a sort of situation not unknown to me personally.

"This is the thing, Sita: when I saw them frozen the what I felt was—cosmic pity. Frozen together there, witho any consciousness of being together. Worst of all, Narf could *never* have known that she came back to him—and s *knew* that he couldn't know . . . Christ, Sita, is that wh hell is?" He broke off and drained his drink.

She went and filled for both of them. She suggested the "Maybe there's another dimension for those two."

"Do you have any evidence, Doctor?"

"None that is scientific. But none against the possibility, ther."

"I keep thinking that those two nuts ought to have chance to learn how to live with each other . . . Ah!" broke off, poured down all of his second drink, stood. "I for the sack. Want me to undress in the head?"

"Don't bother." Already she was shedding clothes; befc his shirt was off, she was nude as a dark skinny herring a heading for Zorbin's bunk, remarking: "I always sleep ra hope you don't mind."

"Be my good guest. I wear pajama pants, it's a ship-ha because of the fast emergencies that come up. Come to thi of it, what's to come up now? Emergencies, I mean—" Drc ping his shorts, he went raw to his bunk, sliding under t sheet which was all that he needed in the controlled cat temperature. "Ready for lights-out, Sita?"

" 'Night, B.J."

Silence.

He, low: "Why are you with me?"

"Sometimes a new woman's company helps mollify the
ng of a woman-loss. I mean, with or without games, just
e company."

"Please know that you *are* helping."

"I'm glad."

Dark silence.

He, low: "I guess maybe you could help me even more."

She, low: "Dear B.J.—I am one who must always be free."

He, low: "Dear Sita—I think I too am one who must al-
ays be free."

She, very low: "Your place, or mine?"

Rigid-cold, immobile, squatting eternally unblinking, wide-
en eyes filled with a mountainous infinity of snow-ice. . . .

Distantly faint help-cry: *Narfar!*

Desperation: she is coming, she needs my help, she is
eezing down there somewhere, no use, I cannot move, can-
t even blink, am unable to send a replying mind-call. . . .

Closer: *Narfar! Help me!*

I see her down there: a speck laboring up the ice-moun-
n. She will fall, I must fly down and help her. I am burst-
g my soul trying: no wing-response, nothing. . . .

Very close: *Narfar, I managed a space-jump, I'm making
I'll be with you, I love you!*

Is Quarfar the devil who has awakened me to face this ul-
nate misery? Quarfar, why did you not leave me asleep?
re, I know, you went through something like this on a
untain with vultures eating the liver of your soul—but you
d no Dorita coming back to you, and you impotent . . .

She appears just in front of me on top of the tooth,
dzyook-swaddled, arms dangling but hands twitching to
ich me, and pours out her heart: *Narfar, I know now what
want, it is you I want, just you and nothing else, to be
th you and help you always, that is my life-meaning, every
er meaning was vain, there is no other meaning . . .*

Narfar?

NARFAR—

She blazes to her feet, sheds her gadzyook fur, sheds all
r clothing. Running to me, she leaps onto me, kneeling on
knees, embracing my neck, crowding her cold cheek
inst my icy cheek. . . .

Gradually I feel her weakening. O gods if it were only v'
tures . . .

Feebly she mindscreams: *Christ, Methuen, HELP US!*

Methuen explodes-awake kneeling and clutching her a
hoarse-yelling "DORITA DORITA DORITA Dorita D
ita—"

He quiets presently. It is coming into him that the wom
he clutches is Sita; that Sita is comforting him, stroking hi
saying: "I dreamed your dream, I understand; they will ha
their time, quiet now, have faith, have faith."

Outstanding science fiction and fantasy

To order these titles,

use coupon on the

last page of this book.

DAW=sf
BOOKS

The really great fantasy books
are published by DAW:

Andre Norton
- ☐ LORE OF THE WITCH WORLD   UJ1560—$1.
- ☐ SPELL OF THE WITCH WORLD   UW1430—$1.
- ☐ QUAG KEEP   UJ1487—$1.
- ☐ PERILOUS DREAMS   UE1405—$1.

Lin Carter
- ☐ LOST WORLDS   UJ1556—$1.
- ☐ UNDER THE GREEN STAR   UW1433—$1
- ☐ THE WARRIOR OF WORLD'S END   UW1420—$1
- ☐ THE WIZARD OF ZAO   UE1383—$1

Michael Moorcock
- ☐ ELRIC OF MELNIBONE   UW1356—$1
- ☐ STORMBRINGER   UE1574—$1
- ☐ THE JEWEL IN THE SKULL   UE1547—$1
- ☐ THE GOLDEN BARGE   UE1572—$1

C. J. Cherryh
- ☐ WELL OF SHUIAN   UJ1371—$1
- ☐ FIRES OF AZEROTH   UJ1466—$1

Tanith Lee
- ☐ VOLKHAVAAR   UE1539—$1
- ☐ SABELLA   UE1526—$1
- ☐ KILL THE DEAD   UE1561—$1
- ☐ DEATH'S MASTER   UJ1441—$1

Many more by the above and other famous fantasy writers. A
for a copy of the DAW catalogue.

THE NEW AMERICAN LIBRARY, INC.,
P.O. Box 999, Bergenfield, New Jersey 07621

Please send me the DAW BOOKS I have checked above. I am enclos
$_____(check or money order—no currency or C.O.D.
Please include the list price plus 50¢ per order to cover handling co

Name _____

Address _____

City_____ State_____ Zip Code_____
Please allow at least 4 weeks for delivery